Harris' Reckless Heart

Sweet McKenna Book Ten

Christine Young

ISBN: 978-1-62420-835-5

Credits
Cover Artist: Design by Ms G
Editor: Sherry Derr-Wille

Chapter One

Scottish Highlands 1757

Music played. Harris Frasier's foot tapped in time to the lively tune of the bagpipes. She watched Ashton whirl her sister-in-law, Maisie, around the dance floor. Hawk, Maisie's husband, leaned, one hip on a table watching the pair. The scowl on his forehead told Harris her brother was not pleased. He was just like all the males in Clan Chaton, possessive. What did he have to be worried about? Maisie was madly in love with her husband. Theirs was the type of love Harris wished for herself. She wondered who Ash would dance with next. Another sister-in-law or someone from the village.

The wedding tonight was celebrating Roc's marriage to Lainie. Just like Kit's wife, Lainie came from another time. Lainie arrived from the future. Somehow in Roc's life...well...if Lainie had not returned they would be fated to never find their one true love. Harris swallowed the lump in her throat, turning away from the dancers. She could not bear to watch the scene. As the days ticked by in her life, she often wondered if she would find her mate. A year ago, she thought Ash would be that man. Now, she wasn't certain. He didn't act like a man infatuated with her. She wanted to see that look in his eyes. The same look Roc sent Lainie. The same one Hawk sent Maisie.

Harris wandered outside to the gardens needing to find a respite from the celebrations. Her head ached with all the questions swirling in the muddied depths. Since Ash returned, he'd acted standoffish, aloof. True, she would never let him get too close. She was afraid if she did allow him to kiss her, hold her as he'd done in the past, she wouldn't be able to think one coherent thought. She would give in to his bold maneuvers. Ones he knew would have her melting at her feet. She didn't wish to melt in a pool on the floor in front of him. Harris needed her feet firmly planted when she was with the man.

Not that she didn't want her brother and Lainie to be happy. She looked back to the hall. Light filtered out from the open doorway. Her mother along with the other women would be taking Lainie to the tower soon. The men would bring Roc after a signal that all was finished. She couldn't go with the women because she was still a virgin, unmarried.

A long-drawn-out breath of air left her trembling lips as she turned to continue her walk down the path. In her case, she was trying to figure out what made her happy. Ashton told her he wanted to marry her. Harris didn't know if she should believe him. The man was Sassenach. He was assigned to the highlands. All Sassenach despised the highlanders. Highlanders reciprocated the notion. Highlanders could not abide Sassenach. Her cousin, Crissie, wed a Sassenach. They were happy. At least it seemed that way when they came to visit. They had two children now. There might be another on the way.

She searched for her mate. Had to find the man who would be hers...had been hers in the past. How the devil could Ashton Wolcott be her mate? She didn't feel the connection as she thought she should. There was no mind changing event that told her the man was hers into eternity. Stopping in front of a rose bush, Harris plucked a flower. Touched the soft velvet of the petals to her cheek. "So soft," she murmured thinking about all the things Ashton told her after he kissed her that first time.

She found she wanted more from him. Acted the outrageous flirt to his arrogant confidence. Thought the world was hers to explore. So, she teased him, challenged when she should have backed off.

A little over a year ago, she made a huge mistake. She ran after Ash when he was leaving Scotland. Harris understood she should have let the man ride away. Watched his back as he disappeared. She didn't. That day he'd been angry. Harris didn't understand the reasons. He always kept his feelings about her bottled up inside. Knowing he'd be gone for months, she had to see him one last time. So afraid he would never return, she...she made a fool of herself.

He told her he would give her a woman's pleasure. As usual the man never asked if that's what she wanted. He seduced her into believing what he wanted was what she wanted. That day while she watched the leaves above her flutter with the soft breeze blowing through the glen, she let him have his way. He made her promise she would not see another man. Told her she was his. Told her she must wait for his return. After that he left her.

The blasted man didn't think the vow went both ways. This was something she couldn't forgive. Harris wished for a partner who would not chase skirts or keep a mistress. Who would be satisfied with the woman he married. After his return from England, they spoke. Ash wanted to know if she kept her promise to him. Of course, she did. She didn't want to allow any other man to touch her, kiss her.

When she asked him if he kept the same vow, he stared at her, his brows furrowed. After that he said, "I didn't promise anything."

His words were harsh. He turned from her, walking away for a few tense seconds. While she stared at his back, he stood stiff as if stunned by her question. After he turned, his face was blank.

Harris' heart hurt. She turned from him unable to accept the salient fact he was sleeping with other women. If she wasn't enough woman for him, she didn't want to have anything more to do with him. She didn't let him kiss her. That wasn't the only reason. Harris understood if she allowed him to get close to her, she would give him whatever he asked for. In doing so, she would betray herself. She couldn't do that. Would never become his pawn.

Keeping her distance was imperative for her peace of mind. She sipped in a deep breath, smelling the tantalizing aroma of the rose she held in her hand. Inside the castle, brilliant lights cast shadows on the grounds. She held the rose to her breast wishing she dared trust Ash. More than anything else, she wished she could.

In the weeks following the incident at the cave that left her brother along with Lainie wounded, Ash did keep his distance. Harris tried to confide with Laine. Roc intervened, threatening Ash with violence. Despite her deep-seated anger with Ash, she didn't wish for her brother to hurt him. Harris needed her fears assuaged so she could move on. Ash never explained himself.

Who was she kidding? Ash was capable of defending himself. He didn't need her intervention. Because of Ash's size, Roc didn't stand a chance in a fair fight against Ash.

Harris supposed she should return to the wedding festivities. If she didn't show her face soon, someone, Ash, would come looking for her. Getting caught alone in the garden by Ash would be difficult to explain. Her brothers along with her cousins were protective of her. As was every encounter she had with the man. Alone or with company, he had this icy way of staring at her. The blue of his eyes filled with thoughts she would never understand. Harris didn't appreciate how he could say he wanted her then look at her without warmth.

Harris shivered. Wrapped her arms around herself.

She didn't wish to return to the McKenna keep. Didn't want to have Ash confront her. Dancing with him would put her in too close proximity for her to think straight. There were places he could take her so they would be alone. Harris didn't want that either. She couldn't be alone with him without coming out of the experience damaged in some way.

The last two weeks he tried to get her by herself on numerous occasions. So far, she'd been successful by surrounding herself with friends as well as family. As the days passed, it was only a matter of when, not if, she would find herself in his arms again. She passed her tongue across her dry lips. Looking at the man made her heart beat faster, made her remember that shattering climax she felt in his arms over a year ago. That day, Ash didn't take her virginity. He stole her dignity. Her pride. Robbed her in part of her purity. In too many respects, her innocence vanished that day along with her pride.

After the single experience with him, she would never be the same. She was no longer innocent. He stole that from her, too. Harris sank to her knees before sitting on the grass, staring at the star-studded sky above. Once, not so long ago she believed in fairytales, in dreams coming true.

Ash never told her why he was leaving. Something about being called home. Elaborating was not something Ash did when it came to himself. He expected her to trust without explanations. Now, he was back. That was the problem as well as the blessing. Harris wasn't certain which was the case. Night and day, he left her guessing as to his plans. A week ago, he told her that he would again have to leave soon. He couldn't stay here until she stopped acting like a petulant child telling her she sulked. He didn't elaborate about his imminent departure. Harris supposed he thought her childlike behavior was because she wouldn't obey all his mannish orders. For all she cared, the man could go to the devil.

The snort she emitted was far from ladylike. Running her hand along the soft grass rifled through her senses. Harris couldn't help what she felt. Ash didn't have the right to call her names. He didn't commit to her. Didn't ask her to marry him. Except that he did ask...once. Never told her he loved her.

Love was something she needed. Wanted. Desired. Even prayed for.

Ash said he was going back to England. Told her she was coming with him. Harris had something to say about that notion. This was a choice about her life she would make. He would need to do something nice to compel her to return with him. Nice, as in marry her at the keep in front of her family along with her best friends. Next week would not be too soon. The women were adept at managing quick weddings. This would never be a hardship.

When he told her that wasn't going to happen. She wanted to toss her wine in his face. His reasons for leaving were not compelling. She would continue to tell him no until he gave in to her wishes. In this one thing, Harris meant to have her way. It wasn't right or fair that he would order her life around him to suit him. He never asked. Wasn't this something that should involve a conversation?

He told her she was acting like a little girl, pouting because she didn't get her way. Harris didn't see this ongoing drama in the same light. She had a right to her feelings. It was only fair that he listened to her. Understood her needs. The devil, he was so closed off. Didn't he understand about discussing something?

A shadow passed across her. She looked up. *No!*

Harris jumped to her feet, her heart flying to her throat. The rose she held fell to the grass. Petals falling around her. "Who is it?"

She didn't know why she asked. She knew who the man was.

"Only me," Ash said, his tone gentle. "You've nothing to be afraid of. Know I won't hurt you." He stepped toward her, shortening the distance between them. He reached out to her before dropping his hands to his sides.

Ash stood too close. Harris caught the spicy tang that was his scent.

Backing away she ran into a trellis. Felt a few thorns from the rosebush prick her back. If she moved forward, she would be far too close to him. "You were dancing."

In a masculine gesture, he lifted his massive shoulders. He was tall. Way too tall. "Missed you. Was going to ask you for the next dance. Your mother told me she saw you wander outside. Decided I would follow. Hear the music?" Ash looked over his shoulder. Held out his hands. "We could dance here."

"Mother gave me away?"

Why? Harris didn't understand why her mother would send Ash to find her. Her mother knew she didn't want to be alone with this man who twisted her heart every which way.

"Because." Again, Ash lifted his broad shoulders in a lazy shrug. He stared at her, his gaze penetrating, uncovering parts of her she didn't want him to understand. "She wants us to talk. To figure out what we want. We both know we won't see eye-to-eye. So..." He paused while he gazed at her with his clear blue eyes. "So..." Ash dipped his shoulder to her waist.

Before she could counter his words with the truth. He spoke again. She was atop his shoulder. *What?* They would never agree on anything. His long strides were taking them from the keep. "What are you doing?" Before it was too late, she should scream. Her voice wouldn't work. She tried to wiggle off his shoulder. Pounded on his back with her fists. A strangled soft, "Stop," let her mouth. The words were so weak no one would hear.

"Taking you with me. Have to go. Waited for you as long as I could. You are far too stubborn."

Perched on his shoulder, she tried to look up. Pushed on his hard back to see around him. "You can't. Where? You can't do this!"

Her mother and father would have his head. Her brothers would tar and feather his big hide.

"Tried to do everything your way. Ran out of time."

He jostled her so she wouldn't work her way off and fall to the ground. She didn't want to land head side down. "Put me down!" Harris understood the words were wasted on the uncompromising man. They were going out the big gate. Soon it would be too late to scream. The devil, no one would hear her shriek over the bagpipes.

"No!"

"Ash," she paused while she tried to think of words that might sway him to tell her what was happening.

"I've both your mother's and your father's permission. If you're worried about your brothers rescuing you, think again. They both know what will happen. Since that day at the cave, they've known all about me." There was an inevitable silence while she tried to digest what he said. "As well as their blessing."

Permission?

Blessing?

"What are you talking about?"

Ash stopped. Just as she was snatched off his shoulder, she tumbled to a seat in a carriage. She tried to rush past him, the need to escape overwhelming.

He stopped her. "Not so fast, love. You aren't going anywhere except with me." Ash stepped inside before sitting down across from her. He thumped on the ceiling. The coach picked up speed.

His last words were an outright lie. Harris understood she could try for the door. Try...he would stop her if that was what he wished. Ash never used brute force on her. She felt as if he did just now.

"Seems I am..."

Harris retorted, a glower of displeasure crinkling the lines around her eyes. She scowled at him even though she felt certain he wouldn't be able to see the expression of disdain she shot him. Tempted to stick out her tongue, she restrained herself.

"Imagine so."

Unable to do anything else, she leaned back, crossing her arms over her chest. Impatient for him to explain, she tapped her foot on the floor. "I'm waiting."

"As I did for several weeks. Now we're doing this my way. I'm going to London. You are traveling with me. After that we will move on to my country home. I've business that cannot wait for your petulance to vanish."

Harris felt his lopsided smile to the tips of her toes even though she couldn't see the smirk. He was grinning from ear to ear, pleased with his accomplishment. She hated being small. Despised not having the strength to get her way. If she were his size, this would not be happening.

"You're abducting me? Against my will? Isn't that against the law? If it's not, it should be. Should be a hanging offense."

As soon as the words left her lips, she understood them for the truth. Ash couldn't get her to leave with him by his sweet-talking ways. He had to result to force.

"For yours as well as my best interest. For our future."

"That's your opinion."

"Yes."

Harris knew his grin was growing. "I object." She told him.

He wouldn't heed her two words. She found herself shaking her head at him. "Don't have clothes." Harris understood he wouldn't mind if she wore nothing.

"Your mother packed what you would need for the next few days. They will bring or send the rest in the next week when there is more time. I will buy you anything you might need."

Mother packed my clothes?

She was pouting. Sulking all the way to the tips of her toes. Ash had an answer for everything. "As soon as we stop, I'm going to find a means—"

"You can try." He was quick to say the words as if nothing she did would work.

If necessary, she would shift. In her cat form, he wouldn't be able to keep up with her. At night they wouldn't be able to travel far. The distance wouldn't be so great she wouldn't be able to get home on her own. The pure confidence she heard in his voice made her angry. *She could try.* Of course, she would try. She didn't wish to go with him to England or anywhere else. Had told him numerous times she wouldn't. He never listened.

"I will," she blurted before she realized she should not have said anything. Why give him a reason to watch her. She was an idiot. Should have surprised him with the deed. Caught him off guard with the effort.

"You can try."

The sheer fact he repeated himself set her on edge. Her nerves seemed to unravel more with each passing beat of her heart. The fact he discounted all her feelings set her teeth grating. She wasn't going to get over this transgression anytime soon. Somehow, she would set the record straight.

"Let's start over."

This train of conversation wasn't getting her the information she wanted as well as needed. Though Harris felt certain her guesses would pretty much be right on the mark.

"Good idea. Where do you want to begin? I'm more than willing to talk. Would be much better than the silence of last week. Speech between us is good. Unusual but good." Ash stretched out his long legs that took up most of the space between the two seats.

"You are taking me to your home. Which one?"

"As I said a moment ago if you cared to listen, the country estate in Dover. We will stop in London first." He crossed his legs then his arms, his pose relaxed, negligent, all powerful. Male.

"Was that so hard?" she asked her words coated with sugar. "I don't want to go. I'm telling you no. Take me home."

"That's too bad. You don't have a choice."

"Why?"

"You're going to marry me," he said the words with no expression. "We will have a life together. Raise children. Love one another. All that..."

"Don't I need to agree?"

"No."

Harris didn't understand how his confidence seemed to overshadow her words. She was negative to his suggestion. He must understand that fact. "So, you are going to force me. Don't see how you can do that. A preacher would never marry us if I say no at the altar."

"Let's just say, I will change your mind."

He sat up. Pushed his too long hair from his face.

"You can't."

Well...he could. Harris didn't believe he would spout tender words of undying devotion or love. A few words of love would, indeed, change her mind toward him. *I love you, Harris, would change everything.* She didn't believe that would happen.

"You want me, want that wonderful climax my fingers seduced from you a little over a year past. Remember? Admit it, Harris. You are just being obstinate."

Seems he cut to the chase. Yes, what he claimed was true. She wasn't going to tell him so. There was more to a lasting relationship than a climax. "No, you're wrong. There was nothing special about that afternoon."

"Liar."

All he said was true. She wanted what he could give her. Nevertheless, she also needed what he couldn't give her. His love. "I'm not going to settle."

At that juncture, Ash closed his eyes. By his silence he was telling her speaking with a child-woman as he often called her was a waste of good time. Harris stared out the window. After that she focused on Ash; at his chest, down his torso, to his feet then back. He was her dream of a man.

For several seconds as the coach rumbled down the road, she turned her attention on his lips. They were firm, sensual. His jaw strong. His nose straight. Since he returned to Coronach, he had kissed her a few times. Whenever possible she resisted the emotions he ignited in her along with the way he commandeered her body. Harris didn't want to like the man.

The heat he ignited.

Dragons seemed to shoot fire into places she'd rather not think about. She fumbled with her skirts. Rubbed her hands down her arms. The night was growing chilly. She needed a coat or a blanket. His chest moved up then down with the easy breathing of sleep. His eyes twitched. Was he asleep while she roamed his body with her gaze, wishing he didn't see other women when she should be the only one?

Honesty.

Integrity.

Sharing her man wasn't possible.

Her fingers feeling like icicles, Harris began her search for a blanket in earnest. There must be something. After looking beneath her seat, she turned her attention to the space beneath Ash. One knee was bent, the other stretched out to the opposite side of the coach. She was kneeling on the floor, between his legs. Her face was at his crotch as her fingers searched the drawers beneath him. She gulped. Years had gone by since she saw her brothers naked. He would have... Her cheek almost touched...

Him...there.

This whole unannounced ride was bad planning on his part. He swept her from the garden in the gown she wore at her brother's wedding without a thought for her comfort. If she didn't find something soon, she was going to freeze to death. She gave the area one last swipe with her hands. Bumped his thigh with her chin. Looked up.

The devil.

What she wasn't looking for was to see him wide awake, a smile forming on his lips. Heat flooded her. Silence circled around her, threatening more mortification if she could come up with a satisfying reason for being here.

Where she was.

She wasn't.

Couldn't be between his long muscular legs, her chin almost on his...

"Looking for something?" The low husky timbre of his voice shocked her. There was humor to his tone. "I'll show you mine if you'll show me yours." His deep base chuckle sent vibrations thrumming.

Harris didn't see anything humorous about this situation. Her chin rested a bit above his thigh. She swallowed down the lump of surprise. "You...you're awake."

"Never been asleep."

"Is this new position, kneeling at my feet, something I would be pleased with? Are you asking forgiveness or praying? You seemed to spend a great deal of time staring at my crotch. If you say the right words..." He cleared his throat. "Never mind."

Her face flamed more. How could he be so insincere? "Why would I do that? Stare at you...your...your...?"

"Crotch?" he added to her thoughts.

"No...well...don't mean..." She pushed back giving herself much needed distance feeling disjointed. Awkward.

"Why don't you tell me why you are on your knees staring at my crotch. Could be an interesting story. Would you tell the truth? Would you concoct an interesting tale? Hmmm...."

"I wasn't...staring there." If she could disappear without a trace, she would do so right this instant.

"If not staring, what were you up to?"

He sat up, catching her chin in his hand. His thumb brushed across her bottom lip, once, twice.

The touch seared... She was shaking. Trembling. "I'm cold. Looking for a blanket." *Take that you over...you arrogant Sassenach.* "You ripped me from the festivities without a shawl or anything to cover myself."

I'm not staring at your male parts. You just wish.

I do wish.

She wondered if the shock on her face showed. How did he know what I was thinking?

Ash patted the seat beside him before stretching out his arm. "I can keep you warm. Come here."

He could do that. Heat her body to an inferno. She wasn't about to give him that opportunity. Harris recalled how she burned when he touched her, stroked places on her body that sent a tempest boiling in her blood. She couldn't give in to her hunger. Wouldn't let him badger her into doing so.

"No."

"Ah...well...a man can hope."

Not too many seconds passed before his frock coat was settled around her shoulders. Even with the coat gone from his broad shoulders, he was covered in more clothing than she wore. Harris pulled the lapels close around her. The coat smelled of Ash. The tangy spice he wore.

"Not going to give anything away about your feelings? Can't compromise even when your lips along with your fingers are blue. If you sat next to me, you would be much warmer." Ash settled back against the seat again. "We'll be at our first stop in a bit. You can warm up there. If you wish, I'll order a hot bath."

Harris found her breath, after that another resounding no. Both of them knew if he closed that distance, if she was curious about his plans. If he expected her to sleep with him, he needed to readjust his thinking cap. As long as he kept his distance, she would be able to tell him no. If he kissed her once, she would be a liquid puddle at his big feet. Would melt all over him just like warm honey. So far, it didn't seem he meant to do any of those things.

"I'm fine now," Harris told Ash through her chattering teeth.

She didn't know when the temperature dropped to frigid. "A warm bath would be nice as long as you give me privacy."

Harris didn't know what he expected. How he planned to move forward. The man would have to understand her feelings about the abduction.

"If you think so, I won't bother to argue. If you get any colder, your shaking is going to turn over the carriage."

Ash opened his arms again as if she would jump at the chance to have him warm her up. Harris turned her head away.

Pulling his coat closer she settled into the seat. The large coat held the promise of the man. She breathed in deep, enjoying the semi-closeness. This was as close as she meant to get to him. It didn't matter what he said or how he cajoled.

Harris had a plan. She would not be with him after he fell asleep. She was going to leave. Tonight.

~ * ~

Leaving Harris over a year ago was the hardest thing he'd ever done. Bloody eyes, he never wanted to leave the woman behind. She had a penchant for trouble. Acted with little to no thought. Had not intended to be gone for more than a year. For him, there'd been no choice. His father fell ill. The older brother who was supposed to inherit the title couldn't be bothered with anything except himself along with his newest lady-bird. Chandler was the family reprobate. He gambled. Drank too much. Spent a fortune on each new mistress. Thought the family's wealth was infinite.

When his father's butler wrote begging him to return, he had no choice except to stop what he was doing and come home. Ash didn't waste any time selling his commission. As a younger son, it had been expected for him to serve his country. He spent five years in the Scottish Highlands. Those years...much of the time was used to protect Clan Chaton. Some members of the clan were reckless. Some a bit wild. As the years passed, they became more cautious. The posters asking for information about the shifters were numerous. Ash burned everyone he found.

In doing so he met Harris. She was young. Beautiful. Vivacious. So flirtatious he had a difficult time resisting her. Until he could not. When he left, she'd been seventeen and full of herself. Harris. He should have taken her with him. Doing so would have been so much easier than leaving her behind.

Harris. His mate. She didn't know that pertinent fact. Had failed to recognize the signs or the potent surge of hunger between them. He'd known her in other lives. Would know more to follow. She would learn. Ash never told her. He wanted her to figure it out for herself. So far, she'd not done so.

She was the spoiled younger sister of two doting brothers. Before he left, she taunted him with the name of another man. Told him if she felt like seeing him, she would. Those few words were his nightmare for over a year. If she saw this man, it would change nothing. She was still his mate. Ash was surprised when he returned to find her working at her oldest brother's office as a doctor's assistant. Hawk told him she was good at what she did. Her stitches were neat as well as small.

At first Ash thought Hawk talked about needlepoint or sewing dresses. He couldn't figure out how she was good in his office. Hawk was a doctor. He didn't believe the Frasier women sewed their clothing. He was certain they went to the village modiste. Doubted if Harris ever sat down long enough to enjoy needlepoint. Ash was also surprised when he discovered Hawk was talking about stitching his patients. Her brother along with her cousin went into enough details he was left with no doubts she was useful at the office. When he realized what she did, he felt proud of her.

Well, his Harris was still full of herself, still spoiled thinking she could have her way in everything. She could have her way with him anytime she wished as long as he agreed. The woman was a fighter. She was courageous. At times, too brave. Willful. Spoiled. He kept coming back to the spoiled part of her character. She wasn't ready to become his wife though if he had his way that was going to happen in a month. The banns would be read as soon as they reached his home in Dover. Her parents along with some of her family would arrive in two to three weeks with the rest of her things. Convincing her this was right would be a formidable task. He smiled. That was what the three weeks were for.

Convincing. Courting. He'd never had the chance to court, romance or anything else with her.

Ash knew he had his work cut out for him. If he told her the truth about his nonexistent sexual activities, she would believe he was lying. His silence cut deep. She wasn't going to forgive that moment when she took him by surprise, left him speechless. Bedeviled by her accusations, he'd not had words to utter in his defense.

Bottom line, Harris needed to learn to trust him. She thought his silence about seeing other women convicted him of the crime. What she didn't understand was that he was too dumbfounded by her inquiry to answer. By the time she made her lack of trust in him clear, he decided silence was the best way to proceed. He was hurt by her indictment as well as her lack of faith. He was celibate now for the two years he'd known her. The brief time they had together the day he left, took all his restraint to keep from making love to her. She was right to deny him. Harris wasn't ready for sex then and he wasn't positive she was now either. He never wanted to risk leaving her with child. Despite her unwillingness to travel, this visit he had to take her with him. Had to bind her in marriage. He couldn't take the risk of her seeing or becoming attached to another man. She was so damn irresistible. Beautiful.

Ash remembered their first encounter. Even though he wore the red and white uniform of a hated English soldier, she flirted with him. Lowered her sooty lashes only to open them wide to show him the silver-blue of her gorgeous eyes. Tossed her hair over her shoulder then had the audacity to wink at him. Did he recall she was flirtatious? The little minx.

He was certain he lost his heart to her the first time she flashed him her signature smile. As if she was a siren, she beckoned to him. Called his name. His body jerked to attention every time he was with her. Ash knew from the first encounter with the pretty girl sashaying her hips as she walked in front of him, she was his mate. What he didn't know at the time was that she was also a shifter. As to this point in time, Ash didn't believe she knew he had the ability to shift. Her brothers knew. That very fact gave him the needed advantage if she tried to shift and run back home. She believed she would outrun him. Impossible.

Their first kiss was in the alley between an inn and the local printer's shop. She teased him as they walked together. When they reached the alley, he pulled her into the sheltered privacy. His hands on either side of her face held her still. He captured her mouth, touched her until she made this throaty beautiful sound in the back of her throat. It was all he could do to stop himself from taking everything she offered. He found out later the printing shop belonged to her middle brother, Cameron. Lainie was the only one who called him Roc, which was a short version of his middle name.

That kiss was memorable. He held the short moments close to his heart. There would be more kisses. Thoughts of that first time still held him spellbound. Harris didn't know the first thing about kissing. She learned. It did not take long for her to flash her pretty smile then get what she asked for. Until that day in the glen, he only kissed her. On the day he left, he needed to show her all he could give her. Needed to bind her to him in ways she would never be able to deny. Ash needed for her to remember how she felt when he loved her, touched her with the intimacy they needed for the rest of their lives.

Roc was the brother getting married tonight. Ash closed his eyes, wondering what plans Harris had for escaping him. He understood she would try. Told him as much. Harris had not been given a choice to come with him. She was with him because of brute force. He didn't appreciate the fact he had to toss her over his shoulder for her to accompany him. What must infuriate her was the simple fact she was with him by her parents' permission. Harris would feel betrayed.

That day, the first time he left Coronach, Harris ran after him. She'd told him she didn't wish to ride with him. Implied she didn't want to see him again. That surprised as well as ghosted him the entire time he was in London. He had not expected to see her again until he could return to claim the woman who was supposed to be his wife. The gamble he was taking left him sweating as well as breathless. When he walked with her, kissed her, he was certain she didn't think of him as her mate. He was. There wasn't one doubt in his head.

Harris had not wanted to promise him to remain chaste. There was a boy she insinuated who could hold her attention. He was furious at the notion another man would kiss her. That she would allow that. When he seduced her that day in the sun dappled glade, he didn't take her innocence.

He hoped to have that privilege either on his wedding night or when she committed to him. When he claimed her in his clan's ceremony. As was their custom, he would declare for her before the marriage ritual. The sooner the better was his thoughts on the subject. In doing so she would see their pasts come alive. Then and only then she would understand his persistence.

Watching her with the top of her head close to his crotch, her silken hair brushing across his hands, his thoughts of celibacy where she was concerned vanished. She had no idea what she was doing to him. His attention was directed on her. He clenched his teeth tight then breathed in deep once and once more to calm his raging body.

She might be the death of him before he could slip a ring on her slender finger. Harris had the most beautiful hands. The fingers were long, slender, soft... The nails well-manicured. When she clung to him, her hands sifting through his hair, it was all he could do to keep his deep groan of desire behind his teeth. Since his return, she stayed as far from him as possible. Ash understood what she needed.

Words of love.

When the time was right, he would say the words she wished to hear. Now, he needed for her to return that love. At every turn, she denied him. Fought her feelings. More importantly, he needed her to move away from his crotch. His pants were growing tighter by the second.

Her body was womanly, soft, pliant. She was passionate. Ash knew she wanted him. Could have made love to her, stripped her of all her clothing that day. He felt the same way she did. Leaving her pregnant to face the consequences alone would have been unconscionable. If he'd had courage that day, he would have taken her with him. Set her atop his horse then left. She would have gone willingly. That day, she would have followed him with no coercion, no abduction necessary. Followed him without her parent's approval.

Harris would try to leave him tonight. They were so close to McKenna land the short distance would be easy for her to navigate. What he didn't know was how. He thought of as many different possibilities as he could. His mind was a muddled mess. He kept coming back to the notion she would shift to get away. That was a dangerous strategy...for both of them. In the highlands there were still factors at play they must guard against.

If she tried to change shape, she would find out he was also a shifter. While he never meant to keep that bit of information from her, it also was never prudent to divulge a secret too soon. She would need to be his before he wanted to enlighten her.

Harris was his now.

The woman didn't know it yet. Maybe she did know. If she did realize, she wasn't accepting.

He smiled. Watching her was like devouring candy. Harris was so full of flavors; spicey, sweet, soft in the center, hard nowhere. She wanted to make all decisions. Needed to control all events. She would learn it would be bloody hard for her to command him. Her parents let her run around the village unchaperoned. Sometimes into the highlands. It was one of those times he first saw her. He was on patrol that day. In her cat form he saw her swimming. Thank the god above he rode ahead of the other soldiers. He was able to lead them away. When he returned to make certain she was alright, she was sunning herself.

Naked. Human form.

The sight remained etched in his head over the years. She'd been young. Her womanly curves just beginning to blossom. Smitten might be an apt way to describe the sight of her. Furious at her stupidity might be another description.

After that, he kept an eye on her. When she flirted with him, he couldn't resist her. Two weeks passed before he was able to spend a few moments with her. Her spontaneity delighted him. She was never boring. Kept him on edge. Still did.

When he looked up, Harris was staring at him, playing with a long strand of hair that fell from the elaborate chignon that had been created for the wedding. She was twirling the lock between her fingers before examining the ends. Ash didn't understand. She noticed him looking then dropped the hair.

"Oh," She lowered her lashes.

Once that was the way she flirted with him. Lowered lashes. Playing with long strands of her hair. Ash wondered if she was after something. Thought to keep him on his toes. She could try to bargain with him. He understood she would like him to turn the carriage around.

"We're almost there."

"Where?" she asked, her voice butter soft beguiling in the extreme. She was searching for a means to get her way. An about face seemed to be her first endeavor. Harris meant to lull him with her complacency.

The woman did want to have things done the way she envisioned them. She was willing to do anything to get her way. He wondered if she would go as far as making love with him if she believed he would return her to her family. He could push that idea when they reached their rooms. The thought shot across his brain. "Believe you know where."

She scowled at him. "What inn?"

"The Witches Inn." He laughed at her new expression. "It is almost Halloween. You do know they change the name during the month."

"There is no inn by that name this close to Carnoch. You're making things up."

"We are close. Close enough for you to try something. I'm warning you, Harris. If you try to run, I'll bring you back. You won't like what comes next. If you do manage to get home before I catch up with you, your father will bring you to me. Suppose we might meet half way. That...would be an incredible waste of my time as well as your father's. We are both busy men." Ash thought of running his fingertip along that vertical crease in the middle of her forehead. Smooth it out. Perhaps ease the tension.

"Did I tell you I don't want to be here?" she asked, her voice petulant with her annoyance. "Doesn't that make a difference? Force doesn't become you." She fell back into the sulk mode.

If Harris intended to look sullen for the rest of the trip, that was her prerogative. While he did care, he didn't have a means to put an end to the grump in her voice. Would love to trace his finger along her bottom lip. Encourage her to smile. Scintillate all her senses until she begged for his kiss.

"Yes, you told me. In this situation, no, what you wish for doesn't concern me. From this point on, we will do this all my way."

The coach rolled to a stop. Ash jumped out to give her a hand down. She stumbled when she tried to dismount the carriage by herself. His hands caught her by her waist. She fell against him. He swore. Held her for several seconds that didn't need counting for him to feel her precious curves flush against him. Something he needed to avoid for a while. Harris was so right for him. Fit him to perfection. His nerves screeched, raced with anticipation of more delights.

Holding her elbow, he escorted her to the inn. Nodded to the man in the front. "Bobo."

Bobo tossed him the keys. "A bath along with a bottle of wine. Perhaps a small plate of cheese." Ash turned to Harris. "Are you hungry?"

"I overate at the celebration feast." She was still in a sulk.

"I'm famished." Ash would rather devour Harris than the cheese board that would be sent up to the rooms. Thought if he could get enough wine down her throat, she would fall asleep. Hoped when that happened, he could rest and not worry about her slipping out in the middle of the night. He resigned himself to a sleepless night. He could always sleep in the carriage tomorrow.

"Should have stayed to partake of the meal rather than kidnapping me. If you'd done that you wouldn't be so hungry."

Bobo grinned. He too had been warned about the possibilities of tonight. Harris would take flight. The man was on duty until the *wee* hours of the morning. How and when were the only questions. Ash bent down close to her ear. "You can try."

Harris stiffened. Tilted her chin.

"You won't get very far."

She still didn't speak. Her back stiffened. That pointed little chin of hers went up even higher.

"There are twenty miles you will have to run. Flee if you wish... Are you that afraid of me...of us? What we can have together if you allow us..." Ash left the sentence hanging in the air. "Let's get you that hot bath. Some wine inside your stomach to relax you as well as warm that chill that keeps you quivering. A *wee* bit of food to blend with the wine."

"A hot bath would be nice." She slipped out of his frock coat, handing it to him. All so prim and proper, she spoke. "Thank you."

"Yes, it would. The door will stay open. As long as I hear you splashing, I won't come in to see if you are still in the room. I'll give you privacy. Unless..."

Wrenching her elbow from his grasp, she lifted her skirts then hurried up the stairs. Fascinated with her pert bottom, Ash watched the provocative display. Every now and then, he caught the view of a slender ankle.

"Fine...very fine... You did find a pretty one." Bobo said with a grin as he also observed her display of pique. "Think you can keep up with the *lass*? She's spirited. High-strung. Going to keep you panting. Run you a merry chase."

Ash nodded then followed in her wake to discover her standing at the top of the stairs studying the closed doors.

"Waited for me? That was full of thought."

He almost laughed at her when she grunted. Harris wouldn't know which room was theirs. Rooms, he amended. They would only use one door. The other one he had Bobo lock it from the outside as well as the inside. When she tried to run, she would have to go through his room. That fact gave him a needed edge. He slept light. His years in his majesty's service taught him to sleep with eyes as well as ears open.

The small bag her mother packed for the trip arrived. After that the hot water for the bath was brought to the room. The bottle of wine along with the cheese board appeared next. He poured her a glass of wine. Brought it into the room he told her was hers for the evening.

"What's wrong?" Ash was looking at the well-known scowl. This time the expression was different. He realized as if she hit him in the gut, she couldn't get out of her gown by herself. When he walked in with the glasses, her arms were behind her back, her breasts taking center stage in a provocative fight with the fastenings behind her. In his line of sight, they were pushed out...so tempting. If he didn't know better, he would think they were begging for his attention.

"As if you didn't know."

"Not at first. Had to study your provocative body posture. Would you like help?" Ash was thinking the line of her spine would be a delight to trace with his lips. All the way down to the crack between her delicious backside.

"You...!" Harris fumed her shoulders shaking. Her bottom lip quivered. "Alright. It's the only way I can get out of this gown. Don't touch!"

Of course he would touch. A brush of his knuckles here then there. Tiny shivers from her body. A bit of foreplay that wouldn't amount to anything except making her want him. He wouldn't be able to touch to see how wet those few caresses would make her. It was just as well. She wasn't ready for anything intimate between them. He wasn't a gambling man. Didn't want to stake his future on one moment of bad judgment.

Ash studied her trying to decide if there was anything he could say that might diffuse some of her anger. "Would never dream of touching you, love. Last thing I want or need. You're too bloody prickly tonight. Have been since I returned. To think I believed you would be pleased to see me. Found how far from the truth my thoughts roamed. All my dreams of a wonderful reunion shattered to pieces."

With a loud splutter she turned her back to him, holding the corsage as if he'd unfastened everything holding her together and the gown was about to reveal all her luscious curves. He expected Harris to call him out on his lie. She didn't. That was another point of confusion for Ash. She ran hot then cold. The little woman confounded him. Never knew what to expect. Didn't know how to handle the confusing aspects of her piques. Women were so damn hard to understand.

Ash proceeded as planned. He meant to tease a few emotions from her. Needed to tempt her passion. See if he could seduce her. The first caress brought a shiver to her slender shoulders coupled with a small gasp followed with a quiver. The response was encouraging. He thought of another ploy.

"You promised you wouldn't touch me," she accused as the tip of his finger settled on one bone. After that the one below then the one lower still. He slid his hand along the contour of her back. Her skin was silken, so soft.

"Never promised a bloody thing, love. Now let me see if I can get you out of the gown then perhaps into the bath, after that your nightgown. Don't want the water to grow cold now, do we?"

Another touch and a shudder. The brush of his palm on her nape to move long hair away from the fasteners. He let strands slide through his finger, teasing the insides. His gentle seduction continued. She held herself stiff. He understood she was fighting her feelings. Was pleased by her reaction. Felt each small quiver. Caught the scent of aroused woman. His sensual evocative woman.

He stepped back, satisfied with all he accomplished. Ash knew she lied. Understood by the soft sound, the little sighs of pleasure, she wanted him. "There, all finished. Don't spend too long in the bath. You'll look like a prune. If you need me, I'll be in the other room. Call my name."

Ash sat. Sipped his wine. Heard her skirt swish across the floor when she turned. Listened to the sound of her clothing hitting the rug by the bed. He wondered if she would leave all her clothing there to be picked up by someone else. No one besides her would pick up her discarded clothes. In this she was on her own.

Water splashed onto the floor when her body filled the tub. He hardened. His imagination spun. Blood roared to life. Those sounds could drive a man mad. He reminded himself this might happen every night on their trip south. No, in the future, he would lock her in then go downstairs for a pint of ale coupled with a few laughs with the locals. He wasn't into torture. His anguish.

After she rose from the bath, he heard everything. Knew when she slipped what would be a virginal night dress over her head. Pictured her sitting in front of the small fire combing her hair. Imagined how the hard tips of her breasts would press against the fabric inviting him to touch.

"Your turn." She stood in the doorway between the two rooms, the glass of wine he poured her in one hand. She sipped. Backlight from her room highlighted her slender form. Even covered by the thin white fabric he could see the outline of her entire body. She was too beautiful for words. The hard tips of her breast did push against the fabric. Her lush curves were outlined in shadows.

His gut clenched tight. He brought in a large breath of air. Nothing calmed the raging heat searing him. The beast within him was awakened. He was so aroused by this virginal apparition, he ached. Bloody eyes, how was he going to last through this trip into his homeland without benefit of touching her? It might be best if he returned her to her family before she reduced him to a pile of ashes. He could do things her way. Marry her here. To torment him, if he gave in to her wishes of marriage in Carnoch, she would still say no. He had his father to think about. His need to be in

England, for him, overshadowed all other desires.

Ash just didn't have the time now to give her what she wanted. He would tell her as soon as she was willing to listen that in another year, they would return to Carnoch. At that time, if she wished to be married in the traditions of Clan Chaton, he would never protest. While he'd been speaking with her parents, he'd told them he would bring her home. Going back on his word was not an option.

"More wine?" she asked while she walked into the room holding her glass out. Her smile flipped his failing restraint.

Ash tried not to look as he splashed the red liquid into her glass, filling it to the brim. Looking down he saw her bare toes. They were small. Exquisite. Hell, toes weren't exquisite. They were appendages. Most of the time toes were ugly. His were. Each had hair growing on them. Her toes, he wanted to...wanted to see how they tasted after her bath. He'd never stared at any other female's toes. Was this some new fetish that would suck him under? Drown him. Incapacitate his mind. He shook off the thoughts to concentrate on this next phase of the evening.

"Is the water still hot?"

"Tepid."

As hot as he was at this moment, tepid would do fine. Freezing would be better. "I won't be long."

"Don't hurry on my account."

"The door is locked." Harris wasn't in any shape to run. Not in that nightgown which hid nothing at all. Her feet were bare. The thought of her running around the countryside in that attire left him sweating. No man except him should see her dressed as she was. He fetched in much needed air catching her scent as he did so. Lavender. Woman. He would end up bathing in her fragrance. That was not a bad notion. He needed to learn her scent, memorize it in case she did slip away. It would be easier to find her. He wouldn't need to search. By her scent he would know where she was.

She tossed him that flirty all or nothing smile that always left him with his gut turning over along with his tongue hanging out, panting. The plans she had would not come to fruition. Ash understood she was biding her time until he let down his guard enough for her to slip from the room. She would wait until he was sleeping. He didn't plan on doing that. Tonight was the most precarious of all.

In the adjoining chamber, he undressed then slipped into the tepid water that smelled of Harris. Ash groaned. Set his head on the lip of the tub long enough for him to bring his emotions under control. Washed then slipped on a clean pair of buckskins. He'd thought to put on a robe. Thought better of that when he realized he might have to make a hasty exit in the middle of the night. He needed to be ready for anything unexpected that might happen.

Once in the other room, he filled the wine glasses again. He hoped she'd fall asleep. Pass out might be better. Ash was pleased. Harris drank deeply. She'd also eaten. He sat down next to her. She moved away as if his touch was abhorrent. How long would she play at this game of hers? He knew firsthand this wasn't the way she felt about him. She was angry. He needed to change that passion to something more fulfilling.

He sat back, stretching out his legs, trying to relax while at the same time tried to see into her pretty head. Wished he could get closer so he understood what she plotted. "Why, Harris? Why have you taken such an aversion to me? I can recall when you wanted me to kiss you. Touch you. You flirted with me. Sashayed your hips back and forth to entice me. What happened?"

"I don't share." She stared at him over the lip of her glass. "Won't be part of a threesome. Want the man I wed to want only me, to think only of me."

Bloody eyes, where did she learn about something like that? A threesome? He wasn't positive, he wanted an answer. "You don't trust, either. There is more. Tell me." Ash needed to get to the truth before she convinced herself they were all wrong for each other. "What if I told you, I was so flabbergasted by your question, I couldn't breathe, let alone think or spout an answer?"

"You mean the one where I asked if you saw other women while you were away in London doing whatever was so important you had to leave?"

"Yes."

"I don't believe you."

"Why don't you try honesty? What else has you so steaming mad at me you turn your back on everything we can have? I've offered marriage numerous times. I know that is what you wish for too."

Ash watched her features pale. Saw the shaking of the wine inside her glass. The red liquid caught the ever-changing light from the fire.

"I didn't see the man I told you about. Expected you to remain...didn't expect you to continue seeing women. Do you even now have a mistress you are keeping somewhere? Is there someone waiting for you when we reach Dover? I won't be a part of that. I cannot stand thinking of you making love to another woman. It's not right!" Her fisted hands came down hard on the table.

Bloody everlasting hell. Ash thought of Abella. She lived in his Dover home. Had played the mistress there for seven years. She meant nothing to him except as a responsibility. He rescued her from a bordello in Paris. She spoke little English. Harris would meet her. He would need to tell her about the woman. There would be another nail in his coffin. Something she would never believe. Abella was a gorgeous woman. Though Abella wished it to be different, he never touched her sexually. She was his best friend's mate. Because of his father he'd not acted on his desires either.

Abella had never been his mistress. He never slept with her. Though she made her feelings clear. She wanted to be in his bed. Harris would never believe that fact.

"What if I told you I haven't taken a woman to my bed since the day I first saw you. That was three years ago when you were barely fifteen."

He sat down, crossing his legs studying her ever changing emotions coupled with the play of shadows across her face.

"I wouldn't believe you." She set the empty glass on the table. "Is that all you have to say? Should go to bed. Imagine tomorrow will be a long day."

"Don't you want to know when that first time was?" Ash asked, thinking she would be shocked when he told her. He wanted to see her eyes when he mentioned to her the minor fact that he watched her sunning herself when she didn't wear a stitch of clothing.

"Should I wish to know?"

Harris didn't get up to leave. Instead, she downed the last tiny drop of wine in her glass.

Good, her curiosity was growing. Her back wasn't as stiff as when they entered the room. "Only if you want. What I will tell you is that it wasn't that first day in Carnoch when your outrageous flirting caught the eye of every soldier in the vicinity. Were you flirting with me or the other men? Everyone wanted a piece of you including me."

Her eyes widened to huge pools of silver-gray. "If there was wine in my glass, I would toss it in your face. If you must know, it will make you more arrogant than before. I've never flirted with anyone except you. If those Sassenach thought I was flirting with them, they were wrong."

Her words warmed his heart. "Since I met you...saw you, I haven't taken anyone to my bed." He would say the words until she realized he spoke only the truth. How the bloody hell long would that take? He wasn't about to beg.

~ * ~

Heather lay in Elliott's arms. She was thinking of all the things she should have done differently. They didn't tell Harris about Ash's plans...or his request that the two should leave during the festivities. Since Harris was still a maiden, she would not be allowed to go with the married women to prepare the bride for the wedding night. They didn't tell her he was a shifter...on his request. There were too many secrets between the couple. They argued constantly. Except at night when she went to bed, Ash never left her side. He tried to soothe her temper along with her constant pique. Their little girl was too stubborn. Spoiled too. Something about Ash spooked her. Before he returned, she meant to marry him. Talked of little else. Harris told them she loved him. For some unknown reason all that changed. For their future, what ailed the couple must be made right.

Ash told them he needed time alone with her. Time to ease the one major conflict that rose between them. He told her he felt as if he was banging his head against a brick wall. She was still too young but as things progressed, he needed to marry her as soon as possible. He expected to spend only a few days in Carnoch. Instead, he spent a few weeks. Told them about the danger circling his father. The sooner he returned the better.

27

"Did we do the right thing by our daughter? I worry so much. Ash is right. Harris is still young...idealistic. She is a romantic at heart. While Ash would love to romance her, he explained he didn't have time. Did we do right by our daughter?" Heather asked a second time as she smoothed her palm across Elliott's chest. "I just don't know what to think any longer."

She felt his shrug against her cheeks. His big hand roamed her back. "We never heard a scream. Who knows she might go willingly. Sometimes you over think. They will be fine. Believe the man loves her."

"I *ken* she loves him." Heather was still attempting to make sense of this relationship that fired hot then cold. At the moment, for Harris, the connection between them was frigid.

"You've noticed the way they stare at each other as if they are star-struck. They are meant to be together. We've seen that same look on our sons' faces when they found the woman meant for them. They are each other's mate. Of course, we did right by our daughter. She is with the man she is fated to be with."

"She doesn't *ken* anything about the man. For the life of me, I don't *ken* why, he wants it that way." Heather lifted up so she could look at her husband. She touched his mouth with her fingertip.

"Our daughter was too young to marry a year ago. By the way she is acting, I'm still not certain she is old enough," Elliott said, biting with gentleness Heather's finger. "I *ken* age wise she is old enough to be a wife." He paused, running the strands of Heather's long hair between his fingers, enjoying the sensation. "She is spoiled. Expects to have everything her way. Ash won't accept that version of our daughter. He will not spoil her to suit her whims."

"Willful," Heather said with a snort.

"Used to getting her way in everything."

"Isn't that overindulged?" Heather trailed small biting kisses down his neck.

"That too."

Don't believe he's a man to allow our daughter the kind of freedom that would put her at risk," Elliott continued as he caught her hand descending lower threatening to end the conversation. They still had a few things to reassure each other about.

"There are no highlands in Dover."

"No Sassenach soldiers to catch her while she runs wild," Elliott agreed. "He was a Sassenach. Was...he told me he saw her first when she was swimming in our favorite loch then sunning herself."

"Imagine he saw her without a stitch of clothing."

"Imagine so...," Elliott said, pulling his wife on top of him. He held her bottom, caressed. She felt him against her. Felt his need. He pulled her up so she could sit on him. He filled her.

"They will have a few rocky days ahead of them. Are we expecting her to come running home tonight? The first place they are staying is not far from here. Quite doable for a stubborn woman bent on having her way about everything. We should be ready to expect our little girl. If she comes here, she will be sent back to the man who is her future."

"I would tell you yes, except I've more confidence in the young man. He will thwart whatever wayward plans she has. Nip it in the bud," Elliott said. Groaned when Heather moved up then down on him.

"If I know my daughter, she will shift then run."

"The man is stronger as well as faster than Harris. My guess is that he won't sleep until they are far enough away from here she won't be able to try anything stupid," Elliott said as he found tender spots that made her squirm.

His hands cupped her breasts. Played with the hard buds he always adored.

She would never get her fill of this man she loved so much, was so lucky to find. Every day he filled her heart with joy. All she wanted for her daughter was to marry her mate and find the same type of love. Ash was that man to fulfil all Harris' dreams.

"We will leave in two to three weeks unless we hear that the wedding has been canceled or delayed. We will see her then. Will have the answer to all our questions," he nipped her shoulder.

"It won't be. I'm praying nothing will be canceled. Ash will never let her return here even if there is not a wedding. Don't know how he will keep her against her will if she doesn't want to stay."

"With gentleness..."

Chapter Two

Harris listened to the night sounds. Counted the ticks of the clock. The beats of her heart. Heard the frogs croaking and the cicadas chirping outside. An owl hooted. Ash's snores pleased her. The sounds were even as well as deep. Told her he slept. This would be easy. She smiled, the first one since he abducted her. Cast her over his shoulder. As the night progressed, his sleep sounds changed, growing more pronounced. Telling her he was in deep sleep. Her heart pounded in her chest. Blood rushed through her ears smothering all other noises. Her stomach did a nervous little flip. Anticipation was heady as well as nerve wracking. Each breath she stole from the night landed in the pit of her belly, somersaulting.

While deep down, she understood what she planned could be dangerous...

She had no choice. Staying with Ash was not an option. To remain with a man who didn't love her...he needed to see things her way. Not his.

Believing his fidelity was impossible, she snorted. Men don't change. Among her female friends it was a known fact a woman's wishes would never sway a man. Patterns had been set that wouldn't deviate. Bah. He'd not been celibate for what...three years? He told her lies to get her to fall into his arms then his bed. How could she ever be certain he wanted to marry her? The words could be more lies with the sole purpose of deceiving. If she reached home, she could make her father run interference with the man. He would side with her. Would never make her go back with Ash if she didn't wish to do so. Harris sipped in a deep breath of air that didn't fill her lungs.

She waited to hear a few more resounding snores.

This was going to happen now. The time was right. The night dark. Silent. A full moon with a soft ghosting of clouds would light up the trail as well as create shadows to hide her progress. As each slow second passed,

Harris was more certain. Ash must be sound asleep. She slid her feet from the bed. Keeping to the side of the room as well as away from the light, she padded to the door. Her feet were cold. Strange to notice that in a few minutes it wouldn't make a difference. Not creating a sound, she slid the bolt. Slow...smooth. Thanking all the gods in the world the mechanism was well oiled as was the hinge on the door, she stepped through the opening and into the hall. One light cast an eerie glow over the floor. She drank in a hesitant breath of air. This was it. She was going to make her escape.

Bye, Ash.

Harris closed the door. A soft snick of the latch followed. Nothing that should alert Ash to the fact she left the room.

Looking over her shoulder and on the tips of her toes, she continued down the hall to the back of the inn. As soon as the door swung open, she stepped into the darkest shadows she could find. Harris pulled on the hem of her nightgown until the fabric was over her head. Wrapped the sleeves of her gown around her neck. Tied them.

Shifted.

The act took only a couple of seconds. Inhaled deep as well as slow, waiting to adjust to the change of her body. Sucked into her lungs a large draft of cool night air. She would need the oxygen for the ensuing run. After one last look at the inn, a smile on her face she leapt through the woods toward Carnoch. She'd done the impossible. Harris was free. No more Ash to tell her how to act or what she should be doing. No one to order her around. To expect all his dictates to be followed. Now, not to wear herself out too fast, she sprinted then she would walk. Once she caught her breath she would run again. Her heart pumped hard. In her cat she was swift...sure footed. The problem was she couldn't run for a long time. Speed was her forte not distance. Pacing herself was important.

Harris felt the exhilaration of freedom. Felt independent. Autonomous. The time was well-past midnight. She would not run into any one. No person would be about. She was safe from possible danger. This was never Sassenach territory. A year ago most of the soldiers had gone back to England. Good riddance. Slowing down to walk, she breathed in deep. The air was redolent. The scent of grass and trees coupled with autumn filled her nostrils. This was her favorite season. It was close to All

Hallow's Eve. A soft wind blew against her cheek ruffling her whiskers. Dry fallen leaves crackled against her paws as she swished through them. In a few minutes she would run again. She was free!

A foreign sound caught her attention. The low growl sent the hair on her back standing on end. She froze, listening. The next growl terrified. Her cat-form tensed. All senses alert. Panicked.

Horrified, she leapt forward, racing as fast as her limbs would take her. Something hard and big landed on top of her, pressing her to the ground. When she hit the earth all her air rushed from her lungs in a huge gasp. Her nose was buried in dirt and leaves. A nettle pricked the tip. Her eyes stung from fragments of dirt. Another nettle dug into her side. She scrambled for air, gasping. Nothing got into her lungs. The beast on top of her was keeping her from breathing. She squirmed then bucked. Struggled. Fought with all her strength. Tried to get the beast off her back. Pushed as hard as she could with her front legs. Powerless.

Shift Harris.

Do it now.

Ash?

Yes, love. It's me. Someone has to save your fool's neck. Shift! My God if you fight me now...Don't. Don't, you stubborn woman. For the sake of your life, shift.

Harris was stunned. How? He was sound asleep when she left. She'd been so quiet. Now, she couldn't think. Couldn't breathe. He wanted her to shift. Couldn't with him pressing her down to the ground.

You know?

Yes.

I can't shift with you on top of me. I'm not a contortionist.

Do it anyway. Now. You can.

You big oaf! Get off me. She wasn't about to give into his demands.

Shift, Harris.

No.

He couldn't do anything to her if she didn't change form. She would stay this way until he understood she could never be with him. Would never share him with any other woman. They would be stuck like this forever into eternity. She could be more stubborn. Out wait him.

His teeth sunk into the fur at her neck. Her eyes widened. No. He wouldn't dare. Ash rose above her. His huge paws on either side of her face. The devil, the man was a shifter! Shock. She caught sight of enough of his legs to realize he wasn't a black panther...a panther of any kind. He was dragging her. He was huge. He'd tossed her nightgown to the side. If she changed back, she would be naked.

No. Stop.

Yes.

Terror set in. He wasn't going to drag her back to the room. He wouldn't. Doing so was far too risky. She had traveled at least a mile from the inn. In those few idle seconds of thinking, Harris decided on the only prudent course left open to her. She shifted.

As soon as she began to change shape, Ash's teeth left her neck. She was once more lying on the ground spread eagled on her stomach. Her bum in the air. Naked for his eyes to see. She'd done this to herself. Felt the cold earth beneath her along with the chilling night above. Yes, now she was naked for his eyes to see. Exposed. No longer caring about her lack of clothing, she was so furious she rose, staring at him, her face set in angry lines. So furious with the beast, she forgot she wore nothing. Her fists were at her sides as she watched the white tiger change his form. Her first thought was that his cat was beautiful. The second...

He's naked.

What did you expect? So are you, love. I do like what I'm looking at. Too bad you're in such a terrible pique. If not, we could make our first time together wonderful here on the forest floor.

He knew her thoughts. Invaded her mind. Harris tilted her chin unwilling to shy away from him. She wasn't about to let him see her fear. In her bravado, she let her gaze wander down his length. Took in all of him. Absorbed his essence into her soul. His person was just as magnificent as his cat. This time she wasn't going to deny where her questing eyes landed. She watched his member grow. Jerked her eyes to meet his. Surprised by the sight he made. She never expected the transformation. Understood a few things about a male. This...

His smile was broad as well as unabashed. He understood what captured her attention. Liked the fact she was looking at that part of him.

The next words showed his amusement. "You've never seen a naked man?" He was grinning. Enjoying her embarrassment. "Put your nightgown on, Harris." The smile vanished as he walked to his buckskins. Before she had her gown over her head, he was dressed.

Still, she stared. "How did you know?"

He must have cat ears as well as cat eyes. He would have sensed her leaving. Ash didn't answer. Her body tensed as his perusal roamed over her, lingering on her breasts and her...

Ash gritted out his voice tense. "Harris...love," He paused, running his hand along the front of his face. "Unless you want to lose your virginity here and now on the forest floor, put your bloody nightgown on...now!" His eyes told her he would put it on her himself if she didn't move with speed.

She didn't understand why she gaped at him. Well...maybe she did understand. The man was gorgeous. His body... He strode to her. Shut her mouth using one finger. Explored her body again with his roaming gaze. She shivered. Why she didn't cover herself with the clothing she brought for just this purpose, she didn't know. Stunned to reality and with rapid jerky movements, she backed away from him then slipped the gown over her head. Her fingers were shaking so hard she couldn't deal with the small buttons down the front. Ash stepped up beside her. Pushed her hands to the side then fastened every single button.

"There." It seemed he breathed a relieved sigh.

As they started walking, his hand on the small of her back, her foot hit on a stone. Harris let out a small cry of pain. In a single fluid movement, Ash swept her into his arms. This time it wasn't to sling her over his shoulder as if she was a sack of grain. This time he cradled her in his arms. To her surprise what she felt was tenderness. She had no choice except to put her arms around his neck so she could hang on. She pressed her forehead against his shoulder. Closed her eyes, feeling him, warm, hard. Heard the resounding beat of his heart. His arms surrounded her. If she wasn't so blasted angry with the cheating man, she would enjoy this moment of closeness. So much time passed. It had been so long since he held her. Since he returned and she discovered his perfidy she'd not let him close to her. Harris missed him. Didn't want to admit to that fact. Wished he would kiss her again. She shook her head, willing the horrible reaction from her mind.

He walked barefoot. She closed her eyes with a small grimace. His feet would be cut by the time they got back to the inn. It seemed to take much longer to return. She found herself shivering from the cold or was it fear. He would be angry. What was he going to do? Tie her to the bed so he could get some sleep? If she was in his position, she would seriously consider that means to an end.

As they walked past Bobo, the man at the desk nodded then, "Seems you found your little lady. Glad to see everything turned out right this evening. Good luck...suppose you might be neadin' that simple commodity."

His voice reverberated in that low growl she remembered just before he pounced on her. "A basin of hot water and a bottle of whiskey. Please. Send it right up." He kept going, never breaking stride as he reached the steps leading back to the room as well as her confinement.

She'd not made headway on her plan to leave the man. By now she thought to be halfway home. She was back in the room. Under his thumb.

"You going to get her so tipsy she can't try anything new?" Bobo asked with a snort of laughter. "I'll get those things right up to you."

"That was what I hoped for with the wine," his voice was dry. "Guess she didn't drink enough to pass out as I hoped. I can try a few shots of whiskey. Hard alcohol might do the trick where a bit of wine would not."

Harris hit him hard on the chest. She didn't appreciate being talked about as if she wasn't there. "Beast!"

"You haven't seen the beast in me yet."

Again, his words were a low growl yet the sound gentled.

A shiver slipped down her spine. The devil, she should have done better. He didn't seem all that angry when they were still in the forest. Should have waited longer. She was certain he was asleep when she tip-toed out of the room. Earlier, he told her she could try. What he didn't know was that he didn't win. She would keep trying until she succeeded. Until he would be so exasperated with her, he would never go after her.

In the room he set her on his bed. She tried to get up. To leave. To go to the adjoining room. He wouldn't allow that. Put his hand on her shoulder.

"Stay put. You're not going anywhere I can't see you."

He pinched the bridge of his nose. Ran his hand down his mouth then his neck. With the knock on the door, he strode over to open it. There was Bobo with the hot water and the whiskey. Ash nodded to the floor in front of the chair she sat in earlier to drink her wine.

"You need some help?" Bobo asked. "Your feet must be bleeding. I can send little Sara up to help you."

"I can take care of them...my feet. No need to bother yourself or your daughter. My feet will be fine."

Harris felt a wave of guilt undulate through her. She did this to him. Caused his pain. Maybe her brothers were right. She was spoiled. Stubborn. Willful. She wasn't old enough to be a wife because she acted as a child. This was proof positive of that fact. The devil, she needed to know what he was thinking. Somehow, she needed to make this up to him. This was her fault. Despite the fact she meant to try to leave again, she would see to his needs now. There was some decency left in her.

How?

She could begin by cleaning his feet. Her brother told her she was good with her hands. Told her she might someday make an excellent nurse or doctor he told her if she wished to spend the time studying. He even explained to her he would mentor her if she wished. In his office, she stitched his patient's wounds.

She did. Harris needed to be helpful. Though she would never admit to Ash she loved him, she did.

Now that she would be living miles and miles away from him that wouldn't be possible. Bobo left. Ash tipped the now open bottle of whiskey to his lips then stuck his feet in the hot water. Harris saw him grimace.

"It must sting." She left for the other room. When she returned, he watched her, his eyes narrowed. He was telling her with the expression on his face that despite the injury to the bottom of his feet, she would not be going anywhere.

At his feet, she picked up one. Used the lavender scented soap to wash. Harris was using her hands to soap then clean the cuts. With the tips of her nails, she pulled small pieces of debris from the wounds. Felt him flinch when she probed too far. "I'm sorry. I *ken* it hurts. I *ken* you carried me so I wouldn't be in the same condition. Thank you. This doesn't mean I won't try to leave again."

"Thought you had a soft touch with the patients. In hindsight if you'd walked back, your feet would hinder all your plans. Harris," he paused again, staring into the dying embers of the fire, "I don't understand this new aversion you have to me. I know you used to care."

"I do have a soft touch," she murmured, thinking he was acting a bit like a baby. Didn't wish to acknowledge the truth of some of his words. The stupid man, she told him the exact aversion she had to him. "You'll be fine." She worked on the second foot. After she finished, she looked at him. He sat in the chair, his eyes closed. She would never mistake that relaxed air for what it was. A tiger ready to spring into action at the smallest hint of disobedience. To pounce. "Do you want me to pour the whiskey on the soles of your feet?"

"I'll do it." He hissed in a sharp breath of air as the alcohol entered the wounds. All through the doctoring process there were no words of recrimination. Now he cursed behind his teeth. She made out some of the words she'd heard her brothers use from time to time.

Ash didn't look up when she walked from the room. Harris came back ripping the fabric of one of her nightgowns. "I've more than enough," she told him, lifting her shoulders. She knew her brothers slept with their wives naked. While she didn't see that happening in their situation, five nightgowns weren't necessary. She would be home soon and could buy a new one or five new ones if he didn't send her clothing back.

"You don't need to do that. I'm capable..."

"I caused it. I do need to help mend the wounds. I do know what I'm about. Watched my brother numerous times."

Harris stopped for a few seconds to look at him and wonder again about his thoughts. She didn't understand why she continued to repeat herself. "As you must know, this doesn't mean I won't try again."

Ash bent over, lifted her chin so she had to look into his eyes. "I'm glad you told me that. Honesty is important for a relationship to last. Tells me how to proceed until we are far enough away you won't be able to get home on your own. I've thoughts. They are too brutal for a young lady whose only real crime is that she is spoiled. A child in a woman's body. You can try to leave me all you want. Won't be successful."

At the harshness of his words, Harris stiffened. "Even if we are two hundred miles away from Carnoch, I will do my best to return to my family. That's where I belong. Not with you. Never with you." She meant the words. He hissed in a breath of air. She meant to tell him she wasn't about to forgive him because she comprehended he would never change for her. This was all so unfair. Harris understood deep inside how much she wanted this man. She loved him with all her heart. He tossed her love away by sharing his body with other women. Doing so went against all her principles.

"How will you leave? Your place in this life is beside me." he clarified for her, his words calm. His anger seemed to have evaporated. "You can't walk that far. I won't take you home until after you are my wife in every way. The marriage in the church. The claiming. Everything. Only then will I consider a visit to Carnoch."

She blinked a few times, surprised at his words. They were untrue. "I've money. I can pay for a coach." Sudden thoughts sped into her brain. She looked at him as if she was reading his mind this time. Tilted her head while she felt her eyes widen with the sudden guess as to what he did.

"No, you don't. No money. I have all your groats. You don't have one single coin to your name. I checked the hems as well as the lining of all your clothing. You have nothing. Don't understand how you guessed my intentions. Nevertheless, you have no monetary means to return to Carnoch." He waited watching as if he anticipated a reaction.

The scream of outrage rising from the back of her throat she pressed down. The man had a great deal to answer to. Counting to ten did her no good. Rage consumed. After she stood, Harris hit his chest. Pummeled him until he caught her wrists, dragging her on top of his huge body.

"Somewhere between here and Dover we are going to come to terms with the falsehood that is stuck in your head. I swear it, Harris. I've not slept with a woman for three years because you are mine. No other woman would do for me. In torment, I've waited for you to grow up. I want you in my arms. I need you in my bed. You will become my wife, willing or not. I will claim you. You will see our past lives. Our children will be yours and mine. They will be shifters. I pray they will. The two of us will teach them about their heritage, your families' as well as mine."

"No, none of what you say will come to pass. Men don't change. I don't believe a word you just said." Oh, the devil she wished she could trust in his word. Her heart cried out at the words he spoke along with what they meant. She wanted everything he did. What she could never abide was sharing the man she loved.

He settled her hands on his chest. Looked into her eyes. Let her go. "Come now, I need some sleep before dawn. Tomorrow will be a long day. Can I have your word you will remain in the bed?"

"Never!"

The long breath of air he let out sounded more like a growl. She understood she displeased him. Too bad. She meant to remain honest as well as true to herself. She would never lie to him.

"We need sleep," Ash repeated while he looked with longing at the bed. "If you could promise..." He didn't finish.

Well, she did too. Harris turned to walk into the adjoining room. He caught her by the waist then carried her under his arm to the bed.

"I'm sorry, Harris. Know you don't wish to be near me. That is where you are sleeping. My bed is now our bed because I cannot trust you. You've said as much."

She landed on the big double bed sprawled on her hands and knees her backside in the air. Harris turned to look at him. "No!"

"Scoot over."

"You can't! We're not married."

"Yet." Ash paused thinking about her words. "Now scoot."

Ash landed on the bed, making her jump to the other side. He pulled the covers over them.

"I'm not going to be able to sleep," she protested.

"Don't care. Except for leaving me, you can do whatever you wish."

His arm came over her body, wrapping her in his embrace. One of his big legs held hers to the mattress. Against her back, he was warm as well as hard. "If you try anything, love, I will tie you to me as well as the bed. Now close your eyes. I'm certain you must be tired. It's been a long, exhausting night for both of us."

Well, she was tired. Nonetheless, she would never be able to sleep with him snoring in her ear. With his body on top of hers. She ached.

"By the way, I don't snore. That was all an act."

Yes, it must have been so I'd show my hand. The beast. The magnificent beast. She squirmed, adjusting herself to the weight of his leg atop her and his arm holding her in place. She felt pushed into the mattress. Harris tried to move away from him, needing distance he didn't seem willing to give. He pulled her back. Her bottom was flush against his...his...crotch! She felt him hard against her. Panic. Terror. He could force her. He wouldn't. Ash could have her with a few kisses. There would be no force because she lusted after him. Most likely more than he lusted after her. Could imagine his touch on her breast. Remembered how it felt when he caressed her in dark secret places.

"Relax, I'm not going to do anything. Your innocence will remain untarnished. When the morning light comes, you will still be virgin."

In this Harris believed him. She sighed, let the air gust out in a long whoosh. Against the nape of her neck, she felt his warm breath slide across her skin. The titillating air was heated, feather soft, leaving shivers where it passed over bare skin. Quivers spiraled down her spine. She closed her eyes tight. Gritted her teeth. All she could feel was his heat. His body. Was this what it was like to sleep with a man? Wasn't there more? Of course, there was more, you ninny. He treated her to part of that "more" when he seduced her in the glade over a year ago.

She moved again trying to distance herself. He pulled her back. Again, she felt his...flush against her backside. She gulped, beginning to understand that he was aroused. He wanted her.

"Hold still, sweet," he hissed in her ear. "Go to sleep."

"I..." She passed her tongue across her parched lips then gulped. "C...can't. Sssleeeppp."

"Close your eyes, Harris. Relax. I'm not going to do anything tonight. You don't have to worry about your virtue." His voice was tender, caressing her again, arousing her still. Her brain was muddled by the rapid sensations searing her body. The sound of her blood rushed through her ears.

Heat streamed through her. She did try closing her eyes. The relax part was harder. Every time he moved, she jumped. The tips of her breasts hardened. She felt wet.

When she woke, light filled the small room. He was no longer in the bed with her. Harris bolted to a sitting position searching the room. Where was he? Maybe she could leave now. She threw back the covers, racing to the door. She tugged on the handle. Threw the bolt to the side. Tugged again. Nothing happened.

"No!" she screeched. The door was locked from the other side. She raced into the adjoining room then came to a wretched halt against the brick wall of Ash. With tight fists, she thudded on his chest. His hands grasped her around the waist, steadying her as she began to tumble backward.

"Good morning." He smiled. "Have a good sleep?" Ash sounded too calm...too confident...

"What's good about it?" She snatched on his comment, fuming. Harris pushed away from him. Stared into eyes that were alight with amusement.

"You are still with me." The smile grew. "Just as I wished. That's what is good. Makes the morning bright knowing I don't need to chase you down."

"Against my will."

His grin vanished. She watched him blow a breath of air from his lips. He looked resigned to her animosity. "Get dressed. I set out a traveling gown for you to put on. Your mother recommended this one. I don't care what you choose. If this one doesn't work for you, there are several others that might suit. There is a cape to keep you warm if it's chilly. While looking for a blanket, you won't have the need to put your chin on my crotch. Though your doing so was no hardship for me. We'll eat on the road. Be ready to leave in ten minutes."

Ash sat down at the table. Picked up a mug to drink.

Her gaze fastened on the cup. She swallowed watching his Adams apple move as he drank. "Coffee?" she asked hoping there would be an entire container of it for her to drink. She needed coffee. Black. Strong.

"Ah, your father did tell me you liked the brew plain. I ordered a large container to go. The coffee will help us on our way." He pushed the second mug toward her. "This one is for you. Told Bobo to make it strong."

~ * ~

The night had too many ups as well as downs to contemplate. He was exhausted. The bottoms of his feet were sore. Ash understood from the beginning she would try to run away. He hoped he was wrong. She didn't disappoint in her attempt to flee. When he heard her leave, he thought to catch her before she could get down the steps. Changed his mind. Decided to let her learn more about his true identity. Hoped she would discover she didn't have a single chance in hell of escaping him. He was bigger. Stronger. In any form, he could outrun her with no effort. Perhaps if she learned he was also a shifter, she would understand they mated for life. Perhaps she would comprehend that he would never cheat on her. His thoughts were a dream that wouldn't come true anytime soon.

His breath caught when he watched her toss off her nightgown. Harris was beautiful naked. He didn't think he would ever get used to seeing her in this natural state. Saw the moonglow bounce off her white skin touch upon the curves of her breasts. Descend lower to caress her belly, the curls at the apex of her thighs. When she turned to look back to the door saw the sway of her breasts, the pebbled rose-colored tips. Her beautiful jewels were larger than he remembered. It had been a year since he held her, cupped the soft globes in his hands, tested their weight. She was older now. Her hips fuller. He tasted her that day. Caught the springtime scent of her that was unique to her. Touched her with intimate meticulousness.

After the fact, Ash didn't believe she learned anything from the effort of the night before. She didn't seem to be impressed that he was also able to change his form. In hindsight, he should have stopped her before she shifted. No, if he'd done that, he would have never felt the presence lurking in the shadows, watching her, spying on them. He understood there was something at play here which he didn't know anything about. Guarding her with more diligence was necessary. He could never let anything happen to her. When he was so involved with Harris, there was no time to follow the dark shadow disappearing into the woods. No time to discover the malevolent purpose. He sensed the evil lurking within that form.

When he landed on her, told her to shift he thought she would do as asked. After she told him a resounding no, bottled rage exploded in his head. His patience ended there. Not that he had a great deal to begin with. At every angle nowadays, Harris tested his endurance. Tolerance to her antics was not his forte. If he could snap his fingers, he would make her grow up. By this escapade she acted as a child would. A child who didn't get her way. A pouting child in a woman's body. Harris loved him. He knew that even though she never told him.

It seemed the entire night he relived the event. Played it over then over again in his head. Ash came to the conclusion the dark shadow he caught a brief glimpse of was a shifter. Then there were the images in his head of Harris wearing nothing. She stood her ground, hands fisted, daring him. Daring him to do what? Make love to her? Ash found he no longer needed to imagine how she would look wearing nothing at all. Now, he comprehended firsthand the curves of her breasts, the line of her hips as they connected with long white legs. He saw her woman's mound a bit darker than her hair. With the thought in the forefront of his head, his breath hitched. Blood roared. She set his pulse on fire.

All her little squirming movements during the night kept him aroused as well as awake. When she fell asleep, her body relaxing into his, he sent a thankful prayer to God up above for allowing him a few hours of sleep. He did close his eyes. Managed to relax as well as concentrate more on this situation that seemed to grow more complicated with each passing second.

Ash didn't want her to despise him for reasons that held no truth. Needed her love as much if not more than he needed to breathe. More than his heart to beat. Still, she fought him at every turn. Wouldn't listen to him when he told her since he met her, she was the only woman who meant anything to him. The only woman who would share his bed. What the devil did she want from him? She had all that he could give. She held his heart in the palms of her hands. If she wished, Harris could crush him.

Frustrated, with both hands he pressed the palms of his hands to his eyes. His feet stung. He'd unwrapped the bandages after he dressed. Washed as well as poured more whiskey on them. They smelled like a distillery. Last night she cared for his wounds. Hawk was correct. Harris did have a gentle touch.

That night, Ash didn't sleep. He listened to her small even breaths whisper through her lungs. Stopped himself from exploring the curves of her body. When he touched her, Ash wanted Harris to be awake as well as aware of her body's response to him. How he kept his hands to himself, he would never know. It was sheer strength of will knowing full well in the end it was what he wished for. What would be best for them.

When he rose, he left her bed to take a hot bath then order their breakfast. In the tub, he watched her sleeping. He hoped this would be the beginning of many nights with her. Nights that would be more peaceful than this one. More conducive to pleasure as well as sleep. If in any way he could ease her way to the marriage bed as well as the claiming, he would. Couldn't help the grin when he recalled the way she stared at him fully aroused. The sight of her naked did that to him.

When she woke then tried to escape again, he watched, fascinated by her antics. The trip to London then onto Dover might prove to be a long one. She was furious the door was bolted. He just didn't feel the need for another race through the woods. Now, while he waited for her, he listened to her muttering. The swear words she must have learned from her older brothers. Heard the fabric of her clothes fall around her. The gown he chose for today fastened in the front so she would have no need of his nimble fingers to either put it on or get it off. The plump of a shoe hitting the rug, the swishing sound of stockings being pulled up her legs. He didn't set out a corset. She would be more comfortable without one.

A few minutes later, Harris appeared framed in the door. Her hair was piled on top of her head in a tight chignon. Small tendrils of her fine hair curled around her face. She was beautiful. Her hands were on her hips. Silver-blue eyes blazed.

"Are you ready?" He extended his hand. Was surprised when she accepted the polite gesture. "We've a long ride ahead of us. This will be the longest stretch in our journey." He needed to put as much distance between them and the highlands as possible.

"How long before we reach Dover?"

"A few days. However," he paused to watch her reaction, "we will stop in London first. Need to check in with my father. Are you trying to figure out where the best place to run from me is? Be advised there is no best place. I'll never let you go."

"Curious what you have in store for me."

"Good," Harris sounded resigned to the fact she wasn't going to go anywhere he didn't want her to go. Today he meant to ride. He needed space from her fuming, from her petulant air. From the succulent curves she couldn't hide.

In the carriage, Ash poured coffee for both then set the basket on her lap. He sat back to study her. She rummaged through the contents. Pulled out a scone. Ate. Sipped the mouth scalding coffee. He'd eaten before so he didn't bother with more food. He was content to watch. Didn't matter to him what she did. He loved to observe every little nuance.

Once she seemed satisfied, Ash tapped on the top of the coach. "I'm going to ride. I'll see you at lunch."

That was it.

The next few days went much the same. He would secure the room for the night. Put her on his bed. Enclose her beneath his arms and legs. In the morning, he would spend the first half hour or so with her then he would ride. It was prudent on his part to stay away. Ash didn't miss the fact she would fume at him every night. The act amused him. She wanted his company in the coach. Told him she had no one to talk to. Asked him if she could ride. The obvious answer to that ridiculous question was, no. No way in hell did he wish to chase her across the countryside.

They reached London in good time. When the carriage stopped in front of his father's townhouse on Trafalgar Square, he tossed the reins to the waiting stable boy then opened the door to the carriage.

"Be on your best behavior," Ash warned. Saw the prickle then the scowl. Her brows drew together. He almost laughed. Thought it prudent to keep whatever humor he felt behind his teeth. He was surprised when she allowed him to help her down. When her feet hit the ground, she stumbled into his arms.

This had been another long day of travel. He felt a moment's guilt. Pushing on the last three hours had been his decision. Spending another night in an inn, sleeping with her encompassed in his arms... He shook his head. Not possible without compromising her. Since the day they left Carnoch, he'd been either in a state of semi-arousal or full arousal. He needed to sleep without her lush body pressed against his.

Though it would be taking a chance, he couldn't spend this night with her. The adjoining room to his would be acceptable to place her. The locks could be checked. Again, the only way out for her would be through him. Sleeping light with eyes half open was a choice to be made.

His hand on her elbow, he escorted her to the door. The butler opened it before he could knock. She shot him a quizzical look. "I always knock. It's not my home. Belongs to my father. When he passes, my brother will own the townhouse. Will never be mine."

What he told her might not be true. There had been words exchanged between him and his father. Thoughts about disinheriting his brother.

"Oh..."

Ash saw the wheels turning in her pretty little head. They stepped inside. Gave their jackets to Smith-Jones. He nodded. "Your father is waiting for you in the drawing room. I will have Stella bring in refreshments."

"A bottle of wine too," Ash said as he ushered Harris to meet his father. They walked through the foyer. "In here." Ash stopped to allow her entrance. Heard the soft gasp of surprise when she saw the man. Ash never had the opportunity or felt the time was right to explain his father's condition. Once she saw him, she should understand why he left along with his haste to return.

James sat in a wheelchair. His body sagged, chin sitting on his chest. It seemed he heard them come into the room. When he looked up, a small dampness slid down his chin. His eyes a deep blue, there was moisture there too. Ash's heart went out to the once vibrant man. A year ago, before his stroke, he was in full control of his faculties as well as his body. He held a seat in parliament. His opinion along with advice was respected. Now, Chandler, his brother, attended. It was too bad his brother wasn't a bit more responsible. Chandler didn't have an opinion on anything except his playmates along with the numerous vices that took up his time and money. More times than he wished to recount, he took the seat meant for his brother. Voted when his brother should have been there.

"Father..." Ash stepped forward, bringing Harris along with him. "I would like you to meet someone very special to me. This is Harris Frasier."

She is going to be my wife. Too bad she doesn't agree. She is also a shifter. Black panther, if it matters.

Ash saw questions forming behind her eyes. He hoped she would ask him later. He also witnessed a small light in his father's eyes when he mentioned she was also a shifter. He prayed his father understood his thoughts.

"Nice to meet you, Sir."

"James," Ash said. "You may call him by his first name. He will soon be your father-in-law."

"He is a lord?" she asked looking stunned. "You?"

"A marquis," he said, realizing this was the first time she showed interest in his family. "My older brother will inherit the title along with the wealth. Though I've no need of more groats." That was the truth. He had enterprises in different parts of London along with a fleet of ships inherited from his uncle, another second son. The spare heir, his uncle called himself then laughed when he raked in the coins. His uncle had a penchant for finding the best deals then capitalizing on what he earned. Ash inherited that trait.

"Please have a seat. This won't take long. After that I'll see you to your room. He brightens when there is company. He has always admired beautiful women." Ash watched her catch her lip with her teeth as if she was trying to keep from saying something they would both regret.

Ash turned back to his father. He knelt on one knee in front of the man. Took his father's aged hands into his. "How have you been?" Ash hoped he could speak better than he did now when he traveled home. Hoped to hear positive thoughts coming from him. When Ash left for Carnoch, he was still reeling from the stroke he suffered over a year prior. A doctor came to see him every day. Ash read what he could on strokes. He didn't think his father would get better. This seemed so debilitating. He lost total feeling on one side of his body.

I know you wish me to recover. I'm not going to get better. I'm ready to pass on to a different world where I'm not in pain. Would love to be with your mother. My passing is only a matter of a few months.

Tears formed in his eyes. One slipping down his cheek then another. This was why he had to leave Harris a year ago. Why he felt the need to rush back to London. His father was the reason he had to return as soon as he could. Given a choice he would have done everything different. He never liked how this affected Harris. How he left her. This woman meant everything to him, his past along with the present then his future. Moving into eternity lay in her small delicate hands.

James moved his lips trying to speak. His eyes reached out to him as if in pain. Ash saw the depression. The lack of energy or reason to live. When he turned his gaze to Harris, she nodded. Her eyes were filled with moisture. He hoped without explanation he turned a corner with her. Prayed she would accept what they both knew they were, each other's mate.

Harris sat in a large chair in a far corner of the room, giving him the space along with the time to be with his father.

The rustling at the door caught his attention. When he turned his focus to the noise, he smiled. Stella, the downstairs maid, carried a tray of food into the room. On the tray there was also an open bottle of wine. He was both thirsty as well as hungry. Was certain Harris would also be in need of food.

The woman set the tray down before looking at him as if she wanted to devour him. His heart gave a quick jolt of surprise. Three years ago on a visit home, he explained to her there was another woman. Ash tried to ease the words but she cried when he told her she could no longer come to his bed. Even in his youth, it had not been wise of him to seduce a servant. He understood now why servants should remain off limits. He tried to find her a new position. She refused. When Chandler took over the household, he might also use the woman.

Stella stood with her hands twisting in front of her. Ash looked from Harris to Stella then back. "Anything else, Ash?" she asked, her voice throaty. Her familiarity with his given name would not make it past Harris. She was bound to notice this huge impropriety. This was something he needed to explain.

He saw the shock on Harris' face. The twisting of her features as she looked from the maid to him. She would guess all wrong. Would believe there was something between them. He'd spent the last several days working to convince Harris that she was the only woman he wanted. Now, it appeared his past might catch up to him. A past that happened before he met Harris. Before he realized who she was to him. Before he tasted the sweetness that was hers. Before he saw her sunning herself naked on that huge boulder by the loch.

"Nothing, Stella. You're dismissed. You may go to bed. Won't need anything else tonight." Ash understood when he watched Stella wince. His words had been too harsh. Hoped she didn't read anything in his mention of going to bed. He meant she should go to her bed. She might think otherwise.

Stella curtsied then left. The damage was done. That fact was written on Harris' face in the tilt of her chin along with the rigid slant of her back. Any progress he might have made on the trip here vanished. Stiff. Anger fumed within Harris. Later he would deal with her reaction as well as explain. Honesty. He would remain true to himself as well as her. He would have another explanation to make before they reached his Dover home.

"Eat if you are hungry." He was learning to temper his words to his future wife. Decided telling her to do something was the best way to get her to do the opposite. "Wine?" He held up a glass knowing she would want wine even if she didn't wish for food. She nodded. "Would you like me to make a plate for you?"

"We are going to eat here?" she asked, sounding confused. "Can your father...?" She looked at the food then back to him.

Ash shook his head. "No, nothing solid. I will tell you more later in privacy." He didn't want to talk about his father's health in front of his father or servants who might pass through the room. His father understood more than most thought.

Harris downed the full glass of wine then splashed more into her glass. She ate the plate of food he gave her concentrating on the cheese. Cheese always seemed to be her selection of choice. Sitting back, she sipped her wine. Tonight, Harris looked at peace with herself. Content. Perhaps she didn't read anything into Stella's behavior.

There wasn't much else to say. Ash sat by his father. Held his hand. He spoke of times in the past. Humorous times. Moments when the siblings misbehaved. Stayed away from anything too serious. The time when he and Chandler rode through Hyde Park pretending they were Indians, whooping...hollering...faces painted. They were only twelve and nine at the time. They'd thought it was great fun. Their father took a switch to their backsides. There was the instance when he was sent home from school for setting fire in a lab. He'd not done that on purpose though the dean seemed to think he did. There was the time he and one of his best friends, Nash, were reprimanded for having girls in their room. He choked when he looked at Harris' reaction. He should have thought twice before recounting another moment when he was with another woman.

Surprised that she smiled, he returned the gesture with a grin of his own.

Her smile warmed his heart. Gave him reason to believe she wouldn't hold his past over his head. Just the future. He didn't know how to convince her he wasn't the man she thought he was. Time would tell the true tale.

They finished the bottle of wine. "I'll take you to your room."

She shot him a quizzical glance. He understood she would be wondering if he was going to have the audacity to put her in his room. What he was planning did take some daring but not as much as putting her in his bed even though that was where he wanted her. He'd grown accustomed to having her in his arms while he slept. Ash knew he could never afford to have her too far away from his cat senses. Even though they were miles upon miles from Carnoch, she might still bolt.

Harris couldn't, shouldn't, try anything. In the city, it would be far more dangerous for her than back in the highlands. Harris didn't know London. Harris believed she was invincible. She could find herself lost in the bowels of London. She wouldn't know what to do or where to go. She was so beautiful. Some man would proposition her. If she ended up at the docks, that could be worse. Parts of London were more dangerous than others. Harris wouldn't know which places needed to be avoided.

Ash prayed she was more intelligent than to get herself into difficulties he would have to rescue her from. Her father did tell him she could find trouble without trying. Thought of the shadow...the shifter who was after her. He knew the person wanted something from her. What he didn't know was what that was.

They walked up the steps to the second floor. A bit farther and they were in his room. She sounded incredulous when she spoke. "Nothing has changed? You mean to flaunt me in front of your family?" she bit out, her anger palpable. "I didn't take you to be that rude to me. It's condescending of you. I'm not your whore. That's what all will believe."

She set a nerve on fire. Heated blood raced into all of his parts that needed no more stimulation. He needed to cool his thoughts. "No, just showing you the way it's going to be. You're right. This is my room. My bed. Expect you to never be far from me at night. I gave you space. You took advantage." He held on to her elbow ushering her through a closet then into another smaller room. "This is where you will sleep. The two doors will be left open. Always."

Harris turned in a full circle while she studied the room. She looked at the door that would lead to the hallway. "Is that door locked?" She pointed to the offending passage.

"Yes."

"Nothing is different." Her heavy sigh disturbed him. "I'm still your prisoner. You will never trust me."

"No," he told her. "Nothing has changed unless you can convince me you don't intend to bolt at the first opportunity. Be aware that my door is also locked. I'll be sleeping with the keys." His heart fell at her expression. "You are only a prisoner by your choice. Not mine. Given time, that can change. Never wanted to be your jailor. Want to be your husband. Since you refuse to listen to reason, I am continuing in the same vein."

He stepped toward her, ran his knuckles along her cheek after that down the long column of her neck. So soft, silken, he wished he dared explore. At his touch, she sipped in a strangled breath. "I want to trust you. Give me a reason." His hand dropped to his side not wishing to prolong her displeasure.

Sitting down on one of the chairs she found the bottle of wine that had been left for them. "You were going to tell me about your father."

She deflected from his statement. He watched her twirl the deep red liquid in the glass. He knew she was thinking about another possible way to escape him.

The door swung open. Stella stood framed there, wearing a thin, transparent gown. She smiled. Tossed her hair over her shoulder. Flirtatious, she lowered her lashes. For a few seconds while he gaped at the maid, time seemed to stand still for him. He'd told her he wasn't going to sleep with her again. Last year she tried several times, slipping into his bed when he was asleep. Standing naked in the room when he came in late from attending to his father's needs. Tonight, she wore little. The transparent negligée covered. Hid nothing. The swell of her breasts apparent along with the tips. Her hand on the ties of the gown. She fiddled with the bow. Didn't seem to notice Harris sitting in the chair facing the fire.

With a small cry, the maid ran to him. Wrapped her arms as well as her legs around him. Ash held his hands at his sides. "You're home. This time to stay? Why would you want that haughty lady when you can have me? She sticks her nose in the air. Thinks she's better than everyone else. I will give you myself. All of myself. I'll be hot and moaning in your arms just as the last time you bedded me. You will discover she is nothing to you. Nothing at all."

"Stella, go back to your room." He tried to disentangle himself from her limbs. "When I told you to go to bed, I meant your room. That last time you spoke of was three years ago. I'm not that man now. I've found the woman for me. I've no need for another. Don't want more than one woman."

His voice was harsh as he attempted to unwrap Stella from his body. Ash felt Harris' rage. Understood her thoughts. She couldn't keep them from him when she was furious.

"She is cold as ice. A bitch. No, I will warm your bed. Not her."

She began to unfasten his britches. Her small fingers touched his belly. "I want to hold your cock in my hand. Lick you. Suck. Devour. Want to taste your seed. Need you inside me too."

"Stella!" Ash managed to set her aside.

"See." She pointed to his crotch. "You are hard for me. You want me. I'm ready for you all wet and..."

"No, Stella, I'm this way because of Harris."

Bloody hell, all he had to do was look at Harris and he stood at attention.

"I'll leave you two alone." Harris rose from her spot by the fire. Downed what was left of her wine then headed for the door.

"No, you don't." Her actions gave Ash the strength to propel Stella away from him. He reached out for Harris' arm. She whisked by him. He caught her at the top of the stairs.

"Smith-Jones!" Ash bellowed, needing someone to escort Stella from his room. His father's man would be prepared for everything.

"Sir." The butler appeared, his face a stoic mask as if nothing untoward happened here. "Do you need something?"

Ash pointed toward his open door. "Need for you to get Stella to her room in one piece. If I do it..."

Ash didn't know what would happen. He might wring her neck.

When Smith-Jones stepped from the room, Stella was slung over his shoulder. "Anything else you need?"

"No."

To his surprise, Harris didn't resist. Once inside his room, she curled up on the chair with a fresh glass of wine. "You didn't have to tell her no on my account. You're a virile man. You can have any woman you want. Well...accept me. You can't have me. I don't share."

That was too much for him to take. He was exhausted. His mental faculties as well as physical stamina were drained. "I want you, Harris. No one else. Since I met you there has been no woman in my life." Ash felt as if he repeated that so many times the words should be etched into her mind. "Go to your room. We can talk more in the morning."

"Talked for ten minutes this morning before you stopped the carriage so you could ride." The pique in her voice didn't go unnoticed. She was fuming. Harris never could hide her emotions from him.

"We aren't going anywhere tomorrow."

She tilted her head to the side. After that she sipped. "You said you would tell me about your father. Since I'm not the least bit sleepy, now might be a good time. I would finish the bottle. Might help me to sleep."

"Agreed."

Ash wasn't ready to go to bed either. Wasn't ready to sleep alone. He'd become used to her curled up in front of him. He wasn't certain he could sleep without her in his bed. After pouring a glass of wine, he sat in the opposite chair regarding her over the rim. He didn't know how to change the atmosphere between them. Imagined nothing would change tonight. Anything that could go wrong did.

Ushering a long breath of air from his lungs, he started. "Father had a stroke. That was a little over a year ago. I had to come home to be with him. The doctor didn't like his chances. Told me he wouldn't last more than a month or two. He seems to be proving all of them wrong. That was why I left so suddenly." He picked up one of her small hands, stroked the back. "I didn't want to leave you. I had plans with you. Father needed me more. You are a strong woman. I thought you cared about me. Believed you would wait for me to return."

Harris was twirling the wine. Thinking. "That was why you had to rush home? Your father needed you? You could have told me. Even then you didn't trust me. I would never have felt abandoned by you if you told me. Family is important."

"No. The letter I received telling me of his condition also warned me not to say anything to anyone. There were extenuating circumstances that needed to be addressed before anyone else could learn. I'd never told you my true feelings. While I believed I could trust you, I wasn't positive."

"Why? What circumstances?" She looked puzzled by the revelation.

"Secrets...government secrets. There had to be...let's just say my father knew too much. He is a man of importance. When the stroke occurred, it came as a surprise. No one knew if he would recover. He hasn't. His chances aren't good. If I wanted to learn those secrets, he would tell me through his mind. We've always been able to read each other's thoughts. We can communicate silently. So far, he hasn't said anything. I'm not about to rush him. He needs time. I expected you to be more understanding."

"I see... When Maisie is pregnant, she can speak to Hawk through her mind as well as vice versa. The ability saved her that first year they were wed. I understand. I don't seem to have that ability to *ken* what you are thinking. I can understand if I'm told what's happening." She set her glass on the table. "Can you read my thoughts?" She blushed. "You talked to me when we were both in our cat. I heard you."

"Some of your thoughts, yes. Does that make you uncomfortable?"

~ * ~

Once Harris was settled into her room, Ash rang for Smith-Jones. A few seconds later the man walked into the chamber. Ash looked up, concerned. Smith-Jones was a big man. When he shifted, he was almost as large as Ash. Ash understood if Harris wished to listen, she would do so. He didn't plan on hiding anything from her. Yet, she was such a powder keg of emotions, he never could second guess how she would react at any given time.

"I'm concerned."

"Thought so. Involves your lady. Is Miss Frasier your mate?" he asked, as he sat down in the same chair Harris vacated earlier. The servant sat back, stretching out his legs. He linked his fingers behind his head. The role they assumed was much more than servant and master.

"Yes. Harris is fighting her feelings. She is young. Immature. I've waited three years for her. Now, it is time to make her mine. She resists because she believes me to be unfaithful. Don't bloody well know how to convince her I'm not."

"You have her now," he said as he looked through the closet into the open door to the adjoining room. "I take it you don't trust her. Will she bolt? I can stand guard at her door. Though how would she get through a locked door...?"

"Trust her to try to get back to Carnoch. She says she doesn't want to have anything to do with me. A year ago, she melted in my arms and flowed all over me. Would do so again if she allowed herself to trust in my feelings. I've not attempted to seduce." Ash ran his hand along the back of his neck. "Could have taken her innocence that day. Could have brought her with me to England. If I'd done that, we wouldn't have the problems we are having now."

"She saw you with Stella?" he asked. "I gather she assumes you are sleeping with the maid. You did make a mistake. That was years ago. You were young."

"I didn't invite that woman to my room tonight. Thing is..."

Ash paused again, directing attention to the door. In his mind, he heard her stirring. Listened to some of her thoughts. She might be eavesdropping. That would suit him just fine.

"You only want your mate," Smith-Jones finished for him, his dark brown eyes twinkling. "What happened that she changed her tune?"

Ash scrubbed his hand on the back of his neck then down the front of his face. "Thing is, before I left to come home, I asked her not to see any other man. Made her promise. Of course, she expected the same of me. A few weeks ago, when I first saw her, I asked if she'd seen anyone. Was pleased to hear her say no. Next, she turned the question on me. I was so astonished, I didn't answer. She took that for a yes, I'd seen other women. Needless to say, she was incensed."

Smith-Jones barked a loud guffaw. "You could have told her the truth. Nothing would be amiss now."

"Could have. Should have. If I'd done so when I realized what was happening, she would be in my arms again. I would be able to trust her to remain with me. Hindsight is everything. As it stands now..." Ash poured himself a brandy then one for his friend. "Was so angry I couldn't think straight. Incensed might be a better description. In those first ensuing moments, I didn't comprehend the fact she was a shifter. Within that same hour, I was able to sense her abilities. Was pleased. After that, displeased, she had no faith in me, her mate. She never found the time to tell me or talk to me about her abilities. She hasn't yet realized she is meant to be with me. If she has absorbed the fact, she isn't accepting of the notion."

"She's still holding the grudge?"

"Not so much that but she doesn't think I'm telling her the truth. Bloody everlasting hell! I've been celibate for three years waiting for her to grow up. I want her for my wife, my mate. She is mine," Ash growled low in the back of his throat. "She will not deny the fact forever."

"Looking at the lady, I believe she has grown up," the butler said, his voice mocking him. "She's beautiful. You are right about that."

"Yes, to both. I also know if I kissed her even one time, held her in my arms, she would want me as much as I want her...possibly more. She is passionate. Has strong appetites. With astounding ease, I could seduce her. Though, she might not forgive me."

"So...what are you waiting for? Seduce her. Make her yours in every way. Your problems will be over. Declare for her in the way of the clan. When that happens, she will be yours once more through eternity. She will see your past lives. Will understand how the two of you are destined to live together...forever. Seems simple enough for the likes of me."

"She will want the marriage to take place in Carnoch with her family. Told her we would return in a year. With my father's health so precarious, I can't be too far away. Can't give her guarantees I might not be able to fulfill. Need to be there for him. While I have you to rely on, there is always Chandler who can derail the best plans. Wish he wasn't in the mix. He is and he must be considered."

"What will she think when she meets Abella? Now that woman believes you are hers. Believes the mansion near Dover is hers. She's been running the household ever since you brought her back from France. You've allowed that. Now, you will have some things to answer for. Again, your mate will doubt you."

"I've never had Abella in my bed. She was too abused when I found her. I've never felt anything for her except responsibility. Not even friendship enters into the mix. We don't like each other. She wants to be the mistress of my home. She doesn't want anything to do with me."

"No? I..." Smith-Jones seemed puzzled by his admission. "Do you mind if I court her? I've always thought..."

"Is Abella your mate?"

"Believe she is."

Ash was surprised when he saw the flush on his friend's face. He was also baffled. "Why didn't you...?"

"Tell you?" Smith-Jones lifted his shoulder in a shrug. "Send her to London. That way she won't be an issue that will come between you and your soon to be wife. What was the other issue since we did seem to get sidetracked here."

"There is a shadow over Harris' head. Something well...someone...a shifter is after her. I can't be certain but I believe it's true. The night she changed to her cat and forced my change also, I saw the shadow. Felt the evil. This man has been sent by someone who means us harm. Not certain if it's me or her this shifter has in his sights."

"Can't be Chandler. He can't shift," Smith-Jones mused, staring at Ash. "What do you think?"

"My brother must be involved. He's never been satisfied with being heir to all this. As we grew older, he always resented me. Sometimes I felt the hate that simmered deep in his soul. Wanted all that I had coupled with what he would inherit. I'm certain if he felt she was precious to me, he would find a way to abuse her. Harris isn't safe from my brother."

"Half your cousins along with your second cousins shift. We have to look to see who might be mean enough to take up with your older brother against you." Smith-Jones was staring at the doorway. "Who are his best friends?"

Ash did the same. Harris stood, framed by the door in her virginal nightgown. Her face, a death mask, the flesh was so pale. The light from the small fire behind her casting her in a warm orange glow. Her hair was down, spreading across her shoulders to slide across her breasts. The sight of her made him catch his breath. Ash had not expected to see her again until the morning.

"How much did you hear?" Ash tempered his voice.

At one point during the conversation, he hoped she was listening. Now, he knew that had not been a good idea.

"You think someone is after me? Why?"

Chapter Three

Last night, Ash never answered her question. Was someone after her? Forlorn as well as terrified Harris, left his bedroom to curl up in the big bed alone. She heard the men as they talked, their voices low. She was more afraid than ever. Missed his big body next to her. Missed his arm draped with possession across her. Missed his scent along with the warmth that emanated from his big body. Thinking about all she'd lost, her shoulders shook.

She thumped her pillow before turning over. Stared out the window watching the night sky. The black velvet of the evening was adorned with twinkling lights. The highlands were so far away. They were unique. She loved the land along with the people. She wanted to return. Going back without Ash wasn't a possibility. Seemed he staked his claim to her. Even though he didn't believe it, she was smart enough to understand she could never venture with safety into London by herself. Would never risk her life in an attempt to escape the man she loved.

As the two men spoke, Harris heard more than she admitted to Ash. She listened to him declare that she was his mate. Smith-Jones told him he should claim her so she would see all their past lives together. If that was true, the part about her being his mate, Harris could no longer believe he cheated on her. Shifters didn't do that. Once they found their person, they were forever loyal. She knew how her brothers along with her cousins felt on that topic. They would never dally with another woman once they met the woman they were meant to spend eternity with. She should believe him. For her sanity, she yearned with all her heart to trust in his words.

Ash was right. If he kissed her and touched her in any way, she would melt into his embrace. She would flow over him as if she was warm honey. She needed to understand what a life with Ash would be like before she condemned them to loneliness. Harris looked through the connecting doors. Wished he would come to her. He wouldn't. Ash wouldn't do anything until she forgave him for spiriting her away without her consent or until she asked him to be more intimate. Harris didn't know if she held the nerve in her heart to ask.

A deep breath of air she inhaled was meant for courage. The oxygen didn't seem to go anywhere helpful. Inhaled again praying for the strength she would need to go to him. Harris didn't want to hide any part of herself from this man. She pressed her lips together then tossed off the covers. Thought better. Pulled the covers over her. Moisture filled her eyes. Tears slid down her cheeks. She didn't want to go to him crying. She pushed all those emotions to the back of her head. With the backs of her hands, she knuckled away the tears.

She was afraid of the shifter who was after her. Had the uncanny notion Ash knew who the man was but wasn't saying. To no avail, Harris tried to read his thoughts. She was supposed to be able to see into the mind of her mate.

Nothing.

How could he be her mate if she couldn't see into his thoughts. Counting to ten, she clung to the covers. Nails gripped the fabric hard. No. Stop making excuses. I'm going to him. I'm going to ask Ash to hold me. I need him. Need to feel his heartbeat close to mine, meld together as one beat. Need to hear the deep even breaths he inhales when he sleeps. Feel the warmth and comfort he gives me when pressed close.

I love him.

Harris cleared her mind of the fear the misconceptions created. She ceased to think. Meant only to act. If she thought hard, she knew he would welcome her into his bed. She prayed he would welcome and not reject. Walking through the doors connecting their rooms, she stopped at the side of his bed. He was lying sprawled out on the mattress, the blanket around his waist. His chest was bare. Harris wondered if he wore anything below the covers. When they slept together on the trip here, he always wore his pants...unfastened.

A moment later, Ash jerked awake. Sat up. His arms bulged while they held him still. "Ash?" her voice was weak. Harris gulped down the anxiety spiraling higher.

"What are you doing here?" The question was expected.

She pulled her lips together, smashed them, biting back the need to spill out all her uncertainties to him. Beneath her breasts, her heart thundered.

"I..."

"I?" Ash questioned, a thin smile forming on his lips. One of his dark eyebrows lifted upward. "Do you need something? Another blanket? A pillow? Perhaps...no you wouldn't..."

"No...! Stop teasing me." She moved her cold feet along the rug she was standing on. They felt like ice.

"Do I need to pull the words from behind your teeth?" he asked, sounding slightly amused. "Can I do something for you? Speak up."

His query was so soft...so tender... She had to find a way to tell him what she needed. "H-hold m-me...please. Ash, I..."

Harris didn't understand why this was taking so much time. She reached out to him before jerking her hand back to her side.

He sent her a half smile. She wished she dared to touch his lips. "Do you understand what you are asking, love?" Ash patted the mattress beside him then smoothed the sheet. "Let me get this straight. Don't want to misconstrue the request. You want me to hold you. You want to lie in this bed with me. Next to me. My arms around you. Do you want anything else?"

Harris tried to swallow the growing lump in her throat. This was foolishness. She looked back through the doors then the dying embers in his fireplace thinking she should run. Changed her mind. "Y-yes...if you don't mind."

Ash cleared his throat. Harris thought she saw another smile. "I'm naked. Do you still wish to climb into this bed with me?"

Unable to speak, Harris nodded. She wanted to see him naked. Needed to touch him. Run her hands along his big body. Explore those parts of him that fascinated her.

"Do you wish for me to dress? Should I pull on a pair of pants?"

That might well be a question she should answer. She found she was shaking her head to tell him no. All Harris wanted was to be held through the night. Needed for Ash to chase her fears away from her mind. Wished she understood why some unknown shifter wanted to harm her.

"Climb in." Ash pulled back the covers.

If he thought she would run at the sight of him, he should understand that tonight everything changed for her. Tonight, she wanted to be with this man. Just as she had from the moment she met him. Harris sat on the bed then swung her legs around so they were on the mattress. Ash put a pillow under her head. She scooted back against him, hoping he would put his arm over her. If he did, she would feel safe.

When he pulled her against his big frame, she felt the heat, his sex pushing against her bottom. His arm was over her as was his leg. Just as they slept before, they would proceed in the same manner. She ran her foot along one of his legs. Felt the rasp of his hair.

Harris inhaled a long deep breath of air. "Thank you."

"Anything for you," he murmured, his breath wafting across her neck. "Just be sure to tell me if there is anything else you would like."

She shivered.

Trembled.

Needed to turn in his arms. She couldn't. Didn't dare put herself in such a vulnerable state. If she did, he could kiss her. Harris wanted that kiss then one after that. She knew she loved the man. Always had and always would.

"Sleep, love," he murmured, his voice soft, soothing her ragged nerves. "I will hold you through the night. You've nothing to be afraid of. I will keep all harm from coming your way. Goodnight."

My love.

That was why she came to him. It was some of what she wanted. With both hands, she clung to his forearms. Soaked up all the heat that was his to give her. Felt the beat of his heart. Heard his long, slow, even breaths.

Harris closed her eyes.

When she woke, Ash was no longer in the bed. She felt bereft, alone. Felt as if something very precious left her. When she smoothed her hands across the sheets where he was supposed to be, they were cold. The pillow where his head had lain still held a soft indentation. After she brought it to her face she caught his scent, male as well as a *wee* bit spicy.

Throughout the entire night, he never touched her except to hold her. Last night, Harris would have given him anything he asked. If Ash wished to, he could have seduced her. Perhaps he sensed that. Maybe he understood while she would have given into him, she wasn't ready. She would enjoy a kiss. Comprehended nothing between them would end with a kiss. The passion he generated was mercuric. Raw. Hungry. Sensual.

Sometime during the night, he murmured, his lips close to her, "I will make love to you after we are wed or after I've declared you as my mate. Our ways are different yet similar to the family of Chaton. When the time is right, we will be one with each other. After there is no more danger, we will be together as mates for life."

There was so much he wasn't telling her. She should also be more forthcoming to him. A piece of paper sat on the bedside table next to her. She picked it up. With her eyes closed, held it close to her heart.

Harris,

I've ordered a bath for you. Pull the cord. Smith-Jones will send a few servants with hot water. When you are finished meet me downstairs at the small nook near the kitchen. We can talk while we eat.

Can't tell you how pleased I am that you came to me in the darkness. Didn't like the fact you were frightened. Though your actions might cause other problems. We will solve whatever difficulties come our way. I understand you were afraid. Nonetheless, I hope that wasn't the only reason you joined me in my bed last night.

Thank you, love,

Ash

Clutching the note to her breasts, she inhaled several times to steady her nerves. No, that wasn't the only reason. She missed him. Had grown used to his warm body next to hers. After this, Harris didn't think she would ever be able to sleep alone.

After pulling the cord, she lay back on the bed, holding his pillow close. Waited for the water to come. Once the bath was filled, she washed then dressed. She wanted to see him. To hear his voice. Harris rushed down to the breakfast nook where he told her he would wait. She stopped while she watched him.

He was there. The sight of him caught her breath. Her clasped hands rose to her chest. She loved looking at him. When he lifted his head from the paper, his smile was tender. His vibrant eyes beckoned her to sit. He seemed glad to see her. Harris wanted to run to him. Hold him. Have Ash hold her.

He nodded. "Come in..." He motioned to a seat across from him.

Harris sat at the breakfast nook, a huge mug of tea in front of her. Ash sat across from her. Last night he told her to go to bed. That he would talk to her in the morning. All that happened before she joined him in his bed. Everything about last night changed when she entered his room a second time. After she crawled into his bed. Well...morning was here. She still needed him to tell her about his father. Where his father was concerned, Ash remained a closed book. He was silent, sipping his tea then staring at the newspaper. She wanted to scream at him. Her patience seemed to lag.

Her egg sat in the eggcup. With her spoon, she cracked the shell while she watched his changing expressions. Peeled the shell away. For the first time in a long time, she wasn't hungry. Most of the time nothing affected her appetite. The thought of someone being after her changed that. Harris needed Ash to explain to her what he knew as well as what he guessed.

She gave up on everything except the tea. *Talk to me.*

Ash cleared his throat. "What did you overhear last night? It's something we need to address. Much was said. I've no idea how long you stood in the doorway listening. Since the words exchanged concern you...you should know every detail."

By the tone of his voice, it was clear to her that he didn't like what happened. He didn't intend to keep secrets. She didn't mean to eavesdrop. The voices coming through the open door made her curious. At least that woman, Stella, didn't return. If Stella pursued Ash, she might be tempted to claw her eyes out. Sleeping in his arms last night created a shift in their relationship she wasn't willing to give up. Harris understood she should tell him everything. She didn't know where to start.

At the beginning is usually the best place.

Yes, when she heard the words that drew her to the door. The truth caught in the back of her throat.

Looking at her hands she decided she needed to be honest. Keeping secrets was never good. "That someone was after me. You know who it is. I *ken* that for a fact. If so, I should wish for you to tell me the truth." Harris prayed he would agree with her.

"You heard right. You're targeted because of me. It's nothing you've done. That's what I think. Except when we were young boys, he always resented me. I will need to solve the problem. You will need to take care. You shouldn't be alone. When I'm gone, I will have Smith-Jones watch out for you."

"Are you speaking of your brother? He's the heir? Isn't that right?" Harris was confused. Bothered that siblings would hurt each other. "Why would he resent you or anyone else? Ash, you are not making sense."

"Yes. You see he doesn't have the ability to change form. He resents me because of that. He also begrudges the fact that father confides in me about certain things. Secret government things. Chandler can't be trusted. That's why he isn't privy to the information. Plus, father and I communicate without speech if that is what we wish to do. I hope that someday you and I will also be able to do that."

"So, let me get this straight. I'm a target because he wants revenge on you." Harris didn't see anything right or just about that. She needed to discover more. "What is it he wants from me? I don't have wealth or position. I've nothing anyone of prestige would care about."

"True. You see, you're my mate. That knowledge is all he needs to pursue you. If he could stop us from marrying, from me claiming you in our traditional way, he would hurt me forever. It wouldn't just be today or for a short time. The pain would last forever. Would stretch into other lifetimes."

Ash twisted the paper in his hands. Set it on the table. He rose to stride around the room. His restlessness touched on her nerves. She'd never seen Ash pace. His nerves must be strung tight. Never seen tension lines radiate from his eyes as well as his mouth. She wished she could do something to ease the distress he must feel.

It seemed she understood all that he said to her. She closed her eyes against the wave of information as she tried to assimilate what he told her. With the new information, Harris felt as if all her blood drained from her body. She looked at him, her eyes wide. "You're my mate? Why didn't you tell me? Why did you pretend to be...?"

She didn't understand anything. Needed to know more. She found herself shaking her head. Disbelief loomed in her head. "How can that be?

You are Sassenach. I don't hear your thoughts…except that one time when I shifted…you shifted…we…"

Ash turned from where he stood then walked to the window overlooking the gardens in the back of the townhouse. His hands behind his back, he continued. "Yes, Sassenach because my parents were English. Do you think only in the highlands there are shifters? They are everywhere." He strode toward her. "More importantly, you didn't trust me. That is difficult for me to understand. Thought you would feel the connection between us. The same way I felt the thread connecting our lives. You didn't. I doubted you would believe me if I made such a claim. Even now that you've seen my cat, you have doubts. Doubts about us…together."

"How do you know I'm your mate?"

Her brothers just knew. As did her cousins. She didn't feel or sense anything. She felt unnerved by the fact. Wanted those feelings of oneness to run through her. *I love him…does that mean…?*

He lifted his broad shoulders. Ash reached out to her then drew his hand back. "How does anyone know? For shifters it's a sixth sense…a feeling in the gut. I'm terrified you don't feel the connection. Afraid you might never understand what binds us together. For some reason, you've no feelings…"

Her trembling fingers tightened on the mug she held. When she looked at him there was moisture in her eyes. She brushed a tear away. Paused a few more seconds before speaking. "I do trust…a little. After last night…oh I don't know. It's just that… It isn't as if I don't wish to be your mate. I do. I've always wanted you. You are so handsome. Your eyes call to me. When you look at me, I have…heat pulses in so many different places I don't understand."

"You don't trust me. I can't live with that. We need to figure this out," he murmured, his gaze narrowed on her, gazing into her eyes as if he could read her thoughts. "For now, I hope you understand the gravity of your willfulness. You must stick close to me for your safety. I'm not being stubborn or arrogant. Nor am I being dictatorial. I'm afraid for your life. Out there," He nodded toward a window. "There is danger for you…maybe for both of us. We don't yet know the direction the threat comes from."

"I will think on what you're telling me."

She meant to do that. As for these next few minutes with him, she hoped he would tell her more about his father.

"Harris, eat your breakfast," Ash acknowledged her presence again with a nod. "The food is good. The tea hot. You must eat. We can speak for a few more minutes. I need to go out. Business. We will leave for Dover first thing tomorrow morning."

She nodded, filling her cup again with the steaming tea. Looked at the egg with growing distaste. Harris looked at the plate of food then at him. There was nothing in front of her she wanted to eat. "Where are you going?"

Ash reached out to touch her hand. He held it for seconds. Rubbed his thumb across her wrist. "Wish I could tell you."

Secrets...seemed he always had secrets. She was an open book. Some things he could never say to her. Harris felt a small ripple of anger rise in her chest. She needed to trust him, in his judgment. If what he told Smith-Jones last night, there were elements at play that might cause her harm. She bit into the scone she spread jam on. The bread was delicious. By the time she finished, she was filled with the sense that her life had become too complicated. She didn't like or trust complications. Back in Carnoch everything had been so simple.

Determined to have faith in him as well as not pursue the fact he didn't trust her with certain pieces of information, she sat back to finish her tea. Picked up a second scone then set it back on her plate. Nothing more appealed. She would wait. Given enough time she would have all her questions answered. "Very well. What should I do to pass the time while you are out and about? Seems there is nothing for me to do here without you by my side. I do grow bored easily. I'm used to family as well as friends around me. Never a minute without something to do."

"My father will be in the drawing room later on. You can sit with him. I've the feeling that if you set your mind to it, you will be able to communicate with him. He will try to teach you how to cast your thoughts toward a certain person. If we are lucky, you might learn how to communicate with me through your mind."

"I don't know how to do such a thing. We've only talked to each other once. Why would he wish to help me? That night..." She did hear Ash tell her to shift. Recalled the anger coupled with fear in his voice. Silently, she refused him. She didn't think she let him into her mind. The fact she refused his command made him angrier. Harris recalled everything about that evening. Her attempt to flee back to the highlands. The first time she lay with him in his bed. The mistrust he felt. He knew if given the chance she would try to leave a second time.

"Ah..." His knuckles grazed her cheek then swept down the column of her throat. They lingered where her pulse beat with frantic haste. "I've been privy to your thoughts since we met. Understand how you feel about me, now as well as when we first saw each other. I swear again that since I met you, I've not been with anyone else. Haven't wanted to be close to a woman who is not you. Still, you plague me with your accusations. Why? I would know the truth."

Harris bristled with indignation that threatened to erupt. "That's not right. It's not right, you know what I'm thinking. Don't want you to be privy to my thoughts. A girl needs a few secrets. I don't want you to know everything I'm thinking."

"I've never used anything I've learned against you. Never will." He dropped his hand. "Before you came to my bed last night, I heard you struggling with your thoughts. Knew you were searching for the courage to come to me, to be close with me. I was pleased when you found the nerve to follow your heart. I pray that where it concerns me you will never deny seeking me out. You are important to me. My life..."

"You did? You heard me?" Found that her eyes widened as she fought against the information he doled out. "Is there nothing private for me? I would not have you know my every thought."

Harris was embarrassed at some of the things she assumed about him. While they traveled, many of her thoughts were unkind. Ash never held it against her. Harris also recalled dreaming about his kisses. The way his hands felt on her body when he caressed her.

"If you learn how to close your mind to me then, yes. I won't be able to get in to see what you are thinking about me or anything else. Father might help you learn a few tricks." His chuckle coupled with a grin had her shaking her head.

"You don't care if I learn how to block you from my mind?"

She was amazed at the idea. Imagined she didn't need to know everything about him. That was it though. He would keep her from his mind when he didn't wish for her to know his secret feelings. Ash had the power to do that. She didn't like that either.

"Yes and no. Need to hear from you if you need me. If you are ever in trouble, come running. If I'm not there, you calling me in your mind would be the only way I would understand that you needed me. Ah, Harris this is an interesting conversation. One I would like to pursue later." He let out a heavy breath of air. "It's time for me to leave. Go see my father. Try to let him into your head. I'll be back as soon as possible. We'll spend the afternoon along with the evening sharing thoughts with father." He leaned over then he kissed her on the forehead.

That wasn't enough; she needed a real kiss. One she hadn't received for a very long time. She watched his back as his long strides carried him from the room. Ash gave her so many new things to think about. Harris finished her tea then decided she would seek out his father. Maybe she could learn something from the man who was Ash's father. They looked so much alike. She'd not seen Chandler yet. She wondered if he lived here. This townhouse was part of his inheritance.

As told, James sat in the drawing room. Harris found him gazing into the fire. When he heard her or sensed her, Harris wasn't certain. He looked toward her. His smile melted her heart. His eyes were the same vibrant blue of Ash's. She tried to open her mind to his thoughts. Wondered when she heard the first ones. Thought it was possible she assumed things. Doubts swirled in her head.

I understand my son's attraction to you. You are beautiful. The attraction goes deeper. He tells me you are his mate. He met you in the highlands. Your brothers as well as your father are shifters. Your clan is the Chaton. We are the Coterie Tigre. The Chaton are well-known by others who shift. I'm thrilled my son was stationed in the highlands. Though his job was repulsive. He despised what he was expected to do. Did everything in his power to stop the violence against your clan.

She nodded her answer. Harris didn't know if she should believe she heard his thoughts. This could just be a coincidence or wishful thinking. Though, she never would have thought to hear him tell her she was beautiful. That would not have been something she anticipated. Ash could have told James about her family.

Thank you. I'm sorry you can't speak in the normal way. How did this happen to you? I would understand if that is alright with you.

I had a stroke. Didn't Ash tell you? My health is no secret. I would have thought he would have said something. His brother is eagerly waiting for me to pass on then leave everything to him.

He mentioned something to that notion. Perhaps I didn't listen. Though details would be nice. If you don't wish to speak of that time, you don't need to. I will understand.

One evening when I was getting ready for bed, I blacked out. That's all I remember. Smith-Jones found me lying on the fur rug in front of the fireplace. Believe he heard me crying out for him. Did you know my butler is not only a shifter but a good friend of the family? He stays with me because of the illness. Believe my other son, who I spoke of earlier, Chandler, would see to my demise sooner than later.

Harris heard herself laugh. *I assumed so when your butler made himself comfortable in Ash's bedroom while they discussed me. He called him Ash. Mere servants don't do that. Knew then Smith-Jones meant more to him than he let on at first. Imagine Ash doesn't feel as if he needs to tell me everything.*

She thought she saw a twinkle in the older man's eyes and a slight twitch of his lips. They spoke for hours of important as well as trivial ideas. The time passed way too fast. James must be tiring. She found it was nearing the noon hour. Someone would serve them lunch. Harris wished to eat with James here in this room if that would be comfortable for him.

I will bring lunch in here.

James nodded. *That would be nice. Go now. Find Smith-Jones. He will be pleased to see we are enjoying each other's company.*

Hurrying from the drawing room, Harris found herself nearing the kitchen. She was looking for Smith-Jones; he would see that all of James' wishes would be fulfilled. Harris knew he would be close by. Ash told her so. She heard a sound behind her. Felt a shadow cross over her. The hair on the back of her neck stood on end. Knew she was about to confront something evil. Harris whirled, horrified to see a man so close. She started to scream but was cut off by a hand across her mouth. This must be

Chandler. He was tall, broad. Had the look of James though his appearance was not as close to his father's as was Ash.

"Found you." Chandler cornered her. Pressed her against the wall. His lips replaced his hand, captured her mouth in a bruising kiss. She struggled against the pressure, twisting her head to get away. His hand captured one breast. Squeezed. She pummeled his back with her fists. Hit him in the side of the head. There was nothing gentle about this man. With his other hand he held her hands above her head giving him free access to all of her. "Ash's little whore. You're quite the pretty little thing. See why he wants you. You spent the night with him. You're a shifter too. This will make my revenge all the sweeter. I'm going to take you. Sully you for my brother. He won't want you after I've had you. After I've left my mark on your body. Too bad you aren't a virgin. Still...the taste I have of you will be sweet. Revenge is sweeter."

No. No, no...no...no...

Get away from me!

Chandler didn't understand her thoughts. Not that if he did, it would make a difference. Her body squirmed and arched in a feverish attempt to buck him from her. She found she was still in her head, screaming to no one. There was no one here to rescue her. "No!" she cried out into Chandler's mouth. With his teeth, he tugged on her lips. Harris bit down hard on his probing tongue. She tasted blood. This man didn't know anything about shifters. He could have her a hundred times, Ash would still want her.

"Bitch!" Chandler yelled, pulling away from her. He slapped her hard. She choked. "Damn bitch!"

Her head flew to the side. Hit the wall behind her. Pain exploded in her temples and left a loud ringing in her ear. Chandler held her chin so tight pain radiated. Covered her mouth with his, bruising her again. He ripped at the front of her dress. Cold air washed over naked flesh. Tears stung her eyes. He grabbed at her breast, twisting, tugging on her nipple. She whimpered. Agony exploded through her. Tears fell in streaks.

Even if James heard her, he couldn't do anything for her. Ash wasn't in the house. He wouldn't run to her rescue. In her mind, Harris tried to reach out to Smith-Jones. He was supposed to be close. He would protect her. She didn't hear him in her head. Chandler's hand was lifting her skirt, his fingers on her pantalets, tugging them down, ripping. His hand cupped her mound. Fingers pressed. She shook. Terrified.

With no warning to speak of, she heard Ash. He was telling her he loved her then he said more.

Calm yourself, love. In just a second, Smith-Jones will be there for you. I've called out for him. All will be well. I'm coming for you. Let my friend take care of you. Go with my friend to our rooms. I will come to you.

She jerked as the body accosting her was ripped away. Chandler was no longer pressing her against the wall. His mouth no longer held hers captive. He wasn't hurting her. Harris thought she would be sick. She slumped to the ground gasping for air. Shaking. Drawing in long deep breaths of air. Her stomach churned. The contents of her stomach emptied onto the floor. Onto the nice white marble. She tried to pull her torn bodice to cover her. Sobs wracked her.

"Go!" Smith-Jones yelled, his voice shaking with fury. "Get the bloody hell away from your brother's woman. You've no rights here."

Harris was certain the butler was yelling at Chandler. She heard the pounding of feet then the cursing. Chandler left. Smith-Jones knelt beside her. Helped her pull her bodice together. Lifted her tear-stained face. "I'm taking you to Ash's room. You will stay there. He is on his way. You've nothing more to fear. I'm sorry this happened. I didn't stay close enough to you. Thought you were safe from Chandler here in the house. I'll stand guard at the door until Ash gets here."

~ *~

When Harris' voice screamed *"No!"* in his head, Ash had just finished his business. He heard her terror. Felt the agony she suffered. Knew the man hurting her was his brother. Understood with stark clarity all that his brother did as well as said to Harris. Ash's gut twisted knowing he was too far from her to help. All he could do now would be to soothe her, tell her how much he cared for her.

In his mind, Ash called out to Smith-Jones imploring him for his help. To hurry. Told him where he would find Harris. To do whatever he felt necessary to save Harris from further pain. Gave him *carte blanch* as to handling Chandler. His brother deserved to die for this. Through Harris' eyes he saw where she was. Knew each time Chandler hurt her. Ash made his apologies before racing from the parliament building. His coach along with his driver waited in front. His heart raced by the time he reached the carriage. His body thrummed with the need to get to Harris. Bloody eyes, he wasn't there when she needed him. How could he ever be with her every minute of every day?

"Home. Hurry!" Ash yelled at the driver then he was inside. He focused on Harris, spoke to her through his mind, prayed she understood. Tried to calm her with his thoughts. As if he was inside her head, Ash felt her pain when Chandler hit her, when her head snapped to the side. Every cruel action Ash knew about. Her mouth would be bruised along with her cheek. She would have bruises on her breasts where he abused the delicate flesh.

Ash knew his brother harbored evil within himself. He had always had that side to him that enjoyed another person's pain. As the man grew older, Ash heard stories about women he abused. What he didn't realize was the extent of the evil that was inside his brother. Chandler didn't understand he could force Harris without changing who they were to each other. Even if he did, that would never alter the fact Harris was his mate. Ash would always love her, always want her. Anger vibrated through his body. Something needed to be done about Chandler's cruelty. There was no way in hell his father should allow him to take over the properties they owned. Chandler would destroy the legacy.

Smith-Jones arrived. When he realized the horrific scene was finished, Ash said a silent prayer of relief. Smith-Jones carried Harris to his room, the one they shared last night. He told her to stay put. His friend would stand guard over her until he could reach her. Ash decided they would be leaving tonight. He wasn't about to wait until the morning.

From what he could tell, Harris would do as told...this time. The countless times in their future, he couldn't be certain. She would learn from this encounter. Chandler would remain a threat to them.

Take care, love. Do everything my friend asks of you. Don't take chances today.

I was careful. The devil, I was with your father. I wasn't doing anything wrong. Just going to the kitchen to bring us lunch.

Ash couldn't help smiling. She was bristling. That was a good sign. Harris was strong. She would bounce back from this ordeal.

I will be there in ten minutes. Telling Smith-Jones to pack our things. We aren't staying at the townhouse tonight. Can't leave you so near to a man who means you harm. I'll return to you in a second. Need to speak with Father.

Ash turned his attention to his father. He told him what happened. Explained to him why they would leave as soon as he made it to the townhouse. There was nothing that could be done against Chandler.

His brother was the heir.

Until that changed, he held innumerable rights others did not. Chandler was arrogant. Filled with self-importance. Believed he could do no wrong. Could do anything he pleased. What he did to others...

As he grew to adulthood, Ash understood the best course of action for him was to stay far away from his brother. Since his father's stroke, distance had not always been possible. His Dover home was a day and a half away from London. If the need arose, he could ride all night and make it here in a day. He was going home. Needed to put his brand on his mate sooner than later. Ash didn't feel as if he now had the time to ease her into his ways. He prayed she would not remain recalcitrant. She was obstinate. Told him she didn't want him because he wouldn't be faithful. The irony didn't elude him. He'd been faithful...loyal to her for three years. His thoughts needed to return to Harris. The carriage lumbered through the busy streets. He smiled when he found himself in her mind again.

I see you are in my room...our room. Smith-Jones stands outside guarding the space well, but he will not go inside unless there is some kind of trouble or I ask it of him. I told you we are leaving. All I want now is to see you, hold you, make certain you will be fine. Talk to me, love. Tell me what lies in your heart.

To hold you too would be heaven. He did hurt me. As I look in the mirror my mouth is swollen...red. My cheek where he hit me is beginning to bruise. I'm a sight. Ash...I'm glad we are leaving. Though I did have a wonderful visit with James. He's a nice man. Much like you. What other surprises are in store for me? Is your brother going to leave us alone after we depart London? I heard about the woman you have in Dover. Will she be a problem?

Ah, I see you heard something about Abella. She is not important to me...that's not true. I've taken care of her for over five years now. We can speak more of this woman on our ride to Dover. While I take care of her it is in the way of a friend...perhaps as an obligation since I took her away from the only life she knew.

You weren't honest about everything...now...were you? You expect one thing from me but not the same of yourself. Don't appreciate double standards. You will have to learn.

In my defense, I forgot about the woman. She resides in my home free of charge. Abella has no duties to perform. In truth, I don't ken what to do with her other than to allow her to do as she pleases.

Tell me more about this woman who is both important as well as not important to you. She does play a role in your life. Does she not? You are making no sense. I'd like to understand. Want to believe in all that you tell me. In the past year, we haven't been close. We've seen each other a handful of times. It's as if we are just now getting to know each other. Am I not right?

Abella has never been in my bed, never will. I rescued her from a brothel in Paris. She'd been abused, kicked out and was wandering the streets. Homeless. The poor lady was starving. She was bleeding because one of her Johns hurt her. I had no other choice than to help this woman. Abella believes herself to be in love with me. That does not mean I reciprocate those emotions.

You had to do something. So, you rescued her. I'm glad you did. What woman who knew you wouldn't be at least half in love with you? You were her knight in shining armor.

Blocking his emotion along with his thoughts from Harris, Ash laughed. He imagined that was Harris' roundabout way of telling him she might be half in love with him...or...half in hate. He hoped for the first. That was good for a start to their new relationship. He supposed what she thought she felt before was lust, hungry desire. Raw, fierce passion.

It seemed true. Today marked the beginning of something new.

Perhaps they would soon reach an understanding. He hoped these new feelings between them would increase quickly. He went back inside her head.

Smith-Jones told me Abella was his mate. I'm happy about that. Once we get to my home, I will send Abella to him. Smith-Jones can't leave father for the three days it would take him to fetch her himself. You see...Smith Jones is my butler. Not father's. He is staying here upon my request. Father needs his protection. I do not.

Oh...

I'm here.

"Wait in the room. Will be down in a few minutes. We're leaving for Dover this afternoon." Ash raced into the house then up the stairs to his room. "Harris!" He cried out as the door burst open. "Harris..." He saw her. She was beautiful even in her dishabille. The stark pain in her face was obvious. His heart lodged in his throat real fear for her surfaced. His brother...damn the man.

She stood in the middle of the room, her hands clasped together in front of her. For several seconds while emotions played across her beautiful face, she challenged him with her head high. As if a damn burst, she rushed to him, her arms spread wide. Harris flung herself at him. He caught her. Gathered her into his arms. Held her close. She nestled her head into his chest. He stroked her back, soothing strokes. Feather light. The painfilled rhythm of her body caught at him. Saw Smith-Jones appear from the closet where he must have been packing for the journey south.

"Your bags are ready."

"Good. We'll be with you downstairs in a few minutes. I need to be alone with Harris." Ash pushed Harris away from him a slight distance so he could see her better. With a light stroke he touched her mouth. She flinched. Her eyes came together, creased lines around her eyes. Not only was her cheek bruised but skin was broken. Her face was turning a fetching shade of blue-green coupled with some purple smudges. She looked like she'd been in a fight.

I was in a fight. I fought for my virtue. For my life. I fought him as hard as I could. He is stronger. Chandler held my hands above my head. He did... Your brother hurt me. I bit him.

Harris spoke through her mind though she broke off with a soft sob that tore at Ash's heart. Silver tears streamed down her face. She was becoming quite good at talking with her mind. His father must be an amazing instructor. She was a fast learner. Ash was proud of her. He wondered if she would also be able to block him from her mind.

It hurts to talk. Are we going now?

"Yes. Does my father know what happened? He will be concerned for you. Father has talked about denouncing Chandler as his heir. My brother will never serve the Parliament or the people who he speaks for in a good way. He will seek only to please himself as well as enrich his coffers. Deep inside Chandler is evil. His mean streak goes to his soul. Is part of his heart. He cannot be redeemed."

"To the best of my knowledge, I told your father with unspoken words what happened. He also understands why you must leave. Under the circumstances there is no choice for you," Smith-Jones said as he backed from the room to give them a few minutes to themselves.

Feeling his warmth, Harris leaned into him. Ash felt her need. Understood with his sixth sense she was giving herself over to his care, trusting him. He needed to cherish her, keep her from harm. Today he failed to protect. His arm circled around her, holding her as close as he could get her, feeling the short sharp breaths that told him she was not as recovered as he hoped. Bleeding hell, he shouldn't have left her here. Didn't know Chandler was in town. Should have guessed as much. Hindsight told him he made a huge mistake.

Chandler would have to die before this could come to an end. His brother would never stop the pursuit. He would come at Harris until he got what he was after. Dear Lord, if his brother forced her, he would kill him with his bare hands. Chandler would never fight fair. He sent a shifter after them. Ash wasn't fearful of another shifter. His cat was huge. Powerful. He had nothing to fear unless he became too relaxed or too certain of his strength. He would need to keep his guard up. Protecting Harris now became the most important part of his life. Chandler wasn't welcome in Dover. His brother understood.

Harris leaned into him, her hand on his chest. The side of her face that had not been abused was against him. She was shaking too hard. Ash wasn't at all certain she could walk down the steps. He didn't know what to do. Didn't want to cause her further pain. She swayed against him. Her arm wrapped around his waist. He would carry her. She wouldn't like that. Would tell him she could walk. She couldn't. Getting back inside her head, Ash spoke to her.

Hush now, don't complain.

He picked her up intending to carry her to the waiting coach. In his arms, she was feather light. His brother was a big man.

I can walk.

Ash laughed having known what she would tell him. "Not so sure of that as you are. A fall down the steps wouldn't get us where we wish to be going, now, would it? A fall would add to the injuries you already incurred today. Don't wish for that either."

No...

"I'm pleased you've become so agreeable. Smith-Jones had a lunch made for us. There is a splendid inn about four hours from here. We will stop for the night. I will hold you as I've done since we left the highlands. Won't allow anything bad to happen to you." *Never again...never again...he vowed with all his heart. Never again.*

Harris wrapped her arms around him. He didn't want to let her go to get into the carriage. Hear the pain-riddled sobs she tried to hide. After he set her on the seat, he jumped in behind her then tapped on the roof. They began to move. The clatter of the wheels against the cobblestone, hoof beats danced in rhythm. Heard hawkers calling out their wares. The city was alive. Vibrant. Fascinating to those strong enough to survive the evil. The decadence. The excesses.

Ash hoped she wouldn't object. What he wanted most was to hold her. Needed to keep her close. After the way she cuddled against him, he felt sure there would be no protest. Letting her sit on the opposite side was not agreeable. He pulled her onto his lap. She came to him. Embraced him. One more time she nestled against him, seeming to hold him as tight as she could. She absorbed his strength.

It wouldn't take much for this sweet surrender to change to more. He needed to hit himself in the head to chase the clouds from his brain. She couldn't kiss. Wouldn't be able to do so for a number of days. Her breasts would be sore from the cruelty she suffered. Suffered at his brother's whim at his jealousy of all he couldn't have. There was so much Chandler had at his disposal. His brother always wanted more.

If it's any consolation, I wish you could kiss me too.

"Too soon in any case. If I could kiss you, it would lead to more, much, much more. Things I want to savor when we are wed. After I've claimed you in the way of my clan, we will make love. All that when you are ready." He wondered if the time would be soon. Wondered how he could wait any longer. She should be his in every way. She wasn't. He needed her heart as well as her soul. Harris possessed his. The exchange was fair.

What if I don't want to wait? I would have you make love to me. Need you in every way.

He groaned. Waiting was part of his plan. It was difficult now that she was no longer putting buffers in front of them. He needed what she asked for. Tonight, that wasn't possible.

"Won't make love to you. I could, however, give you pleasure. Reinforce the ecstasy you experienced so long ago. Harris, love, I'm pleased you've begun to have faith in me again. Trust in me." Ash hoped she might agree to that notion. To touch her breasts, other parts of her would be heaven.

Like that day in the mossy glen. I thought you were going to take my virginity. Believed if you did, I would be left alone as well as pregnant. Didn't know if you would come back for me. I could have been your plaything, you're mistress. Someone to love then leave at your whim. Didn't want that for myself. Didn't want a Sassenach baby when the man didn't care enough for me to marry me.

Harris was letting all her bottled-up emotions out, telling him how she felt. Going back to that sunny afternoon was important for both of them. Ash was pleased she didn't forget that day. Pleased she wanted him to return for her. After he came back, she fought her emotions the only way she could.

Those last hours with her before he left for home to see to his father were seared in his head. "Remember the climax you had in my arms? I'll never forget the way your eyes glazed over with your pleasure. Will recall that vision until I stick my spoon in the wall. I wished to have you in every way. You didn't know it then but I agreed with you. Didn't want to chance you becoming pregnant while I was gone. If that situation came about, I needed to be with you. To be part of the event. You meant too much to me to leave you to the scorn of those who would cast stones."

I do remember the pleasure. I..." Harris ran her tongue across her swollen lips. Winced at the slight pressure. *I never knew anything could be so wonderful. Even though I spoke of other men...boys compared to you, I never wanted anyone but you. No one I mentioned meant anything to me. For me, it was only you.*

"I'd like to throttle my brother. Would love to knock him senseless until he is in as much pain as you. If he ever touches you again in that way, I don't believe I can be responsible for my actions. His head should be on a pike."

Ash's hands tightened on her waist. Moved them higher to below her breasts. Felt the weight. Needed to feel the satin texture. Taste the tips. First though, he needed to control his burgeoning arousal. Even with her bruised, colored face, looking at her aroused him. Made him contemplate long sultry nights with her in his arms. Thinking of the tempting body sitting on him, aroused him. She wanted him to make love to her. He'd waited so long to hear those words. Now...well, because of his brother, now, he had to wait even longer.

Harris brought her head off his shoulder. She touched his mouth with her fingertip. Heat flamed. Slashed into him. Ash touched the tip with his tongue. He found her gentleness, unmanned him. She was fire in his soul. His heart belonged to her. Tonight, he would restrain himself. He could not touch her lips. Would not hurt her more. His brother must have bit her...hard. He caressed the bruising on her cheek. Ran his finger down her neck to stop at the pulse point that throbbed...pounded waiting for his touch. Her hair fell in silken waves against his hands. He sifted the silken strands through his fingers. After the attack she'd not put her hair into the chignon she usually wore. Ash liked her hair down. Thought of the coolness wrapped around him.

When you touch me, the bruise doesn't hurt so much.

I'm a cad for even thinking about touching all the beautiful parts of you. Harris...it's been so long. I do want you. I don't know if I can control myself. I need you so much. I won't make love in this carriage. The first time has to be on my bed. Nowhere else will do. If you like, I will give you pleasure. Watch you climax. Would you like that?

Ash bit back the needs swirling inside him. He couldn't do that with her tonight. Not after what she'd been through. He had to wait no matter her siren's call. Even if she asked, he would curtail his wicked thoughts. He needed to do right by her. She was his love. His mate. Taking good care of her was his first priority.

I want you too.

Not tonight.

No, not tonight.

Soon.

One of the things he did this morning was to initiate the reading of the banns. Ash didn't want to cut corners. He would see to her wedding gown now that he was certain she would agree. The modiste in the village near his home was excellent. The wedding would be witnessed by the villagers as well as close friends. An after-celebration feast would be planned in the extensive gardens at the back of his home. His patience would last the three weeks needed. Not a moment longer. Harris would be healed. There would no longer be bruising to contend with as well as avoid. For them, there would be no special license. A wedding in his church was the proper way to go about their marriage. All must be perfect.

Damn, Harris was Catholic.

He wasn't. Something she might protest. He would wed her in the Catholic Church along with the ways of Clan Chaton when they returned next year to the highlands. He would tell her she could worship any way she pleased. Ash prayed she would agree with that proposition. Nothing else would do. She had to accept.

Almost a quarter mile from his home there was a secluded glade. As soon as Harris was healed as well as agreeable to the wedding, he would take her there. In that private spot he would make her his in the way of his people. Candles would burn. He would chant the age-old sayings that would bind them together in his clan's way. He was the tiger...the white tiger. In his clan the white tiger held the most prestige. He was powerful. Strong.

That night by the laws of the clan, he could make love to her. He would make her his own. When he did, their relationship would be sealed in his eyes as well as his coteries. He didn't need to wait until the vows had been said in the church to make her his. He didn't know how Harris would feel about his intentions.

The declaring was an ancient custom. Passed down over thousands of years. His cat and hers would be joined. Ash wondered if they would have little shifters. Because they were different cats, they might not be able to birth shifters. God, he hoped that wouldn't be the case. Since he knew Harris, he looked forward to having at least one babe who could change form. This was something he'd never thought of before. Surely the ancient Gods would never put them together if birthing more shifters wasn't possible.

I... Harris looked at him. She held his chin in her hand. *...believe that because we are both able to become cats, all our babes will be able to change shape. If we have little girls, they will be black panthers...*

Our little boys will be white tigers? I like that notion. Like it a lot. I pray you were right. Didn't know you were listening to my thoughts.

I was. You didn't block them from me. I understand your need to make this right, to do everything in the correct way. I would also like to marry you in the Catholic Church with my clan watching. Would you also go through our clan ritual? Can you? Would that be possible? Can we have another wedding feast? I'd like that too. Love celebrations. Enjoy eating.

You like drinking wine too.

Yes.

"There are too many questions we cannot answer. Suppose fate will step in and with time, answer all our queries. I planned to have the ceremony in Carnoch in a year when we return. Your father knows my plans. You would too if you had cared to listen. Between us we should not have secrets."

"Tonight, we will remain celibate. Don't want to hurt you. I know you've more bruises on you than just your lips. I saw too much. After we stop, I'll see to those bruises if you'll let me. I plan to take care of you for the rest of our lives."

Harris lifted her shoulders. *What can you do that time won't heal. There is no way to fix what happened. No way to wash away the color with soap and water. No way to rid my mind of your vile brother.*

"You are too fragile. Too delicate for any man to hurt. I would...I wish I'd been there. Chandler would have never done what he did. If father had been whole, Chandler would never have taken advantage of you."

Minutes ticked by while he listened to her breathing. Sometime, Ash didn't know when she fell asleep cuddled next to him. He needed to take better care of his woman. All she had to protect her from harm was him. Even though he knew his friends as well as his under butler, Tindly, would do their best to keep her from harm's way. Harris was his responsibility.

Ash ran his fingers through her hair. Lifted the strands to his cheek, caught the scent. They drifted through his fingers, touching on the sensitive flesh. With care he undid her bodice. Pushed the fabric aside so he could see her breasts. Knew Chandler hurt her. He slid the fabric down until he gasped.

Both breasts were as discolored as her cheek. He saw the marks where his brother bit her. His gut tightened with fury. He'd never seen something this horrific. Harris didn't complain. She didn't whine or moan. She was stoic. Calm in the face of adversity. Told him there was nothing he could do to change what happened.

Harris was right. Only time would heal the wounds. Ash set the back of his head against the seat, thinking, wishing. She moved closer, her hand resting on his belly. He pulled the fabric of her chemise to cover her then fastened her gown. They would be at the inn soon.

He would keep her close. The threat was still out there. When Chandler wanted something, he was tenacious. Ash understood the shifter he saw in the Highlands was hired by his brother.

~ * ~

Chandler walked around the perimeter of the small dank room. He was meeting with one of his friends. A man who shifted. They often plotted in this room. Made plans for whatever foul game one of them wished to play. Women from the vilest places in the city were victims of their schemes. He liked them to beg. He loved them willing to do his bidding. Ah, back to his brother. Chandler hated his brother. Ashton was everything he wasn't. Not that he wished to be like Ash. He didn't. He enjoyed the games he played. He enjoyed his women.

He wasn't a shifter. Ash was. He regretted that fact. Chandler wanted the power as well as the mystery that came with being able to change to a cat. His brother was splendid in his tiger form. The thought that the ability wasn't his had angered him throughout his life. He was first born. All the power should have been his. When they were children, Ash would change to his cat while they were playing. At first, Ash thought he was holding back, teasing him about that ability. Later, Ash felt sorry for him, pitied him.

Chandler didn't want anyone's pity. He wanted strength. Control. Power. Authority coupled with the ability to make others plead for his mercy. When he returned, he would take Stella to his bed. The maid would help him rid the world of Harris. He could do anything to Stella. She liked sex rough. Liked it from as many men as possible. Thoughts started to blur in his head then take root. There might be more women like Stella. Women who enjoyed sex. Didn't care who the man pushing inside her was.

She told him she might join him here. What she didn't know was that if she came here, there would be more than one actor in the play. He understood she would take pleasure from the adventure. She must vow her loyalty. Chandler couldn't afford for anyone to know who conspired with him. His laughter echoed in the room. Stella would never be Ash's. For some reason... Chandler was shaking his head. Women were so gullible. They would give their bodies for whatever they could get. Harris held back. He didn't like that. When he first saw her, he had every intention of hurting her. The revenge on his brother would be sweet. He was pleased with the outcome. The woman would have bruises. The bite marks would infuriate Ash. Chandler grinned pleased with the outcome of this afternoon's dalliance with his brother's whore.

"I'm certain James told Ash about the secrets he was keeping. The government secrets that only father knew. I'm the one he was supposed to tell. I'm his heir. I will have his seat in the parliament. I need the information. Could make a tidy profit by selling the secrets to the highest bidder." He was after money. Enough to keep him content along with his more clandestine habits. Chandler picked up the book he'd taken notes in then threw it across the room to slam against the door. "No!" He was both furious as well as frustrated with the way his life played out. He must do something to change that.

"You've something planned?"

He stopped his pacing, rubbing his chin as a slow grin developed. "I'm going to have his little lady. It was obvious this morning she would never willingly fall into my plans. She's a fighter. Gives me reason to restrain her. I like that. We could tie her hands above her head. Makes it sweeter when I finally push inside her body. She won't beg for pleasure. Doubt if she would beg me to stop. That's alright. I will still make certain she understands she can't win. When I'm finished with her, you can have her for as long as she entertains you."

The man hiked an eyebrow. "She liked..."

Chandler waved his hand in the air then grinned. "Of course not. The girl wasn't supposed to enjoy my attention. I want to hurt her as much as I do my brother. She is a pawn in my vengeance against Ash. Believe I succeeded today. She couldn't talk, her breasts will be colorful. I can imagine my brother's face when he realizes what I did to his charming whore. He will be filled with rage. Fury weakens a man. Women bring about a man's demise. Can bring them to their knees if a man gives a woman the power."

Chandler stared into the small fire that did nothing to warm the room. Yes, yes...yes, he thought he might enjoy stretching Harris out on this bed. Without spending time on the thought, he could see her lying the length of the bed, her hands tied above her head, her thighs parted for him. Defenseless. He would have what his brother had. Everything. By the time he finished with the little whore there would be nothing left for Ash.

"You need to be careful with your brother. The man is strong. Powerful. If he is filled with purpose, he will be a formidable opponent. He won't allow you to get away with hurting his woman. You're taking a huge gamble."

To have her beg at his feet would be nice...beg for her life. Ash would try to rescue her. He would be prepared for that event. There were several men who would welcome the added income. He could pay them well. The funds were his, all but in his name. All that stood between him and power was his father.

As soon as his brother relaxed his guard, she would be easy prey. "I will have her. For now, I'm going back to London. See what I can do about eliminating the old man. He's been alive far too long. I want my inheritance. Am tired of waiting."

"You will have to get by Smith-Jones. Ash left him in London to take care of James. The butler guards him night as well as day. Just as he guarded his woman. The man is also a shifter. That won't be easy. Do you wish for help?"

"Send Smith-Jones on an errand. That could be a good plan. While he's away, I can get to my father. Some kind of poison that won't be detected would be a good way."

"He'll send someone else to keep tabs on him. Even poison won't be easy."

The knock on the door surprised him. "Who is it?"

Chandler grinned when he saw Stella peak around the corner. Smiling, she played straight into his hands. After being with Harris he needed to slake his lust along with the need to kill. He'd not had time to take Ash's woman the way he imagined. When he saw Stella he hardened. Thirsted to have this woman. His body was parched with need. He could already taste her.

"You sent for me? You should know who is at the door," Stella said in a huff while she pranced into the room.

As she took off her cloak to hang by the door, she looked to the other man. "Who is he? Didn't expect company." Her brows drew together. She looked at him again, repeating herself. "Didn't know there would be someone else here. Not that I mind. He's big. That's good." She sent her gaze to his groin.

Chandler hooted his laughter. "Thought it would be fun. Something a bit different than our usual play time. Two men with one girl. What do you think? Want to play with two of us?" Chandler asked as he watched Stella for some sign she might enjoy coupling with more than one man. For some reason he hoped she wouldn't object. He enjoyed Stella. The woman always seemed eager to try new things.

Shaking her head, Stella backed up. She looked at the door as if she might bolt. Chandler wasn't going to lose out on sex with the maid because she might be a bit flighty. He reached out to her, pulling her into his arms. He nodded at Bertram. He wasn't about to take the chance she might run.

Chandler's mouth framed hers. Bertram closed his hands over her breasts. Slid the bodice to her waist. She squirmed. Moaned. Chandler stared down at her. "You want this. I can see it in your eyes." Bertram rubbed his palms on the tips of her breasts. Chandler kissed her again, sent his tongue deep inside her mouth.

"No...no... Oh..." Her fingers wound into his hair. She pulled him closer, meeting the thrust of his tongue with her own. A mewl escaped her when he bit her lip. As Bertram moved lower so did he. He sucked on one of her nipples used his hand to play with the other. Her head fell back giving willing access. Chandler nipped along the column of her neck.

Bertram sent the gown to the floor before kicking it aside. She wore nothing beneath. His hands ran along the inside of her legs to the apex. Separated them with his leg. "You were ready for us. Want this as much as the two of us." Bertram was kneeling behind her. Nipped her fanny. She jumped. Cried out. Moaned.

Chandler laved the tip of her breast with his tongue. Bertram's fingers slid between her parted legs.

"Who do you want inside you first?" Chandler asked as he pushed her feet farther apart with his leg.

"You...I want you, Chandler. After that your friend can have me if he wants." She was panting. Her breaths heavy with desire.

Chandler unfastened his pants. "Good, I knew you would come around." He bit the tip of her breast then sucked hard until she whimpered. He lifted her into his arms, striding to the bed. He fell on his back. She straddled him. Bertram was behind her.

"Oh...please."

He pushed inside. She was hot. Wet. Ready. With a grunt he emptied himself.

"Now it's Bertram's turn."

Chapter Four

Harris stared out the window as the carriage made its way up the long winding driveway to Ash's home. It was a mansion. Huge. Spread out. She thought she would get lost trying to find her way around the house. All her previous fears multiplied at the site of her new home. Appearing excited to show off the house along with his property to her, Ash looked thrilled. His smile stretched across his face.

Since she came to him that night and asked him to hold her, she slept with him again last night by choice. With that act, Harris understood Ash thought all was settled between them. True, she learned he thought she was his mate. Just because they were able to communicate in their minds didn't convince her they were meant to be together through all eternity. She still had a multitude of reservations. They were both shifters. That might be the reason they had that ability to communicate in such an unusual manner. She didn't know. Needed to talk to someone who would answer her truthfully. She wanted Hawk or Cameron to show up. Needed family to surround her. Loneliness seemed to be a huge part of her problems accepting what Ash thought was the absolute truth. He wrenched her away from Cameron's wedding. He stole her. Abducted her. She tried to forgive. Found that impossible though she wished to feel the forgiveness in her heart.

Ash told her that her parents would come for their wedding in three weeks. They decided on the date without asking her. Shouldn't the bride have some say? Shouldn't the two getting married love each other? While she cared about Ash she didn't know if that was enough. Didn't know if she loved him. She did understand she wanted him in the most primitive of ways. Ash cared for her. He wanted to protect her. That wasn't love. She needed the words. Three words would change everything.

Love...

Love was what she wanted...yearned for. Harris wasn't certain if

Ash said the words, she would believe him. Even though she wanted to, needed to believe. Her faith in him had been shattered. With the passage of the last days, she was beginning to trust him. Three weeks might not be enough time.

Love...her feelings about this marriage all returned to love.

There was Abella. Ash also told her the woman was Smith-Jones' mate. Why didn't they do anything about that before she arrived at the London townhouse? Seemed far too convenient for her to accept. Things like that didn't just happen.

The story of the rescue was also expedient. Ash told her he'd never slept with her. Told her he'd not been with another woman since he met her. That was something that was just too hard for her to believe. Her brothers never spent years celibate. They had one conquest after another until they met their mate. They kept mistresses until they found the woman for them.

They were celibate, however, once they met their mate until they wed.

Three years...?

To Harris it seemed he was spinning tales to make her feel better. The carriage hit something on the ground. Jolted her. She groaned. Pain knifed through her. She wrapped her arms around her breasts to better hold them still. She could talk now though it still hurt. At times she chose to speak through her mind.

"Are you alright?" Ash held her hand then brought it to his lips. "We'll stop moving soon. I know the ride has been uncomfortable. I'm sorry. Needed to get you safe as soon as I could. If Chandler wasn't in residence, we could have stayed in London until you healed. That wasn't the case. With my brother around, I fear for you."

I'm fine. Her body ached from the assault. If she were to speak the truth, she was far from fine. Her condition had as much to do with her confusion about the relationship she was expected to have with Ash as it did with what Chandler did to her. It hurt her more to wonder at every turn whether she should believe him.

"Funny, you don't look fine. You've withdrawn from me. What is it? Talk to me," Ash asked her as the carriage came to a halt. He let go of her hand then waited for the door to open for them.

"When we have privacy," Harris tried to reassure him. He didn't look reassured by any means. *I need to tell you how I'm feeling. Not now...*

"So be it. I can wait," Ash said as the door opened.

He jumped to the lawn. Helped her down. Set her on her feet then directed his attention to some of the staff assembled on the porch waiting for their arrival. Smith-Jones must have sent a messenger on horseback ahead of them who would have ridden through the night. "We will begin introductions. Are you up for meeting the staff?"

From the corner of her eye, Harris saw a woman rushing down the steps shrieking Ash's name. In a flurry of arms, she was beside him, pushing her aside. She jumped onto Ash, wrapping her legs around his flanks. From the force of his greeting, Ash staggered back. He looked shocked. Ash knew the woman...must know her well. Her stomach turned over then over again. She gulped down the agony. Pain turned to fury then annoyance. She wouldn't take this from anyone. Let alone the man who claimed to be hers into eternity.

The woman's lips found his. She ran her fingers through his hair. All the while Ash tried to detangle himself from her. Harris gave him credit for that even though a brief thought in her head was that he did it for her. She pushed that thought from her mind.

This lady with more arms and legs than any woman should have, was all over him. Harris watched as she placed kisses all over his face. This woman must be Abella. The lady he never slept with. She was the only woman he thought to warn her about. A rescued lady from the streets of Paris...from a brothel. *He told me he never slept with the woman.* The picture she was seeing flashing in front of her like a nightmare, did not attest to his innocence. Harris heard a few gasps from the servants who milled on the porch waiting for the introductions that might not take place.

After a few minutes, Ash was able to pry her off, setting her down in front of him. When he was able to come up for air, his lips were rouged as well as other parts of his face, his hair in disarray. He looked as if he'd been well and truly kissed.

He had been.

The green bite of jealousy filled her. She fought escalating emotions. Struggled with the knowledge he must have lied to her. Deflated, she waited for his denouncement of the woman or an explanation of some sort. Nothing was forthcoming. All she heard for several seconds that seemed like minutes was silence.

"Abella..." He looked from the woman with octopus limbs then to her.

My God, he was making introductions as if this woman might mean something to him. Shocked. Embarrassed, mortified to the tips of her toes, she stood in front of the couple dazed.

Ash smiled at her. "This is Harris. She will be my wife in three weeks. You need to make friends with her. Respect her wishes."

Despite the fact she was coming to love this man more than she ever thought possible, what he implied was not tolerable or possible. A lot would need to change in three weeks for her to say vows with him. Commit to him. Become his wife. After this exchange, if he thought she would fall into his arms, Ash was delusional.

This woman would never be her friend. She would wait for privacy. For it would be interesting to hear his explanation of this event. Of why Abella assumed he would enjoy her ardent attention. He must have slept with her. The tale about Abella being Smith-Jones' mate must be just that, a story meant to appease her to assist her seeing things his way.

After that infuriating display of public affection, he went on with the introduction as if nothing happened that would make her question her sanity. Seemed he ignored what everyone except him witnessed. Even the servants appeared affronted at his behavior.

She couldn't stay here. Not with that woman in residence. At the thought, her stomach lurched. When he finished telling her the names of the cook, the upstairs as well as the downstairs maids, the groomsmen. There were others but she couldn't recall...a gardener...two of them. Who else?

Abella... The woman did nothing.

He told her he never slept with her. Even if he did, that was the past. The thought did not ease the suspiciousness sweeping through her with lightning speed.

Harris didn't have anywhere to go. She needed to run. Back to the highlands...her parents would bring her right back. They'd given her to him as if she was chattel. Without asking her if she wished this, they let him spirit her from her brother's wedding. Did he pay her parents for her?

That was a horrible uncalled-for thought. She supped in a huge breath of air, trying to temper her feelings to something more normal. There wasn't anything normal about this. Harris found she was shaking. With no means to calm herself, her body quivered.

Ash took her arm. Held her as if nothing happened. He led her up the porch steps into the foyer which was huge. Marble floors just as in his father's home. High ceilings with a stained-glass window at one end. The stairs leading upward were in front of her winding then separating into two different directions. He was going to take her to a bedroom. She didn't want to be left somewhere.

"You must be exhausted," he told her, then turning to address the help, continued, "We will take our dinner in the master chamber. As soon as it is prepared let me know, will you, Tindly? I'm going to see to my...to Harris. After that I will be down to take care of a few details that need attending to. These last few days have been trying for her. For me as well. We have a few important topics to speak privately about."

One of those details better be Abella. Harris didn't want the woman anywhere near her or Ash. Again, distrustfulness stung her. When she recalled the image of the lady in Ash's arms, she felt a knife twist within her. She didn't want to be suspicious. Since leaving London she'd come full circle with her thoughts. She needed to figure out why she needed Ash. Why she wanted him to sleep next to her each night? He did make her feel protected. Cherished. Enjoyed the warmth of his big body next to hers. Even though she didn't say the words, she understood he knew. He could read her thoughts anytime he wished. Harris tried to close her mind to the man. Found doing so was difficult.

He didn't love her. He lied about his women to win her over. That wasn't acceptable to her. She couldn't marry a man who would lie to get what he wanted. If she were to say 'I do' she needed to trust in him, in his word. If he told her he'd slept with women, that was the past, she could forgive him. As it stood now, she couldn't...wouldn't forgive the lie.

What she believed was that he slept with various women over the last three years. That made sense to her. She wouldn't hold that against him in any way if he told her the truth. The future, not the past, was what mattered. When she confronted him about sleeping with women during the year they were separated, he didn't answer.

What she didn't believe was that he'd been celibate for the same amount of time. She wished it was otherwise. Didn't understand why he told her he had been when it was obvious to anyone with eyes he wasn't. Decided she should make him wait as well as wonder about her true feelings. She didn't need to appear too eager. He told her the wedding was in three weeks.

She didn't think so.

Her family would be here.

Damn.

Once inside the master chamber, Ash let go of her arm. Harris walked to the middle of the huge room then turned to face him. Her arms, she crossed below her breasts. She needed to wait for him to speak. The scene in the front of the house haunted her. Knew he would deny again and again any type of relationship with Smith-Jones' so-called mate. She wondered if his butler understood what went on between the two of them.

"That isn't what it looked like?"

Ash sounded uncertain, wary. He pinched the bridge of his nose as if he was trying to think of a plausible excuse. "I..." he paused again as if he still searched his brain for something appropriate to tell her. "You cannot condemn me for something another person did. She flew at me."

That waver in his voice coupled with the exhaustion they both must feel, surprised her. Nonetheless, Harris meant to proceed on the course she mapped out for herself. To her, this man needed to prove himself. "You mean...that wasn't *a woman throwing herself on you, kissing you, wrapping all the limbs she possessed around your body?* Harris could only speak out loud for so many words. She hiked up an eyebrow watching his ever-changing expressions. Seeing his brows knit together. *What you've told me is hard to believe. Would a woman you never slept with do something so outrageous?*

"That's not what I meant." She heard the long breath of air that whooshed from his lungs. "Make yourself comfortable. Your valise is in the bedroom. I'll be back as soon as I talk to a few people."

Abella?

"Yes...I'm sorry. We'll talk. I promise."

With that he turned on a heel then left. He didn't say anything more. Didn't give a clue as to what he would say to the woman. Why would he wish to speak with that woman before seeing to her questions?

Harris found herself wandering around the room, picking up items, turning them over in her hands before setting them back. The carpet was deep dark blue, the curtains a lighter shade of blue. Huge windows adorned the wall facing west. Light from the setting sun sent prisms of color dancing on the floor bathing the room in shades of red and gold. Flames danced in the hearth warming the room. Feeling as if ice encompassed her heart, she stared at the fire. Held out her hands seeking the warmth the gentle flames might provide. Harris looked to the door where he disappeared. Ash was going to speak with the woman. What would he say? After that display was talking all he wished to do? That same knife twisted in her stomach again.

Her valise was in an adjoining room as was the bed they would share. As if in a trance she walked into the bedroom. She opened the valise, rifling inside, looking for something warmer to wear. The doors to the balcony were open. A chilling breeze slipped inside. She should close the door. Harris didn't understand why she picked up her pistol. The need was great...Ash would call the feeling a sixth sense. So she did. A flurry of swishes, soft sounds came from outside the doors. Her eyes narrowed as she searched to find the source of the noises. Hesitating a moment as a quivering sensation spiraled within, she stepped onto the balcony. A second thought had her returning to her room.

More curious than fearful, she decided an investigation was in order. Once more walking out onto the balcony, she stared upward. A huge snake was in the process of falling from somewhere above...a third story window. When the serpent landed, it coiled as if meaning to strike. Without a second thought passing through her head, she shot. Her heart skidded to her throat, stopped for a brief moment. The snake was dead at her feet. Stunned, Harris let the gun drop to the floor. Trembling took over her body. She wasn't at all certain what just happened other than the fact a snake lay dead at her feet.

Someone tried to kill her. Perhaps frighten her to death. Send her running. The ploy very nearly worked. She felt as if an ice chilled ghost passed across her heart. Harris leaned against the outside wall, trembling, shaking from head to toe.

Her hands on her chest, she watched as if the reptile would rise up from the dead. When she lifted her hands, they were quivering. Her knees quaked. Thought she would fall, would topple. The world tilted, turning colors of gray.

The door burst open, hitting the opposite wall. "Harris!" She turned to look at the man who meant so many different things to her. The man who confused her. Terrified her. The man she wanted to love her. He came to her because he heard the shot.

"I'm..." she began but couldn't utter anything else because she wasn't fine.

Ash stood front and center. His pistol aimed at the huge snake. He looked concerned. His eyes glimmered. "What happened? Are you...?" Ash asked as he strode closer to her. "What..."

It seemed he must see the snake on the balcony. The serpent was enormous. She didn't know what kind.

He could have asked how she was. Fine? Not so fine? Harris didn't know how she would answer. Quivering, a finger pointed at the snake. "It fell. I shot. Dead..." The world spun. The shades of gray dancing in her head turned to black spots. She was going to fall. This was it...

Ash caught her before she hit the ground. He carried her to the bed. "Harris..." His voice held a wealth of concern. She was trying to force herself through the blackness to see light, to see Ash. The bed dipped beside her.

Yes...?

You have to tell me what happened?

Whose room is above us? Harris closed her eyes, wetted her mouth. When she opened them, the room continued to spin. Walls whirling into one picture. *Dizzy.*

She heard the soft-spoken swearing. He knew who dropped the snake. She didn't think he would tell her.

Rest. I'll take care of this. Be right back.

It wasn't to be.

The door burst open. Banged against the wall. "She killed my snake!"

I did...would do it again.

Harris recognized the voice. It was Abella. She was in her room, accusing her of defending herself. It was the woman's snake who fell from the window above. Snakes didn't just fall. She dropped the serpent to terrify her.

"He is harmless."

"You dropped the serpent onto the balcony to scare Harris," Ash's voice was calm under the circumstances. "Harris would never comprehend that the snake wouldn't hurt her. It was you who killed the creature. You've no one to blame except yourself. Go back to your room to get packed. Go!" He waved his hands.

I want her gone from here!

Abella is leaving as soon as Tindly can get her packed. She needs to go to London to be with Smith-Jones. He will take care of her. He will see that she behaves. Believe he will wed her as soon as possible.

That was what she wished for. They would be alone. Would have a chance to heal. More confusion rattled around in her head.

I don't lie, Harris. Don't know why the woman threw herself at me. She's never done that before. Nonetheless, I'm not going to beg for your forgiveness. I've done nothing wrong.

Her soft sigh rattled from the back of her throat. Harris wished to sit up. Ash sat on the bed beside her. He stroked her hair from her face, lightly caressed her bruised cheek with the tips of his fingers.

You've been through too much. Imagine I should try to understand this from your view point. I know you're innocent as well as young. Maybe too young for marriage. Too young to give yourself to a man my age.

That would be nice. An explanation.

He smiled then...that heart stopping smile of his. The one that made her heart dance. The one that always stole her breath. Left her mindless. He leaned down, kissed her forehead. He didn't believe his statement that she was too young or that he was too old for her.

I'd like to kiss your lips...

She'd like that too.

His laughter had her furrowing her brows. *You're listening to my thoughts. Is nothing private for me.*

I also heard your thoughts when you confessed to yourself you were falling in love with me. His knuckles continued their exploration down her neck then across the top of her gown. *I want to kiss you everywhere I've touched. Would you like that?*

You want me.

Yes. Wanting you has never been in question. Harris...we will marry in three weeks. You will be mine. I will make love to you, claim you in the way of my clan.

You heard that too. I don't trust you.

Ah...but you are falling in love with me. You said so yourself.

~ * ~

Ash was pleased, very pleased to hear her thoughts. Harris was falling in love with him. While he wouldn't normally listen to her, these were trying times. There were too many elements at play here. With his brother's hatred, coupled with Harris' inability to trust him, he needed to find an edge that would give him the upper hand. Now, Abella changed up his life. Gave Harris one more reason not to trust him. Ash didn't blame Harris for the mistrust. He didn't want to think Abella sent the snake to the balcony on purpose. The woman shouldn't be jealous. He knew first hand that Abella always thought of Smith-Jones first. Knew she loved him. What the bloody hell was going on here?

So, what was happening? For Ash, it seemed his world spun out of control. When he traveled to the highlands to retrieve his woman, she put up such a fuss he left for a few days. He'd needed to leave to gain control of his emotions. Needed to calm himself. He'd been so angry with her for rejecting him, he had to gain a new perspective.

"Sir?" Tindly spoke from the open doorway. "Abella's valise is ready. I'll have the upstairs maid pack all her belongings. They can be sent later, as you suggested. She is ready to travel."

"Thank you. Send dinner..." Ash turned to Harris, studying her pale features. "You were truly terrified of that snake?" He felt his smile grow as she grimaced then scowled as if she didn't wish to admit the truth.

Hate snakes...

Don't like them much either.

Didn't think you were afraid of anything.

"I'm afraid of losing you, love. Afraid of misconceptions that have been perpetrated. Abella loves Smith-Jones. Always has. What she did this afternoon I see no reason for. It was cruel. If what she did was meant as a joke, the act was wrong."

Ash stood up from the bed, walking to one of the windows overlooking the gardens below. He had a great deal to think about today. Harris didn't answer. He imagined there was nothing for her to say. Trust...he'd done nothing to warrant losing her trust. Now, he didn't know how to change that. Time would show her he was a man true to his word. The wedding was in three weeks...less than three. That was all the time he had.

He was bloody tired of defending himself, his actions. Weary of telling her he'd been celibate for three years while he waited for her to grow up. Even now she was only eighteen. That wasn't very old. Wished they could go back in time. Begin anew. That would be nice. If he did that, he would have taken her with him that day. Might have even made love to her, sealing their fate. He would have never left her alone with the fear of a possible pregnancy. He'd not been there when Crissie McKenna was left alone, pregnant, frightened. Because her father was laird, she wasn't scorned publicly. After he arrived, he heard rumors, gossip perpetrated by the soldiers who were under his command. Soldiers who were there when it became known she carried a child. The laughter. The insinuations. It was all hateful. It was all behind a closed door.

Ash would never have wanted that for Harris. He knew he hurt her by leaving with no explanation other than he had no choice. Understood she'd expected to see him again sooner. He came as soon as he could. As soon as his father was strong enough to be left alone in Smith-Jones' care. Ash understood his brother wouldn't hesitate to see to their father's demise if he could find the opportunity.

A sound behind him caught his attention. Harris stood beside him, her hand now rested on his back. His lips twitched with a half-smile. He expected her to stay on the bed. She had been very pale. Her face was drained of color. She looked better now, stronger. He wished he dared pull her into his arms, kiss her.

"Are you ready to talk about our wedding?" he asked as he turned toward her. Setting his hands on her waist, he did pull her to him. She gasped. "We will be married in less than three weeks. Your parents will be here soon. I know..." he set a finger with the gentleness he was feeling on her mouth. Wished he dared take her to his bed. Love her. If he did, she would hurt. Her mouth was still bruised. "Don't protest. You want this marriage as much as I do. Besides, I'll never let you go."

"Tell me about your clan ceremony." She spoke, forgetting the pain of talking. "I would learn as much as possible. Is it much the same as ours?"

He wouldn't have an answer for her question. He assumed there would be similarities. "We will be alone in a small glade. There will be a circle of candles." He didn't know if she should tell him they would shed their clothing. She would be his to look at completely naked for the first time. Yes, he tasted her breasts, touched her intimately. Only saw her that one time naked. Had been so angry. He sighed with all the possibilities. He needed to see her again. To touch her. taste her.

With Clan Chaton our family attends. They watch as spectators as well as witness to the event. The priest, Father Damian, chants to the couple. I don't know anything else. No one speaks of what happens. I understand the actual claiming takes place on the wedding night in the bedchamber. There is something you're not telling me.

Did I say we would be alone?

Harris nodded a vertical line forming between her brows. "You did."

Ash watched the frantic beat of her pulse. Understood she would have fears. Claiming was never easy for the woman.

Imagine I should tell you all I know. Though I'm not going to say what you wish to hear. The ceremony will be private. That is all you need to know until the time comes. Then...and only...then will you understand the privacy.

He wasn't going to tell her they would be naked. If he did so, he would never get her to commit to him. Naked...she wasn't comfortable with him enough to be with him without the benefit of clothing. While that one time so long ago she climaxed in his arms, she'd not been naked. He'd tasted as well as seen parts of her.

Perhaps he should begin to create a bit more intimacy in their endeavors between the sheets. Prepare for their first joining. So far, all he did was hold her close. He should begin tempting her, arousing her passion. If she wanted him, the wedding night would be easier for her. If he gave her pleasure between the sheets, she would not be terrified of joining with him. After what his brother did to her, he wasn't at all certain that would be possible before she healed. He would try.

What are you thinking? Not fair that you can get inside my head any time you find it necessary. I need to know. She let out a soft hmmf...

"Dinner is here."

With the lightest touch he brushed his lips across hers. Harris didn't refuse the contact. With his tongue he swept moisture across her bottom lip. Felt her shiver. Heard the soft sound from the back of her throat.

He could begin charming her tonight. Showing her once more what could explode between them when they were intimate. He wanted her with a fierce desire he didn't understand. Suppose that same desire would always be there between mates. Ash considered himself close to sainthood, he remained celibate so long. That small contact left him wishing for more, his sex hardening with the thought of her body so close to his.

Ash pulled back to gaze at her. She was so beautiful. Bending closer to her he whispered near her ear, "We should sleep naked tonight. Forego the nightdress. Want to hold you with nothing between us."

You always sleep without the benefit of a nightshirt. Why would you say...oh... Oh...my...you wish for me...?

He watched her gulp air. Saw the pulse at the base of her neck quicken. Ash touched the tip of her ear with his tongue. Nipped. Felt the quivering of her body. He ran his hands along her arms then back to her shoulder. He pressed his mouth against that part of her that pounded with the rush of her blood.

"Think about it. Think about the way my hands will feel when I caress you. Think about my lips touching tender, and very sensitive places."

Dinner will get cold. We should eat.

Ash hooted his laughter. "Are you thinking that you might get cold if you wore nothing at all. Rest assured, I would do my very best to warm you. Come, you are right about dinner. Don't want anything to get cold around here before we heat each other until we burst into flames."

Tindly set the table with fine China. Crystal goblets held wine. All the food was served within silver plates or bowls. His people liked Harris. She'd been gracious when the introductions were made, saying each person's name as she shook hands. Her smile created more smiles until the entire staff looked like besotted fools. Her smile could do that to him too. At her whim, he'd become infatuated. She tempted him as no other woman ever had.

Holding up his glass of wine, "Here is to us." Ash waited for her to reciprocate the gesture. While she thought about toasting him, he continued, "May our union be long as well as bountiful." He yearned for a family. Hoped she would feel the same. Until he met Harris, he'd never thought that much about children. Now, he wished to see little shifters playing in the yard, swimming in the sea.

She looked to her lap. Ash heard her thoughts both positive as well as negative.

When Harris met his gaze, she touched his glass with hers, "To us..." She sipped then paused. "I've not said yes to the marriage. As to children, I've always wished to have at least one."

"Even though you are here with me. Sleep each night in my arms." He tried to control his temper. It was becoming increasingly hard to do so. He sipped in a long, deep breath of air. "We will wed in less than three weeks. We will join. I pray you will learn to trust me. I wish to have no other woman in my bed."

"I still have to say yes...or I do?"

Ash wasn't about to argue. He heard the questions in the tone of her voice. Heard her thoughts which so far, she'd not learned how to keep to herself. He was pleased she was not so adamantly against the marriage as she was when they left the highlands. She wasn't trying to run home. He didn't have to fear she'd no longer be here when he returned from whatever business he had that might call him away.

"You do. You will. Eat now."

Harris' mind spun with confusion. Ash heard all the little questions she wanted to ask. He learned in Clan Chaton the two who were being wed were naked beneath a white cape. In his ceremony there was nothing between the couple except air. At times there was not even that much distance. During the chanting, he would hold her close, keep her standing. He would feel her soft curves pressed against him.

Will you sink your claws into me?

The question surprised Ash. His eyes flew open while he studied her. He grunted. Understood he needed to answer something or he would have rebellion on his hands tonight when he wanted to begin easing her into a marriage bed with him.

"That isn't quite how I would describe the declaring, but yes. I will leave ten marks on your shoulders. You will be mine once more through eternity. We will no longer need fear that we will never be together again. This is a very important event. You will see past lives with me. You will understand we are indeed meant to be together."

Wish I could do the same to you. Her little sigh after her words sounded breathy. *Sink my claws into your shoulders.*

"Would be fair. Nonetheless it doesn't work that way in my coterie. I doubt if it does in yours. I talked to your brother, Hawk, about the ceremony. What he told me was that with female shifters there was little to no pain during the process. I was happy to hear that. Hoping it's the same for us." Ash sat back having eaten enough, smiling as he watched her. He sipped the remaining wine then splashed more into each of their glasses. He stood. Held out his hand. Hoped she would accept the gesture and come to him. "It's not time for bed yet. Shall we sit by the fire? I can hold you. We can speak more of our future. Get to know each other better. We've not had a great deal of private time together."

Before Harris could sit on a separate chair, he pulled her onto his thighs. He wasn't going to allow her to put any distance between them. Now was the time to put disparities in the past, to look to the future.

"Ash!" she gasped out surprised by the suddenness of his movement. She pushed on his shoulders, squirmed as if she wished to remove herself from his lap. "Put me back." Her words were weak though. The protest died on her lips as he touched her. Held her next to his heart.

He whispered close to her ear, touching upon the lobe with his lips, teasing, enticing. Knew the warmth of his breath would send heated vibrations down her body. "Hush now. You're not going anywhere. I need to hold you. You need me close too. Would like to see how you are healing beneath your gown. You should get used to me looking at you, touching you. Need to taste you, learn your sweet secrete scent. At one time you enjoyed my attention. I won't hurt you. Would never cause you pain. I've only tender feelings for you."

I'm healing fine. There is nothing for you to look at. She squirmed again, leaned away. Pushed. He continued more explorations. Ash breathed in deeply, holding himself firm. Now was not the time to act on his wishes. She still needed space. Distance to figure out her thoughts. He could give her space even while he closed the gap between them.

"Need to see for myself." Ash enjoyed the way she responded so sweetly to him. "Want to make certain you are recovering. Don't wish to take any chances." He blew on the place where he touched her neck with his tongue. Her hands slipped beneath his frock coat, dug into his shoulders. His Harris was a passionate woman. Ash understood he barely tapped into that raw hunger.

You don't trust me to tell you the truth. I wouldn't lie. I'm fine. The bruises hardly hurt anymore. They are still ugly to look at. Don't want you to see how ugly they are. Don't wish for you to worry about me. I'm fine.

Unable to stop himself, his laughter barked from him. "Truth now. You just don't want me to see you naked. Your stand about this is a battle you will lose."

Her thoughts stopped. She realized what she told him was true. He smiled. Speaking to her now through his mind. He liked to communicate this way. If there were others present their thoughts would remain private. *I want to touch you everywhere. Feel your softness beneath my hands, my fingertips. Look at all of you, not just where you are injured. We will begin tonight as we will proceed in the future. Will never dwell on the past. I will always see to you if you are hurt or in pain. I will support you in every endeavor. You never answered my question about children. I'd like to know your thoughts.*

What if I don't agree? Will you stop if I tell you no? I... Harris ran her tongue across her lips leaving a dewy trail of moisture behind. He wished for a kiss too. From the heated simmer in her beautiful expressive eyes that was what she wanted.

Harris, I would never force you. Guarantee, once we begin, you will not wish for me to cease my attention. Just as that day in the glade, you wanted me. I felt all your precious curves...saw to your climax, to your pleasure. You responded just as I hoped. We both wanted each other, needed more.

He returned to normal conversation hoping to leave her aching for something more from him. The back of his hand pressed against one breast. Ash meant to take everything between them slow. Frightening her was not part of his strategy. "I'm glad to know. You are correct about your mouth along with your cheek. The colors are horrible but fading. Is the same happening to your breasts?" He trailed his finger along the top of her gown. The touch was light. She shivered. He dipped between the twin globes. Touched. Explored. "I would see. Tell me, yes. I would know the truth." Ash meant to look at her. Brush the palm of his hand across the rose-colored nipple. He imagined the color would not be rose today. By the time they were wed, he hoped the bruising would be in the past. In his mind, he was setting his campaign in motion. Tomorrow, he would take her to the modiste. She would need more than a wedding dress. Until her parents arrived with the bulk of her things, she possessed next to nothing. His wife would not want material things or for love.

Harris squirmed. Her hands on his chest pushed. She would have to tell him to stop. His fingers undid the row of buttons down the front of her gown. She batted at his hands, pushing them to the side. "Ash," she cried out. "You are undressing me." Again, the soft voice did not hold conviction.

"You should not be speaking. Even my name, though I do love to hear it when I touch you and see your eyes glaze over with desire, shimmering with fie. They are so beautiful," he told her while he unlaced her chemise. "You wear no corset." Ash shouldn't be surprised. The boning would have pressed against the bruises. He pushed the fabric aside lightly touching the crests as he did so. She was right about the fading bruises. He pressed his palms on the tight buds that hardened when the cool night air washed across them. Heard her gasp of surprise. Hoped it was coupled with excitement too. She arched toward him as if begging for more. For now, that was all. He pulled the chemise along with her gown into place.

Ash kept the smile behind his teeth when he heard her soft thoughts of the pleasure that he gave her. Harris enjoyed the caresses. She wanted more but wasn't going to ask. She would never ask him to touch her. Not when she protested so vehemently a little over a week ago. That was all part of his plan to seduce. To charm until she would ask him for all that she wanted. He meant to lure her. Cajole until she would not tell him to stop. So far, he was pleased with his efforts.

"How many men have you kissed, love?" he asked, watching her eyes begin to cross. Ash understood she would take umbrage with his question. "I know. We had that conversation once before. Believe, at least one time, you lied to me. Now, I would learn the truth. A man needs to learn those things about his fiancée. Would like to learn other things. Have you swum naked in the loch with anyone?"

Her soft sigh told him she might decide to tell him what he asked. His finger ran with light strokes along her neck. Stopped where the fragile blue vein beat hard. Pressed for a moment. *I dinna want to say though... I might have lied to you. What I told you is something I don't recall. You were experienced. I was insecure. I've been kissed but never participated. Only liked your kisses. When I spoke of that boy, it was only because I was jealous and afraid you would take women other than me to your bed. I hoped you would want me more if you knew there might be someone else for me. The boy never interested me. He was a boy. How could they intrigue me after I'd known a man's kisses?*

Her words pleased him. Now all he needed was to convince her he never lied to her. That path was more difficult than he would have ever expected. "You're right to believe I've known women. Never kept count as to how many. In my future, you're the only woman I want to know. You can't erase my past even though you wish to do so. Just as I can't erase yours. The future is ours, not the past."

"Abella?" *What is she to you? Where men are concerned, I don't have a past as well you know. You are my first man. Don't wish to share you with some French tart.*

He was pleased though not surprised to hear he was her first. They had yet to become lovers. Soon... "She doesn't mean anything to me. She is Smith-Jones' mate. We've both known that for a long time. He waited for her to get old enough to wed. Just as I waited for you. She must be jealous of you coming to my home. When she came with me, she was only fourteen. Last year for both of us was...busy. We were occupied with my father...with parliament. There were many things needing my attention. She spent a great deal of time with me. We all loved James."

"Stella?"

"A woman I took to my bed one time. Realized the mistake. Should have never done that. She is nothing to me except a valuable servant. You won't need to worry about her since she works for my father."

"Chandler?"

"Never took him to my bed."

He laughed to see her eyes cross. She hit him on the chest then drew her brows together.

Ash continued, watching each reaction to his words. "My brother wants the title. Father needs to disinherit him before any more foul deeds can be set at our doorstep. Chandler would ruin our name along with our standing in the government. While I don't want the title, I realize Chandler should never possess that much power. With my brother no one can predict what will happen. He could ruin us all. Gamble as well as whore the estate away."

Ash set his hand on her thigh. Proceeded higher, smoothing her gown, touching. Teasing. She leaned into him, her softness pushing against his chest. *I would learn more about your past. You know so much about me. Why is Chandler the way he is? He's...twisted.*

Ash held back the long sigh he felt deep in his lungs. He began a quick explanation. "There are so many ways I envy you. Your family is loving. There are no inner conflicts between the siblings and cousins. I've had the occasion to speak with all the men in your family including your cousins. You are the only daughter except for Crissie. Spoiled. Willful. Sheltered." Again, Ash laughed at the expression on her beautiful face. Her lips were mushed together. Her brows furrowed. She punched him.

I've been too protected. Coddled. I couldn't walk down the street in the village without seeing a relative. They all made sure I would not be hurt by anyone. They knew where you were concerned, they failed me. Father regretted not paying enough attention. When you left, you did hurt me. Tore my heart out when you went back to the city. Didn't believe you would ever return. All knew something happened the day you went home to London. I became withdrawn. I think even my father held his breath waiting to see if I was carrying your child. I told him nothing happened. Though that wasn't true. Father was ready to skewer you through when you showed up the next year. You were lucky Cameron was so involved with Lainie or he might have beaten father to the deed. He was furious.

Ash ran his finger along the line of her brows then down her nose. He was smiling at her. Continuing on to touch her lips. Intrigued by her breathy sigh of ecstasy that couldn't be mistaken. He brushed long silken hair from her face. Held the strands in his hands while he let them sift between his fingers. Tucked them behind her ear.

"Yet every time I was able to come to Carnoch you found time to be alone with me. How did you do that if they were always watching out for you? I wonder. The time at the glade was not the only incident that I was with you unchaperoned. Several times I stole kisses. Touched your breasts. Never went so far as I did that day I was leaving. I felt as if I had to have something more to hold you to me. Knew I would be gone for a long while. Wanted to bind you to me in the most elemental way."

It was a challenge. Two older brothers along with a possessive father made finding time with you a test of sorts. Wanted to know I was able to best them at the game they were playing with my life. I knew I wanted you. Needed to be with you. There were several times I slipped from the house when mother had her hands in bread dough or sometimes dish water. She would always be so distracted, she believed what I told her I was going to do. Most of the times I told her I was going into the village.

"I would know how you did it. What else? How did you get away from your brothers along with your father? Would imagine doing so must have been even more difficult. Would like to know all your secrets."

Harris shrugged her slim shoulders. She touched his mouth with a fingertip. He nipped the finger with his teeth. She shuddered. "Does it matter now? Would you kiss me? I would like that. Would like for you to touch me again. My breasts..." Her eyes darkened with the request as if she dreamed about the way his touch would make her feel. Surprised, Ash didn't think Harris would ever make such an appeal. His endeavors pleased him.

She satisfied him.

He did want another kiss then one after that. Yes, a kiss would be a good way to continue the gentle seducing of Harris. He would need to be very tender. His hand rose to her bruised cheek. He allowed his thumb to pass across the swell of her bottom lip. Pulled until she opened her mouth. He caressed the soft damp inner lining. So wet. So hot. Heat emanated from her. The sensual promise of Harris was mercuric.

"You will tell me if anything hurts. Promise me. There are ways to be gentle. I do wish to explore what we can have together. Tonight, as well as into the future."

Ash never wished to hurt this woman...his woman. She let her tongue glide where his thumb had been. He set her hand on top of his arousal before bringing it back to his shoulder. He could take only so much stimulation. "That is what you do to me every time I look at you. You must understand how very much I need you. Having a devil of a time waiting for the wedding. Barely made it out of the carriage that night when you put your chin on my crotch." Chuckled at her scowl.

"I like the way you kiss me... the way you make me feel. I would touch you some more." Harris wrapped her hands around his neck then threaded her fingers through his hair. She touched his lips with hers, initiating the kiss. Her tongue glided across his bottom lip. *The way it makes me feel deep inside. I get so hot. Feel as if lightning hits me. My body responds as if you've set me on fire. I ache...*

Lightning, you say? You ache for me?

Harris nodded, pulling away from him to study his eyes, his mouth. She leaned into him again. Her tongue wandered across his mouth. Ash allowed her to explore, holding his raging emotions in check. He'd waited weeks for this moment. Of her own accord she was coming to him, heating, arousing. His body thrummed to life with the pure pleasure she gave him. He could give her ecstasy if she would allow him to do so. With the tip of her tongue, she touched the tip of his. Pressed then rubbed. Ash let her explore.

"Yes," she told him with a languid sigh moving back a space as if she wanted to see him better. *Yes, lightning...an inferno of need. No wonder other women want what you can give them. They are not stupid women.*

Your mouth gives so much pleasure. Your hands do the same. I've been withdrawn, yes. I didn't trust you. I want to, need to give you...me...if you'll have that. Am I too late? Even if I'm still not certain about...

Her thoughts sent a cold douse of ice through him. He was no closer to gaining her trust than he was the night they left the McKenna keep. He growled low in his throat, hoarse with anger. He shouted as if the extra volume would convince her of his innocence. "I don't want any woman but you." He didn't know what else to do. Was damn tired of having to say the same thing over then over again.

You say that now... Ash, I don't want to argue. Facts are facts that I can't change. Kiss me. Please. I'm trying to forget...to forgive. As you said, the past isn't important. The future is.

He understood arguing was futile while wishing he could change that one moment where he didn't answer her and she assumed the worst-case scenario. Ash framed his mouth with hers. Felt the sharp flash of pain when he did so. He eased off cursing himself for forgetting she was hurt. Forgetting that he needed to be tender. Gentle. She was his to take care of to protect. He was doing a damn bad job of it.

I should kiss other parts of you. Taste you wherever you would like. I can give you pleasure. Don't need...

He touched upon the lobe of her ear. Nipped down the long column of her neck. Was delighted with the soft whimper of desire she gifted him with. With a soft touch he ran his hands along her shoulders, pushing the sleeves of her gown down her arms. His head between her beautiful breasts, he kissed the valley between them. Turned his attention to each rounded globe. He curled his tongue around one nipple then the other. He would like to stretch out next to her. Hold her tight until she asked for more than she'd ever known.

Are you ready for bed? We could go straight there. Or would you like more wine? I think I would have another glass. Holding you, listening to each breath is wonderful.

Ash wished to prolong these moments. Needed her to relax completely. He wasn't certain how far tonight he meant to take this gentle seduction. Hoped he would sense when to stop. He felt everything she was thinking. She didn't want him to end these tender moments between them.

That was a delight to his senses. She set her head against him. Her lashes fluttered against his neck. His hand cupped her breast.

Another glass would be nice. Harris started to pull her gown up to cover her.

"No, love."

She was so beautiful. Except for the horrible discoloration she was so white. Alabaster. Perfect. He set his bronzed hand on her shoulder, amazed at the difference between them.

You're looking at me.

"Yes, love." True, Ash couldn't keep his gaze away from her. She intrigued every masculine part of him. As he gazed at her the beautiful pink crests hardened further by his attention. His body flamed to life. Lightning split through him.

The glasses were near. He filled them with the sweet Bordeaux they'd been drinking. "Take a sip," he encouraged. "The wine will relax you. Sense how tense you are. Are you afraid of me? Of what we are going to do together?"

She did sip. Then swallowed another small bit. For several minutes they drank the fine wine. They watched each other. Silence along with soft moonlight filled the room. He reveled in the sight she bestowed upon him. Loved to see the slight sway of her breasts as she moved. He wanted to reach out to touch her. Restrained himself to gazing.

While she drank, he continued to look at her wishing there was no fabric between them. After she set her glass down, she toyed with the buttons on his shirt. Soon, it was open. Harris tugged on the tails freeing them from his pants. She set her hands on his chest. Ran her fingers across his chest while she pushed the fabric down his arms.

"Did you wish to see me?"

He felt her desire in the soft caress, the gentle exploration. Knew her hesitation. This was new to her. Though she'd seen his bare chest before. That first night of their trip, she'd seen him naked as well as aroused.

Her eyes wide, she stopped what she was doing. *You sleep naked every night. Even so, I haven't seen you...not...all of you...well, I did that one time.*

He saw the rose color stain her cheeks. Watched as pink darkened to crimson. Her lashes lowered. Fluttered. When he began to speak, she cast her gaze back to him. He felt her embarrassment at her question.

"You never look at me. You always turn your back as if you are afraid. Are you afraid, Harris? I won't hurt you. I want you to see me almost as much as I'd like to see all of you. Touch all of you. Taste every part that intrigues me. You can touch me if you like."

When my brothers were little, I saw them naked. They were very different. Suppose you are different too. She ran her hands across his chest. He sucked air when her fingers paused on his nipples. One beautifully manicured nail sailed lower to his waist band then back. Heat flared. Even with such a light touch, she set him on fire.

Ash kept his laughter deep in the back of his throat. He held onto it when he thought to reply until he had himself in control.

"You saw me that one night when you ran. Maybe it's time for another viewing. Should I unfasten my pants." He paused, watching the dilation of her eyes. "Would you rather I did it?" Ash wanted her to look at him as long as she wished. To shift again with her would be sweet. He needed to see her in her cat again. Play with her. They could run on the beach, swim in the waters. Wrestle. When he ran after her that first night of their travels, there had not been time for him to look at her as he would have liked. To see all that she was. A female black panther...

Believe I would like that...to see you... Tonight?

"We will see." If he tempted her too much, he might... Bloody eyes. "I want you too much. Tonight would not be a good time for that. We will wait until later." Ash didn't realize until this moment just how much he wanted her. Now that she seemed to be more enthusiastic to his desires, he was turning her away.

"Oh..." Harris murmured, sounding disappointed. "I thought you would." Her blush deepened farther. "Thought we would..."

One more time he had to tamp down the laughter that rose up from deep in his belly. "You want me. I like that. How do you feel? Are you hurting?" She was still sitting on him. Her breasts bared for him. He tipped his glass a bit. Red drops splashed onto her nipple. At the contact she gasped in a sweet breath of air. He licked. Curled his tongue around the hardness. Harris grabbed his head, arching her body. He wanted to suck her deep into his mouth. He didn't dare. The raging tempest she created in his blood couldn't be ignored. Lightning, yes, she created the heat in him also.

Ash lifted her, slid her gown to the floor. Harris was left in her chemise. The laces were undone. The fabric parted for his access. He pushed the fabric aside then down her arms. The soft covering went the way of her gown. Naked, she sat on his lap. He tipped a drop of wine on her other breast. Tasted. Nibbled. Sucked on the sweetness. He'd never been so gentle in his lovemaking. Afraid he would hurt her. Harris' nails raked across his scalp. He heard the swift intake of air with each caress of his tongue. The soft feminine sounds that told him she enjoyed his attention. Spoke to him of her passion.

Harris pushed on his shirt moving the fabric down his arms. He knew she wanted to feel him. She set her hands on his chest, ran them across the width. Stopped to toy with his nipples. Ash decided this had gone as far as he wanted for tonight. If he didn't end this now, there would be no stopping. With Harris in his arms he rose, striding to the armoire. Setting her on the floor, he found her nightgown.

"Raise your arms, love."

She looked bewildered but she did as he bade. Her arms were in the air. Ash slipped the gown over her head. Unable to put forth words he nodded toward the bed.

Now? I thought?

"Now, before I do something I'll regret." Ash watched her slip beneath the covers. He would give her part of what she wished for. He disrobed while she stared at him, her eyes wider than he'd ever seen them. He tried not to listen to her thoughts. Didn't know if he could stop himself if he knew she could be his right now.

As if she knew he listened in on her, Harris sat up, throwing a pillow at him. He caught it, mesmerized by the movement of her breast beneath the gown. For a few seconds, he wished he'd not insisted on the gown. Wished also that he had not decided this was all for tonight. Tomorrow, he would take this one step further.

He crawled into bed beside her. As if they'd been doing this their entire lives, she snuggled her bottom against him. His sex was harder than ever before. Ash groaned deep in the back of his throat. This was lingering torture. He wrapped an arm over her along with his leg. Ash brushed hair from the nape of her neck, kissing her, feeling her shivers, the quivering of her slim shoulders. Her hands closed over his wrist. Soon, after she relaxed, he would explore more of her.

For the next few hours, Ash stared out the window at the dark night. Her fingers released his wrist. As if that was an invitation, he settled his hand on her thigh, inching her gown up to her waist. Spread his hand along her hip. Touched upon the softness of her belly. Longed for what he decided he wouldn't take until he claimed her. That would be the night before the wedding. Ached for daylight. In the morning they would move on, deal with the plans he was making.

In the morning Abella would be gone from her life, from his. Ash wracked his brain trying to think of any other women who might throw themselves at him.

He didn't know.

Hadn't expected that from the little French girl he saved. Whatever would happen next, he'd have to be prepared. He was damn tired of defending himself. Thoughts that Chandler was behind this settled deep in his mind. He needed to be more watchful. His brother would have plans.

~ * ~

Chandler looked down on the small form in front of him. He thought this woman might be able to carry out his plans. She was useless. After Stella left they found another woman. The whore did fine until she complained they were too rough. Stella didn't object to what they did. Enjoyed the sensual delight of two robust men making love to her at the same time. Stella understood what they would be about. This wasn't the first time. Wouldn't be the last. Chandler searched for more sexual diversion. He wanted Harris. Would enjoy her as soon as he taught her what he wanted. Ah, his sigh was long as he thought of his father. Chandler was well aware the man who fathered him wished to disinherit him.

His mind sprinted back to the woman. The two of them weren't sated yet. He ran his hand along her face then lower. This dalliance occurred way too fast for his satisfaction. Bertram, his partner, was scouring the docks looking for another doxy they could satiate themselves with. The other one screamed too much. The lady, Sasha was her name, told them they weren't human. He was more human than his brother. Shifters weren't human. They were anything but human. Bertram was a shifter. He was different.

One would think a prostitute would have discovered threesomes long before this. Sasha wasn't very old. She must have been new to the profession. She had no stamina. They wouldn't get rid of her yet. There were still uses for this woman. The girl still had that innocent appearance about her that tempted men. He could set her on Ash. Rock the boat for Ash and his little love interest.

Chandler sat back on the plush chair sipping his brandy. They'd moved to his townhouse in London for Sasha. He didn't like spending much time in the small hovel outside the city. He needed his comforts. Besides, the best prostitutes lived in the city. When he went in search of a virgin, he always found a small hamlet. A farm girl who might not be missed for a few hours but who wouldn't have to be innocent when she wed. Ran less risk of disease with the rural gals. One could never be certain when dealing with a dockside whore. Risk was part of the game, the challenge. He didn't intend to get the pox.

He closed his eyes tight, thinking of his brother's fiancée. Her curves were lush. The breasts that pushed beguiling against her gown filled his hands. She would have bruises for at least a week. Every time Ash looked at her, he would know his brother touched her. If he knew his brother, the woman would be a virgin until he claimed her. By her reactions to him, Chandler didn't think he'd done that yet.

He set his sights on Harris. She was the goal. The main attraction. A man always needed a destination, a target. His imagination playing havoc with his sex, he could see her sprawled on the bed, he and Bertram rocking her until she couldn't take a breath.

Strange name, Harris.

Sometimes he liked virgins. Sometimes he did not. They screamed too much. He didn't like blood and they always bled. Well...his friend enjoyed the blood. He was a bit too much. Too rough. Though they did get along amazingly well. When necessary, Bertram held himself in check.

He thought of James, his father. The father who always liked his shifter son the best. The second son. The hell, it wasn't his fault he couldn't shift. It was his mother's fault, the bitch. It wasn't hard to kill the woman. She trusted him. She thought he loved her. He didn't love anyone except himself. He held a healthy respect for his friend, Bertram. Love was for the weak. The feeble minded.

Bertram loved to defy the laws of the country. Took pleasure in beating the system. They worked well together. The two of them scoffed at the thought of Newgate Prison. Together they were too smart to get caught. Even though Ash knew he assaulted his little fiancée, he wouldn't turn him in. The fact...it would be his word against hers. Who would believe the little Scottish whore? He would paint her as a floozy. Would tell the world she came on to him, begging for his attention. Bertram would confirm the story. She approached him. Not the other way around. Harris begged him. Yes. Perfect.

Chandler didn't know how he was going to rid himself of his father. He heard rumors that James would disinherit him within the week. That couldn't happen. He needed the money. Was in debt up to his eyeballs. The ever-present Smith-Jones always got in his way. The facts stood, he had to kill his father soon.

Tapping his fingers on the chair's arm, he sifted through several ideas. He was torn between two concepts. None of which were perfect. A better idea would come to him. Bertram would return soon with another girl for their mutual pleasure. Together, they would have their fun.

Ah...he turned to see the door to his study opening. It was almost morning. Three women in one night. Not usual but pleasant. He rubbed his hands together wondering what his friend found for them.

"This is Trista," Bertram told him. "She says she doesn't scream. Likes to have more than one man in her bed. Thought after the last lady you might wish to have someone who was a bit more accommodating to our needs." He gave the girl a gentle push into the study. "We should take this up to the bedroom."

"You thought right about my needs. Believe we could do this here. My desk is not cluttered." Chandler studied the young woman. She was a bit overweight. He didn't mind. Just meant there would be more to hold onto. Her breasts popped from the top of her gown. He could see a touch of dark rose, a dusky color which meant she'd had a child. "Take off your gown, sweetheart." He needed to see all of her before he took her. The command didn't faze her. In seconds she was naked. In front of them she thrust her breasts out. They moved with an inviting promise. He was always fond of redheads.

He was pleased. All her hair was a deep red, even the curls at the apex of her thighs. She taunted him by turning one way then the other. Her large breasts swayed as she showed herself to him. Her stockings were gartered at midthigh.

She would do nicely.

Chandler had more ideas in mind for this tempting lady as well as Sasha.

Chapter Five

The next week passed. Harris didn't understand what Ash planned. Every night he teased her body with gentle caresses. Kissed her deep and hard. Now, she slept naked in his arms. Felt his hard body pressed against hers. At those times she burned anticipating the pleasure she recalled from that long ago day in the small glade. Deep in her heart, Harris knew she would gift him whatever he wanted. She didn't intend to tell him. She was in love with him.

Today, he told her they would swim in the ocean. Frolic on a sandy beach near his home. The English Channel was their destination. Harris protested telling him the water would be too cold. He waved her comment aside.

Ash bent low to whisper against her ear, sending a myriad of chills down her spine. She rubbed her arms. Tried to turn to look at him. Needed to see his eyes to know if he teased. She had not learned how to invade his thoughts when he blocked her.

"Hush, love. No more protesting. I've made up my mind. We will change to our cat. We've only seen each other once. One time is not enough. In our cat shapes, the cold water will not affect us in any way. You will see. Trust me with this." He touched her with the tip of his tongue. Taunted then teased down her neck after that back to her ear. The small touches sent lightning zipping through her.

Having trouble forming coherent thoughts, she breathed out the words. "Our...cat?" Harris questioned with complete understanding she would have to disrobe to change. She wrapped her arms around herself. While they slept wearing nothing, she was always in bed when he came to her. Covered by a multitude of blankets.

"Yes." Ash turned her then pulled her hands away from her, watching her as she tried to breathe in air. "I want to see you when the sunlight plays on your body. Need to look at you. Learn everything I can about you. We've only a week and a half now before the wedding." He held onto her hand leading her from the house. "You will need to get used to being with me in every way."

They headed along the cliff. Far below the sea churned. Harris didn't know exactly where he was taking her. A slight breeze blew in from the sea ruffling her hair. A seagull cried out in the sky above. She heard the lapping of the waves against the cliffs. Her body trembled then tightened as she thought about what was going to happen. She did want to see his cat, remembering so little from that one night when she tried to run.

"Where are we going? You never said. I would know." She struggled to keep up until he slowed his pace.

Ash turned to smile at her. "To a special place I know of. It's a singular spot. Never taken a woman there before. Want you to be the only one I share this with." Ash brought her hand to his lips. Kissed the back. Turned the palm over to place a slow languid kiss there. "After we swim, we'll change back. Had the cook pack a lunch; wine, poached fish, fresh baked bread. The spot is secluded...warm because it is sheltered. We won't get cold. I promise you that. Tindly brought the basket down a few minutes ago. Promised to remain until we arrived. Do you think you will enjoy a swim in your second shape."

Harris didn't know what he intended with this little adventure. Seemed he always had some agenda in his head. Always left her wondering what he would do. He seduced her every night. Left her wishing she could ask him to make love to her. The one time she did ask, he told her no. She stopped, turning to him.

"Why are we doing this? What are we going to do?" Harris was so nervous she couldn't swallow, couldn't think. "I don't wish to..."

When he grinned at her, she was swept off her feet. All of her churned. Her stomach clenched tight.

"Believe I told you exactly what I've planned for this lazy afternoon. We could go swimming twice if you like."

Harris tugged back, looking over her shoulder in the direction they'd come from. They started down a narrow trail that led to the beach he spoke of. The area was small. The sand clean. Beautiful. Very private. Perfect for what he told her he intended. "I don't..."

"Yes...you'll love this."

"No, Ash..."

Gulping air, Harris was certain she wasn't ready to disrobe out in the open let alone in his bedroom. She hadn't done that on her own in front of him. Taken off all her clothing. He expected her to do that here. At the bottom of the trail, Tindly waited for them. After he caught Ash's attention, he nodded then started up the track. Harris watched as the man disappeared from view.

Ash's hands rested on her shoulders. Squeezed. The touch was gentle. Meant to reassure. The caress sent other emotions tumbling within. "Should we eat first or swim? I would make this your choice."

Harris shivered as his warm breath caressed the back of her neck. She wanted to put off the disrobing. "Eat..." she breathed out as his lips touched where his fingers had been. Heat welled up inside her. Spiraled. Twisted.

"Thought you would say that." Ash let his hands fall to his sides. He strode to the blanket that Tindly must have spread for their convenience. Sitting down, he patted a spot beside him while he leaned against the cliff wall behind him. His long legs were crossed in front. Unlike herself, he looked at ease. Ash rummaged through the basket, pulling out cups along with a bottle of wine. He uncorked the bottle. Spilled the wine into the two cups. Set one to his side then sipped from the other. His eyes above the rim, Ash gazed at her. His eyes seemed to be bright with unspoken amusement.

She stiffened, understanding he waited for her to make the decisions. Pulling in the cool sea salted air, she decided she could do this. She would surprise Ash. He wouldn't be expecting boldness. Despite her decision, she remained in the same place, her feet unable to move. Her body hummed with tension, nerves stretching thin. She looked to the trail leading to the top of the cliff, wishing she dared race to the top. Ash wouldn't like it if she left. He planned the day. Knew what he wanted to do with the time. Confusion swirled. One moment she wished to be bold the next she needed to hide. She was both eager as well as terrified of the next few minutes.

He wants to see me naked...

He touches me at night. Has seen me twice now with no clothing.

Except...that day when she ran. He saw her then. The night he disrobed her, he saw her then. If she stayed in this secluded location, today would be the third day. Was that so bad? No, but it seemed...seemed that there might be an easier way. She didn't know what that was.

Coward.

You would have allowed him to see you with nothing on that day in the glade. More than anything at that time, you wanted all the sensations he offered. That day he gave you what he called a woman's pleasure. If you'd allowed him to do so, he might have made love to you. Yes, and I might have conceived. Could have been left alone to bring up a child who didn't have a father. She didn't wish for any child of hers to be labeled bastard. Knew what Crissie went through.

While she watched, frozen in place, he dished out two plates. Again, he set one to the side, the one for her. Harris still couldn't seem to put one foot in front of the other. She watched. He was a picture of relaxation. Ash ate. He drank. Didn't say anything else. He was tormenting her. In front of her, her hands were gripped tight. She rubbed her knuckles. Looking for enough courage to carry on with her day, she closed her eyes. When she opened them, he was still sitting, still appearing relaxed, smiling.

Slow, hesitant steps took her to the blanket. She stood above him for long lingering seconds. With a swig of air, Harris sat down facing him, curling her legs underneath her. She sipped the wine hoping the drink would give her the nerve to carry this through. One sip then two. She longed to down the entire contents in one gulp. Instead, she set the cup down.

Ash smiled at her. Pointed to her plate. "The food is quite good. Try the fish..." Again, Ash pointed with his fork to her plate. Encouragement. "The baby potatoes are delicious. Just the right amount of butter." He set his cup on his belly. Closed his eyes. The man was waiting for her. He was patient. Harris supposed they had all afternoon.

He didn't seem to be in any hurry. Ash appeared relaxed. Content. She drug air into her lungs. Ate a portion. The fish was delicious. Just as he told her the potatoes were all fine. Finished off her mug of wine. Played with the remaining food on her plate for a few seconds before she forked another bite of fish. To her surprise, she ate everything on her plate. Her stomach rolled.

It seemed he sensed she'd finished. With no hesitation, he took the plate from her then set it aside. Ash set his hands on her shoulders. It was time. There was no more to waste.

"We should...," Harris began, wishing to find a means to divert his attention from swimming, from shifting. In front of him, she would be wearing nothing. Nerves twitched. "Talk."

"What?" he asked as his hands roamed, touched sensitive places. It seemed he meant to undress her.

By the expression on his face, the brimming smile, Harris understood the moment had come. "I..." She ran her tongue across her bottom lip. Her nerves shattering with each second that passed her by. "Can't," she finished with a long-drawn-out breath of air. Her hands shook. She would never be able to do what he wished.

She could not. Wasn't there an easier way?

"You are shaking. Don't be afraid of this or me. It's natural for a husband and wife. We aren't wed. Soon we will be. I will help. You will enjoy the swim. I promise. Do you like to play in the water? I know you do. I watched you at the loch." Ash reached out to her, pulled her into his arms. She sat in front of him, between his legs. The fasteners for her gown were in the back. She felt cool air caress her skin. The heat of his fingers were against her flesh. Fabric slid down her arms as did his hands. He stood, helping her to her feet while he continued to remove her clothing. He did know what he was about. One by one every item she'd worn today fell from her.

The moment all her clothing was piled on the blanket, she shifted. Ash saw her back, nothing more. The fewer moments he saw her with nothing on the better. When she turned to look back toward Ash, he was naked. Beautiful. Amazing. Proud. Changing to his cat. Prowling toward her. His tail switched. His dark blue eyes focused on her. Once more, she found she couldn't move. Couldn't think.

Tiger...lord he was huge. Picturesque. Masculine. His muscles evident with every movement of his huge body. When they both shifted, she marveled at the way he looked as a cat. That night she never truly saw him. He told her to shift. When she refused, he picked her up by the scruff of her neck to drag her back to the inn. He would never allow her to object to his plans. Now, looking at his cat, she shivered. He was formidable. Intimidating. His word was law.

Ash walked toward her. He shook his head. She backed up a step. Knew running would do her no good. He was bigger, stronger. Harris didn't want to run. Didn't wish to end up with her nose on the ground as she did last time. She wanted to know what he was going to do. Now that she was no longer naked, she should be brazen, bold as well. Didn't want to show him her fear or her hesitation. Swimming with him would be fun. She could do this. A few more deep breaths and she would play with him. This man was her mate. She understood how her brothers reacted to the women who were meant for them. To her brothers their mates were everything. Was she everything to Ash? With him, she didn't know if that was possible. Though she wished she was his everything.

Standing in front of her now, he seemed even larger. More formidable. With his nose, he touched hers. Startled, she stepped back. Her eyes widened. He nodded toward the water. Looked back at her. Blue eyes boring into hers.

Follow me.

Yes, I should follow him.

He loped. Long strides took him to the breaking waves that danced around his paws. Jumping over the crest of one wave he landed in the water. Started paddling. Ducked beneath the surface. Came up for air then ducked beneath another time. He continued, swimming through the breaking serf.

Mesmerized by the sight, Harris stared, mouth open. Tongue lolling. She needed to catch up to him. Would like to feel the water against her fur.

Come play with me. Are you a scaredy-cat? Come...come, love. Play while you can. Dance in the waves. I want to swim with you. Feel you next to me. Maybe next time we can swim in our human forms. Would you like that?

Alright. Bracing for the shock of the cold water, Harris surged into the water. A wave crashed over her as she leapt into the frothing sea. She swam beneath the waves moving toward the beach. Surfaced for air. Ash was beside her. He seemed to wait for her as if meaning to encourage, he touched her nose with his. Harris felt his whiskers against hers. She wasn't certain what he wanted. Diving again, she felt his presence beside her. For many seconds, they swam together. His shoulder touched upon hers. When she came up for air, he did too. They swam in unison. While she dove, he touched her. It seemed he felt as if he had to keep a touch upon her. Would not let her gain or lose distance from him. Protective. Supportive. All things she needed.

Harris didn't know how long they played together. Her breaths were short pants now that she felt herself tiring. Shivers sped through her. The sudden cold surprised her. Panthers did not have a great deal of stamina. He would have more. They were animals created for speed. Wondered if the chills had anything to do with her exhaustion.

I'm tired. Harris spoke to Ash.

We'll go back to land.

Fatigue hit her hard. She tried to breathe in deep breasts of air. Sensing she overtaxed herself, Ash nudged her along. Lending his strength to her. If she faltered, he would catch her by the scruff of her neck. She didn't intend to waver. Harris recalled that feeling. It had not been pleasant. Touching down on the sand, she padded out of the serf. Once free of the waves she collapsed, winded from her exertions. Ash was beside her. She lay her head upon her front paws sipping in the oxygen she needed. He nudged her again telling her she needed to rise. They weren't finished. He had something else in mind. With reluctance she stood. A shiver flashed through her. Her body shuddered.

Follow me.

Where?

Promise you will be pleased. Trust me.

The man had no idea how she felt. Sometimes he could be so elusive. She didn't believe he could promise that. One more time he used the words that triggered her. She did wish she could trust him. Harris understood he would hear her thoughts. She wasn't going to comment so he could be certain she didn't wish for him to know she didn't have faith. In some things she understood he would never lie to her.

Not completely.

Harris did shadow him, watching his tail move back then forth. His paws were huge. One swipe to her slight form would send her reeling. They walked around the cliff that seemed to jut into the sea. The channel's tide was low. Sand replaced water. She bumped into him when he stopped. In front of her was a waterfall splashing down to meet sand along with rocks. The sight was spectacular. Sunlight turned drops of water into rainbows. She heard the soft cadence of the liquid hitting upon the rocks.

We can shift. Rinse off before we dress. Let the cool water pour over our bare skin. If you like, I can hold you. Will rinse you while you do the same for me. Would enjoy feeling your body pressed against mine? What do you think?

My clothes are... Harris looked over her shoulder. She wanted to retrieve them. Getting them would take no time at all. *I'll be naked. You'll be...*

Yes, they are out of reach. Of course, I'll be naked. I won't let you go back until you change your cat form into your human. Yes, I want to see you. All of you. Won't do anything but look. Unless you ask. This time I will see more than your back. I will...see all of you. Promise I will enjoy the view. Your breasts tipped with pink. Your flesh, white as new fallen snow. The shadow of amber at the juncture between your thighs.

As if he expected her to bolt, he leapt behind her blocking her way. *No, you don't. You will be much happier if you rinse the salt water from you. I will be happier too. Once we're done here, we can have more wine. Dress if you like. Remain naked if you choose. Look in the basket to see what sweet confection Tindly packed for us. The man does have a sweet tooth. Believes everyone else does too. What do you say? Water, food then wine enough to sate us.*

Ashton... She was so hesitant. Afraid of the vulnerable position this would place her in. *I don't know...*

Promise you'll feel better. You won't be itchy from the salt water. You need to dig deep inside. Find the necessary courage.

You will turn around? Harris was grasping at possibilities that would never happen. Ash brought her to this place with a purpose. He would never back down.

No.

There was no way for her to argue. His answer was the one she expected. Not a single place she could go to hide. He stated his mind. Blocked the only possible escape route. His intentions were single-minded.

Highhanded. Autocratic All these days she'd been with him, Harris understood the time would come. She was uncomfortable in her thoughts. Uncomfortable with the unknown...with all that changed...everything that was knew to her. Being with a man was very new. Before it had been fun to flirt. To bat eyelashes then send smiles. She'd always known Ash was attracted to her. Wanted her. Now she would be his.

As soon as you change I will also. His voice was calm. Too calm. Harris could see him in his human form, arms crossed leaning against a wall. Watching. Waiting. She would have to give him what he wanted.

She swallowed hard, deciding as soon as she could get this awkward moment over, she would feel better. Quick to change, she tilted her chin into the air then walked to the falls. Felt the heat of his gaze on her back. Once under the streaming water, she accepted the fact she liked the way the fresh liquid made her feel. He was right. She did enjoy the cool clear water rushing over her. In the summer this would be wonderful. The stream of water was cold. Ice cold. Keeping her back to him, she rinsed her hair. Felt him beside her. He didn't touch. He stood behind her. Her body heated. Tensed. Wished he would do something. Needed him to caress her. Wanted a kiss or perhaps two.

You should never hide yourself from me. You are beautiful. You want to look at me. Go ahead. All you need to do is turn around.

Reading my mind is unfair!

Ash's laughter cracked in the private sanctuary they shared. She wanted to understand his thoughts. *Nothing in life is fair if you don't get your way. This is very fair to me. Don't wish for you to ever keep your ideas to yourself. There are notions in my mind that would embarrass you if you heard. Don't wish to do that to you.*

While the water rushed over them sounds of seagulls filled the air, she understood she did want to look at him. To do so she would have to turn around. Doing so would give him a clear view of her...front...of her breasts and everything else that was secret. Places he touched that day so long ago. Kissed.

If looking into your mind helps me to know you better there is nothing unfair about that. Harris, turn. Look at me. See how the sight of you affects me...my body. You will see me then understand how much I need you.

125

All of me is hard, tortured by thoughts of carnal pleasures I won't act upon.
Shaking her head in denial she tried refusing him. The thought-provoking idea tempted her. She would not give in to those desires that also tortured her.

Look at me, Harris. I dare you. Prove you are not a coward. You are brave. The challenge is upfront as well as honest. You can do what I ask. Take a deep breath. Don't think.

The man was tossing out challenges that were damn hard to resist. The devil! Harris straightened her shoulders. Lifted her chin. For as long as she could remember her brothers dared her. Tested her. She always accepted then found herself in a wealth of trouble. Ash was not one of her brothers. She might still find herself in a great deal of misfortune. Sweeping her lips with moisture, she tamped down the fear.

There will be no way for you to retrieve your clothes until you set those pretty eyes of yours in my direction. Today, before we return, we will pass this one hurdle. You will see me. I will gaze on your beauty. What's stopping you? Fear? There is nothing here for you to be terrified of.

I hate it when you are right. She breathed in deeply. Sucked air deep into her lungs.

Her body shaking, Harris turned. She gasped. He was more...much more than she expected. His shoulders broad narrowing to lean hips then rock-hard thighs. She tried not to stare at his sex. Could not help but do so. After she did, her breath caught in the back of her throat. When her gaze shot to his eyes, they were smiling. He understood what she was thinking even without getting into her mind.

"Once you've seen me this way. That night I think you were too angry to notice. Though I know you've felt me at night. What do you think?"

"No...when would I have? Yes..." She reached out as if to touch him then withdrew her hand as if scalded.

He lifted his broad shoulders in a casual shrug, his eyes alight with amusement. "You did well. I do appreciate the view you are gifting me with. Your body is perfection to this man." Ash stepped aside. When she tried to rush past him, he took her hand in his. Brought her fingers to his lips for a tender kiss. "Thank you." After that brief contact he allowed her to leave.

He wasn't going to stop her. Ash was letting her run from him. She breathed in a silent breath of relief. This encounter was as much as she could withstand today.

By the time Ash walked around the cliff, she wore everything. Her gown was unfastened. She couldn't reach the buttons. He would smirk. Hoot with his laughter as he often did. Tease her about the clothing.

"How did you get the dress on this morning?" he asked as he closed the distance between them. His hands swept her hair away from her back then over her shoulder.

"Libby..." Harris was surprised by his question. Startled by the renewed contact. It was not what she expected. "She did the buttons up the back. When I dressed this morning, I didn't know what I would be doing this afternoon. If I had known, I would have worn something else."

"Ah, she took my suggestions. Would you like to have her as your maid? I told her she could be with you if you liked her." Ash fastened her gown. Allowed his fingers to brush across her back as he did the work.

"I like her." By the time he finished with her dress, she thought she might certainly burst into flames. Her knees weak, she dropped down on the blanket.

While he dressed himself, keeping her eyes away from him was impossible. She watched as he pulled his pants over his legs then fastened them. Her gaze never left him while he shrugged into his shirt, muscles rippling body gleaming with the contact of the brilliant sunshine. Ash didn't fasten the shirt. He let the fabric hang open as if he was once more challenging her with something. Harris didn't understand.

"More wine?" he asked as he poured one mug then the second one without waiting for an answer.

Reaching out for the wine, her hands were quivering. She was so confused. Dizzy, her feelings shattered, fragmenting with each new contact. Now she was spent. Exhausted from the immense tension of the day. From the swimming. He spent the weeks testing her, taxing her in subtle as well as bold ways. There was nothing understated about what he did today. She met his challenge.

Harris sat down next to him. Drank the wine. The taste delicious. She wanted more. "What is going to happen next? What are you going to do? I would know." Muddled, disoriented, Harris didn't understand what was happening to her. She ached for him. Her body reacted to everything he did. Even to what he didn't do. Wanted something she understood but didn't. He created a need. A burning need. Her blood pounded within her limbs. There was more. She felt what could happen between them. Harris wanted to experience those nerve fragmenting sensations again.

Ash set his hand on her leg. Touched. Did nothing more. The gentle caress scorched everywhere he touched. Her senses flamed. Ached. Emotions tattered into shreds. He pulled her to him. Held her against his chest while she sipped on the wine. She closed her eyes. Felt each breath he inhaled. Listened to the strong beat of his heart.

When she opened her eyes, his arms were around her. His hands cupped her breasts. As if he had all the time in the world, he caressed the tips with his thumbs. Even through the fabric they tightened. Ash's chin rested on the top of her head.

"Do you think we should go? It will be dark soon. I would not risk the climb to the top of the cliff if there is little light," Ash told her. Still stroking. Teasing. Inflaming.

"I slept?"

"Yes."

"You didn't wake me. Why?" Harris wondered about the time spent here. His hands slipped lower. They now rested on her belly. He caressed the curves of her hips, trailed his fingers along the ladder of her ribs.

"I enjoy watching you sleep. Listening to your breathing. The rise and fall of your breasts." She felt him lift his shoulders. "You were tired. I would have liked it better if you'd told me sooner that you were wearying. Would not have allowed you to swim so long. It's my duty to safeguard you. To see to your needs. Sometimes I don't see into your mind because I'm too involved elsewhere. That's on me."

In his arms, she turned. Touched his chin with her fingertip. "I don't understand you. Why...well I'm not certain you are as good as you seem. Make me wish for certain things. When you say words like you just did, it makes me believe in your word of honor. Then there is Stella...after that the woman you went to see in Inverness when you raced away angry with me. I was protecting myself."

"As well as Abella," he supplied for her. "The first one I bedded once. The other I've never touched sexually. Nor did I ever wish to touch. She was always a child to me. She is even younger than you. As to the woman in Inverness though I didn't deny seeing a woman, there was no woman to be seen. That night I slept beneath a tree on the cold ground with nothing to eat. I thought of you and all you withheld. I wouldn't have bedded you with your brothers in the cave. I never intended to make love to you until you became my wife." His voice began to grate. He was harsh. Gruff with the building anger. There was nothing soft about his voice as his annoyance grew. "I told you before, I'm getting bloody tired of defending myself."

The mood of the afternoon shattered into blinding shards of pain. She felt the hurt she inflicted on him with her words. She ruined the softness of the day along with the gentle way he treated her. "I'm sorry. Ashamed. I cannot give you my full trust. I wish I could."

"Ash! Oh, Ash is it really you? Just as you asked, I've waited for you. I was told I would find you here. That awful man tried to stop me. He was too slow. I'm too fast." The lady was running, stumbling down the trail, waving her arms.

When Harris heard his name called out and the following words, she looked to the top of the cliff. After that she looked to see the stunned expression on Ash's face. The woman barreled into him, knocking them both over. Ash turned to take the brunt of the fall. The woman held his head between her hands.

Kissed him.

Wiggled her body against him. She pulled the top of her gown low so he could see her breasts. They were huge rounded pink tipped globes.

Harris saw red. How dare this woman? How dare Ash? She turned to leave. Meant to walk up that trail on her own. Ash could dally with that woman as long as he wanted. Despite her exhaustion, she could do this alone. Didn't care if he would object.

"Harris, stop!"

She wasn't about to stop. She turned. "No," she shot back, furious with the man she loved for pretending. For lying. He was a womanizer. An arrogant bastard. She didn't need this in her life. As soon as her parents arrived, she would find a means to convince them this man wasn't...could not be her mate.

"I don't know this woman." Ash sounded as if his words held desperation.

Faltering, she looked back at the pair. Heard the sixth sense in her head cry out. A sense of the truth entered into her. For a reason Harris didn't understand, she believed him. Ash managed to push them both to their feet. His hands were on the woman's shoulders. He shook her. "Who the bloody hell are you?"

Honest, I don't have one notion of who she is. Never seen her before in my life.

I know. Harris didn't understand where those two words came from. She should leave. Walk up that path. Let him stumble over his explanation later. She wasn't going to do that. Didn't she just tell him, she didn't trust him. Her faith slipped. Now she was listening to his protest that he was innocent. Perhaps he needed protection this time.

"Sasha," she purred. "My name is Sasha. As if you aren't pretending not to know me. Remember the night...we spent..." The woman looked at her. Her gaze was accusing. "You're feigning for that little whore. I know what the two of you were doing down here." She blinked a few times, tossed her hair behind her. "Don't you remember me? I work at the tavern. You took me upstairs. Made love to me. More than one time."

"I don't take women upstairs in taverns. Never had. Never will. Who put you up to this?" Ash gave her another shake. "Tell me! I'll make you regret this if you don't come clean." His hands still on her shoulders, he gave her another shake. His eyes were cold... so very blue with the ice shimmering.

Harris rubbed her hands along her arms.

"Who put you up to this?"

"No one."

"Don't believe you." He gave her a sudden push. "Go. Don't ever come back."

"You'll regret this day. I promise you."

At the threat another shiver swept through Harris.

~ * ~

Bloody everlasting hell. He was sorry too. Ash watched the woman leave the area. Turned his attention to Harris. She told him she believed him. Maybe this happened for a reason. He would wait.

Now, though, he needed to carry forward with the future. Wished to ignore her lack of faith in him. This incident didn't help. He felt certain the man who paid her to pretend this travesty was his brother. Chandler, along with his buddy Bertram, were part of this charade. They must have promised Sasha some payment in return for this debacle.

If she didn't believe in his innocence, there were no more words for him to say. Someday, God willing, she would learn to have faith in his word. Since her brothers were both wed to their forever mates, she should understand a shifter never looked at another female once he met his woman. He didn't need to wait until they were married. Making love to her now had a nice feeling to it.

He stood. Strode toward her. He brought Harris into his arms. She was light to his darkness. The woman would always confuse him. Tantalize every sense he possessed. He held out his hand. She hesitated. Once more the tiny gesture lit the fire within. He tucked a ragged breath into his lungs.

"The sun will set soon. You look cold. Chilled to the bone." Ashton slipped his frockcoat from his shoulders then draped it around hers. Her health was most important. He could wait longer for carnal pleasures with his woman.

Harris accepted his hand. Clung to him as they started up the path. Ash loved the way her small hand fit into his. He wove his fingers between hers basking in the sensual delight of the tiny yet familiar contact. Small things were important. A hand held, a moment of peace, so important to a future yet to be forged. Tonight would also be another milestone in their relationship. First though, he needed to meet with the solicitor his father sent to him. He hoped the meeting would be news of Chandler's disinheritance. Every day since the stroke his father made improvements. Perhaps the man would report that his father grew stronger.

When he was last in London, his father told him he might be improving. With Smith-Jones' help he was learning basic functions. He could eat by himself. While walking was still difficult, he managed with a device that would support his weight. He could relieve himself without help. Thank all the gods above, he no longer drooled from the side of his mouth. There was sensation in his arm. Writing was coming easier to his hands. He took a full bath with help only to get into the tub then out.

"Are you in a hurry?" Harris panted beside him. Her body seemed to be dragging.

Ash had been so absorbed in his thoughts he didn't realize the pace he set would put her in distress. "Yes and no."

"I can't keep up with you. If you like, you can go on ahead. I will follow."

Stopping, Ash brought her hands to his lips. Placed a chaste kiss across her knuckles. He looked down at her. Her lips were thinned, her nostrils flaring as she tried to breathe. He'd not meant to overtax her. She was already exhausted before his fast-paced trek. He pushed her too hard. "So, I'm walking too fast for you? I will slow. My mind was on something else. Concentrating. The family's London solicitor is supposed to arrive late this afternoon. I was hoping he will be there when we get back." This time he wrapped his arm around her shoulders. Held her next to him. "Never would I let you tag along behind me. Don't wish to have you out here by yourself."

"The basket?" Harris queried, looking from him to his private beach. "You've left it below. Shouldn't we bring it along?"

"Our guard will bring it as well as the blanket." Amused at her expression, he tweaked her on the nose. Her brows were drawn together in thought. Ash ran a fingertip on the crease in the center of her forehead. "You've no need to worry."

"A guard? Whatever for? Thought this country was safe."

"Precautions. You do recall my brother's violent introduction to you. Don't know how that loathsome woman got by my man. Must look into that." He hugged her close. So enjoyed the feel of her small body pressed against his. Yes, he needed to make certain no one would interrupt their play. Couldn't allow his brother or some stranger to discover them when they were in a different form. Wouldn't allow another man to see her naked. Though, when he brought her to the beach, he didn't have every confidence she would shift. He was pleased when she gifted him with her cat.

Harris nodded as if she understood what he was about. "My brothers and cousins do the same when they swim. One of them is always left to watch over the land when they change. As you know, it was a dangerous time in the highlands. Didn't know there were also shifters in England until I met you. For quite some time we always wondered why it seemed you defended us, looked out for the clan. Was always ahead of the trouble when there were English soldiers about."

"Crissie's husband? He is also a shifter?" Ash asked though he knew most of the story.

He also knew before the rest of them why Walker wouldn't marry her. He was already a husband. Wed to a woman who'd been betrothed to him when she was born. Second hand, he heard the story of their marriage. Understood from rumors that his wife preferred women to men. While Walker longed for a divorce, he was too honorable to seek one.

"Irish...a white tiger just as you are. They are happy now...finally after two children were born out of wedlock. It took so long for the two of them to understand what was happening. The betrayal. The fear. She felt abandoned by the man she loved. Crissie was stunned as well as heartbroken by everything Walker put her through. Not until much later in their relationship did he tell her he was married."

Ash had a need to change the topic. Harris should know the schedule of events. "Before your parents arrive, we will go through the claiming ceremony. I wish to have the rituals completed before the wedding. That way there can be no mistaking what you are to me. How I feel about you. Even with your parents here a few days before the vows, you will sleep with me. Stay in the room adjacent to mine. After I claim you, you will be mine. We will be together through eternity."

"Will you tell me about the ceremony? I'd like to be forewarned. Would wish to prepare myself for whatever might be part of it. You did explain the ritual is different from Clan Chaton. How? I'd appreciate knowing."

"Most important to you is the fact that only you and I will be there. No one else is allowed. It's private between the male and the female. Sacred.

It must not be interrupted." If he told her anything else she might run home. He would never allow something like that to happen. "Since I've never seen your clan's ritual, I don't know what else is different."

The rest of the way back to the mansion, conversation stalled. Ash understood her mind would race with different scenarios. She only had her imagination to go on. The ceremonies were much the same. His family was known as the Coterie Tigre. Over time the various families drifted apart. He wasn't going to tell her anything that might dissuade her from the all-important formality. Didn't need to deal with fear or hesitation. In some respects, this was more crucial than the marriage in the church. In this case, the Episcopal church. When they returned to Carnoch they would go through all this again in the Catholic church with Father Damian at the helm. She also wished to be wed as a Catholic. Together they would practice his faith. A wife should follow her husband.

Harris leaned her head on his chest as they walked. Ash knew today his touches heated her. The one time her moan was a soft rumble from the back of her throat, when he passed his thumb across the tips of her breasts, he understood the need to continue with this gentle assault. Headway was being made. She was becoming more comfortable with him. Looking down at the top of her head, he grinned.

In the master chamber, he ordered more wine along with a tray of cheese and meats, bread as well. Tindly arrived telling him hot water would be brought up for a bath if she would like to soak. Ash wished to see to all her needs before he left for the anticipated meeting.

Ash nodded his agreement seeing there was a slight bluish tinge to her lips. Concern for her health swept within him in a rush. The tips of her fingers were also a faded blue color. "A hot bath would be nice. See that she gets one. Warm towels too. Hang them by the fire."

He saw she was still tired. There were slight purple smudges beneath her eyes. Hadn't thought the swim in the ocean would have exhausted her to this extent. They did play in the waves for a half-hour. With a deep breath of air, he reinforced his earlier conclusion that he needed to be more attentive to her abilities. While he might not call her fragile, she was delicate. She possessed half his strength, half his endurance.

She curled up on one of the chairs facing the fire. Ash knelt down in front of her, taking her hands again into his. They were freezing cold. Ice next to his. Anxiety for her swept his insides. He brought up his hand to touch her forehead. She was cold...shivering. A hot bath was definitely in order. He would not give her a choice. Hot tea might warm her from the inside. He knew she liked coffee better. He would see she had both.

"How do you feel?" He ran his hands along her arms. Touched her cheek. "Are you getting sick? You're shivering."

"Never sick," she told him, her blue lips trembling. His hand beneath her chin, he ran his thumb along the bottom lip. "Never." Harris was shaking. "A hot bath would be nice. Believe the ocean might have been too cold for me even in my other form. My fur is not that thick. After that I stood beneath the stream of chilling water."

If she was sick, he would postpone his plans. The claiming along with the wedding would have to wait. Her health was far too important. "Take the bath. Eat something. After that, get into bed. I'll be up as soon as possible. I'll be gone for a few hours. As soon as the business at hand is finished, I'll join you."

She nodded as if understanding even though her eyes had taken on a hazy non-seeing appearance. Ash brushed a tender kiss across her forehead thinking he should stay with her. The meeting could wait. Tindly and Libby would make sure she had all that she needed. He still didn't wish to leave her. Massaging the back of his neck, he thought about all the possibilities.

"I'll return as soon as I can manage," Ash told her, determined to keep the meeting brief. Just the most important details would be discussed. He turned then strode from the room. Harris would appreciate her privacy.

In his office, Marcus stood when he entered. Held out his hand. "Earl." The smile on his solicitor's face told him all he needed to learn. Ash gestured to the chair in front of his big desk. Marcus sat then leaned back, his hands folded in front of him.

"It is done then," Ash said, hearing the relief in his voice.

He poured them both a snifter of brandy. Looked up to wonder if Harris was in her bath, soaking up the warmth of the steaming water. Questioned if the blue around her lips as well as her fingernails faded. He wondered what she would think of the new title or even if she cared. Earl of Greenwood, Ash mused. He never wanted to be an earl. Didn't need the title of lord to preface his name. His soon to be wife would be Lady Harris, Countess of Greenwood. He doubted if she cared. This scenario amused. The man who wanted the title with desperation lost it because he was unfit. Chandler would never see the land along with the family's wealth come to him. He would be both desperate as well as angry to see this changed. He wouldn't be able to alter what was done. The sooner he learned that fact, the sooner his plans of murder would vanish.

Ash ordered lavender scented soap for her bath. Where did that thought come from? He needed to keep his head. Listen to all Marcus told him.

"Yes, it's official as soon as you sign your name." Marcus pointed to the papers sitting on his desk. "Chandler has not been seen at the London townhouse though my investigator has seen him coming and going at all hours of the night from his home. Most times there is a woman or two with him. I fear what they are doing inside."

"They?" Ash arched one golden eyebrow toward the ceiling. "They as in the women or is Bertram also involved.?"

"Yes, Bertram Jacks, his friend, is always with him on these enterprises. They frequent the docks to bring whores to the house. Sometimes they go into the country to find a virgin. All hell sometimes breaks loose when they do find an innocent. Your brother has learned that money can soothe the ire of a virgin's father. They don't use force, just coercion. Chandler has a small country home about twenty miles from the city. They have women there also. Stella met the two of them the other night at that home. During the last hours of the evening just after midnight, another woman was brought to the country home. After that they turned their attention to the women they could find in the worst parts of London."

"I didn't know he was such a womanizer. My time in the highlands kept me from seeing my brother's true colors. Father? How is he doing?"

Ash wondered if the women were willing. If he found virgins in the country, the women would be forced to do whatever his brother and Bertram planned. A sick feeling churned in his stomach. Two men...one woman... From what he remembered of the one dalliance he had with her, Stella would not mind. She liked sex rough. How rough? That he would never know.

"Recovering slowly. We don't wish Chandler to know of the about face your father's health has taken. However," Marcus paused as if to give more credence to what he was about to say. "Chandler will be told about the disinheritance the moment he returns to his father's home. Smith-Jones will see to James' safety. Chandler will also be told he is no longer welcome in the family residence. Your brother is in debt. His gambling has become addictive as has his whoring. He needs the family funds to continue his way of life. Even if he thinks he can come at you, your father has put several codicils in his will that will give the title over to be held by Hawk Frasier until a male child of yours is born. If there is no child and something happens to you, the title will go to Hawk and his heirs. It is as it should be."

"Doubt if he cares about the family-owned townhouse. He will be livid when he discovers he's not going to become the earl. Ever." Ash understood without the solicitor telling him he needed to increase the security here. "I'll put an extra guard on Harris." His mind screamed with the possibility that Chandler could hurt Harris. She would have to be warned. Harris also needed to take precautions. Her life was precious.

"You need a guard also. I would feel better if Tindly wasn't quite so old." Marcus held up his hands. "Not that he's elderly by any means. It's just...well...Tindly is not Smith-Jones. Though he does have training from his stint in the army. I've been told he is good with a blunderbuss."

A half smile formed on Ash's mouth, thinking of his man. Tindly would protect, giving his life if necessary. That wasn't going to happen. "No, there are not many who have the capabilities of my father's butler. I'm glad the man is with him. In less than a week, Harris' family will arrive. I'm hoping the brothers come to visit along with the wives for the celebration of our marriage. Maybe a few cousins will also become guests here. For the time being that should be enough protection. I have one good man who watched our backs this afternoon when Harris and I went on an outing. *Although he did miss the lady.* If you can recommend a capable man and send him to me with your letter of recommendation, I would be open to hiring one more for the interim."

"I will question my investigator if he knows of someone. Good then, if there are no further questions, I'll leave in the morning. Wish to make it back to London by the following day. Will file the papers in a safe place. Your father has copies as do you. Nothing unforeseen will happen that cannot be rectified."

"Is father..."

Ash wanted to ask if he was fit to travel. Would love to have him as a witness to his marriage. He found the thought of the wedding both terrified as well as excited. Yes, Ash wished his father would be able to attend the wedding.

"Not yet..." Marcus seemed to read his mind and answered before he could finish the question. "Your father, while he can now speak almost clearly as well as feed himself, he is still weak. Out in public, his condition might embarrass him. Travel this far would seriously hurt his health. He told me to tell you to hurry up with the first grandchild. He wants to hold a baby, a little boy or girl in his arms before he dies."

Ash rocked back on his heels praying many years would pass before that happened. Yes, he could start working on that tonight if it didn't go against his plans. "Thought you just told me the old devil is improving."

Marcus cracked a laugh as he set down the empty brandy snifter, "He could outlive us all. He is determined to improve. In my opinion, he works too hard in his efforts to change his status. He's not at all pleased he needs assistance with common everyday things. James has no patience. With this disease, he's been forced to acquire some."

That was true. The two shook hands. Bade each other a nice evening. Ash watched the man walk from his office with the signed papers. He put a copy in his safe. Found he was eager to see Harris. Needed to make certain she had not taken ill this afternoon. The sea water was cold. In their cat forms the temperature should not have affected either one enough to make them sick. Not unless they were already ill. Fatigue could have caused the chill. The fresh cold water they rinsed in could have given her the coldness she felt. The hot bath should have warmed her.

When he entered his room, he watched her wrapping a towel around her body. He caught a quick glance of her back before the material covered the length. She must have soaked for a long time. On his way up, Libby told him she'd had more hot water added to the bath. Harris' fingers were wrinkled.

138

When he entered, Harris must have heard him or sensed his presence. She turned. Smiled. Vibrant silver blue eyes simmering with fire stared back at him. She had the look of a wanton dressed in only the towel. Her shoulders were white, slender. Droplets of water clung to the exposed flesh. He wanted to sip each tender drop. With long legs peeking out beneath the towel, tapering to slim ankles and small feet, she appeared breakable. He knew the feel of her cold toes when she rubbed them on his legs. Harris was delicate. One slender fingertip rested beneath her chin.

"You're here. Did the meeting go as you hoped?"

His heart beat hard. He hoped the bath gave her the warmth she needed. The little devil probably found a way into his head so she could listen. "How do you feel? Are you all warmed up?" Ash had many different ways in his mind to heat her.

Her lips were pushed together in a thin line. The smile she greeted him with vanished. She stared at him hard as if he was the enemy. He might be able to guess why she scowled. "Libby told me there was no nightgown in the armoire for her to set out." Her chin tilted up. "Did you take it? All of them? I started the trip with more than one." Her tone accused him of the deed. She was right.

Ash didn't need to read her mind to know the exact content of her thoughts. He would be truthful. "Yes, I took the ones you brought with you." Complete honesty was necessary here. "Did you wish to put it on? I thought after this afternoon..." Ash rubbed the back of his neck. "Guess I was wrong. Hoped you would feel more comfortable around me. If you wish, I'll retrieve your body armor."

She puffed out a breath of air. "I haven't eaten yet. I'd like to curl up in front of the fire. Continue to warm myself. Maybe have a glass of wine with you. I can't do that naked." She told him with blunt sincerity.

Of course, she could. "...and...it would please me to see you again...in the buff. Wearing nothing at all. Hold you. Help keep you warm."

He wanted to laugh when she sent a second scowl his way. After that he wished to smooth the crease lines in the center of her forehead. Ash stepped toward her. He was so close he felt the warmth of her breath. Ran his hand along one damp shoulder. "You never answered me about how you feel. Though, I can tell by looking at you that you've perked up. There are no blue smudges around your lips. None under your eyes." He picked up her hand. "No blue tinges around your nailbeds. Think I would also like to take a glass of chianti with you."

"You've news to tell me?"

Harris changed the subject stepping just out of his reach. She sat down on the hearth, finger combing her hair, attempting to dry the strands. Her towel slipped. She tugged the cloth into place. He thought he might drool. His body reacted.

"Yes. Believe you are growing more adept about getting into my head. Do you know what was said, Harris." He followed her retreat until he sat behind her catching her hands in his. "Do you already know what happened downstairs over the last hour? Can you understand the gravity of this new scenario in the Walcott household?"

Harris turned to look at him. He'd picked up a comb for her to use. "Wouldn't wish to give my newfound talents away. Now, would I? If I did, you would work harder to keep your thoughts to yourself."

"Newfound talents?" he chuckled, the sound reverberated around the room while he pulled the comb through her hair. He liked combing her hair. Never done it before. This was new to him. She stiffened when he caught a tangle in the teeth of the comb. "Sorry," he mumbled. "That's where you are wrong. I want you to be able to get into my head. You do that quite remarkably well. If you would understand the truth, I didn't wish to block you from my thoughts. Sometimes it makes it easier for a man when his woman knows what is going on without having to say the words. There are other situations where a man doesn't wish his woman to understand what he is thinking."

"You are the new earl."

"Yes." Ash was so close he caught the scent of lavender. Saw the tiny droplets of water on her neck. When he entered, she'd just risen from the liquid heat...wrapped the towel around her slim shape. He sipped one of the drops on her neck. Spread her hair out so it would dry faster. He would hold her until she fell asleep. After that they would share his bed again.

"Your brother?"

"Disinherited. He no longer has a seat in parliament. Means we will have to spend more time in London than I'm accustomed to. Do you mind spending time in the city? After we marry you will be a countess. I believe the title will be Countess of Greenwood."

"Your father?" Harris ignored his question.

It was not difficult to ascertain that she didn't care one way or the other. When she first flirted with him, she'd not been after a title.

"Doing better." Ash was thrilled about that piece of news. He was eager to speak with James. Eager to get on with his new life. "He wishes for us to get to the part where he will gain a grandchild."

Her face flushed a beautiful rose shade. "Will he come to the wedding?"

"No."

For several minutes there were no more questions. Ash continued to comb the long strands of her hair. As they began to dry, they stuck to his fingers, weaving between them, clinging. Her hair was soft to the touch. Silken strands fell all around her. As they floated in the air, they seemed alive, vibrant with energy all theirs. He would love to wrap himself in the cool silk of her hair. Needed to feel the silk against his chest. "It's almost dry."

Ash brought her to stand. She faced him, her eyes wide. "I would like my nightgown."

He brushed a tender kiss on her mouth. The outside. The middle then the other side. He touched the fullness with his tongue. Swept his tongue across her lips. Felt the silent shudder as her passion began to grow. Her hands rose to his shoulders. With a tug he could send the towel to the floor.

Against her ear he whispered, sending his warm breath across her cheek. "Drop the towel and I'll bring you your nightgown. It's fair."

An instant stiffening of her shoulders told him she didn't appreciate his answer nor did she agree with him. He rained soft caresses with his lips along her neck, across her collarbone. Waited for her to give in to his request. Framed her mouth with his. When she greeted him with an open mouth, he sent his tongue deep inside.

"I saw you this afternoon. Naked. Can you do that for me? Drop your towel."

Before the claiming ritual she needed to be at ease in front of him. He would hold her close to him. Make sure she remained protected while she grew weaker. The ceremony had a way of draining a woman of energy. By the time the ritual was finished, she would be unable to stand.

"I don't want to."

Ash understood her answer though he didn't appreciate it. He could be just as stubborn. "As you wish." After walking away from her, he opened the bottle of wine Tindly brought for them. Poured wine into the crystal glasses. He held the glass up. "Here's to your decision. May it be the right one."

Adorable. Confused. Her eyes narrowed. She hmphed. "My nightgown." She started toward him. Thought better of doing so then stopped.

He gazed at the rounded tops of her breasts. She would be his soon. He looked forward to exploring all her sweet curves, bringing her to that point where she shattered into a thousand pieces. Once before, so very long ago, it was hard to remember, he experienced that fragmenting of her body. Witnessed the beautiful dazed look of immense pleasure in her eyes.

"The towel for your nightgown." Ash was going to stand firm. This was far too important. If she was healthy, the claiming would happen in three days. Three days, that was all the time he had.

Harris tucked her lip beneath her teeth, thinking he was certain. "How long? How long will you insist on me being..."

Ah...she wished to know how much time would pass while he studied her, ran his gaze over the gentle swell of her breasts, down to her flat belly then her mound. He would spend as much time as she could manage.

"Should I disrobe first?" He sipped his wine. Brought the second glass to her. Shrugged out of his shirt. His hands rested on the fastener to his breeches. Her gaze focused on his crotch. Lightning flashed to his groin. It was all he could do to keep from groaning. When he teased her, it was sheer torture to him.

The silver blue of her eyes wide, she looked at him. A siren's smile formed on her lips. She nodded, "Yes. I would look at you again. Take your clothes off." Her chin went up.

His head jerked. "The towel." In that instant he decided he would disrobe after she dropped the offending piece of fabric. "If you wish to see me, it's your choice. Drop the towel then I will drop my breeches."

A flash of anger swept her expression. "You're impossible."

"As I said, this is your choice. If you wish, you can sit by the fire. I'm certain you will be warm. Your hair will dry."

"Before we go to bed?"

"The towel has to come off."

"Before we go to bed?"

"Yes."

To his great surprise, Harris dropped the towel, the material pooling around her exquisite little feet. His gut clenched. For a few seconds Ash thought he was drooling. His mouth did gape open at the sight of her perfectly formed body. He tamped his emotions into control. His smile grew as he allowed his gaze to touch upon her. To travel the length then back to her mouth. He supposed now it was his turn.

With slow measured precision, he unfastened his pants. Hopping on one foot then the other, he tugged his boots off letting them hit the floor with a resounding thwak. All the while, never taking his focus off her. Harris didn't try to cover herself with her hands. She tilted her chin, playing a waiting game until he retrieved her nightdress. Ash felt proud of her. She would do fine at the ceremony. Three more days of torment then he could make love to his wife. His wife by the sacred ritual.

The rest of his clothing fell to the floor. He kicked the material to the side. Drank wine. Handed Harris the wine he poured for her.

"Drink."

She did. Fascinated by her body he studied every nuance. The way her breasts moved when she picked up the glass, when she sipped. Watched the long white column of her throat when she swallowed. Before she asked again, he turned. Strode into the closet. Brought forth the nightdress along with his robe.

Ash dropped the robe. "Raise your arms." He wanted to put the virginal material on her. Needed to steal a touch here, one there. A few more if he dared. When it concerned Harris, he would dare anything.

As she raised her arms the rose-colored crest of her breasts tugged at him. He needed to sip a taste. He bent to test the flavor. First one then the other. Ash curled his tongue around one tender nipple. Unable to stop himself, he brought the tip deeper into his mouth. Sucked. She inhaled a gasp of air. The sound was sharp. Her body quivered with her desperate need. Once before he tasted her passion. Knew her raw hunger would be unstoppable once the desire was released.

"Raise your arms," he told her again. This time when she did, he slipped the warm gown over her. When the fabric settled, he did the buttons. Saw the hardened tips of her breasts pushing against the fabric. Stepping back once, he saw the darkness at the juncture between her thighs.

"Are you satisfied?" Harris asked with a whispered sigh, her lashes fluttering against the soft whiteness of her cheek.

Ash didn't hear recrimination in the tone of her words. Only desire. A hunger for what he chose not to give her.

"Not yet. Not by a long shot."

Ash slipped into his robe. Taking her hand, he led her to that chair she'd wanted to curl up on. After sitting down, he held her.

Stroked her.

Teased until a small whimper rippled from her lips.

~ * ~

Chandler along with Bertram sat in their favorite tavern, sipping ale, watching their preferred ladies sashay their plentiful butts across the floor. Their scantily clad bodies beckoned to him. He rubbed his crotch, thinking he needed relief from the ever-constant ache. Their breasts were pushed high, nipples revealed by the low cut of their gowns.

"Should we take one or two home with us or just share a room upstairs?" Bertram asked, grinning at the woman bringing them a tray of food. "From what I can tell, you need to forget all that happened today. It's been a bad day. A very bad day. For you. For both of us. How are we going to pay our debts? We do need to find a means to make money. Do you have any ideas? You know. Something that doesn't require a lot of work. Something we can also enjoy. If we could profit from sex that would be nice."

Profit from sex?

He didn't want to think about the news, the bad news as Bertram reminded him. Slamming his hand on the rough wood table, he tried to control his voice. "I've been disinherited. The old codger finally found the courage to rid himself of me. I'll have my revenge. Perhaps owning a whorehouse would garner us enough money to pay our bills. If we did, we wouldn't have to pay for our playtime."

"We rarely pay now," Bertram reminded him.

"True... If the house is ours, we can make money." Chandler rubbed his chin thinking. He did have some ideas bubbling around in his head.

"You've been told of the codicils. What are you going to do?" Bertram asked while one redheaded lady set a second glass of ale on the table for both of them. She bent over so far he saw the rose of her nipples. Bertram pulled her onto his lap, holding onto the curve of her hip, running his hand along her side until his fingers rested beneath her breast. There were plenty of women willing to give away their favors for money. Perhaps he should think about that idea.

Sex for profit...

"I'll kill each and every one of them." Chandler never felt this uncontrollable anger before. He should have been more careful. His father had spies out there. Must have discovered some of his less favorable proclivities. His gambling debts. Couldn't have an earl who deflowered innocent girls. No one could be as perfect as Ashton. He hated his brother. Always had. The perfect son. The shifter. Everything his father wanted. Ashton was the second son. The earldom should not be Ash's. All he ever craved should be his. Now he had nothing except his wits. He would have to figure out how to use the agile brain he'd been gifted with to make money. Had to make money so he could spend.

With a quick stiff breath, Chandler calmed himself. Listened to his friend. "Don't fancy hanging or going to Newgate. Won't be a party to murder. You need to think of some new way to confound your brother. Either that or we go our separate ways and stop thinking about what you can't have. We need to work with what we know as well as understand." Bertram's hand slipped under the woman's dress. He bit the back of her neck. Laved the spot with the tip of his tongue. She squirmed. "What's your name, love?" He found sensitive territory.

Chandler cracked a laugh. Bertram wouldn't care what the woman's name was. Seemed he was enjoying the pursuit. Chandler wasn't in the mood for a gentle session with a woman upstairs. What he needed was rough play where the woman could cry and scream her pleasure. Where no one would run into the bedroom thinking the lady needed rescuing. He wouldn't be a party to murder either. Bertram was right. Neither Newgate prison then the walk to Tyburn Hill for the hanging were viable alternatives to his rage or the predicament where he found himself.

There were other ways to get back at his family. To shame them. A whorehouse...yes...the more he thought about that the better it sounded. A unique whorehouse. Something no one experienced before. A place where men...even women...would pay exorbitant amounts to experience torrid love play. He would have *carte blanche* with what would happen there. Plans formed in his head. Campaigns that might include Harris, his brother's mate. Might involve sex with an audience. Both Chandler and Bertram loved being watched as well as watching. Chandler didn't see anything wrong with adults viewing each other if doing so pleased them. He knew of other men as well as women who enjoyed the spectacle, whether to participate or merely watch. Most brothels had viewing rooms. He enjoyed them numerous times.

"Celine," she murmured as she opened her legs for him.

Spread them wide. So far apart Chandler would see the tops of her thighs. With his teeth, Bertram tugged at the top of her gown until one breast was revealed. He bent. Nipped on the hard crest. She gasped. He held the soft piece of flesh in his hand. Flicked the nipple. Twisted it between his thumb and fingers. "Hush, sweet. When are you through with work?" He bit again. Kept the bites light. She squirmed, pushing her body closer to him. "Got a friend for my friend? We could both have you if you don't mind. Me and Chandler always share. Threesomes are always intriguing."

She looked at him. Let her gaze run the length of him. "Why would I have a friend when I can have the two of you all to myself? What do you pay?"

Nothing.

"You will have to wait to find out. Let it be a surprise."

"Need to know up front," Celine said. Gasped again when he twisted the tip of her breast. "Now don't get rough. Won't go with you and your friend if you're not nice. A little bit rough is alright. Fast and hard as long as I find pleasure along the way. Messy and hard works too. If you don't see to me, I'll do it myself."

"You don't like rough sex?" Bertram asked as he continued to fondle her breast. Tugged on a rosy hard crest. Pinched. "I do. Not too rough mind you. Just a tad. As you say, fast and hard is always nice."

"I'd watch you touch yourself. Think seeing that would make me stiff."

Chandler leaned back, his long legs crossed in front of him watching the display, his arousal growing at the scene. He liked the feelings. Knew he would be satisfied soon. He could wait. Bertram knew what he was doing would help his disposition. Knew Chandler liked to watch his sexual play. Would take his mind off his problems. They could go upstairs together. He could watch as Bertram took her. Darius, the owner of the tavern, would take fifty percent of what she earned. Together they would play with her. That way they both could begin to feel better.

"Just a tad," Celine murmured as she let her head fall onto Bertram's shoulder, her breast exposed in wanton display. "Just a tad. We could go upstairs now. I've a room. Darius will give me the time off. The two of you are paying customers. He has enough help if one of us has the need to give service in a different manner."

Chandler nodded his agreement to Bertram. Looked upstairs.

"We can take the entire hour I've left to work," she purred, moving her butt on Bertram's arousal. "More if you like."

"After the hour is up, we can go to my townhouse," Chandler agreed, scooting his chair back. "Before I decide if we wish to do this, let me taste first." He bent. Took her breast into his mouth and sucked hard. Heard the gasp of surprise when he bit down hard on the tip." She jerked. He continued to suck while soothing the small hurt with his tongue. She moaned a soft sound in the back of her throat.

"Putting my fingers inside you," Bertram said. "Moving them until you find a bit of pleasure. Until you're hot and wet." She whimpered again. Chandler continued to suck and bite. More sounds as she told them she enjoyed their exploration. A tiny mewl slipped from her parted lips. The pair continued on that vein until Chandler stopped to look at the woman.

Her eyes were dazed. Chandler enjoyed keeping a woman aroused for as long as possible. She'd not yet found her pleasure. It was time to stop then continue up the steps to her room. He lied. While he didn't care whether the woman he was with enjoyed the interlude, he never tried to give them the sought for ecstasy. If they climaxed when he came into them, fine. If not, fine. He heard her tell Bertram she could see to herself. He would like watching her while she climaxed.

"It's time," Chandler said, his voice soft.

Bertram set her off his thighs. When her fingers landed on her bodice to tug the fabric over her heaving breasts, he stopped her. "Come along just the way you are. Want everyone here to get an eyeful of what we'll be getting. They'll be jealous as sin. Your sweet jewels overflow my hands. I like that. You've got enough for both of us."

Chandler nodded. "Pull the gown down so they can see both bubbies. We can give the patrons of the tavern a fine show." Just as we will do later when I've rented a room. Invite only those who are willing to pay for a sex show. His ideas would come to fruition.

Bertram followed his orders. Celine gasped. Chandler took her hand in his, leading the way through the smoke-filled room. Eyes followed them, tracking their progress. Her unfettered breasts swayed and bounced, the nipples tight in the cool air. Hard from the attention he, along with Bertram, gave them a few moments ago. They were swollen as well as wet from the hot suck of his mouth.

Inside the room, he closed the door. Leaned against the hard wood while he watched his best friend and the whore they purchased. Bertram tugged on her clothing until the few garments were scattered around the room. She was rounded, curved. Her thatch of dark hair between her thighs gleamed with moisture. Bertram didn't disrobe. He unfastened his britches. His sex sprang free. He turned her so she was on the bed on her hands and knees, her plump butt in the air then pumped himself into her.

Now it was his turn. First, he meant to see if she could pleasure herself. Needed to watch.

Chapter Six

The last three nights went much the same as the weeks they spent together since Ashton took Harris from Carnoch. They slept together. He touched her. Held her breasts. Soothed her fears in the middle of the night when she was afraid, He comforted her. His body hummed with unfulfilled sexual need.

It was the afternoon before he told her she would participate with him in the claiming ritual. One more time in order to assuage her fears, Ash explained the tradition had many similarities to her own clan's ceremony. That didn't tell her much. Since she was unwed, she was never invited to the observance. She heard things. Knew the couple were naked except for two white cloaks that were wrapped around them. Understood by listening in on conversations that the man usually had to hold the woman up to keep her from falling.

Harris imagined that was the reason Ash insisted she get used to being naked in front of him. Ash never forced her. Always gave her a choice as to whether she should remove whatever it was she wore. He did manipulate. In the end, however, she would give in to his wishes. She did enjoy looking at his body. Seeing him without a stitch always left her hot as well as breathless. When he was aroused, his sex was large. Jutted out from a nest of hair at his groin. She wanted to touch it. While she recalled the day in the glen when he gave her pleasure, the memory of the intense sensations faded and was replaced by new memories.

"How are you feeling?" Ash asked as they walked along the boardwalk toward the modiste's store. "We're picking up your wedding gown. You know that. The claiming ceremony is tonight. Your family should be here tomorrow."

"Nervous. Excited. More about tonight than the wedding. Everything important will happen this evening."

Harris thought about the woman who tackled him on the beach. Since then, there had been two more times. She might have believed he dallied with these women if they weren't so cheap looking. That wasn't fair of her.

They were cheap looking.

"Ashton Wolcott. Stay out of my head. You weren't supposed to be listening to my thoughts." She was listening to his though he never allowed her into his head unless he wished for her to know. Those other times, she knew he was shocked. Understood from his mind, he didn't know the women.

He chuckled as he stopped her to kiss the tip of her nose. "Block me. If you can, keep me out of your pretty head if you can."

A huge puff of air sent a tendril that had fallen from her chignon into the air. "You know I cannot. I've tried. You've had too much practice."

"Your family is supposed to arrive tomorrow. Did your mother tell you who all was coming?" Ash asked as they started walking again. He held her hand in his. She enjoyed the closeness. Harris relished everything with him.

"Every one of the McKenna's except Houston and Leah. Neither Hawk or Houston wished to leave the town without a doctor. The silence in the big house will be broken. The children are all little scamps. Almost all are shifters. Feel sorry for the little girls who are not," Harris told him, thanking the fact she had not been left out.

"Here we are." Ash opened the door for her. A little bell chimed announcing their entry. The room was cozy. Stacks of material were scattered around the room. Fashion plates were set on a counter.

"Earl." The modiste clapped her hands together. She appeared very pleased to see them. "Countess. You've come to try on the gown. I know you will just love it."

Seemed most of the little village heard the news about their marriage as well as the housing situation. Unchaperoned. They found most of the villagers greeted them with the title since they got out of the carriage. The first few times Harris cringed. She wanted to race back to the carriage so she could hide. She'd never thought to marry an Englishman let alone have a title placed on her. She would be among the English aristocracy. Her entire life English royalty had been disdained by her Scottish family. Now, she was one of them.

Again, Ash pulled her close, soothing her fears. His arm was around her shoulder, giving her confidence. Whispering in her ear that she would get used to the label. "Lady Harris. It's a fine name. She would make her family proud." The warm whispered breath caused her to shiver with heat.

"You are here for the last fitting. The gown will be ready tomorrow. Understand your wedding is in two nights. I'm certain the gown will be beautiful. It is too bad the weather is too cold to have the ceremony outside where all could wish you well."

"You heard correctly," Ash said while she was ushered into a dressing room. "I would have preferred to hold something where the village people could be part of the celebration. I'm unwilling to wait until late spring for such an event. As it is, I've waited too long. I'm all out of patience where Harris is concerned. Need to make her my wife as soon as possible.

Harris did like the way that sounded. She wanted Ash as her husband with the same intensity. As far as she was concerned, the sooner the better.

After she disrobed, the seamstress slipped the gown over her head, made certain all the closers were fastened properly, then stood back, clapping her hands in approval. The modiste's gaze ran the length of her. The woman smiled.

"You are beautiful. The gown doesn't do you justice. Nonetheless, it is my best work to date. I hear your family will be here to witness the vows. I'm certain your mother will approve of the gown. If I do say so myself, it's almost as lovely as you, my dear."

"Yes, thank you for your kind words. I'm nervous as you can see." Harris held her shaking hand up as she wondered why she confided in the kind woman. "I've..." Harris knew it was the ensuing events of tonight she was anxious about, not the ceremony tomorrow.

The woman waved her hand in the air, shaking her head along with the gesture. "Pshaw...that's normal. Every bride gets the jitters before the wedding. You and your handsome man have been living..."

"It's not like that," she bit out, suddenly irritated with the kindly woman. True, they did sleep together. True, he held her every night. Touched her. Aroused. Brought forth passion and hunger.

I'm still a virgin.

Not after tonight.

"I'm sorry. Didn't mean to imply anything by that remark. We all have heard some of the circumstances that brought you to the mansion unchaperoned. No one holds the situation against you. Nor does anyone judge you. He is a virile man but honest as well as sincere. The two of you are in love." She stood back, her hands on her hips looking over the creation. She put a few pins here and a few there. "Just a few tucks is all that is necessary. The wedding gown will be perfect. Tomorrow, you will send someone to pick it up. Yes?"

"Yes," Ash said. "I will send Tindly for the gown around two in the afternoon. Is that sufficient time for you to complete the adjustments?"

"Plenty of time," she told them.

They finished. Ash took her hand. "Are you hungry? Thirsty? We could stop at the café for a bite to eat. We could also go home. The choice is up to you."

"Nervous. Can't eat. My stomach is doing somersaults. If I knew more, it would help calm my nerves. Tell me about the ceremony."

Harris hoped he would ease her fears. She doubted he would. All this time he kept his thoughts to himself. What she knew was that the ceremony would be private. The ritual was similar. That's all he would expound upon. They would be the only ones there. Ash could have told her so much more.

If there are no witnesses, how will anyone know you've claimed me?

You and I will know. That's all that matters. Everyone we know will have to trust in our words unless you wish to show them.

"Oh...how will I know? Show them what?" Harris understood. He did tell her earlier she would have marks just as her brother's wives did. Believed he didn't want to reiterate the small detail because it had something to do with pain. Just as it would hurt the first time he made love to her, the declaring would hurt. Left in the dark...women were always left in the dark to figure things out for themselves. She did understand since she was a shifter this pain would be less. Somehow that didn't make a difference to her.

It's not fair.

I agree. It's the way of the world. We can't change the fact no matter how much I would like to do so. I never want to hurt you, Harris. Never.

"Would you prefer to go home? Have a glass of wine. Tindly will bring up a plate of meats and cheeses. As soon as it's dark we can leave. If you feel better, you will be able to eat."

He was groping, telling her things that weren't true and wouldn't change her bundled nerves that seemed stretched to a snapping point.

"I don't wish to meet anyone else. The villagers are speculating about my virgin state. They all know I've been living with you. I don't like them questioning my character...or yours." The air she pulled into her lungs was cold. "They all think you ravaged me."

Ash stopped, pulling her into his arms. "Does it matter so much? As soon as we are wed...two days...all of the speculation will be over. You won't have a child too soon. No gossip will follow us."

"I'm certain a few of the ladies will be counting days from the wedding. Ready to proclaim me unfit for you. They all believe you to be perfect. No, that's not right, more than perfect." Harris didn't understand why she felt so bitter. She'd wanted Ash to make love to her. Asked him several times. He always refused. This must be why. He needed to save her from herself. Her father said she had a knack to find trouble.

Wanted to make love to you on our wedding night. Every bride deserves a special night of love. Knew you didn't want me to take advantage of your innocence. Back in Carnoch you worked so hard to keep me from that very thing. Told me you didn't want to get pregnant then be left with the shame. It's very simple. I agreed with all you said.

Didn't know you were such a romantic.

Harris understood how sarcastic she sounded. She was just nervous. Terrified of what was coming.

"Love, we should go home. Have that wine and a bit of food. After that we will prepare for the special evening. There is no reason to be nervous or terrified. I will walk you through every step. I'll be by your side. What little pain there will be will vanish within one beat of your heart."

How do you know? Seems you are just trying to soothe my rattled nerves. You've never claimed your mate.

Listened to your brothers.

"Oh... Am I just being a coward?"
No. Your fears are real.

Leaning her head against his shoulder, she soaked up his strength. His gentle words were what she needed to make her feel more certain of herself. They would do this together. Harris wondered if the other women in her family felt the same nervous anxiety she did. Before the claiming, except for Ash, she had no one to talk to. Wished her mother was here. She would have gone through much the same ritual. Her mother never spoke of what happened or how she felt.

"What do we have to do to prepare? Can you tell me that much?" she asked hoping he would slip then divulge something he was keeping secret. Maybe he was right though. Knowing what would happen might be worse.

"I've a special gown for you to wear tonight. That's all I'm going to say. We will be alone in a private clearing about fifty yards from the house. Tindly and our new man will stand guard while we conjure the spirits from times long gone. My butler has also prepared the area with candles along with a fire that will help keep us warm." He rested his chin on the top of her head.

She still questioned. Wished she could...no she didn't. "You sound mysterious. Conjure spirits?" Harris questioned wondering how he could be hazier.

He laughed. His soft chuckle vibrated against her. She loved the sound of his laughter. Guessed in this instance, the laughter was not about her. About what she didn't know. He would have heard her think she liked the sound of his deep husky amusement.

Ash pointed ahead. "Look, here's the carriage. We'll be home in a few minutes. We can relax then get ready for the night. It's my job to make this as easy for you as possible."

He helped her inside then pulled her onto his lap. His lips found hers. He swept his tongue across her mouth. Just as she always did, Harris opened for him. Felt the warmth invade her soul. She responded to his mercurial touch and the- sensuality he evoked.

His hand rested on the curve of her hip then slipped higher. He held her breast in the palm of his hand. His thumb brushed across the tip. Heated shivers wracked through her. Flamed. Spilled into her veins. Raced. She gulped air.

His other hand touched upon her ankle. His fingers traced gentle circles. Rose against her calf then her thigh. She put her hands around his neck. Pressed herself against him. Enjoyed the kiss. Rubbed her tongue across his. The touch upon the inside of her leg reminded her of another time...a different time. He spread his fingers on her belly. A ripple of a breath left her lips in a ribbon of pleasure. She wanted him to touch her lower, to slide his fingers between her legs.

"Do you like this, love? I know you do. I hear your enjoyment in every movement of your body, in every whisper of breath rushing from you. The sounds you make please me. I love to hear those throaty little feminine sounds."

She wished for more than he was giving. Wished for pleasure to fragment her into thousands of pieces. Harris pushed his frock coat from his shoulders. Unfastened the shirt he wore. She glided her hands across the expanse of his chest. Touched upon his flat, hard nipples. Rubbed her cheek against him. She wished he would touch her there, without the clothing to mask the sensations. Taste her with his mouth. Suck on her. Harris knew so much and so little. She kissed the pulse that beat so hard at the base of his neck.

"You're setting me on fire. We're going to need to stop before I take you here in the carriage. Don't want that for our first time together. I've a soft mattress in mind for the loving. Warm covers to keep us hot."

Harris didn't need covers to keep her hot. All she needed was Ash. She was on fire from this small contact. "I don't care. Feel the same as I did before. More so..." She licked the hollow between his collarbones. Tasted the salt of his skin, his scent evocative, uniquely his, a bit fiery. On his lap, she adjusted herself. Moved her legs so he could explore the most secretive part of her. Once before he touched her there.

Ash slid one finger between her legs, caressed upon sensitive flesh. She felt wet. Ash massaged until she thought she might jump from her skin. Blood pounded in her ears. He sipped a soft kiss from her mouth. Withdrew his hand. Covered her legs.

The coach slowed.

"We are home," he murmured.

He was going to leave her wanting...wishing. Harris felt as if she needed something more. Understood the climax, the woman's pleasure would not happen until he made love to her. He told her that much more than once. Ash was a man who wouldn't change a mind that was made up.

He touched her lips with his. Ran his hand along her back. "It will be alright. Soon, my love. Soon we'll be together the way we both wish to be. The wait will be worth it. I promise you."

His hand rested on the curve of her hips. He no longer held her breast in one hand. He'd withdrawn from her both mentally as well as physically.

Harris found she was damn tired of this. Too many times to count he set her on a course that was never fulfilled. Being aroused to such a height was unbearable time and time again. She understood the blasted man had a scheme. To hell with plans.

Sweeping her from the carriage then into his arms, he carried her into the house, through the giant foyer then up the steps. While he was walking, he bellowed commands to Tindly who scurried from their path.

"Yes, Sir," Tindly said. "Be right there with everything you wish."

Almost as soon as he set her on the chair in front of the massive stone fireplace, Tindly arrived with a tray of food along with a bottle of wine. Harris still didn't believe she could eat a bite until her stomach gurgled telling her something different.

After what didn't happen on the ride back to the house, Harris had no words. She was still aroused, her blood pulsing in shadowy places, clandestine spots that Ash caressed. She sipped in air. Let the oxygen out. Tried again in the same manner to calm herself. All she could do now was to wait for Ash to show her what was planned for the evening. Restless, she stood. Walked around the room then into hers where a white gossamer gown was laid out on the bed. For several seconds her mind reeled. She picked up the lightweight dress.

No... a soft moan rippled from her mouth.

It's the way the ritual has to proceed. The process has been written in all the ancient laws. Passed on from one generation to the next.

Harris could see through the material clear to the other side of the room. She gasped. Blanched. Dropped the fabric. Turned. Ash leaned on the door, his legs crossed, watching her. Relaxed. Seeming to study her. Two glasses of wine were in his hands. He pushed away from the door. Strode toward her. His eyes shimmered, his chin was set. She wanted to argue with him. Understood an argument would do no good.

"Yes, that is the gown you will wear. There is also a cape to put over you so you will stay warm while we walk to our private place. Remember we will be the only two people there. I will be the only person who sees you. Even though it's the beginning of November the night is unseasonably warm. There will be a fire. As to the claiming, there will be little discomfort during the ceremony. You will see some of our past lives flash through your mind. I would like to have you tell me about them. The only way a man learns about the past is if his mate tells him." Ash handed her a glass.

Her fingers touched his when she accepted. "Drink. The wine will help you relax. You look tense. Don't want you to worry."

He was right about that. She was tense. So afraid of what she didn't understand. She downed a good portion of the wine. Warmth settled in her stomach. A gulp of brandy might have warmed her more. She finished the wine then held out the glass to ask for more. He obliged, filling the crystal container to the top. She needed all the fortitude she could find.

"I'm going to wear that?" Harris pointed to the gown. "I can see through it. You can see through it."

"Yes, to all three statements." Ash sounded calm. Determined.

There would be no relenting on this issue. No one could change tradition.

By the deep blue shimmer of his eyes, Harris understood there was nothing more to say. The muscle in his jaw ticked. Harris knew one thing. She needed to get this over with as soon as possible. "Can we do this claiming thing now? I want to be finished with this tradition. Need to have all my questions answered. Put it behind me so we can move on with our future. If you would only tell me the truth, I would not be so petrified of what I don't understand. This is...well...it's your fault!"

His cheeks did flush with her exclamation. "Finish your wine. It is almost dark. We can start out as soon as you say the word. Tindly has prepared the circle for us. It is sheltered for more comfort. Sometimes I forget that this time of year the sun sets early. We wait only for the darkness." Ash downed the rest of his wine then stepped back as if to study her. "After you finish that glass, put on the gown then wrap yourself in the cloak. There are also white slippers for you to wear. You should be comfortable."

Yes...yes there were slippers on the floor. She wanted to become his mate then his wife. Needed to end the uncertainty that plagued her. Harris looked at him. She wanted him to leave. He shook his head once again reading her thoughts.

"Not tonight." With infinite care he began to disrobe. Each article he removed, he folded then placed on the bed.

What she didn't notice on the bed before now was the white transparent pants next to her gown. He would also be all but naked while they walked to this secluded glade he told her about. Her body was shaking so hard, she needed to sit down on the bed. Harris watched him finish undressing. Blanched. Dropped the fabric. He slipped on the transparent pants. She could still see him...all of him. She swallowed air.

"Would you like help?" he asked, his voice polite, gentle. Still the tone held a slight hint of amusement. She bristled. "I would go as soon as you dress in the proper attire. We can get this over with as you pointed out. We would then be able to enjoy the rest of the evening. Your stomach will calm so you can eat. Your nerves will no longer be stretched so tight they might snap. I will love you as well as feed you until we are both quite sated."

Again, Harris gulped air, her head reeling. She felt dizzy. Disoriented. Heard the tenderness in his voice. Staring from the gown to him she knew there was no choice but to square her shoulders then move forward. After that she nodded. He was right. She needed to proceed with haste.

"I'll be naked..."

She didn't know what else to say. That was why he persisted over the weeks. Brought her to the point where she would feel comfortable with him. He told her the ceremony was private.

"Yes."

It wasn't as if he hadn't been with her when she wore nothing. Hadn't touched her, caressed her until her body expired in flames. Determined to brazen this out, Harris stood. She walked to him. Turned her back so he could unfasten her dress, unlace her corset. "I need help," she told him. "Libby assisted me into the dress before we left." Suddenly she stepped away, trembling, shaking so hard again she wasn't at all certain she could stand.

"What?" Ash sounded baffled.

"I need another glass of wine if you don't mind. One more glass. I..." Harris wanted to drink enough she wouldn't know what was happening to her. The entire bottle might do the trick. When she didn't feel his hands against her skin, she looked over her shoulder to see what he was doing.

Pouring me wine.

He does understand. Either that or he has the patience of a saint. Ash would never be eligible for sainthood. So, he must understand a few of her fears.

Before Ash reached around her, handing the glass to her, he smiled. She gulped the wine. The liquid ran down her throat. Warmed her. Settled in her stomach to soothe as well as vanquish her terror. Felt better. If possible, steadier even though she swayed. His hands made quick work of her clothing. Shoes, stockings, gown, corset, chemise, all were on the floor. The clothing pooled around her feet. Ash stepped back.

Harris turned. Faced him. Felt cool air caress her.

His hands were behind his back. He waited. Watched. A half-smile formed on his face. "Do you need more help? Though I would be remiss if I didn't tell you I love the view. Do not wish to see you covered even in this diaphanous fabric."

"Oh..." She was confused. When she turned back the gown was in his hands. He'd reached around her to pick up the translucent material.

"Put your arms up, my love." His voice was husky, rough around the edges. He only sounded that way when she was naked or he was holding her, touching her. At least she had a gown to put on. Cool air touched upon her.

She did what he told her. Stuck her arms in the air. Felt the soft silken material slide down her arms then her body. The smooth glide of the fabric against her skin heated her. Butterflies danced deep in her stomach. The gown floated around her, brushing against her heated flesh. Aroused. Enticed. With every movement the fabric slid over sensitive flesh. The hard tips of her breasts tightened. Flames built.

"Sit."

Unable to think for herself she did sit on the bed. Ash picked up one foot. For a few seconds, he held her foot in his hands. Rubbed his thumb across the arch. He was kneeling, putting her shoes on her feet. After that he pulled her up so she stood in front of him. He wrapped the cape around her. Fastened it then he did the same with his cloak.

"Will you hold my hand?" Ash asked as he held his out for her to accept.

She touched him. Felt his large hand engulf her smaller one. The sensation heated her. He pulled her hand to his lips, kissed the knuckles. Each touch of his lips upon her a tender caress.

~ * ~

Ash spent the afternoon studying the woman he loved. She was at times nervous then flirtatious. She would lower her lashes so he couldn't see her expression. He enjoyed teasing her to a breathless state of arousal. Understood full well by the time evening came they would be able to satisfy all their desires. He understood she wanted him as much as he needed her. This was what he wished for.

Tonight...the devil how he looked forward to the evening.

Harris was still shy about revealing herself. Ash wasn't certain how he felt about her bashfulness. He supposed that after all this time the shyness both pleased him as well as irritated. He couldn't expect an innocent to strip to nothing without blinking. In time, she would become more at ease. Looking forward to that time, he thought of his cat. How he might be able to challenge her to greater heights of her sexuality. He would have to remind her that he was the one pleasuring her, testing as well as arousing. She would find magic in all the different ways he would show her how to explore each other.

When he brought her to the room to eat, he understood her nerves were on edge. Right in front of him she was fraying, unwinding before his eyes. Her lovely shoulders shook, her hands...all of her. He had to agree the sooner they got on with the ceremony, the better off she would be. He wanted to make love to her. Teach her all the ways he could pleasure her as well as the places on his body he would like her to explore.

Over the course of their lives, he intended to give her everything she wished for. They would have children...as many as she asked him for. Complying would be a delight. He would have to inquire as to how many she would like. Before they left Carnoch both her brother as well as Houston, her cousin, lectured him about being careful not to keep her with child year in and year out. Ash never intended to do that. He respected her along with her physical needs.

Nor did he mean to withdraw from her body to keep her from having a child until after she conceived the first time. Houston told him he should get to know Harris better before having their first baby. Hawk made certain he pointed out that children took up time. Lots of time. He would not be able to give Harris all the attention she deserved if they had a baby too soon. After the child was born, the babe would be their first concern.

What Ash made certain to tell the two doctors was that there were no guarantees conception would be easy. They all knew of couples who waited months, sometimes years for the woman to increase. There were some pairs who could never conceive. Ash wasn't going to take any chances with this endeavor.

Now, Harris walked beside him. He slipped his hand from hers then into the sleeve of her cape. Keeping her aroused was his first priority. When he removed both the gown as well as the cape from her slender body, he didn't want her to balk. His hand settled on the curve of her hip. Embraced. She jumped, seeming startled by the languid caress down her leg then up to cup her pretty jewel with his hand. He set the palm of his hand against the crest of her left breast. Rubbed with a gentle caress. Pinched. Tugged upon the tip. He felt the shiver of pleasure rip from her. Heard the tiny sound of delight.

Ash wished he could taste the sweetness he found there. He had not done that yet. Tonight, most of the pleasures they could enjoy would be new to her. They would be at the small clearing in a few minutes. He continued the gentle assault on her breasts, the flat of her stomach, the curve of her hip. Heard another soft whisper of air. The tiny mewl of desire.

This would all happen soon...not soon enough. They had just left the house. Ten minutes more and they would be on sacred ground.

A man stepped in front of him. He held out a piece of paper. "A message from your father. Hoped to catch you before you left. Failed that. Read it. If you have a reply, I'll wait at the house for your return."

"My father?"

What would his father want to tell him? Perhaps a bit more advice? He'd been informed the claiming ceremony would occur tonight. His father taught him the words he would need to say for all to go as it should.

"Yes, I believe he was just hoping to wish you luck among a few other things. Smith-Jones did not tell me what else he might have written. The words in the letter are not for me. Please..." the man implored.

With Harris beside him, Ash stepped into some light given off by a lantern. "I'll be just a minute. Have to read this." He brushed a chaste kiss on her cheek, let his hand run down the long column of her neck.

She was nodding, accepting that he would have privacy. Even seemed relieved somewhat with the short reprieve. Reprieves only tended to make a person more nervous about an anxious situation. Ash opened the letter.

Ashton,

By now you would have heard, via Smith-Jones, about your brother's newest ventures into the seamier side of London. He has fallen to new levels. I'm appalled to have heard about the sex showings. Entertainment for both men as well as women. Some say he's a remarkable businessman. I say your brother has no morals though he claims all participants are willing. No one is being forced to perform. Each time there is a show, the audience grows. His women have names. They follow the four seasons. It all began with Winter Snow, the Ice Queen. Next came Spring Mist, the Flower of Woman Hood. I can't imagine the names of the next two seasons. Chandler has yet to introduce Summer as well as Autumn.

He's making money for the first time in his life. If it wasn't such a despicable way of earning a living, I would applaud him for actually doing something other than gambling and whoring. Well, I've heard he is also participating in the shows. So, he hasn't stopped whoring. His favorite lady seems to be Winter Snow. I hear he won't allow other men to touch her. Can you imagine Chandler keeping one woman to himself? He's always said he was willing to share.

I want you to understand he's not yet been informed by me that he has been disinherited. Since his departure that night he attacked Harris, he has not visited. Thought he would have come for money. Now that he has an enterprise all his own, he has no need of anything from me. Thank God. Though by his actions it's obvious that he knows the hard cold facts. Smith-Jones told me you have increased your security around your home, though God knows with this new enterprise your brother would hardly have the time to seek revenge. Perhaps he is reconciled to the prospects of no title. He was never interested in politics, only money along with women. Would have been a poor member of the House of Lords.

Whatever you do, keep young Miss Harris safe. By now you will be considering the ritual that will make her your mate through all time. I pray there are extra guards outside the glen. Chandler, if he knew what would be happening soon, would not stop to either put an end to the ceremony or end Harris.

I know my son. He has always despised you. He will find some means to humiliate you or hurt your mate. Even keep you from declaring for her.

Take care.

Your loving father, James.

The letter gave him more things to think about. He did have two extra guards around the clearing tonight. Tindly even volunteered to be part of the entourage guarding them bringing the total to three.

"What is it?" Harris asked, turning to place her shaking hand on his arm. "Should I know? Does this concern me?"

Ash gave her a little half-smile. Yes and no. He didn't wish to give her anything else to worry over "The letter is about my brother. He has a new enterprise that is making him money. Chandler has never lifted a finger to work over the entire span of his life. Imagine this could be a good thing. My brother was in debt. He has always been in debt. Before this he's been able to access the family funds. He can no longer do that. The astronomical amount he owes could send him to debtor's prison."

"The work is questionable. Is it illegal?"

"No, what to tell you? Not exactly, yet it is questionable. I would guess he would pay off the local constables. Perhaps we can put this conversation off until there is a new day and we've finished what we need to accomplish this evening."

"Ash, please..."

"If you must know..."

"I must," she smiled at him.

"In short, he's providing entertainment to anyone with enough funds to pay to watch other people having sex."

"He what?" Harris blinked a few times. The expression on her face was left blank. "People would do that? Pay to watch...other people...?"

Ash surveyed her face for a few more seconds. Thought he might laugh. His little innocent would not understand that some people enjoyed that type of entertainment. "Yes, my brother always enjoyed doing so. Told me about the peep holes in the various brothels he visited. He and his friend Bertram share their ladies as well as watch the other having sex."

"I don't..."

"Harris," he began with a calm he wasn't feeling. "This is the last we will speak of this tonight. Though, I will explain more later. After we've been intimate...more intimate, you will have additional knowledge."

"Alright then..." Harris tucked her bottom lip between her teeth as if she was in deep thought. "I won't ask any more questions."

"Shall we proceed?"

A few days ago, Smith-Jones wrote to tell him about Chandler's new enterprise. The first night, his brother rented a room in the back of a tavern. Advertised the coming attractions. Somewhere around forty men and women bought tickets to the show. They sold the vouchers at an astronomical price. To see the entertainment, there was an assortment of dukes and earls and a viscount was tossed into the mix. There were wealthy members of the merchant class along with some politicians. It seemed now his creative mind brought in new ideas with the ladies. Winter Snow...how on earth did he come up with that name...Spring Mist. He could imagine Summer and Autumn.

All participants were there to view the women having sex. Chandler claimed all the entertainers were willing participants. Told him they liked others watching them. Stella was among the women. She was the first. Stella waltzed into the audience naked. Found a man who was also willing. The man disrobed. She did all manner of things to the man then opened herself up to whatever he wished to do with her.

The thought gave his gut a twist. Never would have believed Stella was a whore. The two had sex in front of the forty or so people in attendance. Coins were tossed their way in appreciation. There were two more women who participated on the dais with a man Chandler hired then walked into the crowd to find a willing mate. The audience even had to sign a waiver saying they would participate if chosen.

Ash was told Chandler watched in the front row. At the end of the first show a woman from the audience stood in front of his brother. Stripping. Her breasts swaying. No one knew if she bought a ticket to the show or if she was a plant. By the time all was done, Chandler participated to a roar of applause.

When Harris stumbled, Ash was brought back from his deep musings. Chandler would always land on his feet. Smith-Jones told him the next showing occurred a week later. This time there were well over one hundred in attendance. Seemed the word got out about the event. Chandler was raking in the money; not only on the show but the liquor he served. Auctioned off individual rooms for the men or women to buy for a night of pleasure with any of the entertainers.

Rumor had it that Chandler was going to buy a home where these shows could take place. There would be numerous rooms upstairs where men as well as women could have discreet affairs if they didn't want others to view them having sex.

Harris stumbled again. He needed to pay better attention to her. "Are you still so nervous that you cannot walk?" Ash asked, feeling very solicitous to her. This event they were walking to was a milestone in both their lives. He needed to concentrate on Harris, not his brother's new business.

"Nervous?" Harris looked at him, her eyes wide, dark, shimmering in the moonlight that bathed her face. It seemed she tried to smile. He respected the effort. "Whatever would give you that idea?"

Ash didn't miss the sarcasm. Patting her hand, he spoke. "If it's any consolation, I'm also nervous. Not as much as you, nervous nonetheless."

Yes, he was thinking he didn't want to hurt Harris. She was so small.

So delicate in her proportions. What if his claws dug into her shoulder too hard, too far. What if something went wrong and he scratched her. There were to be only puncture wounds. Wounds that would leave small indentations. Scars...tiny scars.

"I would put this off another night if you asked. If we did, you would feel the same nervousness tomorrow as well as the night after that. Is that what you want? Once this time has passed, you will have no more fears." Ash told her. While he was giving her a choice, he was also praying she would not ask him to wait longer.

She was shaking her head. No, she would not stall. Earlier Harris told him she needed this to be over. He could oblige her in that wish. Tonight was for them to be bound together in the ways of the coterie.

"We must go on." Her shoulders shook while she said the words. "I'm afraid. Know that bothers you. As you say, we have to do this now. To put it off another night would be foolhardy."

"Then we will continue on our way," Ash told her, pleased with the decision she made. Harris was courageous. She wasn't blind to the fact this would happen despite her reluctance.

Once again, he set his arm inside her cape. He pulled her close, enjoying her wonderful curves as they molded against his body. Soft met hard in a delightful way. Above them a full moon slanted light between the branches of the trees to dance on the forest floor. Leaves glimmered where the same beams touched upon them. To Ashton there was something magical about the evening. Enchanting. Mesmerizing.

Somewhere above an owl hooted. Could hear wings whistling against the air. The bird would be searching for food. Some luckless rabbit or squirrel would lose their life tonight, while his and Harris' lives would be renewed. They would be free to find each other after that they would find love in another lifetime.

This was the way of the shifters. He was lucky he was sent to the highlands instead of India or some other territory of Great Britain's. If not, how would he ever have found his mate? Would he have gone there on some pointless vacation? Met her that way? Those were all questions he found no answer for.

Realizing they were nearly at the private glen that would become such an important part of his life, he pulled up short. Harris stumbled into his back. He turned. Touched her chin to see into her eyes. She looked at him, confused.

Ash tapped her on the nose. His smile generating a warm response from her. Her small smile gave him the reassurance that she would be fine. "This is where we will seal our love for another generation. Are you ready? Do you need more time?" He didn't understand why he asked that question. More time was something he didn't want to give her.

Harris tugged in a huge breath of air as if she was using the extra oxygen for courage. "Yes. I'm ready. Believe so. I'm ready. Impatient even." Beneath the cape he felt the rise and fall of her breasts as she tugged several breaths of oxygen into her lungs.

They stepped through an archway of branches. Inside, candles burned in a wide circle, pouring light into the small space. A structure sat in the middle, for protection in case the skies decided to let loose with a downpour. To shield them from the cold a small fire burned in the center, the smoke going through a smoke hole. They would stay warm tonight.

They would enter into the tent. Ash knew what it looked like. Tindly helped him prepare the structure for this evening's events. He moved the flap aside so she could go through. Harris walked in. Stopped a few feet from the door. There were also candles inside burning around the circumference.

Beyond the fire, there was a bed with blankets. It stood about a foot off the ground. Harris looked at him, eyes wide.

"Is that where it will all happen?"

He felt the lump in his throat grow. All he could do was nod his head. Yes, the mating, not the claiming. Though we will stand beside the bed. Wine might relax her. Tindly gave him twice the bottles he asked for, just in case, the butler told him. Tindly had been with his family for years. His butler wasn't a shifter. Nonetheless, he was trusted. Knew as much as possible about the traditions.

Tindly knew some things about the ritual. Ash noticed there was a bowl along with two pitchers of water. One to clean the wounds he would leave on her shoulders more if necessary to cleanse the blood of her innocence. By the time the ceremony coupled with the bedding ended, he might need all the wine.

Beneath his calm exterior, Ash cringed. Thoughts of hurting Harris made his stomach cramp. When he turned to look at her, Harris seemed to be searching the room, her gaze roaming to every nook and crevice.

She swept her tongue across her mouth. Moisture lagged behind. He tried to reassure, running the back of his hand along the softness of her cheek. Ash decided speaking with her through their minds would be easier.

Wine. Would you like a glass before we begin? I find I also need a bit of false courage. What do you say?

Two...maybe? The smile she graced him with was weak. Almost non-existent. Harris was nodding her head as if the few words weren't enough.

As many as you would like, my love. No, perhaps not. You need to be able to begin this standing by yourself. In silence, Ash cursed himself for that thought. He needed to take a great deal more care.

You mean at the end I won't be able to stand? Heard as much through rumor. My sisters-in-law sometimes forgot I was still innocent, unclaimed.

I've no idea. Every declaring is different. Every woman is unique in how they feel as well as what they see. Want to be honest with you now that you are here. I've heard at times the woman is weak. The male has to support her. Promise I won't allow you to fall.

Promise...seems you've promised a great deal of things.

I have. After the next hour or so, you'll have no more fears. I can guarantee that one last thing. No more fears.

No more fears...

Ash brought her the wine he poured. Handed the glass to her before watching her drink. She sipped instead of gulped as he expected. Harris decided to lengthen this. She could prolong the event for another hour or more. He would still claim her tonight. Nothing she did now would change the ending.

They would make love.

She would be his in every way possible.

When she finished, he took the glass from her. Set it on a small table near the bed. His hands rested on her shoulders. They stood together, looking at each other.

"What is going to happen first?"

Her fingers played with the ties on her cape as if she expected him to remove it. He would if she didn't.

Ash stepped back, his arms crossed over his chest. He didn't understand how he could possibly reassure her more than he'd already tried.

"You did tell me you wished to get this over with as soon as we could."

"Yes."

"I'll relate to you the process as I know it. Since no man or woman is allowed to witness the exact ritual between two people, all I know is what I've heard from those who went before me. Other than that, all I know is what concerns me."

"That has to be good enough."

"My father, James, taught me the chant that creates the magic of the night. A father is expected to teach his son. To pass down all he knows. That way the traditions continue. The coterie endures."

"In my clan, Father Damien says the words that create the mystery along with the enchantment. All married family members are allowed to witness the ceremony. Obviously, I've not seen it. What does the chant..."

He set his finger against her lips. "You will experience our past lives together. I will not. You will have to tell me what you see. How you feel. If I tell you the words too soon, all might go wrong. Do you want to risk that?"

"No, but..."

"Still, you wish to learn before this happens. I see nothing wrong with that now that we are here. You won't leave. Didn't wish to explain anything sooner because I was terrified I would lose you. Petrified you might not accompany me here."

"Now, you stand in front of the door to the outside."

"I do."

"It is time, Harris."

Ash stepped toward her. Pulled the ties on his cape. Let the garment slide down to the floor. "Will you do the same?"

Her hand shook while she undid the string. Eyes wide as his cape also pooled on the ground by their feet.

Ash couldn't help but let his gaze roam over her. Harris' curves were perfect, her breasts firm round globes with tender pink nipples. With the candle light he saw all of her. Before tonight he'd held her breasts in his hands. Tonight, he would taste and savor the crests. Pull them into his mouth to orchestrate pleasure for both of them. He found she was gazing at him too. Thought her eyes would be captivated by his sex.

They weren't.

Harris stared at his eyes. It seemed she saw beyond them, into his head. While he knew in time she would have that ability, she didn't now.

"Lift your arms, my love."

~ * ~

Chandler sat back, relaxed, his arms spread across the sofa. Auditions for roles in his new adventure were taking place. He was pleased with the idea of his. Bertram confirmed that his idea would make them more money than they knew what to do with. When he advertised, he didn't expect this many men along with the women would show up to try out for roles in this new endeavor of his. He was delighted by burgeoning prospects. Never in his life would he have thought to find such enjoyment in work. Of course, when one enjoyed what they were doing, it wasn't work.

The woman who stood naked in front of him was named Winter Snow. To his immense delight she was beautiful. Her body slender as a read, she possessed the largest breasts...ripe to taste...to savor on a long cold night. He wanted to pluck her nipples. Her eyes huge, deep blue while she stared at him. Her lips full, kissable. Pouty. Long legs, white alabaster flesh. He longed to caress. The length of her ebony hair fell well past her waist and played peekaboo with the tight hard buds of her breasts.

He placed her with two men, Jimmy and Johnny. They were brothers, twins. Both were tall and lean. Their shoulders broad, hips narrow. The two men were blonds with distinctive brown eyes. Their chins square. Chandler always loved threesomes. Seemed when there were two men making love to one woman every erogenous zone the female possessed could be fondled or tasted at the same time. He grew hard watching them touch...explore Miss Snow. This threesome was good. He decided they would begin the next show. Not tonight but the one coming up in three days. He would charge extra. Her name could have top billing. He would need to figure out a suitable title to go after Winter Snow.

He clapped his hands signaling the end of the night's audition. Nodded to Bertram who would take care of the details, the contracts would be signed. Everything would be above board. He would explain the procedure along with what would be expected of each participant. After their part in the show, they would each walk through the audience to pick out the person or persons who would entertain everyone who bought tickets. Chandler thought that idea to be a grand one. The audience would participate in a new sexual encounter.

Before anyone was allowed into the theater, they would have to sign a document that stated if chosen they were willing to have sex in front of everyone with the male or female who picked them from the vast array of candidates. Chandler never thought life could be this much fun. This was his dream come true. If he didn't know better, he would believe he had gone to heaven not hell as he once expected.

Other women he interviewed who were not willing to participate in the group entertainments were given the opportunity to show their skills in one of the bedrooms upstairs. If they proved competent, they would be given an individual room where they could be independent. These females were also expected to serve drinks during the biweekly shows in scantily clad costumes. Chandler understood males enjoyed seeing glimpses of the women's bodies. The gowns would be made special to enhance each woman's best attributes.

Ah...the good life.

Stella had become one of the star attractions. From the beginning, Chandler knew Stella loved threesomes. She accommodated him and Bertram many times over the last few weeks. Celine, the little whore they encountered in the tavern, worked once a week performing for his guests. Men liked her. She was round, very curvaceous. Her breasts were huge globes of temptation. She found pleasure flaunting herself. Enough to wet any man's appetites. Celine had no trouble parting her legs then showing everyone how she could give herself pleasure.

When she traveled the room to pick out a man, she always seemed to be able to find a male who was shy yet wanted to be part of a unique sexual encounter. One man she found, Chandler was certain, had been a virgin until that event. Now, he was a regular. Attended each performance. Chandler had thoughts of putting him on stage. He could be part of any threesome. The other male could show him what to do. An experienced female could do the same. Next show, he would have Bertram present the idea to the lad.

Before Bertram took Winter along with Jimmy and Johnny to the back room, he wanted to taste her. She tempted. Fascinated. Intrigued. Tasting her once would never be enough. That bothered him. Still, he wished to savor all her unique feminine charms. Perhaps tonight he would send her to his room.

"Winter...come here." This woman wasn't as large as many of the whores he employed. Winter was slim, her waist tiny. Though her bubbies were magnificent, huge rounded globes tipped with more enticement than most men could handle. He wasn't most men. Handling Miss Snow would be his delight. While she walked to him, the globes swayed, bounced when she stumbled once.

Winter seemed comfortable in her nudity. Chandler appreciated that asset in a woman. She never once thought to cover herself with her hands or an arm. If he was right, she was also relatively new to the profession. There were times during the interview, she didn't appear pleased with what was happening. She would make this tiny noise of distaste. She would need to get over that. Though he did appreciate the knowledge. In this short time Chandler found that he was able to read her likes along with her dislikes. He understood her without talking to her.

"Sir?" she questioned but she stood in front of him, her head tilted a bit to the side. Her lashes lowered as if she wished to hide her emotions from him. Ash saw moisture left on her lips from the two men who'd been with her. Her nipples were still elongated as well as hard...damp from their attention. He gazed lower. Her stomach flat. Her mound of dark hair tempted his fingers.

"Straddle me." He smiled at her as she moved to do his bidding. She started to sit. "No. Free my sex first. You can taste if you like."

God, he wanted her lips on him, sucking him deep into her warm mouth. Her eyes were a deep dark blue shining, lips almost the same color as her nipples, soft rose. Chandler needed this woman for his own. Winter did all that he asked. She kneeled. Brought his penis into her mouth. He arched back, enjoying the sensation she created. He felt the scrape of her teeth along his length. She looked up. Her eyes wide. That small caress was not enough. Never enough.

This woman didn't come here as a virgin. Startling, the very nature of her was innocent. Her lips formed around him again. From her point below him, she stared at him as if awaiting further orders. He set his hands on her head so she could not leave him. "Suck on me. Suck hard." With that said, his hips lifted. Pushed himself between her lips. He exploded into her mouth. "Swallow me."

He could have laughed at the pained expression he read in her luminous blue eyes. She didn't like what he asked. He heard the tiny noise she made telling him something more about her. That pleased him. She didn't need to be taught who to obey. Winter knew her benefactor.

"Would you like to sit on me now?"

Winter nodded. In this situation, what else could she do? The girl knew her welfare depended on his generosity...on her ability to please him. As all whores did, she would need the income. Perhaps that was why very few of the whores he saw this last week told him they weren't willing to share their bodies in front of an audience. That was an intriguing thought. He meant to find a way to capitalize.

"Turn around."

Her surprise was registered in the tilt of her mouth as well as the shimmer in her glorious eyes. She didn't understand the order.

There were several women and men still left to audition for the jobs he offered. Ash realized in that instant his show would never be the same. He meant to have different entertainers on different nights. What he had planned would always be unique. Each night would be scripted with an unusual theme, different scenarios. Winter Snow, ah, the Ice Queen...his Ice Queen would star in one show a week.

After she turned on him, he lifted her. She settled on his rod. He felt the pulse of her desire. "Pleasure yourself." Though he would like to watch her eyes when she reached her climax, he would settle for watching those of the people still in the theatre. Chandler found she was a novice at this. Winter had no idea what he wanted from her.

Chandler brought her small hand to his mouth, wetted her finger then found the perfect spot, the one that would send her soaring, fragmenting into thousands of pieces. He helped her. Showed her what to do, how to massage that spot. After she understood what it was she should do, he brought his hands to the full round jewels he admired. Focused on the tight crests. Needed to savor. He twisted. Tugged. Heard the soft moan ripple from her lips. Felt the increased pulsing of her core on his sex. He smiled. Just when she cried out, he emptied himself inside her.

The applause from those left in front of him was loud, the calls ribald. He saw a flush of color across her back. She was embarrassed. That pleased him too. He had ideas about how to present her when it was her turn to act. He wasn't going to give her much practice. Didn't want her to become jaded. Given time and too much experience she would no longer portray the innocent that she was.

He held her hips down, unwilling to allow her to rise. He nipped the base of her neck. Sipped upward until he felt her move against him. To his surprise she had a passionate nature. Her body needed his attention again. Not here though. There would be no more show for the interviewees this evening.

Chandler set her away from him. Placed his hand on her butt. The muscle there was firm. A life of leisure had not been hers. After she stood, he saw her legs were sleek, firm. There were no little dimples on her thighs to mar the attraction. An active life would give her those attributes. An avid horsewoman would also have well-toned muscles. He had more questions about this woman who was going to bring him a fortune.

Winter Snow was not all she presented to him.

He would find out who she was. The information might garner a bit more money or blackmail. It was obvious to him, she hid something.

"Bertram. Take Miss Snow to my room. Gather her things from the room she was given. She'll be staying with me for a while."

She gasped, looking at him as if he'd gone mad. He saw her lips form the word no. Her lips thinned while she kept the words to herself. This was another pleasant thought. This girl didn't mind having sex with him...or...she didn't show her displeasure. Kept her face a mask. Nonetheless, Winter did not wish to stay in the same room with him.

Another puzzle to an anticipated discovery.

"Next!" Chandler called out.

There was an hour left before this evening's show would begin. This would be the third one over the course of the last two weeks. Every night there were more observers, more money exchanged hands. Chandler decided when he presented a new lady, the price of the tickets would double. For Winter Snow he would triple them. She was special. He watched Winter walk naked with Bertram out the door. She would be in his personal suite of rooms when he finished the work here. Indeed, he did look forward to the evening as well as his future dalliances with the intriguing lady.

Celine would be up first tonight. For Celine there would be no costume. For Winter he had all types of scripts running through his head. He thought he would present her as a debutante. Perhaps she could be at her first ball. Dressed in silks and satins. The gown would be cut very low, exposing the pretty tips of her breasts. He would have a slit in the front of her gown from her slim waist to the floor. As she danced, the audience would receive titillating glimpses of her most private places.

He sat back, watching the next hopeful with her two male partners. Chandler tapped his fingers together beneath his chin as he planned the interlude. There would be a dance. A seduction on a balcony. The ripping of clothing as she succumbed to her aristocratic suitor. He saw it all. She would pretend to dislike the attention. He would coerce, seduce, charm. He would be her suitor. Jimmy and Johnny would be the extras in the play. Perhaps there would be no tearing of the gown. He would enjoy disrobing her one garment at a time.

Chapter Seven

With slow precision, Ash drew the filmy gown over her arms. His hands skimmed her body. His action generated heat. Once she was free, he dropped the material to the floor. Watched her with the intense shimmering stare she was growing used to seeing. He smiled at her, giving her confidence. He touched the tips of her breasts. A light caress. Nothing more. Ran one hand down her side to her hip.

She gasped at the touch of his fingers. At the warmth they produced. Flames filled her. Shot through her as if she'd been hit by a lightning bolt. He had not begun yet. His eyes narrowed, a crease forming between his eyebrows. In his mind he was apologizing for the end of the ceremony. He didn't need to do so. Now that it was upon them, she was no longer terrified. All that needed to be accomplished would happen soon.

He prepared her for this. Taught her not to fear him. Taught her she should stand with him. He would always cherish her body. The night was chill. Cool air surrounded her. Touched upon her as she stood in front of Ash...her mate. Tightened the hard tips of her breasts. The night would be frigid. She looked to the bed. When they were through with this phase, the covers would give warmth. Ash would make love to her. When he penetrated her, he would cause pain once more. Unable to stop herself, she flinched. Her gaze shot to meet his. He seemed to understand.

The small fire gave out enough heat to keep a few of the chills at bay. He stood next to her. Brought her hands to the ties of his pants. She saw him swallow. His muscles were tense. A small tick at his jaw told her he was tense. Her nerves stretched thin.

Harris understood he wanted her to pull the strings. For a beat, she felt frozen in time. Her fingers fumbled with the ties. She did manage to pull. Watched the material fall away from his lean body which was now exposed to her view. He kicked them out of the way. She always admired the sight of him. Reaching out she wished she dared touch his sex. When she looked up to see his eyes darken even more, he nodded, giving her permission.

She shook her head. Could not touch. Not right now. Didn't know if she would hurt him. He was so large. So, intimidating. His cat, white with dark stripes, also intimidated. He brought her hand to meet his. Brought both lower until he showed her how to hold him. A few more seconds passed while she struggled with her misgivings. She sensed he wanted to begin the ceremony. Was eager to start the second phase of the night.

Without saying anything more, Ash brought her so she was pulled against his flesh. Her breasts touched upon his chest. His arousal nestled against her belly. She sighed, enjoying the feel of his body so close to hers. She never felt him this way. Never felt his sex against her stomach. When they slept together, she always lay her back against his front. He would hold one breast in his hand while they slumbered. Sometimes he would caress the crest. There were also occasions when she felt his arousal pulse against her. This was different.

Tonight, she would know this man intimately. He would mark her, claim her as his own. He would breach her maidenhead. Dear God, both situations would cause pain. Against him she trembled. Ash's fingers tightened their hold upon her. He stroked her back as if he understood what she realized. With a delicate touch his fingertips explored each vertebra.

She closed her eyes tight.

His hands were placed around her waist. Fingers tightened. Tension filled her. Anxieties strained. Heat pulsed within. She felt the calluses on his hands. He did work. Used his hands for many things. She'd seen him help build the corral holding the horses. He liked to chop wood. There were many other chores he did.

Absorbing the sounds of the night she tried to concentrate on what was about to happen. Ash told her his father taught him the chant, the words that would bring them together now as well as into the future. The letter...about Chandler. She couldn't remember if he told her or if she saw the words in his mind. While...if he didn't tell her, he must have forgotten to barricade his thoughts from her. She understood what his brother was doing...exploiting women for his personal gain. The women were willing.

So she was told.

Ash began. His voice soft. She heard his words. He repeated some while he proceeded. Didn't understand what he said. As the tempo increased so did the volume. His voice resounded in the small space. Echoed. Filled her with something undefinable. A sense of the past along with the future.

The sound was an ancient chant of sorts. Harris recognized a few Celtic words she'd heard before. Never understood what they meant. This was pagan in origin. A ritual passed on from the dawn of time through each generation of shifters. The ceremony had to be completed or the line would end.

She heard the word for earth, *talam*. The breath she inhaled caught in her throat. She choked. Coughed to clear the terror. He smoothed her back. Rested his hand upon her derriere. It was as if Ash shielded her. The realization he would do that, defend her, for the rest of their lives was assimilated into her. This man would always be there for her. Shelter her from harm. Despite his father's illness, he returned to the highlands to fetch her. She'd been an incredible idiot. A child would have reacted with more maturity than she had. He'd been disappointed in her. She accused him of things he didn't do, never listening to his explanation.

Something happened. Her body shook. She gripped him tighter. Her nails bit into his flesh. As if amused by something she didn't understand, he chuckled. She wanted to look up but didn't intend to do so. Her nose was pressed flat against his chest. She caught the spicy scent of him. Felt the rippling of his muscles. He was unique in every way. Different from every man she'd ever known.

With minimum energy, the small room began to move. To turn. To spin. Slow. Methodical. She bit down on her lip, feeling queasiness in her stomach. She sipped in a small gasp of air as she realized all was starting. This was the beginning. Her head whirled. A strange dizziness assailed her as her stomach churned. Nausea threatened. She leaned into him, pressing against him as if she could get closer. She held onto his arms. Her nails bit flesh. Needing him. Panic filled her. Swept through her bones. He never lied. There would be pain. When, she didn't know. Harris fought the fear. Reminded herself, he would shield as well as shelter her.

Stay calm. This is Ash. He won't do anything that isn't preordained.

He doesn't wish to cause pain. Don't let your nerves get the best of you. She talked to herself until she couldn't. Opening her eyes, she saw the solid wall of his chest. Her lashes fluttered against his skin. His hands tightened again giving her courage where there was none.

She absorbed what strength she could from his lean body, until it seemed her knees would give way. He would never allow her to fall. Ash would support her throughout the ceremony. She tried to hold anxiety at bay. Was unable to do so. A moan filtered with a soft sound from her lips. She moaned. His hand smoothed her back. The room continued to churn. The scene rolled. Heaved. Felt as if the ground beneath her feet moved in ever more undulating waves. Her hands on his arms tensed.

His voice grew deeper. The singing clearer. The words louder now than when he started. Seemed he was bent on a mission. All sounds flowed together into one. Harris sensed his confidence grew as the ritual continued. She was spinning now. What little she could see of the walls whirled into a blur before her eyes. Even with her eyes closed she had trouble remaining on her feet. He supported her.

What did he feel? She wished she would know. Wished he could tell her. Needed to understand his part in all this. Just as he asked her to tell him what she saw...how she felt...she craved the same information from him. Other than the ever-turning room along with her escalating emotions...the dizziness...the sickness, nothing more happened.

She began to calm. Her stomach quieted. The breaths she inhaled deepened as if the worst was finished.

Without warning, all she witnessed changed. She no longer saw his chest or felt the warmth of his skin. The scenes moved forward with lightning speed. All that she saw was new to her. Panoramas flashed through her head faster then faster still, everything a jumble. She shrieked. One hand settled on the back of her head, pressing her closer.

He chanted. The sound droned within her ears.

Harris felt as if she spun with blinding swiftness. Over and over again the world spun. She tumbled through space. The earth departed her feet. She gripped Ash as tight as she could manage. Harris felt an all-encompassing weakness burn through her. He held onto her as if she would slip to the hard floor beneath her at any time. She found she could not inhale.

The ground tilted, swayed. Rippled. Undulated. She sunk her nails into his shoulders in an attempt to remain upright. Her ears rung.

In her mind she saw...

Moving in motion that slowed and from the depth of the earth a white tiger rose. He stared at her as if he knew her. She shook her head. Tried to focus on the animal. He was... Just like Ash. Bold. Brave. Audacious. Magnificent in his power. Muscles rippled beneath the fur covering him. His roar reverberated in her ears. Loud. Masterful. She wanted to put her hands over them. Couldn't release her fingers from his arms. Couldn't let go of Ash. Behind the tiger a small black panther followed. Harris understood this pair were her and Ash in a different time. A different world. By watching, she had no sense of the era. The highlands looked the same. Rugged. Imposing. The panther trotted behind the male. The female was so much smaller. She looked delicate next to the tiger's bulk, the massive array of muscles. The huge tiger grinned. Stared at her as if he understood she was being watched. The uncanny sixth sense shifters possessed enveloped her.

The pair played. Cavorted as if there was no one near. *Just as we did in the ocean.* They would sense trouble. Rolled in the deep green grass. She pounced on top of him. Licked his face. His paws wrapped around her, rolling her over so he was on top of her. Staring down at her. On her back, she let him nuzzle her. The drama changed. Became more intense as the seconds ticked by. More moments passed while he wrestled with her. Once again, she lay on the ground. He was above her. Straddling her. Cleaned her fur with his tongue. Nuzzled her beneath her chin. He stood. The female shadowed the male doing whatever he decided. They would communicate in their heads just as she did with Ash. To Harris, the two seemed as if they were one with each other. They acted in unison. Appeared to understand what the other would do. Would she ever feel so much a part of Ash that she would know him that well? Would they ever exist as one?

She wondered if the panther held any control over the tiger. If the male would do what the female asked. A small smile formed. Her thought was true. Harris recalled all the times her sisters-in-law received their wishes from their mates. Hawk along with Houston would cater to their mate's needs, desires. Whims. She would have to see if the same would hold true with Ash.

Jerked by the rolling of the land, she set her cheek against Ash's chest. Touched his flesh with her tongue. Tried to inhale a sip of air. Caught his unique scent. Heard the strong, resilient beating of his heart. Knew he was concerned for her.

Without a doubt Harris knew what he wanted from her, from this ceremony. She only suspected before. Ash would expect her to tell him about this scene she witnessed. Would want to know in detail what happened. Though, in this, she felt as if she was an interloper. That she was spying on two people who would soon be engaged in intimate behavior. Even when she closed her eyes, she saw them.

The tiger along with the panther; were the two of them in a different time? The pair shifted. Naked, they stood in front of each other. The woman had long dark hair. Her eyes a silver blue. The Frasier eyes, McKenna eyes. Eyes of Clan Chaton. Her body, perfectly formed, caught the attention of the male. He responded to the sight of the beauty of his naked mate. He reached out. Circled her neck with his hand. Brought her to him, possession in the tenor of his eyes. His hair was light in color, appearing so much the same as Ashton's. His eyes brilliantly blue, deep and dark. He was large, well-muscled. Tall, so very much taller than the woman. Just as Ash was so much taller than she. He dwarfed her.

The man's finger beneath her chin, he beckoned her to come closer to him. He was aroused. It was obvious he wanted her. She swept her tongue across her bottom lip. He bent to kiss her, touched her lips with his. Framed her mouth. Tasted. Savored. Explored. She gripped him tighter, running her hands along his arms then twining her fingers in his long hair. Harris heard the purr of sensual delight. The woman wanted more. Standing on the tips of her toes, it seemed she wished to get closer to him. The hard tips of her breasts pushed against the man's chest.

He tossed his head back and laughed with delight. His hand rose to touch her breast. His palm circled the tip. He picked her up then into his arms. Twirled with her. Set her back on her feet. He reached out his hand for her, beckoning her to come with him. She followed.

The scene changed. The earth still whirled, twisted, slanted until she could no longer remain on her feet. She felt the dip in the earth. Stumbled.

Found she was upon her knees still pressed against Ash who followed her down. She wished she could have watched more of the couple...then she understood why the scene ended. They would make love. No one would wish to have another watch them when they were intimate.

What was happening here was far too complicated. The earth stopped moving. Harris brought in a deep lungful of air. Exhaled with a soft sigh against his chest. Relief filled her. She breathed deep again. Her stomach ceased to churn with the dizzying whirl of the ground beneath her feet.

The ceremony was over. That was not too bad. She didn't feel the bite of his claws. They were on their knees. Ash urged her to stand. Helped her when she faltered. Held onto her when she would sink back to the ground. Harris found she was very weak. Discovered each breath of air she tried to inhale came at an alarming price.

Still, the chanting continued. The words changed. Slow. Measured. Deep. Picked up speed just as he began again. Harris heard the Celtic word for wind, *gaoth*. They weren't finished. What she thought she saw had been an illusion.

Cold air, warm air, whirled around them. The winds touched upon her flesh. Heated her in places then chilled her with the frost of its touch. Her hair swirled around her, teasing in places, wrapping around Ash's hands, clinging to his fingers. She found herself chilled to the bone, shivering with cold. She held tight onto his arms. Ice seemed to slither down her spine. Wind appeared to come from the north. from the glaciers close to the north pole. They were once more standing on the wild craigs. Heather. Pillars. The land swept with tuffs of lavender broom. She caught the scent of the wind. Saw wild highland cows in a valley. Watched elk wander over the rugged ground, foraging.

Harris recalled days where cold winds swept across the highlands. Days when one needed to take shelter or they would freeze. Frost lay on the ground. Snow began to fall. The white flakes were beautiful. Whiteness coated the heather as well as the barren ground along the rocks. A waterfall was iced over. Rocks below the falls were coated with ice.

She shivered, huddling closer to Ash, searching for his warmth. Clinging to him. Bone deep the cold reached for her. Harris waited for the next vision. Assumed she would see more. Would be gifted with the sight of another couple. They would make love. Show each other the depths of their feelings for each other. Winds continued to swirl and shift around her. Her fingers along with her toes felt numb.

This time she recognized the black panther first. The cat was alone. The female stood on the top of a cliff, searching below. Harris understood she searched for the tiger. Her mate. She felt danger surrounding her. Understood this woman would need to run for her life. Where was he? Why wasn't he with his mate so he could protect her from the demon stalking her?

The sensations ripping through her were not good. Her stomach heaved in fear for the panther. There was something terribly wrong. Harris didn't understand what that could be...nonetheless what was happening here wasn't right. Pressure stretched her nerves to the breaking point. She needed to cry out. To warn the panther. Scream at her to run.

Helpless. Bereft of power Harris could do nothing to right what was so powerful here. A man appeared. A Sassenach soldier stood behind the panther riding slowly toward her. This man meant her harm. Fear tumbled through Harris. Tears slid down her cheeks. She didn't want to see this. Death hovered. Threatened to rip this woman from her mate. Harris felt the female's fear.

Where was the tiger?

Run!

The command terrified her just as the bellowed command startled the panther. Harris felt as if he yelled at her. Thought surely she should obey the directive. As if Ash sensed the deep fear, he held her closer.

Run as fast as you can. Don't stop. Don't stop until you can run no farther. Go to the cave. Hide. Wait for me.

The devil knew she would not be able to run far. True, the panther could race sleek and true for a short way. If she didn't find a place to hide, she would falter. He sent her to a cave. There must be one close.

The next man she saw rode a huge black stallion. He also was dressed in the despised red uniform of the English. It had to be the panther's mate. He came to save her. To warn her that danger threatened. Ash had been that person. More than once, Ash saved her brothers and cousins. What was she doing alone? Why wasn't he with her? Had she done something foolish? Why did she shift? Surely, this was not taking care. Her mate was an officer. He warned the man to take heed. She heard the other tell him about the panther. That he would capture her. There were wanted posters for shifters. Money to be gained. He needed the money along with the prestige of capturing one of the illusive shifters that populated the highlands. The man told him the tale about shifters was old wives' tales. Nothing more.

Harris found she was holding her breath. Waited for the officer to dissuade the man. Saw the anger in the soldier. Felt the greatest relief when the man turned his horse before heading down the hill.

The officer let out a very sharp, very loud whistle. The sound had to be part of his communication to his mate. After that she heard the caution in the Sassenach's voice while he spoke to his mate.

Shift. Dress. I will come to you. If you are in the cave at the bottom of this hill, stay right where you are. If not, tell me where I can find you. You must hurry. I'm not at all certain this man believed my story. He was positive he saw a panther...a shifter.

She saw him close his lashes over dark blue eyes. He was both disturbed as well as angry with his mate. Harris knew the woman did something stupid. Could hear the words that he chastised her with as if Ash was reprimanding her. She had been caught swimming at the loch. Been seen naked there. Her mate was angry.

With unhurried meticulousness he turned his horse to skirt the edge of the cliff. A few moments later, she watched his back as he descended a narrow path. Harris assumed he rode to the cave. Against her will, she held her breath, waiting. Wondering. She didn't know if she would see anything more of this pair. Hoped the female did what her mate told her. Harris recalled when she shifted to run from Ash. He'd been angry with her that night. Furious that she'd been so foolish to put herself at risk. All he wanted was to keep her safe from herself.

What had the woman done wrong? If she'd been caught out by herself, he wouldn't know where her clothing could be found. He must have had something to do with the disaster that almost occurred. He'd been able to come to her. To find a means to dissuade her would be captor. She would not be able to see the finish to this story. Though she felt them together. Felt their heart and soul merge as one. She rubbed her cheek on Ash's chest. Found she was reassured by the strong thump of his heart.

Winds changed. They were warmer. She felt the images in front of her transform. The heat lulled her. She thought she might sleep. Comfort assailed her. The scene was cozy. Warm. Yes, very warm. Hot. When the images cleared, she saw the woman dressed, standing in front of a fire. Her hands were reaching out as if she wanted to warm the frozen fingertips.

Even though the man entered, a deep scowl on his handsome features, she smiled at him. Held her hand out to touch him. To wait for his touch. She knew he would be furious with her. Understood he rescued her.

I should hog-tie you. Keep you tied to our bed. You had no right to risk your life in such a fashion. If I hadn't sensed your fear, the very panic within your heart, you might well be caged as a specimen for the wealthy aristos in London to watch. How dare you risk yourself in such a stupid impulsive fashion?

I wasn't going to get caught. Everything was in control. I could out run as well as out think that despicable man. Didn't need your rescue. I can take care of myself.

With a soft curse, he tugged her into his arms. Framed her mouth with his. The kiss was deep and long. When he looked up, pushing her straying hair behind her ears, he spoke. You do know you are pregnant. You must not take risks with our child.

She gasped. Pushed back from him. Her eyes wild with happiness. Her thoughts were on her womb. On the beginning of new life.

When I touch your belly, I feel the babe inside you. The boy is a little shifter. He didn't like his mother putting herself into trouble. He called to me. How do I keep you from finding trouble? You cannot fight the entire British army. You should not have been where you were. What? Did you mean to lead that man over a cliff? That would have been impossible.

He peeled her clothing from her. Her breasts were bared to his gaze. She touched his chest. Fiddled with the brass buttons. Staring at her, he touched the hard tips. He bent to suckle her breast to tug the globe deep into his mouth. The picture went black. There were two couples she could tell Ash about. Would there be more?

The warmth from the fire in the cave increased. Heated...an inferno blazed around her. Touched upon her. She burned. She felt as if her skin was scorched from the flames she saw rising around them. She tried to push away from Ash. To escape the searing heat. The red-hot fire surrounding her. He held her close. His voice deeper...harder than before.

Crushed against him, she could not move. Could not escape the fire, *aingeal*. The flames. Fire licked all about her.

Chants. More chants. His voice husky. Hot where his breath touched upon the flesh of her body. Red painted the walls of the structure. Flames danced, leapt high. She gasped as the heat intensified within her. She was on fire, standing within an inferno.

On her knees one more time, she bit into Ash's shoulders as her body cried out with its need to escape. What had been cozy as well as comfortable turned to searing pain. Who would she see now? A witch burned at the stake? She could not bear to see something so horrible. Would this woman's mate save her? Rush through the flames to snatch her from death before she suffocated from the smoke? She prayed that would happen. Didn't want to think that in an earlier time she burned to death.

Ash soothed her, stroking her hair, hushing her cries of fear. The mantra sounded ever clearer. That was before the words began again. What she saw was nothing so dire as a witch's execution amidst flames. A small hut burned. Went up in flames while other crofters rushed to douse the fire. Perhaps this scene was just as terrible. A woman staggered from the home. Her skirts were caught up in the fire. Flames licked against her skin. She screamed. Began to race toward the tall man riding toward her.

Don't run. Drop to the ground. Now! Stop where you are. Fall down. I'll be there. Put out the flames. Do it now. Roll on the ground.

I... The woman stared at the man issuing the command, her eyes wide with terror. Harris thought she might continue to run. The female did as he said. In one swift movement, he was off his horse. His jacket covered her. He beat at the flames with his hands putting them out. The woman cried out. Pain caused the woman to faint.

Harris breathed in a swift rush of air. Relieved. Let the oxygen out in a slow glide of air. When they rose, she saw little damage was done to the woman. Her skirt was scorched. Ragged around the edges. She was safe.

He held her. Kissed her on the lips as if it was the first time. Ran his hands through her hair. Seemed he wished to check out every part of her.

He led her into the woods. A crystal-clear stream rushed down from the nearby craigs. Sunlight shone through the swaying leaves touched by a gentle breeze. They stood together in a small space. Harris saw she was shaking. Her arms were wrapped around her body. Eyes wide, simmering steel-gray she stared at him. Red curls bounced around her face. She heard the Celtic word for water, *uisce*.

No one will dare follow. We will be alone. I need to hold you. You need to cool the flesh that might be red from the fire. Need to see if your injuries are worse than I believe.

You are so sure? Always certain. Don't wish for anyone except for you to see me without clothing.

The need to laugh at her sarcasm assailed her. The man was so much like Ash. Certain in all things. This was not the time to laugh. The couple were about to make love. The man undressed the woman. Swept her up then into his arms. He strode knee high into the stream flowing in front of them. He tossed her into a pool of water, laughing. She hit the water. Liquid splashed over her then onto him.

The woman came up sputtering. Angry. Her brows creased together. She slapped water his way. He laughed again. Shed his clothing then dove. He came up beside her. Held her within his embrace before capturing her lips with his.

Harris didn't know what happened or when. Water dripped from her. Doused the searing flames that had seemed to consume her. She was cold now, shivering dripping in Ash's arms. The floor met her bum. She could no longer kneel. There was no strength left in her body. She tried to recall the three couples. They were all so much alike.

Now she was sitting. Cradled in his strong arms, her cheek still pressed against his chest. While she traveled back in time, he remained here sheltering her, protecting her. Supporting her. Something told her he'd not yet claimed her.

The visions vanished.

Opening her eyes was impossible just as moving seemed to be. Her breathing was slow. Even. She felt the tips of his fingers as they ran along her spine, touching against each vertebra. His hand rested on the curve of her hip. Sometime, she didn't know when he pulled his cape around her.

It is time.

What?

I'm sorry.

Before her eyes, his hands changed to huge paws. The paws of a tiger. His claws long. Sharp. She put her hands up to stop him. Tried to draw back. Shaking. Trembling. Fear rushed. No! She'd forgotten what the ceremony was all about. He had to claim her. She gulped a twinge of air. His nails sunk into her shoulders. She cried out. Screamed. Her world became black. Pain slashed across her shoulders. Burned. Seared as the fire could not. Harris fainted.

Black darkness rose up to meet her. Just as the first encounter, she felt as if she was spinning in a void. There was nothing except black in front of her. No light. No feelings save emptiness surrounding her.

Still, she heard the soft cadence of his voice. Whispering close to her ear. Telling her all would be alright. Until the pain vanished nothing would be good. Over then over again he apologized for the anguish he never wished to cause. For the stinging...left to him to give. *Wake up. Open your beautiful eyes for me. I need to see you. Need to know I've not done more damage.*

The time it took for her to see the candles flickering in the structure, she didn't know. Shivering, frightened, she was sitting on his thighs. He rocked her as if she was a child. His hum soothed her. Brought back thoughts of his hands touching her in the gentlest manner. She moved against him. Pressed close for comfort. Cuddled as she absorbed the heat of his body. The fire was burning low. Embers crackled then spit. He would need to add wood or they would be chilled to the bone.

Ash lifted her chin. Touched his knuckles along her neck. He smiled. His voice soft when he spoke to her. "How are you?" *What did you see? No, it's too soon for you to talk. I can wait. Do you want wine? Something to put in your stomach? Do you want me to hold you?*

Harris blinked a few times. Needed to make him feel better. She didn't know how. Turned to sarcasm in hopes he would understand. "My shoulders sting where some heathen savage sunk his claws into me," she told him, trying for a *wee* bit of humor. She understood he was hurting. With her words, Ash grimaced. She felt his anguish as if the pain was hers. Harris didn't intend to lie to him to ease his fears. *I apologize. I should not have said those words that might increase any guilt you might feel. I realize you don't wish to hurt me. There can be no remorse or shame in something that is so essential and fundamental to our clans to our lives. The pain is fading. As to food or drink...not until I can sit up by myself. For now, the next few minutes you will have to hold on to me. Seems the result of all this is that I've no strength left to me. My energy is drained. I've no reserves.*

"I'm so very sorry. If I could bear the pain for you, I would." He stroked her arm. Touched her shoulders. Lingered over the spots where his claws dug into her flesh. "When you feel as if you've the strength to move, I can carry you to the bed. Give you something to eat to drink. Tindly has put together a feast for our enjoyment once you've recovered from the ordeal. We've wine when you feel up to sipping liquid. I will need to wash the blood from you. The wounds will heal. You will have tiny scars there for the rest of your life. They mark you as mine. I cannot regret that small fact. Even though I'm sorry for the hurt, I would never change what we did. You're mine now in every way."

"Was I unconscious for long? I saw the flames. Felt the inferno burning around me. Thought... Was doused by water." She looked at herself. "I should be dripping with water. Felt as if I was tossed into a pool. Did you dry me while I was lost in that black void?" *The other woman did land in the deepest part of the pool before she was joined by her mate. They played. Lobbed cool refreshing water at each other. The two laughed. They made love in the stream.*

Ash touched the tip of her nose with his fingertip. "No water here except in the pitcher. I will clean your wounds." *You saw someone...our kindred spirits. He tossed his mate into the water? Clothing and all?*

I can't recall if he took her gown off first. It had been burned. Seared by flames. Ragged. I should start from the beginning, not the end.

However you like.

Keeping the cloak tucked around her, he brought her to the bed. Set her down so she leaned against the backboard. She was trembling as well as fatigued. Harris felt as if she'd run for miles upon miles. He poured her a large glass of wine. Handed it to her. She sipped. Sipped again then drank long...deep. The renewal of energy would be slow.

Ash left her bedside. While she watched, Ash poured water into a basin. Dipped a cloth into the water. After he sat down beside her, he pushed the cloak behind her shoulder. With careful strokes, he meticulously washed the blood away. When he finished, he tossed the rag. With a soft plop, the material fell into the basin.

She set the glass down. Wished to be clear headed for a little while. She needed to breathe. Gain strength. Wished to slow the rapid pounding of her heart. Ash sat down behind her cradling her so he could be closer to her. He kissed the top of her head. Rested his chin there. She leaned her head against his chest, concentrating on each breath. He wanted to hear what happened to her. She wished she could tell him all he needed to learn.

Recounting anything at the moment was difficult. Thinking was near impossible. She closed her eyes, going over the events from the instant she saw the tiger rise up from the earth. His roar such a loud bellow it caused her to tremble. Harris imagined Ash's roar would be just as terrifying. Just as bold. The sound would horrify anything in its path. If she heard the roar before she came to know him, she would have fled.

She breathed in, willing her body to continue to heal. "It all started with the rolling of the earth," Harris began in a soft tremulous voice. She told him all of what happened with the first encounter. How the two loved each other. She felt the love...the caring...bone deep. They played together in their cat form. The male licked her as all cats do, cleaning her fur. He was so large. So very gentle with his mate. There were so many things she wondered about. If he would touch her while he was a cat and she was human. A heated shiver swept her. In his cat, he would still be Ash. Still the same one she wished to be with. That was for another day.

His arms were around her. Settled just below her breasts. Pushing against them. Reminding her they would make love soon. She placed her hands on his forearms. He wanted more. She needed to give him all he required.

"I saw you...us three times. The second time all wasn't fine. Not like the first sighting. The woman, his mate, did something wrong. Something he didn't like. That time reminded me of the instant you found I'd shifted.

You came after me. You were furious with me. When all that happened, I didn't understand. The way you took me from my home, I was angry too."

"Yes, I was furious with you," Ash agreed. "Couldn't believe you could be so reckless as to put your life at risk. In the highlands, in the open it could be deadly to shift. Even then we were being watched. The observer was another shifter."

Ignoring his words, she continued. "A Sassenach soldier saw the female. He meant to capture her. The other man, who was also Sassenach, sent her running to a cave. No, not our cave. Not the McKenna cave. Somehow, he dissuaded the man. I don't know how. When the images caught up with them, it was just before they would make love."

"You saw us more than twice? I didn't know that was possible."

She smiled at his question. Lightly, she ran her fingers along his arm. "The third time, wind swirled around me. I was cold then hot. The images were horrific. A small crofters hut was burning. A young woman stumbled from the home, her skirts on fire. He put the flames out then took her to a pool. He tossed her into the pond then followed. That was when I was soaked. I felt as if I was also catapulted into the water."

His bark of laughter surprised her. "What did you do to get tossed into the pool? You were trouble then too?"

Too weak to hit him as she wished. She snorted her displeasure. "Don't believe I did anything wrong. Perhaps just in the wrong place at the wrong time. What happened might not have been my fault. The hut was in flames. I've no idea why. My skirts caught on fire. You now know as much as I."

"You find trouble wherever you go," he repeated seemingly for her benefit.

"Not now, Ash. I'm too tired. Don't wish to argue."

She drank more wine. Began to feel stronger. He fed her a piece of cheese. His fingers touched her lips. Her tongue.

~ * ~

Going back to the start of the ceremony, Ash recalled the innate sensuality of the ritual. There was nothing more stimulating than feeling her small body pressed against his. He couldn't touch her except to hold her up. Even when he felt the tips of her breasts, the hollow of her stomach, the soft roundness of her little butt constrained tight against his frame, he could not touch. Her legs were forced against his.

He could do nothing except soothe whatever fears she might have. He fought his emotions, the mercuric need she generated within. She was soft everywhere he was hard. Trying to soothe her when she trembled, when she shook, he ran his hands along her back, down the elegant column of her spine. There were times he caressed her bottom. Held her even closer. Wished deep within his soul this would end.

One time, she bit him with her small white teeth. Her nails dug into his shoulders leaving tiny little marks. For the situation at hand, he thought that was somewhat appropriate. She didn't draw blood as he did.

With all his heart, he despised that moment when his claws grew. When he pressed them into her soft flesh. Remembering sent his mind reeling. Her cry of anguish turned his stomach inside out. At the very thought, he shuddered. Drank the wine that was meant for courage. He stroked her hair. Wound his fingers in the silken length. Tugged until she turned to look at him. He needed to see her eyes. The sweet flush of her skin. After he claimed her, when the ceremony ended, she was pale. Her face bleached white as new fallen snow. He feared for her. When she fainted, his heart catapulted inside his chest.

Ash was pleased when her eyes opened, when she told him so much in vivid detail about their lives in the past. He imagined there might be more flashes of the previous times together when they made love later tonight. He hoped so. Learning about the past was always important to the future. Now, all he could do would be to tantalize as well as tease her body with the promise of pleasure. So far, that was all he'd ever done.

Holding her through the ritual hardened every part of him. His thoughts sped to more pleasurable pursuits with his mate. He hoped tonight would bear fruit. As far as he was concerned the sooner she started to increase the better. He promised himself as well as his father heirs. His father hoped to hold a grandchild before he passed on. He meant to do his best to make that happen.

He was ready to claim her innocence. To breach her maidenhead.

Tonight, she would be his wife in every way possible. In every conceivable way. After that there would be no more pain. Only pleasure would follow. He hoped they would be able to spend the next week in bed, getting to know each other better. Learning all that pleased as well as displeased. He would make love to her as often as she was willing.

Patience was what was needed now. The ordeal weakened her. Sapped her strength. She needed food. Wine. He pressed another piece of cheese to her mouth. Her lips touched upon his fingers. After that he shared a slice of apple with her. Trailed the slice along her lip. Followed the path with his tongue, tasting the juice of the apple. The food was good. The taste of his mate better. He found that he was hungry for food, but more famished for her. He'd waited so long. Their joining was more than a year in the making.

He recalled the one wedding he attended at the McKenna keep with amusement. To all in the room, it was obvious the groom seduced the bride during the feast. Touched her with intimate precision beneath the massive table that hid what he did from view. Nothing could hide the enchantment of the bride's expression, the pleasure. The ecstasy he gifted her with. The groom caressed the softest hottest wettest part of her. All the men as well as the women knew what he did in front of all the guests.

That scene occurred the night before he left to return to London. Hawk's wedding to Maisie. She was adorable in her discomfort. Perhaps when they feasted for the second time at the McKenna keep, he would proceed in the same manner. That night there would be no more pain for his bride. Only pleasure. Even though the clan ceremony was different, he'd claimed his mate. He'd breached her maidenhead. All would be pleasure.

He harbored such intense feelings for Harris. Because her father understood the expediency of the situation, he'd been allowed to attend the feast. His presence there was not appreciated by most of the clan. Trust was not there. To them he was Sassenach. Highlanders would never trust an English soldier. There was too much animosity between them.

Putting his stamp of ownership on his mate, the next day he seduced Harris in the small mossy glen where she led him. He'd been leaving. Never expected Harris to chase after him. He touched her. Kissed her. Could not resist a more intimate taste of her. She was so aroused. He could have taken her in that out-of-the-way clearing. Just as Harris didn't want to be left to bear the consequences of their loving, he didn't wish that for her either. A babe out of wedlock wasn't something he intended for the woman he loved. At that time, he knew he would be gone at least a year. If she became pregnant, she might never forgive or forget.

So, in the time he had with her, he gave her a woman's pleasure. Taught her passion. Reveled in the strength of her hungry desire. Watched her eyes glaze over while she splintered into a thousand pieces. She cried out his name at the culmination of their interlude. Tonight, he would watch her eyes when she climaxed. First, he sighed with wistfulness, she needed to regain her strength. He must be patient.

He would test. Tease. Wait for her to respond. Ash ran his hands along the top of one thigh. Her legs were folded beneath her as she sat sideways against him. Reached to her ankle. Touched upon her toes. Found a tender spot behind her knee. Against him she changed positions. Her sweet rounded jewels pressed against his chest. Because of the cool night air, her nipples pebbled.

She exhaled; the sound whisper soft against the silence of the night.

He brought his hand higher. Set his fingers on her belly. Stretched them so they touched her hip bones. Dipped into her navel. Followed a path higher to circle the rouged aureole. One more time, she moved against his body. Enticed. Seduced without understanding how those little movements created a tempest of need within him. A little ripple of a sound gave him good reason to continue the sweet seduction of his mate. Harris gained strength with each passing second. This evening they would begin the quest for a son or daughter, a grandchild for his father. After him, the next Earl of Greenwood.

Before he entered into her warmth, he wanted her to climax. To feel the ecstasy she'd known one other time. Needed her to embrace as much pleasure as possible. Immense pleasure would vanquish the hurt from her mind when she remembered this night. He would much rather see the pleasure in her eyes than the next hurt she would encounter. Didn't wish to hear her cry out with pain, only ecstasy. See the silver glide of tears slipping down her cheeks.

Touching her chin, he turned her to face him. Brought his lips to hers. With a butterfly kiss, he touched upon her closed lips. After she opened for him, he explored deeper, longer. Heat from her small form ignited him. Emotion flared inside. His blood thundered through his ears. She created a tempest of yearning. His hand ran along her shoulder touching upon the red marks left there by him, by his claws. He scowled.

As he bent to touch each mark, he sipped, kissed, laved where the redness stood out, where the sight yelled out that Harris was his though eternity. Reverence caused him to touch again, to soothe with his tongue. His kisses were meant to make amends for the pain caused by the tradition of the coterie.

She touched her hand upon his cheek. Her eyes were deep pools of silver. He saw moisture glistening. "It's alright. The marks no longer hurt. As you told me the pain would vanish." With her hand settled on his chest, she ran her palm across the breadth. Touched upon him. She must have felt the shuddering of his body. His blood pounded with fierce intensity. His head reeled. He heard the loud rush in his ears.

Ash touched upon her lips. Kissed her along the column of her neck. Her breasts, he cupped in his hand. Touched the pebbled hardness with his thumb. Ran his hand along her torso, to her legs as she whimpered softly. A soft mewl filtered into the air.

Setting her between his legs, she stretched out. She seemed content in her nudity. That pleased him. He fed her a piece of ham topped with cheese. Handed her the glass of wine she set on the table. Ash sipped his own. Watched. Waited. He brought her legs over his. Moved his hands across her thighs then higher to seduce her breasts. Palmed the tips. Tugged.

Following his example, she trailed one finger along his thigh. Then the other one. With each passing second, she grew stronger. Bolder. She could be brazen, this woman of his. The thought delighted him. Everything about her tonight thrilled him. He stopped her roving fingers. Didn't want to climax before he gave her pleasure. He'd been aroused, in need of her throughout the entire ceremony. Nothing had changed. He looked forward to the rest of the evening. She swiveled in his arms. Her breasts touched against his chest. He captured her lips with his. Tasted the mint on her breath mingled with the wine.

Passion as well as a deep intense hunger was what he hoped to draw from her tonight. To proceed with her deflowering too fast might ruin his plans. Yet...he fought hard to suppress his increasing desire. He slipped one finger between her legs. Touched. Caressed. Discovered the soft petals hidden there. Heard her gasp of surprise or pleasure he hoped. Found the small jewel that would bring her ecstasy. He hoped she remembered the delight. Raw hunger filled him. Felt the clenching of her muscles. Desire so penetrating she couldn't deny. She moved to give him easier access. Opening. Ash sensed they approached that point where he could not hold back.

Harris was hot.

Wet.

With each gentle caress, her hunger seemed to flame. She arched against him. Coiled. Thrust her breast outward as if demanding more attention. The tight hard crests tempted. Enticed. A wild air echoing from her into him scorched. His mouth descended on hers again, raw now with her hunger as well as need, demanding, expecting so much more in return. Her hands lay on his legs, fingers curling against his skin, stretching then curling again. Her nails raked down his thighs as she gave in to raw hunger. With her siren's call she lured him. Beckoned all that he was. His restraint dissolved.

Ash kissed her until he had his fill of the sweetness of her mouth. Kissed her then kissed her again until her breaths followed in short delightful spurts. Her breasts moved with each breath of air she attempted. He delighted in the tiny little noises she made. Sounds of a woman pleasured. He kept his eyes focused upon her...on her eyes. As he did, he lowered himself to capture a breast within the palm of his hand, cradling the soft globe, stroking the sides, running his thumb with tenderness over the hardened tip. Deep in the back of her throat, she whimpered. He needed to taste. Savor. Relish as well as cherish. He needed a slow hand. Didn't wish to rush this first time with her.

Her breath caught. Froze. She ran her tongue across her lips. Moisture left behind stared back at him. Briefly he tasted. Still, he kept his gaze on her, on her eyes until he closed his mouth over her nipple, teasing the tip with his tongue, swirling it around the crest. His teeth raked across the hard bud. His lips surrounded the peak with the fullness of his mouth, sucked upon it until the nipple hardened. Pebbled. Stood elongated and damp when he pulled away. She appeared astonished at the change in her body.

A sweet siren's sound escaped the back of her throat. Her nails bit into his flesh. Harris closed her eyes. Her face gained color. She was recuperating. She still trembled. Quivered. Was weak. Nonetheless, every second brought her closer to her full strength. He brought his lips to her other breast. Tarried there in the same manner with the same attention he gave to the first one. He turned her so she now lay on her back. Ash rose above her, looking down on her delicate features. He moved his legs between her thighs. She reached for his shoulders. Ran her hands there. Tarried around his neck. Swept her fingers through his hair.

While he seduced and charmed with his mouth, he brought his hand to the curve of her hip, to explore her stomach. He stroked her, hip, belly, thighs. He pushed her leg apart. She was open to him. Damp where he wished. Hot where he touched. As he swept his finger into the hot wet petals of her sex, she gulped. Pushed. Her nails dug into his arms. She closed her eyes. He kissed the lids...the tip of her nose. When she opened them again, he saw the hungry desire. The passion shimmering in her eyes.

She arched. Whimpered.

He parted her. Stroked her. Enraptured. Sought out the most evocative, dark places then delved deeper, with slow intimate care. He tested, pushing a finger then two into her core. She was tight. Small. He would fill her. Touch her womb. That first day in the glen, he didn't stroke her core. Only the tempting pearl resting with such enticement at the apex of her thighs. Tonight, he felt the kiss of her body on his fingers as he moved them in then out. Again. Slow. Faster. Needed to stretch her. Felt the proof of her innocence. He continued the slow assault while he watched her eyes. The slant of her mouth. The small crease in her forehead. Her lips parted. She tossed her head. She gripped his arms. Nails biting into him. As he moved lower with his kisses, her fingers wove into his hair. Raked across his scalp.

Touching her warmth, her innocence, the movement of her body in response created all the fires of hell within him. Ash found himself fighting the demons clawing at him from the inside out, the raw hunger for her he'd known for over a year. It seemed he wanted...needed her forever. In his dreams, he'd relived that single moment when her orgasm took over her. Dreamed of the next time. The next time was before him now. He stroked her everywhere. Kissed all of her. Reveled in the raging passion he brought forth with each caress. Every stroke. Kiss. Touch. Taste her body vibrated with raw passion.

He found himself fighting the power of his hunger for her, the ache in his loins. The tempest rampant inside. He was going to bring this to its proper conclusion. Before he stole her innocence, gave her more pain, he would give her pleasure, the ecstasy she'd known once before.

"Look at me," Ash spoke to her knowing the discomfort, the ache was all caused by him. There would be more to come. He loathed the fact. Despite the abhorrence of the situation, had to go through with this.

When she did meet his gaze with the silver-steel of her own her eyes were huge, shimmering and questioning. Luminous in passion. Dazed slightly as she fast approached that place where her body would splinter with its pleasure. He smiled realizing at that moment all would be well between them. There would be much more to experience in their lives. They still had issues to contend with. He prayed in time she would come to fully trust in his word. Understood, she still harbored doubts.

He smiled. Touched. Lowered his lips to her, again tasting wine and mint along with the raw passion she couldn't conceal. She rose to meet him. Her hips pushed against him. Parted her lips to accept him deep inside. Their tongues dueled for supremacy. He sought the depth of all her secrets. He knew then she wanted him. Perhaps as much as he yearned for her. Inhaled the flash of her breath before his mouth devoured hers. Savored the urgency seeming to grow within her. Fought his need to impale himself deep inside the velvet channel of her core. He continued the slow seduction of her with his fingers. Hoped he stretched her and readied her for his intimate invasion. In then out, again and again he brought her higher. Longed to thrust inside.

The first stirring of her climax fluttered across her stomach, milked his fingers that were still deep inside, muscles clenching. He heard the soft gasp. For a few seconds, she held her breath. The moan meeting his tongue as he deepened both caresses. All left him breathless with need. She evoked strong, intense passions. Her hot sheathe kissed, throbbed against his fingers that were deep inside her moving with a languid pace.

Her tension grew. She heaved, seeking. Seeking...

Relax, my love. Let it happen. This time I won't hurt you. Only pleasure to feel. Don't be afraid of your passion. Desire. I hunger for you as well. It will be just like last time. Violent pleasure. The fierce shattering of your body. The moon and the stars will all be yours to feel...to see...let me rock you.

Her eyes widened. Darkened. A deep blue rim formed around the silver. She cried out as violent, fierce sensations took over her body. Her hips bucked. Her fingers dug into his arms. "Ash." Her head moved wildly from side to side as she let her body convulse with the sheer pleasure of all the hunger invading her body.

Moving with lightning speed so she would have no time to fall from the plateau he orchestrated, he withdrew his fingers. The pleasure humming still with her. Not allowing for time to ease the pulsing of her body, Ash eased his sex into her. She was so bloody small. Tight. His jaw grated together. Sheer willpower kept him from a quick deep thrust. Her moisture rained down upon him. Again, Ash gritted his teeth, holding back his hunger. He met the barrier within her tight sheathe.

Now.

He thrust into her. Stopped dead when she screamed. Deep inside he felt the quivering of her pain. The clenching of her muscles in an effort to push him away. His stomach churned and rolled while she pressed on his shoulders. Struggled against him. Frantic for him to withdraw. She hit his shoulder. Bucked her hips in an effort to get rid of him. She pushed him deeper. He touched her womb. Tears slipped from her eyes to slide down her cheeks. He placed his forehead against hers.

I'm sorry. The words seemed to mean nothing. The pain of his entry was still there. He didn't want to continue with the apologies. Ash understood she would rally. Knew in a few seconds she would find pleasure in his arms. He waited. Held still. Rose above her. Braced himself on his forearms. Watched her. She opened her eyes. He placed a hesitant kiss on her forehead.

As she began to relax, he felt the tightening of her muscles around his sex. Knew when she no longer felt the pain. Her body acknowledged the desire. She arched. Whimpered. He captured her lips with his. Nipped. Laved. He kissed her with light strokes then hard. Kissed her until he felt her complete submission, her heated response. His fingers smoothed across the tips of her breasts. She curved against him. Her body rounded upward. Moaned. With gentleness he continued the smooth assault on her senses.

I no longer hurt. Ash...I'm fine. I want you again. Want to feel the crest of the wave you create. Need to reach that pinnacle of desire. Want to soar to the sun then fall with gentle ease to be held by you.

He understood the soft pleas. Control he prided himself with vanished. He thrust again then again, slow then fast. Changed the rhythm. Rocked her between his thighs. Brought her with him. She was clinging to him. Small teeth bit into his shoulder. Her fingers raked into his hair. Her body met each thrust of his own. When he felt the fragmenting of her body, he thrust one more time. Hard. Deep. Touched her womb. His climax shook him to the core. The moment was incredible. He let his body descend on her. Still, he braced himself above her not wanting her to feel his full weight.

Ash pushed damp strands of hair from her face. Her eyes were open, dazed, gazing up at him with what appeared to be awe. Ash memorized this moment. Placed soft kisses on her lips, nose, eyelids. He traced her eyebrows with a fingertip.

Thank you.

Withdrawing from her was difficult when he wished to remain in the dark heat of her body. He slipped from her. Saw her virgin's blood on his sex. Grimaced.

I will never hurt you. Never, ever again. That's a promise.

Rising, moving away from her so he wouldn't take her again, he padded to the second basin before pouring water into the bowl. Found another cloth which he damped. She would protest. He held no doubts. Nevertheless, he would clean his seed along with her blood from between her thighs.

When he sat down on the bed, she'd raised herself in order to stare at him. Harris leaned on her elbows, watching him. Quizzical, she tilted her head one way then another. "What are you doing?"

He spilled more wine into her glass. "Drink." Grinning at her he handed her both the wine along with another slice of apple. She appeared wary of him as she sipped the wine then bit into the apple. Another moment of mistrust for her. She had good reason to wonder what he meant to do.

Replying to her question would only garner a protest. He was going to do this. After all, he did owe her. Methodically, he placed his hand on one leg. Slipped the wet cloth along the inside of her thighs. She gasped, pushing at his hand in silent protest, trying to close herself off from him.

If it would work, he would ignore her. Deep inside he smiled at the look of chagrin. There was no reason for her to feel that way. He saw as well as touched every evocative part of her. Would do so again before the night was done. Sent her a look of amusement. After all this time, she was shy.

"What? W-what do you think you are doing?" Harris appeared resigned to his plans. She must know what he was about.

"Sip some more wine. Have a piece of cheese for me. Relax."

His half-smile of amusement put a scowl on her forehead. He kissed the tip of her nose. Brushed another light kiss across her lips. Her eyes narrowed.

"You..." She sipped in air when he caressed her more intimately with the cloth. Touched upon her again. Swept the material between the feminine petals that were still bloody. "No..." she squeaked. The sound was amusing to him.

After he brought his gaze back to her, he winked. "I'm done." He sent the cloth to the basin. The material landed just as the first one did with a splash of water. "Relax. Let's eat our fill. I find I'm famished."

After she ate again, he thought it would be rather pleasant to make love to her. This time she would feel only pleasure.

Ash sat down, his back against the wall. In front of him, he crossed his legs. Ate. Drank. Watched his mate. In two days, she would also become his wife. The mansion would be full of people. There would be children. Chaos. Pandemonium. He found he was looking forward to having a full house of guests.

"Tomorrow your parents, brothers, and other relatives will descend upon us. What should we do to amuse them?"

Ash didn't know her family. Because of Harris he gained permission to attend one wedding. After he returned, he made certain Heather and

Elliott both understood his intentions where it concerned their daughter. They allowed him to take her the night of Roc and Lainie's marriage. They agreed to come to his home for their wedding. Her parents put a lot of trust in him.

Harris looked as if she would rather toss her glass of wine in his face instead of answering the easy question. Her thoughts seemed to be miles away. What did she think?

He cleared his throat, thinking he would have to begin this conversation. "Your mother, Heather, will want to have some hand in planning the wedding feast. Perhaps help with the flowers. We never thought to purchase any for the ceremony. She can sit down with Tindly. What do you think?"

"I don't like what you did."

Ah, she would voice her opinion about his earlier actions. She wasn't even listening to him. He thought she'd been in a different universe. That was all true. It seemed to have taken her quite some time to voice her protest. "You wished to keep the evidence of your virginity along with my seed between your thighs?"

Perhaps that might have been too crude. He arched an eyebrow in amusement while he watched her sputter.

"N-no—no."

"Well?" Ash wondered where she would go with this conversation. He understood she could have done it herself. Truth was, he needed to touch her again. Couldn't resist.

"I could..."

Harris gulped the wine. Her cheeks stained a beautiful shade of crimson. She set the glass on the table. "Never mind. I've learned once you set your mind on a course, you will never change your mind. You will do what you think right without asking."

"True."

"Still... Will you ever negotiate?"

Laughing, he lifted his shoulders. "I wanted to touch you again, my love. Can't seem to get enough of you. You are too tempting by far. I've waited more than a year. Can you say the same about me? Would you like to touch me again?"

Her confusion at his question gave him another reason to grin at her. He was amused. She was staring at him. Looking at his sex with wide eyes. He was certain what she was thinking. With a few quick strides he rinsed the cloth then returned. He handed it to her looking from his member to her.

"Would you like to?"

She sipped in a deep breath of air. "You are..."

"Yes." He was going to agree with her no matter what she would say. "You may."

Without barking out his laughter at the sight of her confusion as well as the hesitation, he watched her swallow air. To his surprise as well as delight she used the cloth to wash his heavy arousal. After she finished, he tossed the cloth back to the basin. This time he missed.

~ * ~

Chandler sat back in his overstuffed chair that looked out on the audience who came to see Winter Snow, the Ice Queen. She was the last attraction of the night. Winter waited behind the scenes. Over the week he interviewed more than one hundred women for this position as well as others. For each season he looked for specific characteristics. Not only did they need to be willing participants in group sex, they could not be revolted by coupling with the same sex. One never knew when he would put extra enticements into the performances. Each new arrival had to be willing to go both ways. He was well aware that not all who would pay money to come to be entertained were heterosexual.

After he found Spring Mist, the Princess of Rain, he delighted in the young lady's quick wit along with her willingness to participate in all that he thought of. She was tall, her woman's body lush. She enjoyed her nudity. Long brown hair reached to the middle of her back. Amber eyes stared out from the perfect oval of her face. She possessed full red lips, plump, so very kissable. Some might say too full. Chandler would never agree. Her nose tilted at the end. When she smiled her eyes seemed to light up with amusement. She was so lovely, one would believe her innocence. She wasn't. Spring was a contrast in delights.

Her first night out would be titillating for the audience. While he loved threesomes, Bertram relished arousing a woman, watching another participant caress as well as fondle her. Bertram also liked to have sex with two women or more. Bertram would have Spring Mist for his own. Each night she performed he could choose the third partner either from the audience or from his employees.

Several days passed after securing Spring Mist that he decided on the role for the next season. Summer Passion would be her name. Summer Passion, the Innocent Virgin. While after the first time with him she would no longer possess her maidenhead, she would have to portray innocence. In order to find Summer, Chandler along with Bertram spent a few days surveying the countryside outside London. They spoke with farmers, blacksmiths, cooks...every trade imaginable. They visited families. Offered incentives.

When they found the young woman he wanted walking alone down a country lane, Chandler knew immediately she was the one. If she would come to them, willing to do everything, he would make her a star. Her hair was blond, a very light blond, nearly white. Her eyes a deep crystal blue. She had yet to fill out, to blossom into a mature woman. Her breasts small, slender hips, long lean legs that would reach around a man's flanks with no problem. When he asked, she told him she would be seventeen in a month. That was the average age of most debutantes seeking a husband during the London season. Her innocence would win her a role in the company.

The girl was lithe, agile as well as quick. Her fresh-faced look was perfect for his plans. They followed then cornered her in front of the pastry shop. Afraid, she fought them, wiggled against them. Chandler pinned her to the building, her hands above her head. The movement told Chandler she possessed more curves than he'd thought. When Chandler subdued her with a few kind words then a chaste kiss to her forehead, she listened to the proposal. By the crazed look in her eyes, he understood he had his work cut out for him. It might be difficult to procure her as a willing participant. He would need to give her along with her family the proper inducement.

As he discovered, the girl came from a poor family. Six younger siblings resided in her home. She helped support them by doing odd jobs around the village. Told him she wasn't a whore. When approached, her father was more than willing to accept the pounds he was offered for her compliance. In the end, he was certain the girl would come along. It was apparent to him, she loved her family far more than her father loved her. They needed the money her work would bring. The father guilted her into agreeing. The littlest boy needed medical attention they could not afford. All was in his favor. She was his new Summer Passion.

Chandler was smart enough to let the protesting girl have as much time as she needed with her father. To talk, the man told her. By the time she emerged Chandler was pleased with her easy compliance. With the promise of money coming to him every month, the father handed his oldest daughter over to him without blinking. The money offered would change this family's life for the better. Summer Passion, if she was good, would rake in the pounds. Chandler intended for her to be very good. He would personally train her. Show her how to come on to the men who would watch her. How to posture. What to do to earn the most for her endeavors. Told her of the extra money she would earn when she was auctioned to a man for the night.

Ah, Summer Passion. His attention returned to the show. He'd not made love to Summer yet. Stella along with Celine were preparing her for her role as an innocent maiden. It wasn't too far from the truth. He would receive her virginity for providing the chance to act in his shows, for the opportunity to earn money for her destitute family, for herself as well. In two weeks, it would be her turn on the stage. He'd yet to pick out a man for her or decide on the scenario for her introduction. He wasn't about to rush the young lady. With her long blond curls and pretty blue eyes she was a delight to any male who looked at her. He wanted her around for a long time.

For Autumn Bounty, the Countess of Harvest, Chandler knew the exact woman he needed. The lady needed to possess generous curves, large breasts, wide hips along with a well-rounded belly. No man would need search in the dark for the parts of her he wanted to caress. He didn't care if she was a seasoned whore or an innocent. Her scenario still needed to be invented. Autumn would be up on the dais in three weeks. He was still searching for the perfect seductress to play the bountiful role.

The tickets for these stellar, unique performances would be limited. Auctioned off to the highest bidders. To see Winter Snow, the last two tickets for the performance tonight went for one thousand pounds each. The viewing was limited to fifty people. All the other presentations were to sold out crowds of one hundred. The upstairs rooms were also auctioned to the highest bidder. His women were well-paid. He could be generous with them.

Stella finished with her show then found a man she wanted for her own. She brought him to the platform pulling him along with his frock coat. He stumbled after her, grinning, drooling if he wasn't mistaken. It was obvious the man was pleased to be chosen. Chandler felt certain the man's tongue lolled from his mouth. He was tall, reed thin. His light brown hair ragged, his chin weak. By the time Stella disrobed him, he was fully aroused. Only a few seconds passed before he came inside her, panting with the exertion.

Celine was up next. Chandler watched with jaded, narrowed eyes. He was waiting to see how Winter would do after Celine finished. Impatient to be with her. Again, his mind drifted to Winter. He didn't appreciate the fact the woman was a constant in his head. No woman had ever held his attention this long with so much intensity.

Celine's partner wasted no time. He had her legs over his shoulders and was pumping into her within the first few seconds. Chandler made a mental note to tell the man this was a show; a performance must be savored by the audience. He was supposed to entertain. While the main theme was sex, there needed to be something more. The people wanted to be titillated, aroused to a fever pitch. If he couldn't control himself, he wouldn't have a job. After Celine picked out a man, had sex with him, he and Winter would be the next characters on stage. Chandler looked to the back of the room. Caught the music as Winter walked through the crowd. She was regal, poised, graceful. Ice. Frigid except when he took her. Every eye focused on her.

Background music played, the sound soft while the two couples finished. The noise of their groans, the yell along with the scream when they climaxed. After the entertainers left the stage, Chandler stood. Looked to the back of the stage watching Winter glide toward him. Felt lust, violent lust stirring, the sensation fierce.

She was dressed just as he imagined from the first. The seamstress created his image to perfection. Her gown was made from a light blue transparent material. The corsage rose to a point below her rose-colored nipples enhancing her large breasts, pushing them up to provoke. To entice every customer. He was surprised when his mouth watered with need. The fitted waist emphasized her tiny waist. The gathered skirt had slits from the bottom of the gown to the waist that were three inches wide. With every step the skirt swayed. Oscillated. Covered then uncovered. Tantalized. Incited. Teased every male in the room as well as a few females. Hushed silence filled the chamber.

Bloody eyes, this dress was all he imagined. As she walked the fabric parted, moved with ease, flowing around her. Everyone caught glimpses of her legs, the apex between her thighs. A collective groan went up from his audience. There was nothing a person couldn't see of Miss Winter Snow. She was perfect. This picture was impeccable.

Chandler pulled her into his arms. They danced around the room. His hands settled on her derriere. Moved the fabric to the side so he touched bare skin. He wanted every person in the audience to see her perfection. Gliding with ease, the woman was graceful. Smooth. No emotion. His Ice Queen. This woman would prove to be worth more than her weight in gold. He had big plans for this tiny lady with the huge breasts, ones that would overflow his hands.

Magnanimously, he stepped back. Allowed both Jimmy and Johnny to dance with her. His gaze focused upon her. He studied her elegant lines, the graceful curves of her hips, her breasts. After a time, he took her into his arms. Stopped in a shadowed corner of the room. His lips met hers. Captured her quintessence. Tasted. Savored the essence of her. His hand slid the fabric of her gown down her arms. Her breasts rose in front of him. Large. Ripe. Succulent. Exposed for all there to see. He bent to taste each one. Curled his tongue around each nipple. Teased. Bit.

She gasped. Chandler felt her passion rise. Beneath his tutelage, her beautiful body stirred to life. There were things she enjoyed along with things she did not. It pleased him when he felt her stiffen, the movement slight but obvious to the man who held her. To him. He took her by the hand to the waiting chair. She stood. Her hands were held at her sides while he disrobed from the waist up. Jimmy took his discarded clothing, folded the garments then set them on a table. Chandler splashed wine into two crystal goblets. He handed one to her. After his nod of approval, she drank. Johnny took the pins from her hair, finger combing the length as they fell down her back, stroking her as he did so. The dark ebony strands swirled around her cascading to her hips. Hiding parts of her while revealing other parts just as her gown had done. He didn't know how he would devise a more perfect and captivating scenario.

When he sat down that was the cue the entertainment would begin. Beside him, she stood waiting for his directives. Just as they practiced before, he would continue in the same vein. Next time she would be a British woman captured by Turkish slave runners. He was pleased with the idea. Thought the scene would arouse everyone in the audience.

"Take off your gown," his voice was gentle even though the tone allowed no argument.

The single fastener was in the back. When she reached behind her, her voluptuous breasts swayed, beckoning to all the men in the crowd, some of the women too. Everyone there would hope to explore, taste, cherish his Ice Queen. He knew which women would rather play with a person of the same sex. Winter would never dally with another man. But a woman... Johnny had been directed to find the exact right woman for Winter. He would bring her to his Ice Queen. She wouldn't like what he orchestrated for her pleasure. She would do nothing. The transparent fabric fell to the floor.

He turned to Jimmy and Johnny. Nodded. They held her by her arms. Paraded her across the floor, stopping, turning her so everyone would see all of her. After, they walked her down the aisle into the main seating. They stopped.

"Would you like a taste?" Jimmy asked a man.

He nodded, standing. Yes."

"Just a small one." Jimmy cupped her breast holding it out to the man who put his mouth on her, touched her. He closed his eyes as if savoring the taste of his Ice Queen. There were more men who were allowed a small discovery of his Snow. Jimmy stopped in front of a woman. "You may kiss her." She did. Her mouth closed over hers. She wrapped her hand around her neck. Chandler was certain she deepened the kiss. Then the woman sucked on her breast. Snow, his Ice Queen, didn't flinch. Didn't move a muscle. Stood as if frozen in the ice she was named for.

Jimmy brought her to stand in front of him. She looked at him. Her eyes flashed fire. Ah, she didn't like that bit of the performance. Snow didn't know about what he planned. The strategy to show her off was last minute.

"You want to see me. Don't you love? Work your magic. Savor me. Everyone is looking at us...you."

Winter nodded. Moved in front of him. Opened his pants. He leapt from the stifling confines, hard, eager to be part of the entertainment. Cool air caressed him. Chandler liked to keep the room cool. He kept the windows open. Even without stimulation her breasts would be tight hard buds.

"Take me into you. You know what to do."

Her hair fell around him. Teased and tickled his belly. Swept across his thighs as well as his sex. She did as he commanded. His hips thrust upward, seeking her warmth, the hot wetness along with the suck of her mouth. The sharpness of her teeth raked against his length. The wet mouth surrounding him, sucking. Provocative. Treasured. He ejaculated into her. His hand was on her head keeping her from moving. This was something else he understood she didn't want to do. The slight flinch didn't go unnoticed. He treasured these instants. Winter would never voice a complaint.

"A moment now," he told her, smiling at the audience who watched with avid interest.

He felt as if they held their breath waiting for the next scene. "Jimmy, wine for Miss Snow."

She drank long and deep. He knew she washed the taste of him from her mouth. That pleased him too.

Chandler released his hold on her hand. Stroked her cheek when she looked up. He smiled, a half-smile. His lips twitched upward telling her of his approval. "Come to me. I need to touch your mouth with mine."

Chandler drew her up to meld his lips with hers. Deepened the kiss. Touched inside the secret depth of her that no other man would taste. The brief intimacy complete, he ended the kiss. Broke off pulling her higher.

Tasted each tender breast. Savored the sweet taste. He let her go, inspecting the audience. Viewing each man and woman's expression. Satisfied with the performance.

"They are watching you, my Ice Queen. All are pleased. You know what to do next."

Winter nodded. She turned. This had all been rehearsed. No more words needed to be said. She sat on him. Placed her long white legs across his thighs. Chandler nodded at Jimmy as well as Johnny. The men also understood the next part in the play.

Jimmy came down on his knees by the side of the chair. Holding her breast in one hand, he played with the rounded globe, sucked, kissed, bit. She gasped. Writhed on him. With each caress, Winter moved. Heated. He felt her muscles clenching around his sex. She'd been told to make it last as long as possible, holding back her pleasure would garner her more money. Everyone stared at her. All of her was revealed. Nothing about his Queen of Ice was secret. Winter Snow became everyman's dream tonight.

"Are you alright with this?" he asked, whispering into her ear.

Touching his tongue inside to be rewarded with the flinch of displeasure he was coming to know all too well. He was pleased. Touched again. Swirled. Knew she wished to tell him she didn't like what he did. Interesting. He never encountered a woman who didn't like a man's caresses around her delicate ears. Something else that made this woman unique.

She nodded her compliance. Chandler thought she did enjoy the exhibition they put on. Miss Snow understood her worth. She would capitalize on her beauty. Would make more money than she could have dreamed. The boys continued to play with her. As planned, she reached to touch herself.

"No." He held her hand away. She started, surprised. Winter turned to look at him, eyes wide. Confused.

Chandler didn't know why this delightful woman needed money. Nor did he care. If she was running from a man, didn't matter to him. She was his now. He would give her whatever she needed for a price. Winter understood. Complied.

The boys were on either side of her playing with her jewels. He kissed her nape. Ran his hands along her shoulders then down her arms. Felt her convulse. Shiver. The constricting of her muscles greeted him. Knew when her body could hold back no longer. He gave her his seed. He felt her shudder.

His words whispered close to her ear. "You think that was unfair of me. You missed what you want. Your beautiful climax. Now you can see to your pleasure." He placed her hand on her beautiful pussy. She complied with his command. She would always do as he asked.

That was something she didn't mind though the first few times she'd been hesitant...uncertain of what he was asking. Now, she comprehended the ecstasy she could give herself. Once given permission, she didn't hesitate at his command. Tonight, he would come one more time inside her. He would wait. The next step they'd not rehearsed. She knew nothing of his plan.

After she touched herself and he found her body responding again, he held her hand. Pulled her fingers away from the nub of flesh that would arouse and excite to greater heights. She wouldn't appreciate what he planned next. Winter would not protest except with the flinch of her muscles that only he would feel. She would hide her distaste behind the mask of ice she cloaked herself with. The money garnered made all this worth her while. She was a whore, an intriguing whore.

"Jimmy." The man knew what he wanted.

They discussed his role in Winter's setup an hour ago. He wanted a real woman from the audience who would see to Winter's pleasure. Who would touch her with her mouth. Fondle her intimately with her tongue. He'd thought that perhaps either Stella of Celine would be perfect. Jimmy dissuaded him from that notion. Believed the audience would be teased by one of their own.

Now, Jimmy perused the audience. He tapped his finger on his chin looking from one woman to another as if trying to decide on the perfect specimen. Settled on a plump woman with rounded cheeks, a wide mouth with just as chubby lips. She must be in her forties. Her hair had begun to gray around her temple. Her breasts, well-endowed, would overflow Jimmy's hands. Chandler was certain her breasts would sag would no longer be firm-tipped, inviting sensual play. Nonetheless, she was pretty in her own way. At one time, she might have tempted men to carnal pleasures. Tonight, she would receive what she most likely hadn't enjoyed in a long time. If she wanted sexual pleasure, her money would be well spent.

"Me?" she questioned as Jimmy selected her.

She giggled. Her hand on her large bosom. She blinked a few times. Looked around the room as if she was mistaken and Jimmy decided on a different woman. Jimmy knew how to smile at a woman. How to make her feel special. He understood carnal needs. Comprehended how he could use his masculinity to tempt.

"Yes, you... Is this what you want? I would bring you here with me. Show your assets to all. Are you still agreeable now that you've been chosen to be the one to give as well as receive pleasure. I would wish to touch all your lady parts."

"Yes...yes...a thousand times yes."

"Good. You've come to the right place as well as the right man. I will see to all your needs."

He reached out his hand to her. Pulled her forward as if he was in a hurry to jump her. When they stopped, he kissed her. Captured her mouth with his. She moaned. Whimpered. Fascinated with his choice, Chandler paid close attention. There were many beautiful, young women in the audience. Why this one? Though he understood she would be the perfect foil for his Ice Queen.

Jimmy had her gown unfastened by the time the two reached the stage. She was turned facing the audience. Her back to him. The ties on her corset fell away. Jimmy tossed the garments on the floor. Tugged on her petticoats. She was naked. Jimmy stepped back, his arms crossed over his chest, looking her up then down. An admiring expression on his face. He turned her around in a complete circle so she once again faced the audience. His hands closed over her breasts, fondled. Caressed the hardened tips. Tugged on them. He brushed kisses across the back of her neck. Suckled. His mouth found the tip of one breast. Gave that hardened crest his full attention. The lady moaned. She clung to him.

"Are you ready?"

"Oh...yes. What do you..." she broke off her words halted by his command.

"Show the lady what to do." Chandler stroked Winter's arms. Ran a finger down her spinal column. She arched. Her breast pointed to her audience. Provoking every person there. Johnny continued his assault on Winter's breast. Sucking on her. She writhed with attentiveness. Chandler moved his hand to her other breast. Rubbed his palm across the tip once then twice again while he watched Jimmy with the woman. Bit on the nape of her neck. Twisted the crest until he heard the soft whimper of her passion. Her shudders pleased him. She squirmed. His sex pulsed inside her heat.

When he looked back to Jimmy he was kneeling in front of the woman. One of her legs was over Jimmy's shoulder. Her hands were fisted in his hair as she tried to maintain her balance. Jimmy licked her femininity. Circled the knot of ecstasy. She cried out. Quivered. From excitement or shame, Chandler didn't know nor did he care. He couldn't see her face. He was pleased. Felt Winter's arousal throb. She kissed his hard member with her need. Within her pulses vibrated. This was what his show needed to step up the games. He thought of Harris. Knew she would never be here as a willing participant. Maybe he could find a way to humiliate his brother with his new wife. It could be done if he thought long and hard. He didn't wish to jeopardize his business venture that proved to be fruitful in multiple ways.

He would have to be careful. He could get her here. If he did, what then?

True to his cat, Ashton, the new earl, would follow. Ah, back to the scene. He needed to focus. Jimmy looked at him for his approval. Again, he nodded to proceed.

Jimmy pointed to Winter.

The older woman's hand flew to her throat. "Me? I couldn't. To her? To a woman? You wish for me to touch her..." She paled. Her voice vibrated. She flushed. "On her..." it seemed she couldn't say the word.

"You!" Chandler boomed. "Will you? Do you wish to forfeit your pleasure? As well as the enjoyment you can give my Ice Queen?"

She was shaking. Her head was bobbing as she hurried to fulfill the deed. The chosen lady knelt in front of Winter. Jimmy stood behind her and brought her bottom into the air. The woman's mouth settled on Winter exactly where Chandler directed. Where Jimmy showed her. When she licked, Chandler felt the shudder from his Queen of the Ice. This was perfection.

Chandler smiled. Another swipe to her feminine parts gave him exactly what he needed to understand. Felt Winter's flinch of displeasure. Was pleased with the results. He also felt excitement rise within his Ice Queen. Knew when her body responded. When her core milked his rod. She wasn't completely against this. She could refuse at any time. Would be giving up the money if she did say no. Chandler's sex reacted to the deep pulses. Leapt to find the final expulsion of need. Lightning tore in his loins. Tempest rose in his blood. If he didn't control himself this would end way too soon. From behind her, Jimmy thrust into the woman, his hands on her broad hips keeping her in position. Winter's contractions built ten-fold. She cried out. Yelled her pleasure. Her body fragmenting as he emptied himself inside her sultry depths. It was over too soon. He would need to figure out how to prolong this pleasure. The audience would be aroused to a fever pitch. They would pay over the top for their enjoyment of any of the women.

"Good girl," he whispered close to her ear before he swirled his tongue inside one more time just to tell her who was taking charge, despite her efforts to remain frigid with this new invasion. Winter stiffened. "You were spectacular. We are done here."

He nodded to Johnny. That was his cue to find someone in the audience. Jimmy pulled the older lady into his arms then with a swat to her bottom, he directed her to her clothing. Helped her with the corset. Whispered loud enough for the audience to hear. "If you find yourself increasing, send me a message." She giggled.

While Johnny found a woman to have sex with. Chandler brought Winter to stand in front of him. She was regal. Queenly. Everyone swept their gazes the length of her. Everyone in the audience wanted her. They would hope soon he would tire of her so they could experience her exquisite charms. It would be another month before she performed again. The price for her would increase. He would start the bidding at two thousand pounds.

He waved his arm to her, bowed low. After he stood, "I hand you Miss Winter Snow, the Ice Queen. Give her the applause she deserves for tonight's spectacular performance. She is not available for auction this evening. Perhaps another time."

The crowd erupted, with clapping yells along with catcalls. Threw money at her. He nodded to Jimmy to collect. This would become extra earnings for his people.

"Is Miss Snow going to pick someone to have sex with?" Despite his earlier words the question was asked.

"Not tonight."

Becoming possessive of this woman, Chandler wasn't certain he would ever allow her to choose an audience member, even another woman. The Ice Queen was his.

Chapter Eight

The day of the wedding arrived, the temperature cold and the sky was clear. Shivering, her arms wrapped around herself, Harris looked out on the grounds. She felt the cold bone deep. Wanted to stand in the sunshine to soak up the heat of the day. What there was of it. The garden area behind the mansion swarmed with people bustling around to prepare everything. Ash had awnings put up in case of rain. There were stacks of firewood, bonfires laid in strategic places to keep the guests warm through the feast. Tables were stacked high with plates. He managed this in such a short period of time.

The cooks, the staff and especially Tindly worked for two days putting this all together. Many times, she saw her mother huddled with Tindly working on details for the wedding. In the kitchen Scottish foods were found on the stove as well as in the ovens. Harris let out a huge sigh of pleasure, content with all that was going on. The cake would be white. The frosting would have a swirl of chocolate. The flowers were lavender.

Ash stood behind her, his hands now resting on the curves of her hips. She gasped. She'd not heard him enter the room.

"Hush. It's me." His hands moved up then down her arms. "You're cold. You should sit by the fire, warm yourself."

Harris found herself smiling as well as shaking her head. For such a large man he moved so quietly. All cats, he told her once, moved in silence. He was right. Her brothers along with the cousins were the same. They had great fun as children sneaking up on her. Would scare her. Laugh at her fright. Not that she didn't have a myriad of ways to seek revenge in much the same manner. All was done in good humor. She was going to miss her brothers. Already missed them before they followed her from Carnoch for the wedding.

His hands were on her shoulders, massaging, easing the tension she felt. He always knew what she was feeling. He told her he would know when she conceived. Would she have that same sixth sense? She wanted to know that pertinent piece of information before he did. The oxygen she tugged into her lungs did nothing to help ease the wedding jitters. She knew she had nothing to be nervous about. She turned in his arms. His lips brushed on hers, the caress light, chaste. They did not have time for anything serious.

"I would that all this was done. Finished. I'm tired of all the company. Her laughter was soft. How ironic when she fought to stay at Carnoch less than a month ago. We've..." Though she loved having family with her, she wanted some alone time with her husband of two days. Supposed she needed to say mate of two days. Until they wed in the church, he wasn't her husband.

In a few hours all the missing details would be complete. They would be man and wife in every conceivable way.

"Not had much alone time." He tapped her on the nose having read her thoughts. "You know as well as I that you will miss all of them once they are gone. This entourage will leave in less than a week. It will then be a year or more before we shadow them to Carnoch. You will beg me to take you home so you can see them all again. So you can wed one more time in the Catholic church."

"A year?" she questioned. That would be a long time, she conceded. "That is a long time. I imagine I should make the most of the last few hours they have remaining with me."

"Yes," he agreed with her. Make as much of your time now with your family as you can. Spend time with each sibling. I would not have you begging before it is time. Go shopping with Heather. Ride with Elliott. With your family, we could have a meal or two in the village." His arms were around her. She loved the way she felt when he held her in his arms. His body never failed to heat, to arouse. Even now when the women would descend into the room, he challenged her, inflamed her.

"The bonfires? They will keep us warm?" She was wondering. The last two nights the temperature dipped to where the water in the fountains froze. "Once the sun plunges behind the hills it will be freezing outside. The ceremony won't be over much before the sun will set. We will need to..."

"The fires will keep the villagers warm. Us too for the short time we will spend outside. Would not wish for my bride to catch a cold in the freezing weather." He pushed strands of her hair behind her head. His eyes shimmered a deep dark blue. Sizzled. "There is enough food and drink for the villagers to celebrate into the wee hours of the morning if they wish," he amended her statement. "While I plan to make an appearance with my new bride on the lawn, our feast will be in the ballroom along with the dancing and the cutting of the cake. Until you wish to retire for the night we will dance as well as eat. I've arranged for food in the bedchamber. A bottle or two of wine. Tindly will leave us three. Would like to keep my new bride up for the entire night. The next day we can sleep or play with each other as long as we wish. There is no reason to rise until it's what we want."

"Couldn't we have two cakes to share with these fine people? We could cut one out on the lawn before we head inside. Dance a dance or two with them."

Harris thought that was a grand idea. Hoped Ash would agree. As far as she could tell the only issue would be the baking of more cake.

"Grand idea. The cakes are baked. Our handy chef along with Tindly made enough cake for everyone who will be in attendance," Ash said, a short bark of laughter following. "Everyone wants this to be a grand occasion. It's not every day the earl takes a bride. They will all want to toast to our happiness as well as the children we are hoping for.

Harris set her head on his chest. Heard the beating of his heart. Steady. Strong. Ran her hands along the width, thinking of the wedding night to come. She had nothing to fear. No pain. Pleasure only. They made love both nights since the ceremony. She was pleased all the necessities were over. A simple traditional wedding would be enjoyable. "What seems to be my entire family is here. You..." He didn't have anyone to celebrate with that she knew of. "I wish James could have attended."

Ash set a finger on her lips. "Hush. My father is here in spirit. I appreciate the fact he is healing faster than expected. However, he won't be able to resume his duties as the earl or in parliament. There is so much to do along with the businesses we own. There is another estate that needs to be tended too though our manager is a capable man. The stress will be too great for his health. Believe we will accompany your family to London when they leave."

"What about friends? You must have childhood friends. School mates you..."

"It's nothing to worry over. My best friends are in the service of the crown. Those friends were also second sons. The spare son to the title usually joins the armed services, sometimes the ministry. My friends are not in London or they would be here to celebrate with me as well as congratulate both of us. The man I've known since childhood is in India. Another has been stationed in the colonies...believe he is in North Carolina."

"I'm sorry. Smith-Jones?" Harris continued to hope that someone would be there for him. She didn't think it would be.

"Has to stay with my father. I don't mind. Father needs the protection. As you must guess, I don't. Though..." Ash seemed to think...tapping his chin with a finger, "I wouldn't be surprised if my brother showed himself. The banns were read in London, the wedding date set and announced in the London Times."

Harris inhaled a sharp breath. Chandler wasn't welcome at her wedding. She didn't want him there. "Don't want to see your brother. What would happen if he makes an appearance then we send him away?" She knew Ash would not wish to see him either. "We do still have the added guards? Hawk and Cameron will be vigilant along with all my cousins."

"Nothing will happen. If he tries, he won't be able to get close to you. No one will let him near. Besides, if he comes, he will be escorted from the premises."

"He could remain with the villagers. Make trouble there."

"He hates the cold. Come, stop worrying. Nothing has happened yet. Nor will it. If he is at the wedding, I'm certain he will either behave himself or find he is escorted from the festivities.

"We won't have any time to ourselves after the wedding either. Suppose we're lucky to have this moment."

Harris let a long slow breath of air slip from her lungs before she spoke, "My mother would be angry if she knew you were here with me. The groom is not supposed to see the bride the day of the ceremony until she walks down the aisle. It's supposed to be bad luck. How could it be bad luck?"

Harris didn't like to think about bad luck along with the thoughts of Chandler. They seemed to go hand in hand.

"Superstitious, are we?" Ash chuckled as he bent to kiss her again. The kiss was light. Soft. Held no demands. There would be more of that to come. He told her little of the wedding night other than there would be plenty of food and drink. "Don't suppose the groom is supposed to do that either until the minister tells him to do so. It doesn't matter. There will be no bad luck for us. Luck is something one makes for himself. You will see... all will be well." He stroked her cheek. "What could go wrong?"

"We could defy all the falsehoods. You could make love to me before the wedding. I would enjoy that. Would you?"

Harris didn't like the wistfulness she heard in her voice. She did wish for the closeness the intimacy would bring. The devil if her mother discovered...

His laughter barked from him. "We can't. You understand there are not enough precious seconds left to us. I won't challenge this time you will have with your mother along with your brother's wives to prepare you for the ceremony. That time with the women is important. I believe I should make myself scarce before they come upon us. Besides, I've an appointment with those brothers of yours. A bit of ale to drink. A few bawdy jokes if I don't miss my guess. If I'm late, they will come looking. Don't wish for them to find me making love with my almost wife, her skirts tossed over her head. Afraid you'd be too discomfited for them to see you."

Even while he spoke, the knock on the door told them the wedding festivities were beginning. He cast an eyebrow toward the ceiling telling her he knew what he was talking about. On invitation, servants entered bringing hot water; after that, behind them the women who were related to her through marriage to brothers along with uncles. One after the other they filtered through the door until the last woman stood in the doorway.

Her mother's hands on her hips she looked them up then down. With a snort, she spoke, "Why am I not surprised? The two of you are here. Ash is not supposed to be in this room with you" Heather announced when she stepped through the door. She was shaking her finger at them. Tsking.

"My ardent apologies." He bowed low. "Had to see Harris. Couldn't let it go another second. A very important discussion." Ash set his hand on his heart, looking skyward as if that would appease her mother. "Your daughter is in my thought's night and day. I had to see her before the wedding. Forgive me this small *faux pas*?"

It surprised Harris that her mother included Ash in her reprimand, not just her. Now that he saw the interaction, she understood. Ash wound her mother around his little finger with no difficulty. The man knew just what to say. How to smile. He could charm a saint. Her mother adored the man. Even after he left her for the year, she still loved him. Believed him to be the best man for her. Did Ash do the same to her? Yes, Harris admitted she would give him whatever he asked. She was well and truly caught as well as wrapped around his finger.

Ash looked at her in that charming way that never ceased to make her heart flutter then race like a tempest beating down from the highlands. Now that she understood what it felt like to be completely in his arms, her pulse beat more rapidly. At the door, he bowed. He looked at her. "I will see you soon."

He was gone. Her breath caught. The silence in the room changed to women chattering about the wedding. Hypatia, Pippa's monkey, jumped from table top to table top chattering along with the wives. She landed on her shoulder before putting her hands on either side of her face then kissing her. Harris adored the little monkey. Pippa was Roby McKenna's wife. Roby met Pippa along with her pet one moonlit night. Pippa was about to be hanged for stealing then killing a rabbit to eat. She'd been starving. With a leap of faith, Roby's sixth sense kicking in, Roby agreed to marry Pippa while she stood on the gallows with a rope around her slender neck. It was the only way he could save her from the hangman's noose. She was forever grateful. After the first night, he was a man well-pleased. Roby along with Kit traveled to the colonies in hopes of finding their mate. Both found them in the highlands.

Before Harris set the adorable creature down, she kissed Hypatia on the nose. The monkey made a kissing sound then found Pippa's shoulder. The women filled the tub with lavender oils. The water steamed. Looked relaxing. Aila, Kit Stuart's wife, handed her a full glass of wine. She drank deep. Crissie McKenna, the only other female child in the group of McKennas, Stuarts and Frasiers, pinned her hair on top of her head. Crissie was Walker Endicott's wife. They lived in Ireland. Walker's cat form was also a white tiger.

She looked over the group, thrilled all her relatives were able to come to her wedding. Surprised Crissie and Walker were here. It had been several years since she'd seen Crissie, a cousin of sorts. Crissie's mother, Wynnie, was Heather's daughter. The story was a confusing tale. They were all related by blood or by marriage.

It didn't take much effort to lose the robe she wore. Harris let it slide to the floor. When she got out of bed this morning, Ash was gone, the bed cold. Harris missed him, his warmth, the feel of his lean body next to her. She didn't know how long he'd been up and about, tending to their guests.

Her wedding dress hung in the armoire. Heather handed her a scone dripping with honey. Just the way she liked them. Her stomach told her she needed to eat. From past weddings, she understood this would be a long day. Eating was necessary. Nothing would go wrong. There would be no bad luck. Chandler didn't dare show himself.

The scone eaten and the wine gone, she finished washing. The chatter from the other room was lively. She heard stories about the children. Good as well as bad escapades. Heard tales of the first times the toddlers shifted.

Harris placed her hand on her belly. As far as she knew there was nothing there. For a few more seconds while she gathered her feelings around her, she listened. Everyone seemed pleased with the marriage. They all adored the man. Knew his cat wasn't a panther but a white tiger. Only Lainie, Roc's wife, knew the full extent of her misery when she waited for Ash to return for her. Lainie also understood how difficult it had been to resist him after he did come for her.

Lainie, not even her mother, was the only person Harris confided with her feelings. She reached for the bath sheet that was warming by the fire. Wrapped the cloth around her after she stepped from the now tepid water. She stared at the fire caught up in the dance of flames. She was both impatient as well as nervous for the ceremony. The celebratory feast would be fun except she didn't relish being the center of attention.

Someone set her petticoats and corset on the table near the tub, her stockings as well as her slippers. She dressed then walked into the main bedroom where the other women were. Again, she was handed a glass of wine. The prewedding gifts were given to her with explanations as to the old as well as the borrowed then new.

Heather brought a box to give her. "This is from Ashton. He said the gift would enhance your eyes. It is something blue for you to wear. This is all for good luck mind you. Even though the two of you *dinna* seem too concerned about the superstitions."

Harris' breath caught in her throat when she saw the beautiful sapphire necklace lying in a bed of pale blue silk. Her eyes were usually a silver blue. Ash told her when she climaxed, they turned dark, sapphire blue...dark. He loved her eyes in those moments. She brought the single pear shaped stone to her chest. Closed her eyes remembering the exact moment he told her. Her breath hitched. She looked to her mother, holding out the exquisite piece of jewelry.

"I'll fasten it for you," Heather told her. "Turn yourself around."

The rest of the preparations flashed by so fast it made her head spin. Now, she sat in front of her dressing table staring at herself. Her hair was fixed, piled neatly on top of her head. A few artfully placed strands framed her face. Her gown pulled over her head. Hair rearranged a second time. Stockings along with her slippers adorned her legs and feet. Ash would take his time removing each article. Thinking of his hands, fingers, lips eliminating the clothing, touching her, heat swept through her. She felt the rise of heat to her cheeks. Placed her hands there to cool herself.

Oh my...

She heard his soft chuckle. Damn him, he was listening to her thoughts again. Intruding on this moment. He had no right to delve into her most private thoughts. She wished she knew what he was doing this moment. More than that, she wished she could read his mind. Know what he was thinking at any given time.

As if Heather knew what was happening, she spoke with a soft warm voice. "The men are on their way to the church. They will have a glass of ale as they wait for us there. Talk about the wedding night I'm certain. The carriages are downstairs waiting." Heather stood back to look at her. "Are you ready? Last chance to change your mind. You are beautiful."

"You understand I would never change my mind."

"Yes. Ashton is your mate. The two of you are destined to be with each other, to live on through the future generations," Heather continued to say, her eyes filled with moisture. She opened her arms. Harris flew into them, hugging her mother fiercely.

They stepped apart. She thought she might cry. Sipped in air hoping to stave off the tears. Harris let out a slow breath of air, a tug of wistfulness capturing her thoughts. All these women played an integral part in her life. She would miss them. All were so far away. How did Crissie survive the distance? Nostalgia swept through her. A deep breath brought her back to the present.

"I wish we were at the McKenna keep. I would like to help prepare your daughter for the night to come. I have lingerie. Bought it as well as brought it," Wynnie spoke with a huge smile. "Suppose we could do that here. Prepare the bedroom for the couple. We will have to speak to Tindly to be certain the room has enough food along with wine for the entire evening." Her hands were on her hips, her chin tilted. "What do you all think about that? We can whisk her away after the cutting of the cake. She will be ours before the wedding night begins just as it would have been if we were all home. This is the way of traditions," Wynnie McKenna, said a wry smile adorning her beautiful face.

"Her husband to be might not be pleased by us keeping her from him as was mine. He even understood what would happen. Knew he would need to wait. Still from what he told me of the events downstairs, he was a wreck before Heather beckoned for him to follow her," Lainie said with a small laugh, her eyes sparkling as if she recalled that night. "I'm certain he has his own plans. We might be interfering."

"There is no tradition like this here. Is there? We would not intend to infringe on a time-honored custom." Crissie turned to Harris searching for an answer. She repeated as if she needed to make a point. "We wouldn't want to intrude. From what I understand, you will have a traditional wedding when you return to Carnoch. When you are there all will happen the way it is expected."

"No, I don't believe so. James, Ash's father would be able to tell you. He couldn't attend. I'm sorry." She wondered then if Father Damian would do the claiming ceremony with them. The white cloaks would become part of the ceremony. Harris didn't think the groom claimed the woman during or right after that ritual as Ash did the other night. She didn't want twenty tiny claw marks. If necessary, she would protest. Enough was enough.

"Well then, I agree. We should take charge of the bride after the cake is cut. Whisk her upstairs to this room. I'm certain the men will be pleased to play their role too," Maisie, Hawk's wife said. Hawk was Harris' older brother. One of the doctors in Carnoch. He was always full of advice. Of course, he was the oldest. So, he would always claim he knew best what all his siblings needed. "Nonetheless, this is agreed. We need to adhere to a few traditions. Ashton will have to wait to have his bride until you are ready for him. When the time is ripe, we will whisk you away. The groom will not know what is happening." Maisie set out a sheer nightgown that Heather brought for the occasion.

"He will be blindsided, of course," Heather said with a tiny laugh while she smoothed the fabric. When she looked up to speak again, she smiled. "Always love the look of chagrin on a virile man's face when he doesn't know how to proceed. The expression is so adorable. Men are so used to being in control, of taking charge of every situation."

"As do all women," Wynnie agreed with a wink to Harris. "That look is always memorable. Tonight, it's Harris's turn to shine. Let's make certain all here is as it should be before the wedding as well as after the ceremony. I will speak with Tindly. He will see to the food as well as the drink. There should be enough for the entire night."

"Stand back then turn around. Yes. Need to make certain everything is where it should be." Heather grinned at her daughter, taking in all of her as she turned. "You are so beautiful. No wonder this man can't keep his hands off you. Oh..." She put her hand over her mouth. "A mother shouldn't say something like that to her daughter. Though I know it for a fact. The man is besotted."

A smile tugged at Harris' heart. Her mother always managed to blurt something that would cause embarrassment. Though everything her mother told her was true. She was also besotted with him. The man's smile never ceased to steal her breath. "Thank you. I feel as if I'm a princess. I appreciate your sentiments. All of you. What you say is true. I'm certain my father felt the same about you," Harris said, her voice soft, her gaze touching the velvet softness of her mother's eyes. "Believe after all these years he still feels the same. I've seen the two of you looking at each other. I hope in twenty some years, Ash will still feel the same about me. Will still look at me with the same shimmer of fire in his eyes."

"Speaking of your prince charming..." Lilly, Brady McKenna's wife laughed. Brady was the first of all of them to find his mate and marry. At the time, Lilly worked in the kitchen at the McKenna keep. Brady followed her home one night to protect her as well as discover a few truths about her. What he discovered was that she was not what she played at being. A servant. "I did find my prince charming in Brady. We are all so lucky that our men love us. Would do anything for us."

Wynnie held up her glass of wine signaling for a toast. Heather topped off the glasses that were empty or nearly empty. When they were all filled, she held hers up. "A toast to our bride. Here is to your forever happiness with your mate. Just wish you weren't living so far away. We will all visit as often as possible. You will come see us. Don't want to miss out on the *wee* ones when they come along."

At the mention of babies, Harris felt the rise of heat to her cheeks.

"We all love you," Aila, Kit Stuart's wife said.

Aila came from the past to unite with Kit. She ventured through the Kinnel Stones. For a few months Kit was lost inside the stones trying to find his way home. Aila was faithful. Rarely left the stones during the night or the day even though Houston was concerned about her health. She was carrying Kit's child.

"We will miss you," Pippa added.

Hypatia jumped from her perch, tipped the bottle up, drinking the few drops of wine that were left within the bottom. The little monkey burped then covered her mouth.

Laugher spilled around the room. The knock on the door followed. Elliott's booming voice came next. Heather opened the door. Harris saw her father. So handsome in his tight-fitting britches, white shirt and dark blue frock coat. If the wedding had been in Carnoch, even though it was forbidden by British law, he would have worn a kilt, the plaid of their clan. Her gown would have a sash of the same plaid.

"I'm taking my daughter to the church. We've less than a half hour to get there. Don't want to be late."

He held out his arm. With a deep breath she accepted. Together, they started down the stairs. The rest of the group followed down the steps then outside to the waiting carriages.

~ * ~

Restless energy driving him, Ashton paced the small room in the back of the church. Every few rounds, he would stop at the window to peer out. His wife had not arrived yet. Soon though, he would walk through that door. In a matter of minutes, say his vows. The brothers poured drinks while they waited. Ash didn't think he would be nervous. With all his heart and soul he needed to marry Harris. He felt stretched thin as a wire. His hands were shaking. He was sweating. Thought his knees might give out.

The men took turns checking on the congregation. The pews were filling with old family friends. After that they would look to the spot where the bridal carriage would park. Ash couldn't help himself; he looked out the door searching the sanctuary. Ash invited business partners. A few men who his father was close with. The wives of her cousins along with one husband, Walker, were sitting in the pews.

The clock struck three times. Where was she? Harris was late for her wedding. His gut tightened. Prayed she hadn't changed her mind. She couldn't change her mind. Harris was his mate. She was claimed. The marks were on her shoulders. He rubbed his hand behind his neck. Pressed his fingers at the bridge of his nose. Looked into the sanctuary again.

"The carriage is here," Hawk slapped him on the back. He walked away laughing. "See, there is nothing for you to worry over. Father wouldn't fail you or her. Believe I felt much the same before my wedding."

"She will take a few minutes in another room to freshen up. Women need that time. Her hair must be perfect. Her dress free of wrinkles," Roc told him with a hoot of laughter. "The church is still filling up."

"My father must have invited some of his friends to the wedding," Ash said feeling confused. "Told him I didn't care. Just wished to be married as soon as possible. Seems I've waited a long time for this event."

"You had an eye on little sis even before we knew it. Suppose we were all too caught up in our lives to think our little sister was seeing a man. She was too young," Roc accused, knowing he'd seen them kissing a little over a year ago. "Understood from a few things Harris confided in Lainie that she'd seen him a few times at the cabin in the craigs.

"I waited. Never touched her until she was old enough," Ash retorted, not liking the chastisement. The waiting had been so bloody hard. "You should be grateful. There were several times I headed off English soldiers when she was being careless. Always thought she could do what she wished. Being the only female child, she was spoiled by the lot of you." Ash peeked out again. He sucked in a deep breath of air. Stunned, he looked again. Closed his eyes as if he wasn't seeing straight.

"One of the cousins will come when she is ready," Hawk tried to reassure him. "Today, of all days, they are on their best behavior."

Ash didn't hear the words from Harris' brother. "The bastard came. Was afraid he might be here to taunt me."

"What bastard?" Hawk stood beside him, his hand on his shoulder. "If you tell us who wasn't invited, I'll have Kit or Riley escort him out. Don't wish to have interlopers here. It's a private affair. At home we can close then lock the gates to the keep. Done that on more than one occasion."

"No." Ash rubbed the bridge of his nose again trying to stop the advent of a headache while he thought about what should be done. "Don't want to make a scene at my wedding. I would, however, ask that two of the cousins flank him along with the woman he brought with him." Chandler was the reason he was nervous. His sixth sense kicked in. He just didn't know why until now. What would Harris think when she saw the man who accosted her in London. She might not notice him when she walked down the aisle.

"We can do that. Tell them not to be too obvious. Bring their wives also," that from Roby who chuckled before speaking again, "Hypatia could sit next to the man or better yet, on his shoulder. She has a way of making grown men nervous. The little monkey would play with his hair. Kiss the man. That would send him scurrying for cover."

"Wouldn't wish for the sweet monkey to get hurt. Chandler sometimes has a mean streak. My brother wanted Harris. Hurt her before we left London. For good reason, she despises the man. She will not be pleased to see my brother at our wedding."

Ash's blood seemed to boil. He hit his fist against his palm wishing it was his brother's face he bashed. Would love to see his nose broken. Thought of the bruises Harris suffered on her mouth and breasts left there by his brother. The bastard had gall to show up at his wedding.

"Hurry," Hawk told Roc. "We can't walk out there until this is taken care of. I want to see the man flanked before Harris walks down the aisle."

Roc was back in minutes looking a bit ruffled about the situation. His tie was slightly askew. Hawk fixed it. Music began to play. Ash's nerves skyrocketed. His pulse raced as he waited for the cue to enter the church.

"It's time. I do love a wedding. This one I've waited for years to see," the minister told them as he walked past them to stride with confidence into the sanctuary then stand at the altar.

The brothers followed as did Ashton who now stood by the minister. His hands clasped behind his back, he stared down the aisle then at his brother. His gaze fierce. For a few seconds Ash focused on Chandler. After that his gaze switched to the regal woman sitting beside his brother. Who the hell was she? One of Chandler's mistresses? That would be something Chandler would do because bringing a mistress to an event like this wasn't proper.

The woman was beautiful, frigid. Ash thought her body must be coated with ice. Though she held herself with grace befitting royalty. Her hair was perfect. Her gown fitted, displaying regal curves. Her skin flawless, alabaster. Rose tinted lips. A pert nose. Her chin was slightly pointed.

Who was this woman?

What the bloody hell was that lady doing with Chandler? She was lovely. They didn't belong together. Ash held the distinct impression she was good to the tips of her toes, soul deep good. The opposite of the man she sat with. His sixth sense...?

The music changed. The two matrons of honor stood framed by the massive double doors. The flower girl, Maisie's and Hawk's youngest stood, in front of the women along with the ring bearer, their oldest. The little boy shifted from one foot to the other. The pillow fell from his hands. Maisie picked it up. Said something to the boy. The girl held onto her mother's hand, her little thumb in her mouth. The sight of the two children gave him good reason to smile. They were adorable.

On the way to the altar, petals were strewn in haphazard fashion. At one point she stopped to return to her mother who motioned her to keep going. She did. After that the little girl stopped to pick one up then tossed it again. When she reached the end of the red carpet, Heather claimed her with a big hug coupled with a kiss to her cheek. The ring bearer wasn't far behind. He stood in front of the minister then turned to watch his mother walk toward him. Maisie went first then Lainie walked the aisle. Each standing opposite to the men, Harris' brothers. With another change to the music, Harris, standing beside Elliott, her hand on his arm began the slow, majestic march toward him.

She stole his breath. Her gown moved softly around her with each step. She held her flowers in front of her. A circlet of flowers had been placed around her head.

When he caught her eye, he smiled then nodded, hoping to keep her attention focused on him. Harris appeared nervous. Her fingers were held tight around Elliott's arm. Ash was certainly pleased he wasn't the only one with shaking hands. Elliott spoke to her. Whispered something else as they approached.

Yes, the gown was lovely.

Harris was lovelier. She was half the distance. It would not be much longer. Harris would be his bride. Seemed he waited forever. When they reached the altar, her father handed her to him with a few words from both the minister and the father. If he was asked later what was said he would never be able to recall the words.

The ceremony passed by him in a blur. He held her hands within his. Rubbed her knuckles when he felt her hands shaking. Responded when prompted. Was relieved when he was told he could kiss the bride. Ash pulled her into his arms. His mouth captured hers. Stopped himself from deepening the kiss though it was what he wished for.

The minister announced them to the congregation as the Earl and Countess of Greenwood. It was done. He brought his hand to her lips as they turned to walk down the aisle. Ash knew the second she saw his brother. Felt the stiffening of her body. She paused. Stumbled. He held on to her. His brother's brows drew together then he grinned as if acknowledging he'd done what he came here for.

Chandler nodded, a grin lighting up his face. Harris tilted her chin. Lifted it high. Walked past the man along with the woman who didn't smile. A smile would change her features. Ash wondered if the woman knew what went on between the brothers. If Chandler told her what he did to Harris? He imagined not.

They chose to forego a receiving line until they reached the mansion. Until then, they cut cake on the lawn then danced together with the villagers watching. Ash didn't intend to speak to Chandler yet he understood that might be difficult if his brother had other ideas. He wished he could ignore the fact his brother came uninvited. If he chose to attend the feast, he would be flanked by the cousins along with the two men he hired. He would not be able to do anything to ruin this day. Though his being in attendance put a damper on the event, he wasn't about to let Chandler ruin this special day for Harris.

Ashton helped a trembling Harris into the carriage. Tapped the roof after they were settled. Ash sat beside her. Pulled her into his arms. He meant to kiss her. Wished to erase the sight of his brother, at least for a short time. His pulse raced. He leaned in close then whispered to her, "Feel the fire...don't think about anything else..." He kissed her then parting her lips with his tongue, he captured her essence. Searching within for the heat. For the fire. Flames scorched. Tempest flared. He savored the moment. She responded with more sweetness than he could remember.

Ash wished for nothing more than to forget the uninvited guest. Forget he might need to confront him. He didn't think she would allow a confrontation. "Why?" she asked after they separated for a moment. Her hand rested on his chest. "Why did he come uninvited? Who was the woman? How could any woman want to be with that monster?"

He wished he could tell her he didn't know. Couldn't. Didn't have an answer to even one of her questions. Just as he knew her thoughts, he knew his brothers. He lifted his shoulders a bit. "Chandler wished to upset us both. For a reason I don't understand, he wanted us to see the woman. She was speaking to him in her head. Ash realized then the woman was a shifter. Odd. The Ice Queen is what he calls her. She is also known in his circles as Winter Snow. Though that is not her real name." Ash paused.

He heard that before. The description fit the woman. While Chandler wanted a bit of revenge, the woman apologized to him. She'd wished to keep his brother from attending. He cared little for her wishes. Did what he pleased.

"Ice Queen, that sounds harsh. She did appear as royalty though. Held herself aloof," Harris told him. "I wish he did not attend. I also understand if you knew he was here why you allowed him to stay. We both *ken* my cousins along with my brothers would have extricated him from the church if you gave the word."

Ash touched her cheek with the back of his hand. "Might still need to do that. I wouldn't wish to hurt the woman. She is his pawn. Didn't wish to cause a scene at our wedding. Didn't want this day ruined any more than his showing up did."

"How could anyone give up their autonomy to become under that man's control?" Harris questioned.

Ash lifted his shoulders, wondering if he should tell Harris the truth. He imagined that was the only way to proceed with this. "It's fairly simple. The lady loves him. I did look into her thoughts as I did Chandler's. Was surprised I could read hers. I don't know anything about the woman. It seemed, when she felt me breaching her mind, she closed it to me. That woman does a much better job than you."

He heard Harris' gasp of surprise. "She's a shifter."

"Believe so."

"Does Chandler know about her abilities? He wouldn't force her, would he? That's a stupid question. The man had every intention of forcing me."

"My brother has not forced her. Everything the woman has done with him has been fine with her. She's been willing to go forward with his plans for her. Though I do think what they've done is tawdry. Like I say, she closed her mind to me. There are things she doesn't wish for me to discover. Chandler was focused on me, not on what the pair did together in privacy. Don't wish to know."

In his arms, Harris shuddered. For the rest of the trip, he meant to attend to his new bride with more finesse, pleasanter thoughts. His hand slid along her leg, lifting her skirts. Her flesh silken. Teased. Explored. Touched upon her thigh. Higher then so he could spread his fingers across her belly. It was a gesture to discover if a child had been conceived. There was no indication of life. He was disappointed.

"Devil," she whispered as his free hand cupped a clothed breast. Moved his palm across the tightening nipple.

He'd not had enough of his wife. Didn't think he'd ever get enough. He knew she wanted him. In this short distance from the church to his home, there wasn't sufficient time.

"Witch," he murmured, his voice soft. Needed to arouse the raw passion that came to a peak so fast and furious. Tugged the sleeves down so her breasts were exposed to the chill air then to his mouth. His tongue curled around one hard tip while he explored other delicious places. He slid a finger between her legs to discover her hot. Wet. Needing him. Desperate. Willing. Her head fell back. He slid his tongue along the column then across her collarbones. Sipped at the hollow between them where her life's blood catapulted. Captured her mouth again. Tiny cries of pleasure whimpered from the woman he adored.

"Don't think I can wait through the feasts, the cutting of the cakes. Two cakes. The dances. I need you so damn much. You're on fire. You've set me on fire. Created a raging tempest within." He set her hand on his stiff sex. "Do you know how much I want you? Feel me. Touch me." He wished there was time for her to free him.

There was none.

Harris gave him a tiny whimper as the carriage slowed. Came to a halt. They arrived. In haste, he pulled the corsage into place. Lifted the sapphire she wore. For a moment held the gem in his hand.

"Behave yourself," Ash told her with a hoot of laughter at the expression that painted her lovely features.

She snorted. Poked him in the chest. "Me?" Her brows lifted upward in question. Then, with another poke to his chest. "It is you who needs to behave."

He set her on the seat. She sent him a fierce scowl of denial. Unable to help himself he traced the small crease between her eyebrows with his thumb. The door opened. He leaned back. "You look fine. Everything is in place."

Hearing his whispered words Harris shot him a second glower. His laughter barked. She delighted him in every way. Later, he would unfasten everything she wore. With light sure strokes, he would relieve her of her wedding finery. He would take as much time as possible to savor each delicate porcelain spot he uncovered. His loving of her tonight would be slow, mesmerizing. She would beg.

Harris didn't know but he ordered a table for them. It was set on a platform in the front of the room. A bridal table with a huge tablecloth that touched the floor on three sides. There was one tradition from Clan Chaton he meant to continue. During the wedding feast he intended to seduce his bride in front of their friends and family. Wanted to see her eyes glaze over when she climaxed. Though doing so would be pure torture for him. He would enjoy every second of the seduction.

Once safe on the ground, Ash led her to the prepared gardens at the back of the house. He held her hand high as they walked down the long pathway toward the revelers. A loud cheer rang out as the villagers saw them. They walked through the crowds greeting each person. Chatting about mundane topics, shaking hands. The weather being the most often commented on. Ash didn't know the name of everyone but he made certain they stopped for each couple to exchange a few words. The tables were set with an abundant amount of food, ale and wine as well. The bonfires were lit. Musicians played. The crowd lively.

A lilting song picked up the pace making toes tap to the rhythm. Bagpipes played a familiar tune. This was their dance. All waited for them to begin. He bowed low. "Would you like to dance, Lady Wolcott?"

"Would love to, Lord Wolcott." She curtsied gracing him with a smile that sent heat straight to his loins.

He pulled her into his arms, dancing on the soft grass. Held her too close. One hand splayed on her delightful butt. He took liberties. She wouldn't complain. Knew her brother's along with her cousins did the same on their wedding night. Their feet flew with the energetic tune. Another song played, haunting as well as slow. Another dance followed that one. At the sound of the music, the guests formed groups. Exchanged partners as the dancing continued. By the time she was back in his arms, she was breathless. Smiling. He kissed her soundly on the mouth. They drank ale. Accepted the toasts of the well-wishers. Listened to the bawdy jokes about the night they would share. Her cheeks flamed with heated color. How much she understood, Ash was never certain.

Hawk stood by the table that held the four huge cakes baked for this occasion. He tapped a fork on the cup of ale he'd been drinking. The chatter slowed then stopped. All faces were turned to him. He bellowed, "Time for the cutting of the cake. I've been told that as long as the musicians wish to keep playing and all of you people wish to party, the food along with the ale will flow. We have servants who will provide for the guests all night. We wish for you to enjoy the evening as will we."

Another rousing cry went up around the gardens. The lit bonfires were tended. Sparks raced skyward. A partial moon stood out on the horizon. There were added servants to keep the fires burning. More to keep the tables filled.

Ash stepped up to the cake, Harris' hand in his. "Shall we?" He arched a brow. A half-smile formed on his face. "Cut the first cake of the night."

"Yes, of course." For a few seconds she looked down. Ash felt certain she didn't want him to look into her eyes. She was hiding her feelings. Suspected what she intended. This was the first, she'd been able to keep him from her head. She wavered.

Ash caught a glimpse of her thoughts. His new wife was up to something. He bent over, "As I said before, little witch, if I were you, I would not try what it is you are thinking. You will regret doing so."

"Don't say that too loudly. There could be repercussions." She laughed dancing away from him, her skirts twirling around her legs giving him glimpses of slender ankles. She gave Hawk a huge hug. Her big brother lifted her off her feet. She tossed her head back laughing again as she caught his eyes on her. Unnerving him with her easy laughter.

"We'll see. You go first. Be advised that whatever you do I'll follow tenfold. You cannot win this game you might choose to play."

He didn't think she cared about his threat. She would please herself. Would never care if he left cake on her face to be licked off.

Growing up with two older brothers made her more daring than a woman should be. He imagined that was why she pursued him. Chased after him even when she was too young. She'd let him kiss her when she was only sixteen. He recalled that scene with a clear vivid picture. The recollection pleasant. Even then he felt the fire of the caress including her response. After that kiss behind the mercantile, he stayed away from Carnoch. Made certain his orders would remain farther north in the highlands. Even then he couldn't escape Harris along with her easy beguiling ways. Her family often visited the cabin that was near the fort. In most cases, she vacationed with them. Once he caught her swimming in her cat form. Had to stay put in order to guard her from a nearby British patrol. She didn't know he was watching her. When she shifted from her cat to her human form, he tried with desperation not to look at her. It was to no avail. Impossible. She stretched. He turned away. She sat down on a rock to sun herself. After several minutes passed, he turned to look at her positive she would have clothed herself by then.

His jaw gaped open, stunned by her beauty, rare beauty. True, she was young. Not fully matured as a woman would be. Even in her youth her breasts were rounded with rose colored tips. Her hips flared. She possessed curves everywhere he wished to explore. Everything about Harris beckoned to him. He couldn't go to her. If he did, he'd terrify her. She would have had no idea he was also a shifter...not a black panther but a white tiger. He understood all too well the danger of discovery she courted.

Weak kneed he sat down. Leaned against a solitary tree to wait for sounds that she was getting dressed then leaving. He didn't dare look or go to her. Didn't dare stand to catch another glimpse of her maiden's form. He needed to remain observant but hidden. By the time she turned seventeen, relief swept through him. Without guilt, she was now old enough to steal a kiss from. He wished for far more than a kiss from this tempting woman.

At their next encounter, she was still young. He stole another kiss. She made it clear she liked the kiss and made herself available for more of the same. Harris understood how to lead a man to foolishness. How to make him mindless with need. She would come upon him at the most startling times. He was only a man. Knew he couldn't take this to the conclusion he wished until she was older.

He'd been leaving Carnoch to return to London. His father was ill.

That day when she ran after him, he lost the ability to resist her sweet seductive charms. She came for a kiss. When he took the process farther than the kiss she intended, he frightened her. Then...well...then the fire erupted. Flames ignited in both of them that couldn't be doused. A tempest stormed between them. She gave him her heart that day. He gifted her with ecstasy. He didn't take what he most wanted.

He left for London. Wished he dared bring her with him. She had just turned eighteen. He couldn't. Her parents would storm after him then demand his head on a platter. Both his father along with the family business needed his attention. He returned a year later. Now, they were cutting their first cake. He knew she meant to smear the sweet confection on his face. If she did, he would return the favor. The taste of her along with the icing would be divine.

Ash wasn't wrong. Before he could grab her hand to stop her, the cake was smashed on his face. To his delight she licked his face. Touched the icing smeared there with her tongue. Sipped on his skin. The villagers cheered and laughed. Urged them to be more daring. Cried out his name then hers. Told her he should do the same.

He did. She was in his arms. He was kissing her, savoring the sweetness that was both the cake and Harris too. He slipped his tongue deep inside her mouth. Ran it across her lips. Relished the frosting lingering on her cheek coupled with the satin finish of her skin. After he pulled away, he was pleased with the beautiful smile he saw on her face. A portly matron with silver gray hair handed them both damp towels. With gentle hands, he wiped her face. She did the same for him. The moment was erotic, evocative. His body hummed to life. With this done, he was ready for the consummation, not another group of people and another cutting of the cake.

"Are we going to do this again in the house? Are you willing to call a truce?" He wasn't positive his body could handle much more temptation. His sex throbbed, ached for release. Ah, he did intend to seduce. To charm. To make her eyes glaze over with her pleasure. They had all night coupled with a meal to eat. This, with the cake, was nothing but foreplay. What he did beneath the table would be more of the same. Hoped to have her so stimulated they would run to the bedchamber shedding clothing on their way.

She was laughing now. "A truce would be nice. Can we trust each other that far?" With a flirting lift to her brows, she tilted her head. Slipped her tongue along her bottom lip where he realized she encountered more icing. Harris understood what she did. Knew the gesture inflamed. He didn't trust her with a cease-fire.

"Remember, I will know the instant you change your mind. You are still unable to hide your thoughts from me. If you break this armistice, I will retaliate," Ash reminded her, his voice soft. In some ways, he wished she would give in to her impulsive nature. "Come now. Wave to these folks. Toss them kisses. These are our people. Good wishes abound. Let's go eat. We've a wedding night ahead of us that I'm famished for. We must have enough energy to last the night through." To the delight to all watching, he swept her into his arms.

"Put me down." Harris pounded on his shoulder. "You big oaf. You can't carry me all the way." She was laughing though. Laughed until Chandler stepped in front of them. The confrontation was unexpected.

Chandler turned to Brady who had been his ever-present shadow. Brady, hands on his hips watched. "Just wish to speak with my brother for a moment. You can give me some privacy. I don't intend harm to either one. Though I don't know what my brother told you about me. Here to congratulate him on his fine marriage to a beautiful woman."

Ashton did put Harris on her feet. He nodded, sending Brady a small distance away before turning to his brother. "You have a minute." His voice was harsh, demanding. Ash didn't want anything to do with his brother.

"Wished to tell you how happy you've made me. To my delight, my new life is much more satisfying than the old. The disinheritance is wonderful. Turned me into a new man. No more obligations to fulfill for the old man or anyone else. Have no one to answer to except my pleasures. My life as well as my time is mine to do with as I please."

He turned. Pulled the woman standing behind him to his side. His hand rested with possessiveness on her hip. "This is Winter Snow. I'm quite fond of her. She is one of the stars in my new endeavor. I call her the Ice Queen. Actually, Miss Snow is the star."

The woman flinched. Stiffened. The movement perceptible only to a man who was used to observing. Ash felt it though as did his brother.

Chandler smiled. Whatever it was they did together, Miss Snow didn't like it. Though even now, she held her head high, impervious to his leering brother. Chandler meant to discomfit her too.

"You must come to the show sometime. It's delightful. You might enjoy the entertainment. It is unique. Exciting. Bring your wife. I could give the two of you the stage if you'd like. You could have an audience. Everyone there is willing. Don't employ anyone who is not."

Ash nodded. There was so much the man wasn't saying. While Ash delved into his brother's head, he was beginning to catch the drift of what this enterprise was about. Some of the information had been provided by the letter from his father. His brother's thoughts rifled through his head. He felt sick to his stomach. He stared at the woman standing next to his brother. Needed to dismiss the pair. "Miss Snow. Chandler."

He turned on his heel. Brady appeared.

Walking away he forced his mind back to his wedding along with the feast awaiting them. Harris walked beside him, clutching his hand as if she too heard Chandler's thoughts. Felt the woman's chilled gaze on the back of his neck. The woman was...intriguing. Perhaps that was what attracted Chandler to her. His brother didn't deserve a woman such as her. Without a doubt, Ash understood his brother used her. He sent his thoughts to Miss Snow. Delved into the truth of this entertainment. She remained reticent.

Whatever happens, if you need me. Send for me. You know how. I'll be there for you. Don't let Chandler hurt you. Understand you don't enjoy what the two of you are doing. It isn't necessary unless he holds something over your head.

That won't happen. I can never come to you for help or understanding. You see, I love him. Chandler is my mate. Will never tell him no. Can't. He owns my heart as well as my soul now as well into eternity. You understand. Somehow, I need to orchestrate my claiming. Otherwise, we will end. I won't chance that. Need to teach him how to shift. Yes, Chandler is also a shifter.

His stomach heaved at her last words. Words that would seal her fate to everlasting hell if she remained with him. How could she not? What she thought couldn't be true. Chandler could not be her true mate. He was never able to change form. She had to be mistaken. Chandler was so wrong for this beautiful woman.

"Ash?" Harris' concerned voice snapped him back to the present along with the delights of his new bride.

He covered her hands with his. Let's celebrate. As I said earlier, I'm eager for the night. Eager for the seduction of my wife during the wedding feast."

"You can't. Won't allow it to happen."

"You can try. We both know you will fail."

Upstairs in the ballroom, Ash wasn't disappointed. Heather along with all the ladies did a spectacular job decorating. Flowers were everywhere. Servants carried trays of champagne straight from France. The bridal table appeared just as he wished. He led her to the table. Wine had been poured. With a wink, he handed her a crystal glass.

"We will now see what happens next. If nothing else, I'm planning on at least one tradition of Clan Chaton being carried out tonight. What do you think? Are you up for a gentle persuasion? Do you wish to be charmed until your toes curl? Want to watch you as your eyes glaze over with your pleasure. Private, just between the two of us. No one will see. Though they will all know."

~ * ~

Chandler, accompanied by Snow, were back at the home he purchased for employment as well as living. He was still looking for the perfect Autumn Bounty. So far, none of the women lived up to his expectations. To his misfortune he found the perfect woman at the wedding, Lainie Frasier. She was married to one of Harris' brothers. Since the perfect woman wasn't available, he would need to settle for second best. In this group of females, there had been a few promising applicants. He was settling on one.

A long breath of disappointed air left his lungs. If there was any way...no...the woman would never be willing. He couldn't even approach her. The Scottish clan circled every woman there as if he had designs on all of them. No, only one...

Now, his second choice stood in front of him. She was clothed in a gown of yellow satin. Lace edged her bodice. Tiny fasteners lined the back of the dress down her spine. She stood in front of him, an earthy beauty. Perfect for Autumn Bounty. The striking simmer of green eyes stared back at him. Auburn hair curled around her shoulders falling down to a trim waist that flared to generous hips a man could hold onto when he took her. He wondered if the triangle of hair between her thighs would be the same bewitching color as the hair on her head. Her breasts might be her best features. First, he would need to see them. Savor the taste. Test the hardened crowns. Her flesh a delicate ivory in color. No freckles decorated her skin. That was rare for a redhead.

A restless energy seemed to possess her. The straight back along with the tilt of her chin spoke of defiance. Still, despite the obvious dislike of her new profession, she signed the waver. Perhaps she wasn't one hundred percent willing. He would discover what she would as well as would not allow in the next few minutes. If she intended to remain employed, she would learn she might not always get what she wished for. What he could tell from what he witnessed so far was that she wasn't an experienced whore. Neither did he think she was a virgin. This woman had been used at least once. Though her story intrigued him, he didn't need to know why she was here. The simple truth was that she walked through the front door of her own accord. Would most likely sign the contract that would bind her to him for at least a year.

He nodded to Jake to begin with the second phase of the interviews. The first phase was to rid her of her given name. To sign the papers while making certain she understood all the terms. Nothing of what was expected from her was withheld. From here on out, if she passed the second phase, she would be known as Autumn Bounty. She would comply to what was asked of her. Autumn would also be well-compensated for her work. If she invested her new found wealth, she would amass a fortune that would tide her over in her later years.

Jake stood behind her. Swept her long hair into a tight bun that he pinned on top of her head. Chandler needed to see all of her, inspect those parts his audience would love the most. He decided he would drape her in sheer fawn colored fabric that would be decorated with silk leaves the color of fall. They would highlight her hair. Frame the near perfect oval of her face. Other than that, he'd not settled on a scenario for her first performance. He tapped his chin. Understood the program would need to be unique.

With her gown unfastened, Jake slid the sleeves from her arms before pushing the fabric to the floor. Chandler was pleased with what he viewed so far. Her tiny waist was cinched in tight by the corset she wore. The tips of a man's hands could touch when they spanned her waist. Her corset pushed her breasts high. Large rounded globes showed above the fabric. The dark rouge of the aureoles could just be seen peeking above the corset. Sheer stockings covered her legs to mid-thigh. Tiny yellow slippers were even now being tossed aside. As Jake lifted each leg to remove stockings, Chandler saw provocative places. Thighs dimpled in delightful spots. She was nothing like his Ice Queen. Perfect. Each of his ladies were very different. Each would tantalize as well as arouse different men with different tastes. This lady, while not as fetching as Lainie, would add to his coffers. She would also demand a huge price above stairs where she would be auctioned for a night of pleasure with the man or woman willing to pay the most.

Chandler was delighted by his find.

The ties of her corset were undone. The garment fell to the ground. Her chemise followed. Pleased, ah, yes, thrilled very much. Beneath his chin, he tapped his fingers together...thinking. Jake turned her around so the small audience could see her then back so she faced Chandler. Her breasts swayed nicely as she moved. Her butt well-rounded. While her spine was straight, stiff, it was beautiful.

"Carry on..." Chandler smiled at Jake. "You know what to do."

Standing behind Autumn, he set his palms over her nipples, rubbed and teased. Explored with more intimate strokes while all watched. Her hands remained at her sides. Chandler told her to show no emotion. To keep her eyes open. She followed orders quite well. She was what he wanted. Autumn Bounty would be Jake's as well as Bertram's if he wished. The woman seemed to please this man. She would bring top dollar at the auctions as well as for the rooms upstairs. He was doubly pleased. Doubly rewarded.

"I wish to see her expression when she reaches that point of no return. When her body takes over and she cannot control what is being done." Chandler watched intently as Jake had sex with this woman. She moaned softly, a siren's song in the silence of the room. A sweet tempest arousing all who watched. While she climaxed, the men in the audience adjusted their pants. The women in the audience squirmed. Her body, the innate sensual appeal of her, captivated the viewers. The perfumed scent of a woman well-pleasured wafted through the air. Chandler loved the scent of sex.

When the pinnacle was reached, she cried out, screamed as sensations rippled through her. Bucked. Heaved. Her hips met each fierce thrust. Jake let out a hoarse yell when he left his seed inside her. Yes, his patrons would love this woman, Autumn Bounty. He would have to think more on how he wanted Jake to take her. She must be positioned so her bounteous curves would best show.

One week...he had one week to set up this thrilling evocative experience for his customers. His mind was at work.

"Autumn is perfect," Chandler said as he stood.

He was hard. Ready for a private encounter with Winter before the next show. Summer was on tonight. This was her first time on stage with one hundred men and women watching her sensual journey. Johnny was her main man. He would be the male performing with her. She, of course, true to form would choose an audience member for a second dalliance on stage. After that, as with all the women except Winter, she would be auctioned for the rest of the evening to the man willing to pay the most for the use of her feminine charms.

As he walked to his suite of rooms, he was reminded that Winter had not been pleased to attend the wedding of his brother. She never spoke about the affair. He knew though. That almost imperceptible flinch told him the truth. Despite her stoicism, she couldn't hide her feelings from him. Winter did try. He gave her credit for that. She always wished to delight him. Wasn't always successful though that fact also pleased him. No woman was perfect. Chandler was also pleased she came very close to that ultimate goal...flawlessness. Something to strive for.

Chandler wanted to understand the circumstances of her life that led her to him. She was the only one of his employees he cared about. On that subject, Winter was a closed book refusing to give him a shred of information. When he entered the living room, he found her curled up on a chair reading. She looked up. The shimmer of her eyes betrayed her feelings. Winter rose. She understood what he wanted. As she walked toward him, she shed her clothing. Was not difficult. All she wore was a blue silk robe he gave her after that first performance that brought the house down. That one presentation set the stage for the next few weeks.

He hired an accountant. Decided to pay his ladies as well as his gentlemen handsomely. He could afford to be generous. With the added incentive the better the shows became. The cast put their hearts and souls into the telling of their stories. Evocative. Titillating. Vibrant. Sometimes the players adlibbed. Fell from the script in delightful sexy ways. They accommodated all avenues of sexuality. All the strange diversions men and women wanted, wished to see fulfilled.

Three weeks passed. They were going on the fourth. Chandler was certain Winter must be increasing with his child. They made love every night. Sometimes during the day. He was pleased with the thought of an offspring of his. In the mornings he looked for signs. When she entered her ninth month, they would perform just as they did during their first encounter. The gown would be reconstructed with two openings, one in the front, the second in the back. He hardened thinking about the delightful picture Winter would make swollen with his child. All would know the babe was his. All understood he didn't share this woman. Perhaps after the birth, he would reconsider.

Winter stood beside him, her hand on his chest, ridding him of his shirt. As the fabric fell to the floor, she kissed him and made a trail down to the waistband of his pants. Freed him. Touched him.

He swept her into his arms. Strode to the bed. Fell down upon it with her beneath him. Kissed her mouth hard. Deep. The hot suck of his mouth encapsulated hers. Tasted mint along with a hint of sweet red wine. The mating was swift. Almost savage. He ravished her mouth. Her breasts. He would take more time when he returned from the theater tonight.

"Would you like to watch this evening?" He asked, sweeping hair from her damp forehead.

Her orgasms both on stage as well as in private delighted all his senses. Winter was everything he'd ever wanted in a woman. Intelligent. Sensuous. Curvaceous. She was even loving. Never expected that emotion from one of his women. When he once thought he wanted the lady his brother possessed, he laughed. Harris was nothing like Winter. She would never fulfill all his wild desires. Come to him in the darkest of storms. Fulfill his wildest dreams. Winter melted in his arms.

"No..." Her voice was soft, hesitant because she didn't ever disagree with him. If he insisted, she would make an appearance by his side.

Yes, Chandler understood if he insisted, she would acquiesce. Winter would stand by his side, while the characters he created cavorted in front of them. He found he wished for that tonight. Needed the warmth of her small body next to him. She gave him confidence. Whetted his appetite for carnal delights.

"Why?"

He would know the reason. If he asked, she would be honest.

Her smile was weak. She lifted her small shoulders. Her tongue slipped between partially open lips as she hesitated with her response. "Do you wish for me to be there?" She looked at him, her eyes burning fire from the climax.

Chandler ran his palm over the tight hard bud that was forming again. "You want me still? Again, before I go downstairs by myself?"

"Always. I'm tired. It's not that I don't wish to stand by your side. It's..." Once again, she hesitated to tell him. He didn't appreciate her reluctance.

"Are you pregnant?" Chandler asked, hopeful. He discovered he wanted a child.

She blinked a few times. Ran her tongue across her lip. Turned her head to the side then back to him. "It's too soon to know."

"You think you are."

"Maybe. Will I still perform?"

"Your increasing will be a delight to your fans. Each month you will look different. Your body will swell with our child. All will believe the baby belongs to me. You've had sex with no one else. Except for a couple of women."

Even now with stronger feelings toward this woman he couldn't call what they did making love. What they did was too hard, too savage, primal. They had sex. What they did together was loud, chaotic. A mating of a man and a woman. That was all. Chandler didn't know if he could simply make love to her. To anyone?

"He...she...will be a bastard."

"What does that matter?"

Chapter Nine

Ashton led Harris to the table set up for them. She understood what he'd done, shooting him a fierce scowl. Knew what he meant to do here. Heard rumors to his intentions from family as well as friends. Harris wasn't certain if she would be embarrassed or mortified. All would understand he was seducing her. She could hide her face in his chest but her entire family would...know. If she could figure out how to do so, she would change this around.

She would seduce Ashton.

This was different than in Carnoch. At home the female was exhausted from the ceremony. She was weak. Could not protest. Would never wish to object. Now, tonight, she was able to take charge of all her faculties. She should tell him no. Tell him he had no rights here. Again, she thought about the alternatives. Yes, what she should do would be to change this up. Seduce him. Watch him climax while all her family tended to their meal in front of them. That thought caused a wide grin. She turned her head so her new husband wouldn't see. Tried to block thoughts.

He would never allow her to do that.

Harris found she was still reeling from the brief encounter with Chandler. She didn't wish to think about the man. Ash filled her wine glass. One arm wrapped around her waist in a way that shouted possession.

"Drink."

The wine was delicious, sweet... She could forget what he would do if she drank enough. If she got tipsy, he would take wicked advantage. She found that she wished to remember every minute detail of this, their wedding celebration along with the night to come. Ash took their glasses then set them on the table.

"A brief kiss for our audience of well-wishers. A fine way to begin the seduction of Harris. Don't you think? I would have your compliance in this. Newly married couples kiss." His hands were on her shoulders, slid to her waist to pull her to him. His lips found hers, touched, stroked. Heat rose. Tempest soared. Flames spiraled. She did want him. He created magic. Could feel his arousal press against her belly. It would not take much stroking to send him to heaven. This might be too easy.

"We should sit," Harris said as she began to formulate a plan of attack. If she wasn't circumspect, he would know her plans. She would need to be quick, sure in every move. Ash might put her aside. Move her hand from him. He might well read her thoughts. She tried to block him from her head.

Ash tapped her nose, grinning as if he knew what she was thinking. "What do you have up your sleeve, love? You're plotting something. Let me into your mind. I won't like it if you block me. Don't wish for you to learn that skill."

Harris was trying very hard to block her thoughts from him. If she thought about this night, she might be able to keep him from learning what it was she had in mind for now. He knew she was planning. Plotting. She brought a deep breath of air into her lungs as she continued to formulate her plans.

Her smile sweet, she lifted a shoulder. "Nothing...something, you are right to be suspicious," she whispered, her voice soft. "I'm famished. We do need to eat. Seems it has been forever since I ate a scone at breakfast," she told him sitting, watching the servants pile the table with food.

She understood they would eat. The haggis smelled divine, the stew and soup as well. She loved the neeps and tatties he'd had the cook make special for her Scottish family. Her stomach rumbled. For the next few minutes, she needed to fill her stomach. Needed the strength to proceed with her plan of seduction. She could charm her husband to her will. After that she would see what could be accomplished with this man. His hand rested on her thigh while he piled a plate with food.

"We will share," he whispered, squeezing, stroking, moving her gown along her legs. Inching the fabric higher then higher still.

It seemed she would need to take the initiative. Too bad he didn't wear a kilt. Since she had both hands free, Harris reached beneath the table.

Set one hand upon his sex. He jerked. His eyes narrowed. With the other she deftly unfastened his pants. This might be easier than she thought.

"Little witch," he whispered, touching his tongue to her ear. His warm mint scented breath whispered across her cheek. "I see what you've planned. Know now what was up your sleeve." Again, Ash jerked when she touched his sex, wrapped her hand around his hard length. He was sleek, solid, satin steel to her touch. He set his gaze on her.

"Devil," she told him as he slowly pulled up her skirt. His fingers toyed with bare flesh. She moved her hand up then down. Stroked. Tempted.

The tips of his fingers caressed naked thigh. Explored higher. "Open for me. Two can play your game."

She moved her hand. Watched him clench his jaw. Fight for control. Knew he would be hard pressed to remain untouched by her actions. When he saw her smile, "You will..." he was cut off as his arousal grew. He gripped her wrist trying to stop the climax she initiated. She decided the orgasm could wait a few more seconds.

With other plans in her head, she dropped her fork. Slipped beneath the table to retrieve the fallen cutlery.

Don't you dare.

Why not? I find I cannot help myself. You are too virile. You need me too much. I feel your need. You need relief. I'm the only one who can give you that. Try to stop me.

Harris moved his knees apart. Came between them. Kissing the tip of his penis, she moved lower until she touched the length with her tongue. After that she moved back. Swept him into her mouth. Sucked hard. Laved. Nipped.

Harris...Elliott is here. He's standing in front of the table.

No!

Frozen on the spot, she didn't know what to do now. Of all the people in the entire world the last person she needed here at this time was her father. Heat stole through her body. Rushed to her face.

"Where is my daughter? Thought I saw her here a moment ago. Did she go somewhere?"

"She a..." His low throaty voice would give all away.

His sex was encompassed in her mouth. Even though her father stood at their table, she didn't remove her mouth from his member. His hand on her head, Harris gulped. Touched him with her teeth. Her nerves seemed to be snapping one at a time. The thunder of her heart pounded in her ears.

You've got to come up here for air.

I cannot. He will know. He cannot know.

"Dropped something..."

Harris saw his fingers on the cloth as it began to move to the side. Elliott was going to lift the cloth to help. Her father would see what she was up to. No!

"Sir...I would not do that." His words were husky, drawn with tension. Throaty. Telling anyone who'd ever been in his position what was happening was not possible.

Elliott's hand fell away. He rocked back on his heels. Snorted. Harris imagined the look on his face. The sudden realization of what his daughter might be doing beneath the table. Why did her impetuosity always get her into trouble?

"I see..." Elliott's deep voice echoed in her ears.

She'd heard that voice before. No, she had not. This time the sound held a bit of a chuckle. Brought more embarrassment to her. His hoot of laughter mortified.

From beneath the table his feet disappeared. She heard the sound of his boots as he left. Breathed a silent sigh of relief. Remembered what she was doing before she was interrupted. All would be fine if no one else came to see where she disappeared. Harris meant to finish what she so impulsively began.

With her mouth, she worked him. Sucked. Rested her hands on his hard belly. Explored the insides of his thighs. Cupped him. Felt the muscles constrict then quiver as she continued her assault on his person. His fingers slid into her hair. Pins fell to the floor. This would be something she would need explained. Prayed she would not. If she were lucky no one would notice.

Felt the spasms of his release begin. Drew on him harder. He lifted her away.

His seed spilled onto her hand, on his belly. She reached for the napkin in his lap. Wiped his belly clean then her hands. Kissed him there.

Touched the tip of him with her mouth, Kissed again.

His hands under her arms brought her up to him. She found herself flattened against him. Her breasts against his chest. He kissed her. Swept his tongue deep inside her mouth. Ran his hands through her hair. What was left of her pins landed on the table as well as the floor around them.

She was shocked by the ferocity of the kiss. Amazed at the savagery. Responded in kind to him as his hands ran along her sides to beneath her breasts then back to her hips. The clearing of a throat behind her stopped them both.

It was Cameron as well as Lainie. "You two should lay low for a while. Too much pleasure before bed time can backfire."

"Go away, big brother."

"We will take care. Listen to your words of wisdom." Ashton said with smooth finesse that Harris didn't understand how he could possess after what just happened.

She was shaking. Trembling from the knowledge of what she did. While...Ash was the picture of composure. He pulled her up so she sat on his lap. Watched as her brother walked away.

"You will... that's what you said before you dropped beneath the table to charm me. "I would know the rest of what you were planning to say."

"I will?" She arched her brows, smirking while at the same time wondering what it was she was saying I will to. Pleased with herself, she gasped when his finger found hot wet flesh beneath her gown.

He would seek her capitulation. Retaliation. Would find the means to embarrass her in front of her family, his friends. He knew where to touch, where to stroke. Just as he had, she would climax before the feast would end. His long fingers tantalized, fondled. She opened more fully for him. Gave him greater access. He held her head against his chest. She heard the thundering of his heart.

Her body heaved. Writhed. Vibrated with the force he created within her.

"Not a sound...hush...let it come. I know you can do that. No one is watching us. If they were, they are looking away now. I will see to your pleasure. Close your eyes. Keep your pretty face against my chest."

She did. The first pulses grew, shattered within her. She sucked in air. Bit him through his shirt. He stroked her unbound hair as her body quivered. Smoothed his hand down her back. As her body quieted, she heard his soft masculine chuckle. The possession evident.

"You thought you would dissuade me from my purpose. Tell me if I'm right." Ash continued to stroke. Didn't remove his hand from beneath her gown. If Ash could, he would have his way with her a second time.

"Yes..."

They needed to tend to their guests. Dance. Cut the cake. Fly upstairs to their room before he...she could embarrass herself further.

"Have some wine. Drink up. I know your mouth is as parched as mine. You do understand you cannot best me. I allowed you to have your fun. Knew from the moment the thought was conceived. Your father almost put a humiliating end to the sweet-talking. Seems the man was astute. Is your mother as impulsive as you? He caught on to the machinations of his daughter while she hid beneath the table. Was able to walk away. We are married, Harris. Married folks do these things. Saw Elliott take Heather outside. What do you suppose they are doing?"

She hit him, wishing to do more damage to the arrogant man. "You did not know." The next pause was lengthy. She comprehended what Ash implied. "My father took my mother outside to do..."

"Privacy I'm sure was what was needed," he told her without skipping a beat.

"To do what we just did?"

"It will do you no good to argue the point as to whether I knew what you were thinking or not. You are still unable to block your thoughts from me..." Ash handed her a full glass of wine. "Drink. Eat another bite of this Scottish fare you love. After that we will dance, cut the cake then retire for the night. I for one also need privacy, as your mother and father do."

With her head resting on his chest, his arm around her, she did drink, did eat more. Wondered at the women bustling around the room, her mother, Wynnie, Lilly, Aila, all of them, all her cousins' wives. Pippa and Hypatia as well, giggling, looking her way. She sensed they were up to something.

"What are all your cousins-in-law doing?" he asked, having also noticed the women skittering about. "They seem harried."

Harris pushed away from him, staring into his eyes. "I don't know."

She felt confused as well as bothered. There was something afoot no one told her about. She didn't know what it could be. If they were home, in Carnoch, the women would be planning to spirit her away from her husband. She inhaled a sharp breath of air.

No.

"You don't...?" He brushed the back of his hand along her cheek. "That's the truth. Think it not. Believe you just figured out what the women are planning."

"You are encroaching inside my head. I don't like it," Harris protested, watching him, the glide of his eyes as he followed the women around the room. The women who would disappear then reappear carrying all manner of items.

"Come, let's dance. After what we just shared, I've a need to find privacy. A secluded balcony somewhere. I've a great desire to discover your lips. To taste the sweet wine. Catch the scent of my woman. I would have no more public displays of affection. One time...two times was too much for me."

She snorted, hitting his chest again. So you say. "As you reassured me time and time again, that was not public. No one was even looking our way when you spilled your seed. I would have taken it into my mouth. You know, it's impossible for you to..."

"Shush... Your father was about to look under the table. What do you think he would have seen? When I hinted doing so would not be a good idea, he stopped. Was certain he understood your predicament." Ash framed her mouth with his. Kissed her hard and deep. Kissed her again. Pushed his tongue against her lips, opening her to his strokes. She dueled with his tongue. He pulled hers into his mouth. Bit. Rubbed. Plunged deep into the hot depth. Intensified. Retreated. Held her head with his hands. Stared into her eyes. Kissed her again. Hard then gentle. Fast then slow.

Gasping for air, she distanced herself. Pushed on his hand that now covered her breast, his thumb moving across the covered tip. Inflaming her. The gesture sent more heat into her. "Stop." Her voice cracked. Wavered. "You said..."

His hand dropped away as if he realized with a start that what he was doing would be evident to anyone looking their way. "My apologies. Didn't mean to be so blatant. Know you don't wish to share what we do together with the rest of the world. Neither do I." His voice was harsh. She understood he was angry with himself. "We need to finish with the necessary duties. Want to be alone with my wife. Seems I've waited forever for this moment."

Harris felt as if he knew something he didn't want to tell her about. She sensed what he was thinking concerned his brother. He took more from the short encounter outside than she did. Had something to do with public displays. Something they nearly participated in. Except for a long tablecloth...

Ash stood, extended his hand to her. "We'll dance. Your father and brothers will wish for a dance. We'll cut the cake... For now, we will forget about the seductions. In our future, all will be private between us. Don't wish to share you with anyone."

He did have ideas he didn't block her from viewing. She heated. With the tip of his finger, he touched her flaming cheek and followed a path down her neck.

"A delightful shade of pink. Do you want to continue to see my thoughts? If so, you will be the color of a beet." He waved his hand at the guests. "All here will understand what you are thinking about."

On the dance floor, he whirled her around the room. Brought her close, too close for propriety. Cupped her buttocks with his hands. Brought her flush against him so she could feel his hard shaft. She flushed from the intimate contact. All understood they were a newly married couple. They would be looking forward to the marriage bed. With a tap on his shoulder, Ash gave way to Elliott.

Both her brothers danced with her. They did not find the time to search out a secluded balcony. Had not been able to walk onto the grounds for a kiss. She was winded when Cameron brought her to the large table that held the cake. Ash waited for her. The knife and plate for them were ready.

Do we still have that truce? I would know. Need to be prepared for whatever you decide. If there is no truce...

Don't threaten me with soft spoken innuendos. Once was more than enough for me. I dinna *want more icing on my face even if you mean to lick the sweet confection off. Need to go with you. Get out of here as soon as possible so we don't have to play any more games.*

I feel the same.

The cake tasted. They shared chaste bites with each other. Set the plate and fork on the table. Someone filled their glasses. Hawk toasted to the newlywed couple. Heather stood beside her. Wynnie on the other side. Each took an arm. She dragged in a long breath of air. This was not going to continue in the manner either one of them hoped or planned. She understood from past weddings, she was being kidnapped.

"Come now. We all are going to prepare the bride. This is our custom. You would have regrets if we didn't follow through with tradition. Would always feel as if you missed out on something important."

Heather smiled at Ash, shaking her head as he started to take a step then protest what they were about. The two continued on their way.

Hawk held him back yowling with his laughter. "Not now, Ashton. A bit of diplomacy is needed here. We will take you to your bride when the women let us know she is ready. In about ten minutes Heather will appear."

Beside him Roc snorted. "We both understand it will not be ten minutes. The mothers always take as long as possible. They try our patience until they believe we can endure no longer. Never so long the prospective groom breaks down the door. By the time Heather arrives back, you will find yourself pacing and drinking. Gazing at the stairway as if you want to race up those steps to be with your bride. Of course you do. All here *ken* that for a true fact. The thoughts will only burn brighter if you don't douse them soon. You must wait the allotted time. Be patient. It will all be worth the postponement of your plans.

Harris turned to look at him, dismay written clearly on both their faces before Heather tugged her away.

No, I didn't see this happening, Ash. Don't know when mother planned this little diversion tactic. Would have told you if I'd known...if I'd had any idea. No one let one clue drop this was planned. Instead of playing with each other we might have found a way to leave without cutting the cake. That would have been the only way to avoid them.

It won't be long?

Shouldn't be. They don't have to tell me anything about the claiming or the breaching of my maidenhead. We've done it all. Though most of the wives were intimate with their mates before the wedding night. Don't know of one who was not. Not even Lainie. Even though my brother thought to wait for the sacred occasion, he did not. Even he gave in to his need to touch, feel...become a part of his mate.

How long?

Mother always said fifteen minutes. I think most of the time it is longer. Ask Hawk and Cameron. They will commiserate. I hear that is what the men always do. They will ply you with ale. I heard mention of that. I was always too young to go with the women. This is just as new to me as it is to you.

I would follow. Snatch you away.

Hawk has a tight hold on one arm, Cameron on the other. Am I right?

Yes.

The last yes was a begrudging reply.

"This blatant kidnapping is for your groom," Heather told her, a sly smile on her features. "He needs patience to be with his wife. He has none, just as your brothers along with the cousins had none. Still don't."

"A learning experience. All men need to understand they cannot always have their way despite their superior strength. Cunning along with wit will always play an important part of a woman's life with her man. She must hold on to those virtues to use when her way is right," Wynnie shared a piece of advice.

"What you say is true. I cannot get an upper hand because he always knows what I'm thinking when I'm thinking it. Don't understand how to block my mind from his." She found herself rushed up the steps. Winded, she looked through the open door to the main room then farther to see into the bathing room.

Inside the bathing room was a tub with steaming water. Seemed she'd just been in that tub this morning. She imagined this was all part of the ritual. Traditions were important. Mother was right. If she'd been denied these short moments of bonding with the women in her family, she would always have regrets. The soft scent of lavender wafted her way. The women stripped her of the wedding gown, the slippers and stockings. She stepped into the tub.

Crissie poured her a huge goblet of wine. Aila brought her a sweet chocolate confection. Heather wrapped her hair into a knot on the top of her head. Harris sunk into the water. The liquid was hot. Relaxed her. She didn't wish to admit to the tension. Tonight would not be her first time. Yet...this evening would be the first with a husband. She looked forward to the night. Thrilled there was nothing for her to fear. Thought of the moment under the table when her father appeared, looking for her. The thrill. The fear of discovery. Excited.

Maisie sat down beside the tub, sipping her wine. She looked a bit wistful. "I fell in love with Hawk the moment I saw him. He tried so hard. Your brother was always afraid he'd scare me if he moved too fast. As it turned out he moved too slow." She drank again. Sipped the wine with a thoughtful expression. "Referring to Ashton, that man adores you. He is besotted. Head over heels in love. He didn't look pleased when we abducted you."

He's never told me in real words that he loves me. She swallowed then sighed, wishing he had. She would feel so much more secure if he would tell her. "I hope so. I adore him. Though sometimes I'd like to toss my wine in his face he can be so opinionated. Autocratic. High Handed."

I heard that.

Go to the devil.

His laughter came through her head loud and clear. He amused himself at her expense. Listened to what she told the women in her family. While she understood his immediate frustration, she was also annoyed by this turn of events. On the other hand, she was thrilled the women sought to include her in the tradition. This was not what they planned. Ash told her he intended to take one article of her clothing off at a time. Kiss. Stroke. Fondle all of her as he unveiled her. Supposed he would need to wait for some other time.

Jerked back to the thought the sooner she took the bath then dressed, the sooner they would bring him to the room. The sooner the two of them would be alone. There would be a conversation before that. What they would speak of she had no idea. He would not wish to talk first. That much she did know about her man.

"Perhaps you should take your time," Lainie said with laughter shadowing her words. "Always does a man good to have to wait for what he wants. We could make this kidnapping last an hour if you're amenable."

An hour might well have him breaking the door down. Harris lowered her eyes before she met Lainie's vibrant gaze. After her mother, she felt the closest with Lainie. Had shared feelings as well as frustrations about Ashton with her. At times, she opened her heart to her brother's wife. "You were my confidant when I thought Ash was seeing other women. He swears now that since he first kissed me when I was sixteen, he hasn't been with another female. That's hard to believe."

"You must trust in his word. Mates don't lie to each other. It's not possible to tell untruths to each other. What else is there if you don't have trust?" Lainie asked, lifting her shoulders. "You were distraught at the time. Fearful he didn't want you. Confused from misinformation. You also didn't know he was a shifter or your mate. Now that you do, the knowledge should change everything."

"I was. Terrified of even a kiss from him. I understood if I gave in and allowed that one kiss, our relationship would escalate too fast. I wanted those kisses. Had to tell him no so many times my words...my actions hurt both of us. He grew angry with me. When he stole me away from your wedding, I tried to run that night. That was when I learned he was a shifter. Tried to defy the man. Learned that was impossible. His cat form is formidable, strong. He wasn't having anything to do with my defiance. Thought he would tie me to the bed just so he could sleep."

"I think we've all been pelted with those same types of decisions. Once these men decide what they want they are relentless. Even when I didn't wish to return to the portal, Roc was determined I would do so. He told me he had to make certain I would never get caught up in the black hole by accident." Lainie stood, smoothed her skirts. "Now, drink your wine. Dress in that sheer gown that will delight your man. Come join us when you are done. We will chat for a while. Tell stories about each other's wedding nights. We mean to prolong this to a certain point. Don't want to have him rushing up here then barging through the door."

Left alone with her thoughts, they drifted to Ash. He was on his third glass of ale. Harris didn't realize so much time passed since she found herself dragged away from him. If she didn't get out of the water soon, she would be a wrinkled prune. Water sluiced from her naked body when she stood. The warm towel by the fire felt good as she dried herself. The gown Heather left for her was sheer, a soft peach in color. Thankfully a matching robe was laid out with it. She put everything on.

Barefoot, her hair falling around her shoulder, she picked up her glass of wine then walked into the main room.

"What now?" Harris asked, sitting on a chair near the fire. "I would see Ashton. Don't wish to wait longer. He is pacing, drinking. My brothers along with my cousins are teasing him. Not that I mind the teasing. It is my wedding night. I'd like to be with him."

"We don't have much to say to you. Lainie tells us he's claimed you. When?" Heather asked, her curiosity shining through. Yet she sounded saddened by the thought. "At one time I thought of being a part of that ceremony. Even brought the white capes with us. We were ready. Though Father Damian was unable to travel the distance. He is aging well. Nevertheless, he didn't feel as if he could travel this far. Suppose it was a good thing the deed was done when we arrived."

"Ashton told Elliott the truth. His clan's ceremony, I believe, is different from ours. The ceremony was a private observance. I experienced the sighting of other lives. Don't know if it is like ours but it is singular in the respect that we were the only two there. Naked. Without the benefit of capes. He claimed me that night. Since I was his mate, he made love to me. If you're worried about the wedding night, don't be. There will be no pain. Now, since we were married in the church, he is also my husband."

"I'm thrilled there are no fears for you," Heather said, still sounding disappointed. "We should wait only another ten minutes. After that I'll retrieve your groom. I'm certain he does grow impatient. It is the way of all men."

"Ten more minutes? Ash will not be pleased."

"No, I *dinna* imagine he will." Heather laughed.

~ * ~

Waiting felt like an eternity to Ashton. Every few seconds he looked to the stairs. Rubbed the back of his neck. Wiped sweating palms on his pants legs. Hawk as well as the rest of the clan tried to soothe his rattling nerves with ribald jests. Told him humorous stories of their wedding night. Congratulated him on the fact he would not be claiming her as well as initiating her into the ways of lovemaking. The wedding night would be flawless. Nothing to get in the way of all the pleasures the evening would bring.

The fact the men knew so much about his personal life disturbed him. Ash drank too much. He walked the length of the ballroom too many times to count. Gazed at the doorway searching for Heather. The oldest of the clan told him to buck up. Every male went through the same practice. He had the rest of his life to share with her. He swallowed down another pint. Stuffed his fingers through his hair. Looked for Heather. Swore a silent oath. Searched for Harris' thoughts.

Thinking of the moment when she slipped beneath the table to retrieve a lost fork, he chuckled. Recalled the first night in the carriage when she was on her knees staring at his crotch. She'd been inventive. He would give her credit for that. Wanted her to continue on that vein. Needed to talk to her. Touch her. Hold her. Bloody everlasting hell he wanted to make love to his wife. When he reached out to her thoughts, Ash found she was busy with the women folk. He was unable to find a way into her head to know what she was thinking.

Then...she was in his mind. Harris plucked at a peach-colored gown. He could see through the transparent fabric. Saw all her beautiful parts. Her breasts were ripe, the tips the color of peaches. After she slipped a matching robe over her shoulders, he was disappointed. Ah...he would, after all, be able to disrobe his wife. He would take everything off. Perhaps he would make love to her with the sheer fabric still covering her. Taste her veiled body. He was pleased. Anticipation for the night ahead escalated. Would she be able to reach her climax if there was thin fabric between them?

The men were right. He had all night as well as the rest of their lives. Yes, he had the rest of the evening as well as into the morning hours. He could be patient. As he was told, the rest of their lives together was his. Elliott stood beside him, handing him more ale, patting him on the back. Ash shook his head. He didn't want anything more to drink. Needed his faculties intact. Last week before he claimed his beautiful bride, he sent a messenger to his father, requesting that he send Smith-Jones to discover the true nature of Chandler's new enterprise. Now, after the confrontation this afternoon, the knowledge seemed more important than ever before.

Today, while he was dressing before the ceremony, he received the missive. The letter told him something of what he expected. His brother had been creative. What he owned was a glorified whorehouse. Prostitution was considered a nuisance by some, a convenience to others. The practice was an economic necessity for many poor women. Tolerated by society. Men of all social status considered prostitution a necessity. The institution was not illegal. Female prostitutes were condemned for their behavior. For some of the women, selling their bodies was the only way to survive.

Ash's brother tapped into this need. On some level Ash didn't understand yet, Chandler was here to threaten him. Despite what Chandler told him, he would seek revenge. If he could, he would shut Chandler's house of ill-repute down. He could not. Chandler boasted all his women were willing as were the men. The public viewing titillated his audience. He paid all the participants well. No one was expected to do anything they didn't like or want.

Of course, Ash realized if the necessity to eat as well as clothe ones' self was important, the woman would say they were willing. He also asked if Smith-Jones could discover Winter's story. Was told finding out this information was impossible without her real name. Seemed she left the name behind when she stepped into Chandler's keeping. Winter told him Chandler was her mate. If they were to live on through eternity...what then? It was rare that the man would not be a shifter while the female was. Would she need to claim him? That posed an interesting scenario that left Ash's mind reeling. She told him he was a shifter. Ash had trouble believing that.

Hawk nudged him. Heather stood at the doorway with an angelic expression on her face, Her hands clasped in front of her. She nodded at Elliott then the other men gave the cue to proceed. Ashton stepped forward eager to trail Heather to the bedchamber, startled when the clan gathered around him. Without saying a word, they hoisted him to their shoulders. Carried him to the bridal suite. Their suite of rooms.

He lay still uncertain of what the men intended. Seemed over that excruciating hour he waited someone might have explained what exactly was proposed. Bawdy jokes followed him. He heard the male laughter around him. The men carrying him joked as well. Elliott, in the lead, opened the door.

They stepped inside.

Lowered him to the ground.

The sight in front of him caused a surprised gasp of air to whoosh from his lungs. His jaw gaped open. Even though he'd seen all of her before, he was still awed. Harris stood in front of the women clothed only in a sheer gown, her hands clasped in front of her. A robe that would have concealed more of her lay on a chair. He wanted to rush forward, to cover her. No one else should see her this way. If he could see every part of her in minute detail, so could all the other men.

While he stared at his wife, jaw still gaping open, the men took his shirt off, his boots then his socks. His chest was bare as were his feet. The continued sight of her sent a stream of lightning straight to his groin. He gulped oxygen. Waiting made him even more eager, more aroused than if they'd gone straight to the wedding chamber. He looked to the bed then to her.

She smiled, a siren's smile. Her fingers wove into the fabric of her gown, tightening the material over the hardened tips of her breasts. Watched the frantic pulse thunder at the base of her neck.

Hawk handed him a glass of wine. Harris held one of her own. All the men held a glass of the red Bordeaux. Elliott lifted his in a salute to the bride and groom. "To the newlyweds." Everyone cheered. Harris was shaking. A bit of wine sloshed from the glass to slip down the side onto her hand. Cheers followed. The women retreated. The door clicked shut. Bootsteps pounded down the hall. He hoped the men returned to the festivities.

A second later he was alone with his bride. She ran into his arms. He enclosed her within his warmth. She trembled. Her head rested on his shoulder. Fingers weaving into his hair. He stepped back to look into the beauty of her silver-blue eyes.

I never kenned *I would be naked in front of all those men. How could they? Mother told me that was tradition too. All the wives had been presented in the same fashion. She also said none of the men would look at her because they were all enamored of their wives. Is that so? Do you ken it could be true?*

I've no idea about that question. Neither did I, in my wildest imagination, think you would be all but naked when we burst into the room. Had no clue they would bring me here on their brawny shoulders. They should not have seen you. I don't like that. Enough of this talk. We will forget what happened here. This is our wedding night.

He pushed back from her, held her chin. Once again looked into the silver-blue shimmer of her eyes. "You are beautiful," he mouthed to her before his lips descended on hers. His body throbbed to life. She touched him in so many ways both physically as well as mentally. He needed her to keep his soul intact. Wanted her for the physical beauty she possessed. Hungered for her in ways he never thought to feel.

That night they made love, touched each other deeply. Felt the raw passion blaze between them. Desire leapt fanned by untouchable flames of love. Sealed the night with memories they would never forget. Together, they drank the wine. Ate the treats the women along with Tindly supplied for them. Spoke of everything they wished for in their lives. Talked of tomorrow then the days after that.

Harris told him she didn't wish to go to London even though he would be there. Needed to stay in the shelter of this home. Said it was her sixth sense. She felt danger if she left. He told her he would protect her. She had nothing to fear. Though she wished for the time with her family. She finally acquiesced, ensuring him she would not venture out alone. Why should she? She had strong brothers as well as cousins to guard her back.

Ash confirmed to her in two days they would travel with her clan to London. The time spent would be all about business. He would show them some of the sights London was known for. They would visit the London Wall as well as the well-known Tower of London. If she wished he would take her to Westminster Palace. There were other places they could visit when he had the time. Ash reassured her he would make the time.

After that he told Harris about the whorehouse called a spectacle by his brother. Mentioned the women other than Winter Snow who she met. Ash felt she should understand all his brother did now. He also didn't understand why he didn't think Chandler would harm her. What his brother wanted was to humiliate him in some way. Perhaps lure him to the glorified brothel.

With that thought in mind, Ash pulled her closer. She lay with her head in the hollow of his shoulder. Her breasts were pushed against him. The soft breath of hers whispered across his chest. She settled her fingers on his belly. Teased him. Moved lower to stroke his sex. He ignited. In one fluid motion he swept her beneath him. Entered her. Made love to her until they both cried out their pleasure.

With Harris cradled in his arms, he pushed damp hair from her face. She snuggled against him, her hand resting on his chest. "While we are in London, you must understand that Chandler cannot be trusted. If you see him, turn away from him. Walk in the opposite direction. No," Ash reiterated, "run. Don't be alone."

"After what he did to me, I would never trust that man. Your words confirm what I feel. He has not suddenly lost all cruelty. A man cannot change that fast. He still means his family harm. Would hurt me if he found a chance." She traced the middle of his chest down to his erection.

That was all it took for his sex to grow hard. A moment ago, he believed he was sated. He wasn't. "My brother told me he's a changed man. Wants no revenge. Says he likes his new life that holds no responsibilities. Spends his time doing what he wishes. Is enamored of the woman he calls Winter Snow. Is making more money than he ever thought possible. He doesn't wish to ruin this new life he created for himself."

"Isn't he responsible for the people working for him? For Winter? She is a lovely woman. Winter is sad." Harris closed her tiny little fingers around his sex. Stroked. "She wants something from Chandler he doesn't wish to give. I hope it's not marriage. A lifetime committed to a man such as your brother would be a sentence to a living hell."

He held her hand still. Kept her from her exploration. This conversation was too important to him to be interrupted. "Yes. Winter told me Chandler is her mate. She would do anything for him, go anywhere he asked. While I would question that fact, I cannot. She seemed positive. No confusion in her mind. If I tried to dissuade her from the idea, I would fail." What he wanted to understand was how his brother planned his retaliation against him as well as his father. He'd not told Winter anything about their circumstances. Ash worried about Harris. Understood his sibling would involve his wife in his revenge. He would have to wait. Would take every possible caution to secure her safety. Smith-Jones would help. The butler was already scouring the town for information about Miss Winter Snow.

Here, residing on the cliffs of Dover, he felt she was safe. Felt his wife was also well protected. Once they were in London, he would make certain she didn't go anywhere alone. The first few days doing so would be relatively easy. After that...well...after that she would give her word to remain inside the townhouse. While he believed she wished to stay as far away from Chandler as possible, one never knew what his brother would attempt. Chandler now had men in his employ who would do his bidding. Had the money to pay them for their efforts. Harris would never recognize Bertram, Chandler's best friend. She was in danger.

"If you..."

She moistened her lips. Rose to pour them both more wine. Her breasts moved provocatively. He adored watching her. She was now becoming at ease with her nudity. He'd like to change to his cat. Set his head next to her breasts. Perhaps if he could convince her, he could wind his tongue around a nipple, explore lower to taste her darkest secrets between her legs. Wanted to see her climax while he was in his cat. Cry out her pleasure. When he sipped her nectar in his cat, he would change to his human then thrust inside. Maybe another time. She was still too new to lovemaking for him to be so audacious. They would need to spend more time in their cat form for her to be comfortable. He enjoyed the day they played in the water. More of that before...

"What is it exactly that your brother does to make his living? I'm curious. Have heard bits and pieces when you and Winter communicated. I should know. Don't you think? He runs a whorehouse? Did I hear right?" She sat against the back of the bed, sipping the fresh poured wine.

He nodded to her. Took the glass from her then drank. "Yes, as much as I dislike the fact, you should have some idea what is going on at his new place of residence. Don't want you going anywhere near that house. Not even with me. Chandler lives as well as works at the brothel. There are rooms above his suite where the women as well as the men sleep. Play for money." Perhaps he should be more direct with his words.

"I won't. I promise. The women sell themselves in these rooms? The men too? Is that what you're trying to tell me without saying the words? Isn't that unusual...men selling themselves? It's a glorified whorehouse, isn't it? Am I right? Too bad prostitution isn't illegal. You could..."

"Bring a constable to arrest him? His eyebrow slanted upward. "He is my brother. I would get no joy in seeing him behind bars. As you say, prostitution is legal. There is more about what he does though. I've heard from Smith-Jones that my brother is raking in the money. He hires only the most beautiful women along with the most handsome men. Men and women others would covet. They perform nightly shows. One must buy a ticket sold at auction to become a spectator. They are all bought with the knowledge they might become a participant in the show if selected by an acting member of the cast."

Ash felt the constricts binding him. Chandler would always be his older brother. One he held no respect for. Nonetheless, the man was family. Disowned by the family.

Chandler was his brother.

"What...?"

Ash placed a finger on her mouth. "Hush...I will fill you in on what more I know. Will also make a few guesses."

He didn't know how he could explain the depravity practiced in that home. Men and women liked sex. They played at feeling good. Shared intimacies. The ecstasy as well as the passion could be coveted. Money changed hands. Chandler was growing rich. Previous to this he was a man in debt.

These places were...convenient for men who did not have wives. For men who did but found little to no pleasure with the woman they married. Women survived by selling themselves. Chandler capitalized on both aspects.

Harris nodded, gazing into his eyes. Puzzled. Mulled over what he told her. Brought her exploring fingers up to rest on his chest. "Go on," she said, her voice soft. It was obvious she needed to hear more.

He wasn't certain what should be said. A woman shouldn't know certain things. In this instance, it might be more prudent for her to understand. He'd always believed knowledge was important. Information could impower. Naivety could get a woman into trouble.

Clearing his throat, he began to speak. His brain was in a muddle. This was not something he wished for her to learn. In his mind he tossed out pros along with cons. Though she needed to comprehend the dangers if she was going to survive his brother's wrath. She should be prepared.

Ash had no doubt that something would happen between the three of them. Was certain he wouldn't appreciate the way Chandler would proceed. Didn't know if he could protect Harris from everything his brother might toss his way. Time would tell the tale. He realized he might not be able to keep her safe. If not this visit, they would live in London a few months out of every year. Chandler always possessed a wealth of patience when it came to getting something he wanted. His brother yearned to humiliate him. Coming to Dover for the wedding, his brother showed his true colors.

Stroking her cheek, he spoke. "While the entertainment, as my brother calls it, occurs all seven nights of the week, he has four special women who perform for expressly chosen audiences. Each of these women performs once each month. Chandler auctions off the fifty seats in the audience to the highest bidders. The last auction he started the bidding at one thousand pounds. The last seats went for over five thousand pounds. He might well begin the bidding even higher this time. Believe Smith-Jones said this coming week would be the fourth special showing."

"Winter is one of those special women? Isn't she?" Harris asked as she wound the soft hair on his chest between her fingers. "Does she reap the benefit of all that money? I would guess that would keep her returning to the stage if Chandler pays well."

"She is called Winter Snow, Queen of the Ice. Her first time she entertained the gallery with my brother. Don't know all the details." He lied.

Telling the full story to Harris would shock her to her pretty little toes. How could he tell her what the men did as well as the woman who was chosen from the audience? "They had sex in front of those fifty people. From what Smith-Jones heard from the gossip, he took her at least three times that showing." Even though she should know what happened, he couldn't tell her about the rest of the script.

"In front of people? Fifty you say?" Harris turned her face into his chest. "Why? Why would anyone wish to do something so private in front of all those people?"

"Yes. After they finished, a man found a woman in the audience, then brought her on to the stage, stripped her then had sex with her." Ash could tell her that much, never the details. "Every night there is a show. Chandler has other women who perform on a daily basis. In these cases, there is no script. While the tickets to these shows are not as expensive, the price is still high."

"I would have scratched his eyes out," she told him with fierce conviction. "No one could make me do something so tawdry. *In front of an audience?* How... Winter Snow seemed to be a lovely lady. She does all that?"

"Yes."

"The woman who was brought from the audience? Why? She must be...I don't know what to say."

"The lady brought forth to have sex with the man who chose her was willing. Every person who buys a ticket has to be willing to be brought onto the stage. Was told she giggled. Enjoyed the attention. Also was told she was in her late forties. Plump. Vivacious. If you can believe that. The woman was not only willing, she was eager. She also possessed the money to pay for the ticket."

Her hand stilled, twitched. He felt her nails scrape against skin. "The men and women go into the audience to pick out a partner? I don't see how that can happen. I wouldn't do this with anyone except you..."

Her pause concerned him. She frowned at him. That little crease in the middle of her forehead that he adored, deepened. Ash wasn't certain he'd like what she was thinking.

"You've had sex with other women. What's it like?" She paused again. "No. Don't tell me. I don't want to know."

He held her hand in his. Watched moisture filling her beautiful eyes. Didn't wish for her to be unhappy. Facts were facts, "Before I met you, yes," he reminded her. His voice soft, deepening as he fought the urgent need to feel her heat surround him. "You knew that. I'm only a man. I had needs. Then..." He drank in a deep breath of air. "I still do. You fulfill all of my needs. As I hope I fulfill yours."

"You said there were four women. One for each week of the month...?" she asked it seemed she wished to take the questions in a different direction. That was fine by him. "I don't wish to speak about your other women. Thinking bothers me. I find I'm jealous."

"Jealous?" he asked, feeling pleased with the emotion, while there was no reason for jealousy. He had trouble holding back a grin.

"Yes." She punched him.

"We won't then. Yes, one woman for each week of the month. They are all unique. Pleasing in different ways."

"Winter was the first week. I'm guessing now, spring, summer and fall are the remaining ones. So, fall will perform sometime this week."

"Yes. You are right. One for every season...Winter Snow Queen of the Ice I told you about. Spring Mist, Princess of Rain, Summer Passion the Innocent Virgin and last, Autumn Bounty Countess of the Harvest."

"Where did all these women come from? How did he go about finding women who do...do this in front of people?"

"Chandler advertised in the London Times. Wasn't explicit though. When the applicants arrived, he explained his intentions. Brought a few from brothels he frequented. Except for Summer Passion they all interviewed for the job. Came to him eager to be selected. Was told he wished to have a real virgin for Summer Passion. He bought a young lady from her father with the offer of payment every month after she performed. The lady is fifteen, soon to be aged and jaded beyond anything imaginable. Believe the women get extra money tossed at them during the show. Smith-Jones told me he gives the women as well as the men five percent of what they make. The four seasons make ten percent. The money tossed their way is theirs to be divided equally among the participants."

Harris was silent. No more questions seemed to follow. When she turned to him again, she dribbled a bit of her wine on his chest. Bending over, her breast passed softly across him. She sipped where the drops pooled. Laved then teased more. He was aroused. Ready for action.

I find one explanation is enough to last forever. Would you ever pay for a ticket to the show your brother puts on? Would you toss coins at the women because you liked the performance? I understand I've no right to ask.

Would never. You're my wife. You've every right to inquire. Would you pay to see what goes on? You are a curious lass. Would you allow me to take you?

Believe you should know the answer to that. Though I am inquisitive about what others would do. Is it always the same? You know...the way they do it...make love. Like you make love to me?

He couldn't help the laughter from bubbling up inside at her question. This was much nicer than answering questions about his brother.

Do you mean...will I always be on top of you with your legs open to me? No, that is not the only way for a man and woman to make love. Would you appreciate a new way? I would. Indeed. Pouring wine on me, licking it, you are straddling me. You could. Come down on me. Take me into your body.

He looked at his swelling sex then took the wine from her hand. "Would you appreciate the fact you could sit on me. Set the pace? Take charge? I find the thought delightful. I would be at your mercy." He held her breasts in his hands. Stroked the crests with his thumbs. "I could hold your pretty round globes in my hands while you move up then down on me. Penetrate then retreat. Would you like to do that? I would enjoy watching their movement."

Harris tilted her head a bit to the side. Looked at him. Paused. Licked her lips. "I could sit on you. Is that a way you like to make love? We both *ken* I'm new to this."

"If the woman is you. Yes, I would like that." Smiling down at her, he saw the bewilderment in her features. "The act should not be too difficult to comprehend," Ash told her, his voice soft, husky with the raging desire the thought provoked. With no imagination he saw her riding him. Realized the joining of their bodies in this way would be delightful.

"I... Are you certain? I would please you but..." Harris sounded hesitant.

Ash intended to reassure her. "Very certain."

His hands circled her waist. Lifted her. Brought the tips of her breasts to his mouth. Pulled one deep within, twirled his tongue around the tip. Enjoyed the tiny sounds of pleasure she gifted him with. He set her atop him. She must feel the tip of his sex against her.

"Now?"

"Oh, yes."

Of her own accord she slid down his length. He filled her. Felt the heat. Embraced all the mercuric magic. She wiggled. Tested. The spell she wove around him mercuric. Still, she didn't move. Her hands rested on his chest. Her rounded globes easy on the eye. So close, he could pull them into his mouth. Tease the tips. "Is it done this way?" she asked, her eyes wide with an expression he wasn't certain he understood.

He tried going into her mind. She blocked him. He laughed. Pleased with her. Decided against trying harder, enjoying the tiny moment of her success. If she didn't wish him to comprehend her thoughts, that was fine for now. He wouldn't remove the barrier.

"It...is done in many different ways. Should have explored them sooner with you. Look down. See how we are joined as one." His hands rested on her splayed legs. He ran his finger upward to the juncture between them where he touched. Found the jewel hidden there. "Move on me, love. Set the pace. The timing is up to you."

She did as he said. He loved the way her body moved with each thrust she made taking him ever deeper inside. She bent over him to touch her mouth to his. Slipped her tongue inside him. The magic she created, he would always adore. Her fingernails scored across his chest, touching his nipples again then again.

Her cry of release came before he wished. He wanted to prolong the moment as long as possible. With her climax, he emptied himself inside her heat. Harris lay atop him. Her softness pressed against him. He cupped her buttocks with his hands. When she tried to rise off him, he held her until he slipped from inside.

"I love the moments you hold me after we've made love. These times seem as precious as the other. More in some ways. I can feel how much you care for me. That it isn't just the sex between us that is special. With you everything between us feels magical. I..." She moistened her lips.

Her poignant thoughts touched him deeply. "I'm glad you say that as I adore every second with you. Sleep now. The sun will rise soon. I doubt if anyone in this household will expect us to rise with the sun."

One more time, she rested her head on his chest. He stroked her hair, the line of her back. Followed her spine to the base. Heard the soft, easy sound of her breathing when she fell asleep. His mind traveled to his brother. He feared more now for Harris that she carried his child. A boy, a shifter, was created tonight.

He would need to take great care.

~ * ~

Chandler sat in the background. His audience cheered for the first actors. Tossed coins on the stage. Celine added to her coffers tonight. The pounds thrown to her were more than she made in a month of whoring at the tavern she worked in before he brought her to this new place of business. She was natural. One with her nudity, she didn't seem to mind the constant stream of attention or sex. Celine smiled as she collected the coin. Bowed low. Moved so her breasts swayed. Created a provocative pose. More cheers went up. More coins were thrown her way. Chandler employed a boy to collect the coins for the entertainers. He was busy putting everything in a bucket. Celine turned sideways, circled her hips. Stuck out her fanny. She was good. Very good. Knew just how to position herself. She moistened the tip of her finger, twirled it around the rose-colored tip of one breast. More coins were tossed her way.

Stella yes, there was the little maid. She quit her job at the noble Wolcott's townhouse. She was all his now. Thanked him profusely for the opportunities he gave her. This little lady liked the sex. Loved the attention, threesomes, men as well as women were her preference. Told him when she had more than one lover, every part of her would be caressed at the same time. She loved the money more than the sex. The combination was perfect. He brought in Sasha, a woman who he, along with Bertram, shared a few months ago. When she saw the money, she welcomed whatever he asked her to participate in. Sasha was becoming quite good at entertaining. She watched both Stella and Celine. Mimicked. Pranced nude. The audience adored her.

All the new women began their career above in their private rooms. If the auction brought in enough pounds consecutively, then he would allow them to work the floors. All strived to be chosen for the entertaining shows. That's where they made the most money. Chandler allowed Bertram to sample the women before they were hired. His friend had *carte blanch* with the ladies. He could ask anything he liked. From what Bertram told him, he explored a myriad of different avenues with the females he interviewed.

Chandler leaned back, his hands resting on his stomach. A glass of brandy on the table beside him. This evening, he would have Winter attend the show with him. She wouldn't like watching. Never did. That was alright. There were times Winter needed to be challenged, her loyalty to him tested. As with his four special women, she'd been on stage once. She was pampered. Yes, he made her watch all the important shows. Tonight was just that. In the background, he might take her tonight. His doing so would add another dynamic to the entertainment. No one would expect to see them together on stage this evening. It wasn't in the script.

Having made up his mind, he tapped a finger on his chin. Turned to Jimmy, "Bring Winter. Tell her I need her tonight."

"Yes, sir."

"She is to come like she is. Don't let her change her clothing. Not even a robe if she isn't wearing one."

When he left her, she was clothed in a sheer gown of pale blue. She was barefoot. Her hair spilled around her shoulders. He doubted if she'd had any time to put anything else on. It was not her practice to clothe herself after they made love.

Chandler had Jake set up a plush chair in the back of the room. The light was subtle. They would be in provocative shadows. When he stood in the audience, looking at the shadowed corner, he could imagine the erotic silhouettes that would dance to the tune he set. They would be seen. Just not clearly. The audience would understand what they were about as well as who they were. Would be curious appreciative too. Winter would not expect what he planned. They would not interfere with the main attraction. They would perform before Autumn while Celine and Sasha were playing with the customers.

He grinned. This would be a new incendiary enticement to the shows.

Celine was up first. She slipped from her clothing. Jake was with her as he would be with Autumn Bounty later in the evening. Their show was meant to stimulate the audience to a fever pitch. Provoke as well as inflame emotions. The sensual play, hot. One woman tore off her blouse. Then the rest of her clothing. She sat naked among the fifty guests for this performance. She must hope to be picked for something.

"I'm here, as ordered." Winter told him, a slight edge to her voice. Annoyed with the intrusion on her free time.

Ah, yes, Chandler heard the flinch in the words she spoke. There was a note of displeasure in her voice. A mild note. Chandler wondered what he would need to do to make his Ice Queen angry. He wanted to see her anger. Appreciate her fury. She stood beside him, as expected clad only in the pale blue gown. He recognized the moment the audience saw her. The noise stopped. Gazes were fixed on them. A mild rumble began. He heard soft chanting of her name. Winter...Winter...Winter...

Patting his lap, Chandler smiled at her. turned his head to the side wondering what she would do. "Sit. Make yourself comfortable. We will watch the entertainment tonight. Provide some of our own. It's a new beginning for the evening."

She hesitated. Her body shook. "This is not my night. I..."

She bit down on her bottom lip before she lifted her chin. She wouldn't argue. Would do all he asked. He meant to take this further now that she arrived in a tiny snit. His queen of the ice needed to learn her place.

"I want you, now." His words were simple. "Don't wish to wait for the end of the evening."

She wouldn't deny him though he understood she wished to do just that.

"We can return to your suite. You can have me as many times as you like," she made a small protest. Looked at the entertainers in front of them. Gazed at the audience. She caught their attention. While many watched the two people frolicking naked in the center of the stage, most were looking at them, at her. Wondered at this unique turn of events.

His hand moved over her thighs again, lifting her gown in the process. "Want you here. Need to watch my new star, Autumn. With you at my side. Sit down. Want you naked. Will you do that for me? Your benefactor?"

Her mind was working, searching for a way to change his mind. Chandler recognized the instant she gave it up. She sat down. His hand rose to cup her immense breast. Fondled. Touched. Pulled on the tip until the crest was elongated. He replaced his hand with his mouth. Laving as well as nipping her through the sheer fabric.

"You seem less than enthusiastic. Do you wish to be replaced? You must show more loyalty to the man who sees you fed as well as clothed. Show more enthusiasm. Cater to his needs. Do what he wishes."

His threat would be very real to Winter. What she didn't understand and never would, was that she had no replacement. In his mind, no one could ever replace her. Chandler hoped she would never understand the full extent of her power over him.

"No..."

She gulped air. Her breasts heaved with the confusion he ignited.

He needed to keep her guessing. In the last three weeks she'd become complacent. That wouldn't do. She needed to be enthusiastic in this pursuit of sexual pleasure. "Proceed as you did the last time we were on stage."

The expression she tried to hide from him gave him a small chuckle. Her loyalty now was coming along just fine.

"You want me naked?" Winter asked as if trying to keep her voice steady. She wasn't successful. "Didn't believe you meant it."

He heard the tremor. Was pleased. Gratified. Controlling her emotions was important to Chandler. Winter would never dictate the course of action between them.

"Not yet. Perhaps not tonight. But then... You do know what I want. Remember?" He ran his hand along her leg. Touched upon the tip of her breast.

Winter nodded. Stepped in front of him. He opened his legs for her. Before she continued, she looked at him. Her eyes were luminous. Flashed fire, simmered. She looked down. Unfastened his pants. Kneeled between his legs then stroked him with her mouth. Ah, perfection. He groaned his pleasure, a rough husky sound in the room. All eyes focused on them. She continued until he emptied himself inside her. Again, she swallowed, taking his seed inside her mouth. He pulled her to him. Spread her legs so she sat upon his thighs. Ran his hands up her legs, once again lifting her gown so the fabric pooled around her waist. He would see to unveiling her further in a few minutes. Now was not the time. He needed to keep his audience enthralled. Wondering what was about to happen. Chandler wished to keep them on the edge of their seats.

This time her back was to the audience. The spectators would be able to watch him caress her buttocks. He impaled himself on her. Just as he expected, Winter was hot...wet...tight. Ready for him. Waited until Celine climaxed. He thrust deep. Emptied himself. She whimpered. He knew what she wanted. She didn't have her orgasm though he felt her walls clenching around him. He would wait until Sasha performed to give her pleasure. Maybe until Autumn was on stage. He wasn't going to give her what she wanted without a bit of work.

Chapter Ten

They were in London. The trip took two days. The weather was pleasant for the first part of December. Ash was pleased neither snow nor pouring rain held them up. The two days they'd been blessed with sunshine. When they arrived, Smith-Jones met them at the door of the townhouse. James waited in his library for Ashton to talk to him. Smith-Jones told them his father had a great deal to say along with warnings about his brother. The conversation couldn't wait. He kissed Harris on the cheek before sending her upstairs to rest.

"I'll be with you as soon as possible," he told her, his voice soft.

"I could go with you to see your father."

Harris didn't appreciate being set aside. She felt as if she became less important. What could he say to his father that she shouldn't hear? Nothing. Absolutely nothing.

"No."

She scowled. Despite her position, Harris found herself whisked upstairs. Given a bath. After that her clothing for the evening meal was laid out. She didn't see Ash. He didn't come upstairs to join her. Time slipped by. She wandered downstairs. Looked into the main room. After that, found the library. Roc along with Lainie stood in the room. The conversation was low. What was being said didn't sound private. She walked inside.

James sat in the wheelchair. Ash was gone. Gone where? He was being elusive. "Ah, I see you made it down."

"Where is Ash?" she asked, curious now that he didn't seem to be anywhere in sight.

"He's changing for dinner. Come sit with us. Roc was telling me stories of the highlands. About how he met his wife. It's quite an interesting story. Would you like a sherry?" James asked as he wheeled to the sideboard to pour her a drink.

"A sherry would be fine. How are you? Yes, her story is remarkable." Harris accepted the glass then sat in a chair.

Looking to Lainie, "Did she explain to you that she doesn't remember most of what happened to her?"

Harris didn't know what more to say. Ash's father looked remarkably well. Much better than the last time she saw him. His face had color, no longer the shade of ashes in the fireplace. With sparkling, vibrant eyes, he watched her. Eyes so very much like Ash's. They were dark blue and seemed to see into her, read her thoughts. He was a shifter. Harris hoped he could not know what she was thinking. At that thought, heat flooded her face.

"Yes, I am. I wouldn't wish to see into your mind if that is why you are frowning." His smile was also much the same as Ash's. "Doing so is always between a husband and his wife. Never anyone else."

She looked down, her lashes briefly fluttering against her cheeks. "Your son is not as polite as you. He finds the time to probe my mind. Does it with infuriating ease. Never apologizes. I would learn how to block him when I wish for my thoughts to be private."

Harris looked at Lainie. "Does my brother step into your mind when you least want him there?"

"He does. I find I've grown used to him interfering with my thoughts. Sometimes it gives me comfort to know he is always with me. At first when I met him, I found it offensive. A girl needs her privacy. Roc wouldn't allow that. Told me he was in my mind so he could protect me."

"The two of you believe it's unfair." James said with a soft chuckle. "Perhaps you should know a bit more about your husband, Harris. Can't tell Lainie anything about hers other than it seems she has married a fine man. Now, as to my son, you've not known him for that long. Some of what you do know is new to him also." He scratched his forehead as if thinking. "Let me elaborate a bit. As you must have learned, he is the second son. Should be the spare as the second son is sometimes known as. You should be pleased as he will now become the earl though he never cared about the title. I'm guessing you don't either. Second sons most often join the army. I bought him his commission. That act brought him to the highlands. Who knows how long it might have taken him to find you if not for that little twist of fate. His mate. If not for the fact he was born second. Contrary to the norm, he is now my heir. I disinherited Chandler, his older brother."

"Other than what is obvious now, what made you disown Chandler?" Ash never told her the exact reasons. "I understand a bit of what he does with his new business enterprise but that wasn't the case before the disinheritance."

"There was never one thing he did. The problems accumulated over the years. Multiplied until the multitude of misdeeds could never be overlooked. As soon as Chandler left for school, things began to happen. He felt as if everyone owed him. That his title gave him privileges he didn't earn. The title did but not to the extent he imagined. A man who inherits a title should owe as well as look out for the people beneath his status. There was always trouble around him. Rumors. Gossip. In time a father must believe some of those tales are true even if he doesn't wish to believe."

"I'm pleased Ash met me. Sincerely happy that he was commissioned to the highlands to subdue the Scottish people. When he returned the second time, I was ecstatic until he acted the autocrat then refused to understand my feelings. He thought he could do what he wished, damn the consequences. I couldn't allow that. My refusal to allow him his way angered him."

"Believe he learned early that the Scottish cannot be subdued." James laughed as he watched her. "Why did you fight my son?"

Harris whirled when he walked into the room. Startled, she sipped in air. She could never tell his father the truth. Didn't know how to prevaricate.

Ash cleared his throat before he spoke. "She didn't trust me. Hope that little problem has changed. A man does wish for his wife to trust him...believe in him. Understand that what he says as well as does is honest."

Ashton walked into the room, splashed some brandy into his glass. Refilled his father's. His gaze remained riveted on her as if he expected her reply.

"With good reason." Harris snorted, turning away, unwilling to meet his gaze. She had no intention of speaking more on this. Ash's father didn't need to know their problems. Though he could probably see into her mind just as Ash did.

He cannot. You are only his daughter-in-law. I'm the only person who can hear your thoughts. The only one who is connected to you. Forever. Don't worry about giving away our private battle. Besides, my father would never try to search your mind unless some type of emergency presented itself. As you well know that is not the case as we stand here in idle conversation.

Am I supposed to be grateful? I swear to you, I will learn how to keep you out of my mind when I dinna want you there.

Harris knew her tone was sarcastic, encased with a bit of anger. Harris remembered Lainie's words. Knowing she could talk to him even when he wasn't close was comforting. Would she also come to feel that way? Ash heard her words but did he understand the underlying tone?

Yes, I heard. I've no problem with the tone of your voice. In time you will learn the ability. Even now you are picking up some of my thoughts. Though the block I put up is minuscule. I'm proud of you. Keep testing yourself.

"The two of you should talk to me. Don't like to be the odd man out. Not polite of you, dear boy. As I was telling Harris, there are numerous reasons Chandler was ousted from the family. Not to mention the fact that he is a liar as well as a cheat. He gambles and is always in debt. Not a good trait for the next earl. In short, Chandler is a wastrel."

"Chandler as we know him is not a shifter," Ash told her. "My brother always resented that fact. While he could give us away, he has kept his knowledge to himself. The family appreciates that fact. Though," he paused tapping his fingers, seeming to deliberate what he meant to tell her, "one of his friends shifts. His name is Bertram Wendell. Believe he is the shifter that was after you that first night when we left the wedding. The night when you were..."

Foolish?

"I wasn't going to say that." Ashton turned to his father. "Harris didn't trust me to keep her safe. She wanted to return to her family even though her father and mother gave me permission to take her with me. They knew I was what was best for her. Understood I could and would keep her protected, even from herself. Back to Chandler..."

"Yes, my oldest was always impetuous. He made too many rotten decisions to overlook. Took up with the wrong people. He didn't want responsibilities. Wanted all that went with the title except the restraints we put on ourselves. Though he did manage to find many other aristocrats who felt the same as he did. He has friends. Other wastrels."

"Now he seems to have found his niche. From what Smith-Jones has told me, he is raking in the money. Somehow the life of sinful pleasure he is now leading suits him quite well," Ash said looking around the room, seeing the pallor on his wife's face.

Roc knew what was happening. Lainie did not. "You must be on guard. I cannot tell you more often. Do not go out unless you are with me or Smith-Jones after your family leaves. Don't take your sisters-in-law with you unless their husbands are also along. Chandler might not keep his revenge centered on me. He might reach out seeking other ways to hurt me."

"I've told you I won't," she said in a huff.

How many times did she need to reassure the man? He told her enough times to be wary. Knew she despised his brother. She didn't know what his brother could do to her? There were laws. She wasn't a prostitute searching for a means to survive the streets of London. Nor was she willing to do something so tawdry as what was described to her. From what she understood, the participants must want to be part of his spectacle of his making. She would never agree.

Ash came to her. Stood behind her with his hands on her shoulders. Possession came to her mind. There were times she appreciated that aspect of his character. Now was not one of them. The need to shake off his hands was strong.

"We are meeting with your brothers, also their wives tonight for dinner. The others, including your mother and father, are leaving in the morning. James has told me is tired and wishes to retire early. We will leave as soon as Smith-Jones takes him upstairs."

"What? They are leaving? So soon." Confused, Harris turned to look at him. "No. I thought..." What she had thought was that there would be one more week. Believed they might shop. She needed a few things. Would have enjoyed spending more time with her mother doing girl things.

He massaged her shoulder. "I did too. They have been away for a time. It's nearly winter. The roads can become impassable at times. They are all aware that you don't need their protection. I've assured them we will see them within the year if possible. Would depend on the weather."

"A year seems so long."

Harris let out a small sigh. Her family would leave in the morning. There was nothing she could do to change that.

"Yes..." He squeezed as if that would alleviate her disappointment. "Yes, hopefully by then there will be a grandchild to bring with us. If so, we might have to wait a bit longer depending on the time of the birth or the conception."

"That would be nice."

She sipped the last of her sherry in a daze. A child. She might even now carry a *wee bairn*.

"Get your coat, love. We'll be going. We'll meet Hawk and Maisie at the restaurant. Roc and Lainie will ride in the carriage with us."

Harris kissed James on the cheek. "Good night. It was nice speaking with you. Perhaps tomorrow we can have another conversation. You can tell me more about your son. Things he might never tell me."

She laughed at Ash's expression. She supposed he would have secrets he wouldn't wish to be told.

They left then. The restaurant was elaborate. The décor beautiful. Maisie along with Hawk arrived first. They were led to the table. Wine was served. Harris watched the people all dressed in extravagant attire. She felt a bit out of place in the surroundings. She didn't own anything that nice. Did Ash care? He never spoke to her about her clothing. It was clear she was underdressed.

You will do fine. Get used to this. While we are in London, I must behave as expected. Tomorrow, if you wish you can shop for more appropriate clothing. Smith-Jones can take you if I'm busy. He makes an excellent bodyguard. He also gives good advice on women's clothing. He is well-versed in fashion trends.

I do understand. It's just... Harris brought a deep breath of air into her lungs. *Until we arrived here, I never expected you would have the title. Never knew your father would disinherit Chandler. I don't care about titles or fashion trends. I would never wish to disappoint you.*

The disinheritance was new. When we set out for London, I didn't know either. My intent was to resign my commission. Live with you in the south of England. Intended to go to the highlands once or twice a year to keep you happy. None of this mattered to me. Just expected that sometime Chandler would grow up then assume his rightful place in society.

Oh...

The first course was served. A soup she didn't care for. Harris understood she needed to eat and drink only a bit from each serving. She felt terribly out of place in this atmosphere. Opulent, everything here was over-the-top. Drinking the wine from each course, she felt a *wee* bit tipsy by the time dessert was served. During the many courses, they had pheasant. After that, salmon. Some type of beef dish was set in front of her. Each serving held an array of vegetables. Thinking of all she was eating, she thought she might be sick. Her stomach twisted into a knot.

Setting a hand on Ash's arm, she spoke softly, "I need to go...for a moment. To the powder room." She looked to Lainie who nodded as if understanding she needed to relieve herself and didn't want to say as much in front of everyone.

Ash nodded, seeming distracted by the conversation between him and her brothers. He looked up, "Don't be long. Don't wish to come after you." He sat back, enjoying the after-dinner brandy that was brought to the men.

Harris smiled. Kissed him on the cheek, wishing they were home enjoying the fire in the bedchamber, "I won't. We will be right back. Need to splash some water on my face. Feeling hot." She and Lainie left.

"That was easy," Lainie told her with an unladylike snort. "The way Ashton has behaved; I expected an escort to the lady's parlor. Would not have been surprised if one or all of the men stood guard at the door while we freshened up."

"Or...followed us inside."

Harris giggled, finding amusement in the situation for the first time. It was fun having Lainie to herself again. She missed Roc's wife. Their chats at the dinner table while she cooked. Lainie created the most amazing dishes. Inside, she used the facilities, then washed. She rearranged her hair. Pinched her cheeks. She looked to her sister-in-law who nodded.

"Are you ready to go back?" Lannie asked, taking her by the arm as they left the room. The hallway wasn't empty.

Startled, Harris' breath caught. *No.* She recognized the man standing in front of the door. She started to scream. A hand was clamped down over her mouth. She struggled, trying to lash out with arms as well as her feet. She kicked. Scratched his face. Bit the hand that covered her mouth. The arm he wrapped around her neck tightened.

"Now... Now, Harris. It won't do you a bit of good to struggle. I'm much stronger. You will come with me. I'm taking you where you'll have fun. Expect your husband to show up to rescue you. The fact I also find my first choice for Autumn Bounty is here with you is wonderful indeed. I plan to introduce the two of you to my audience tonight. You will stand in front of the fifty people in the room. I've thought of this moment for over a month. Didn't expect it to come so soon or so easily. My brother is slipping. Believed he loved you. Would be more protective. Ah...'tis a shame."

The blow to her jaw left her reeling. For a few seconds she heard voices. From the slight cry of pain, she knew Lainie was also hit. Blackness enveloped her.

When she woke, she was dressed in diaphanous material. She sat on a stage in front of a leering audience. Held by a man. Her breath caught in the back of her throat. Lainie sat next to her, dressed in something similar. Harris saw Lainie's breasts, the hard rouged tips. She looked downward to gasp at the sight of herself.

"No!" Harris screamed trying to stand. Hands behind her pressed down on her shoulders. No one heard her over the roar of the audience. The people watched a pair of women fondling each other. Touching. Kissing. Heat rose to her face. Dread filled her. Blood pounded inside. This was the nightmare Ash tried to describe to her. The one she was supposed to avoid at all costs.

"I see you're awake. Good. Are you enjoying the show? There will be more. Believe I'll have Jimmy find a suitable man for you. Would you prefer a woman? Anything here can be arranged. Just state your preferences," Chandler asked from behind her. His hands rested on her shoulders. Caressed. "It will be your turn soon."

"Ash will kill you." Harris clamped down hard on her jaw. She didn't understand what was happening. Everything she'd been told was false. "I'm not willing. You can't make me do anything I don't want. Everyone here has to be agreeable, eager to perform. I'm not. I won't. If you force me, the law will shut you down."

"Don't believe so. Your husband has too much to lose. Committing murder would rob him of everything he covets, including you. He would hang. Do you want that? In order for your husband to live you will be acceptable to all I propose." He squeezed again. Loosened the ties at her shoulders. She didn't dare move for fear the gown would slip to her waist. While the fabric left little to the imagination, the material was protection.

She heard the soft moan beside her. Lainie was waking up. Chandler turned his attention to Lainie. He kneeled in front of her. Brought her chin up so he looked into her eyes. Cupped her breasts in his hands. Fondled the tips with his thumbs and fingers. "You are perfection, my dear. I saw you at Harris' wedding. Did you know you were my first choice to play the role of Autumn Bounty. Your hips, thighs, breasts are so large, so beautifully rounded. Your face is so perfectly beautiful. With you a man would not need to look for the desired female parts in the dark of the night. I know men who would give everything they owned to possess you. Ah, but you would not be compliant, would you? Well...I'm not certain that in your case it will matter. We will give your husbands a choice. You or them to perform at my discretion. One way or the other there will be willingness. Coerced maybe. Yet...still...agreeable. They will sign documents that say as much as will the two of you if it becomes necessary."

A choice?

Harris understood neither of them were agreeable to this. There was no incentive he could contrive that would cause herself to let anyone except Ash make love to her. Touch her. What did he mean by giving their husbands a choice?

"Perhaps I can find something that would make you more amenable to perform for my spectators. A threat to your husband's life? Perhaps to your unborn child's? Those threats are always heeded. So far, I've not needed to do anything so horrific. The two of you are here. At my mercy." He searched the audience for a moment. "Watch. See what they do? You might like your body put on display."

"You wouldn't dare kill either man," Harris cried out stunned Chandler had taken her and Lainie with ease. "That would be murder on your part."

Chandler stroked his chin, grinning. "No one would be the wiser. Besides, I would pay someone to do the deed. Have the money to do so. Would never get my hands dirty. What do you say? Would you allow me to make love to you? Jake? Jimmy or Johnny. They are my best men for the task. I save them for the best women. The most beautiful. Perhaps Bertram. He covets beautiful women." He nodded to the man who was now caressing Autumn. "That's Jake." After that he found the twins, pointing toward the men, "Perhaps Jimmy or Johnny? Or both?" He looked toward the other men on the floor. "You have your choice of men. I would oblige. Do the job if you asked for me."

One was walking through the audience. He picked out a woman then led her on stage, disrobing her as he strode to the dais. By the time they reached the platform her clothing lay scattered on the floor in different places. The man tipped her over a chair, fondling her breasts. Another man stepped to them. He ran his hands along her thighs. Touched her intimately. "She's ready." The first man thrust into her over and over again. The lady cried out as the man yelled his pleasure.

Harris moaned. Gulped air. How did this happen? Had to stay strong. She and Lainie left only for a few seconds. By now Ash as well as Roc would have missed them. She knew her husband along with her brother were powerful shifters. They wouldn't attempt something like that here, in front of all these people. Doing so would ruin their lives. Being caught here would ruin Ash's life. What would James think? He would believe Ash was just as depraved as his brother. He would disown Ash also.

Oh God.

Ash would come for her. As Roc would come for Lainie. She sipped in a deep breath. What was the choice Chandler meant to give them? Chandler would either force her or force Ash to do something he would never agree to under normal circumstances. "I won't give in to your threat. You are a weak man. My husband is strong. He won't give in either."

"We will see." Chandler's smile was pure evil.

"He won't."

"What about this beautiful lady?"

Chandler touched her breast, the tip. With a sharp gasp, Lainie drew back. Tried to stand as if to run. A different man standing behind her pushed her down. "You aren't going anywhere, my love. At least not yet. Not until I'm ready for you to depart. I'm going to give the two of you a chance to show off your bounteous charms for my audience. Soon you will find yourselves escorted around the floor. I might auction your charms to the highest bidder. Again, I might not. Depends on your behavior. After that we will see how long it takes for your husbands to arrive here. You will have a seat where all can see." He leaned close. "Keep in mind, I might auction you each to the highest bidder. Might not. Depends on what your husbands are willing to give for your return. We will see now. Won't we? Also depends on the choices you make."

"Sit back. Relax." He handed each a glass of wine. "Watch the ladies perform. Learn from them. Doing so will give you some ideas. Your husbands can be treated with your newfound knowledge."

Harris didn't wish to look at anything that was going on around her. This was far worse than anything Ash described to her. Her stomach clenched. Tightened. In front of her as if Chandler told them to be there one woman was with three men. They touched her everywhere at the same time. The lady moaned. Arched. Heaved as she cried out.

Unable to watch more, Harris closed her eyes. Felt the whisper of Chandler's words against her ear. "If you close your eyes to what is happening in front of you, I will untie those cute bows that are the only things holding your gown up. You must be willing to watch my show. You understand the choice? Naked or your eyes open. What will it be? See...this is only for the willing."

She held her breath. Felt his fingers on her shoulders. One bow untied. He worked on the second. "Stop. Please...retie it."

"As you wish. That is, if you're willing to watch. Swear to it."

She nodded.

"Swear."

His fingers once more danced on her shoulders, played with the bow. Teased the ties. "I swear."

His hands left her. Though he remained behind her. Another woman from the audience stood in front of her with Stella. Stella the maid who Ash once took to his bed. She didn't want to think that he'd made love with this woman. Touched her with gentleness.

His breath was against her cheek. Chandler moved her hair from her neck. "My esteemed brother took that woman to his bed. Of course you know that. Played with her. Sucked on her breasts. Entered into her. Spilled his seed into her hot, wet channel. What do you think? Isn't she something else?" His fingers were on the bows again. "Answer me. What do you think?"

Gulping air, "Something else," she agreed.

"Would you like Stella to play with you? Or...would you rather have Jake touching you? Which would you be more willing to have fondle your breasts? You could have me."

"Neither... no one."

He ran his hands down her arms then back to the bows. One came untied.

"That's not the right answer. Not what I asked you."

"J...Ja...Jake." She closed her eyes tight then remembered what he told her. Opened them.

"You're learning. You see. Sometimes complicity is about options. Many of these women need to feed themselves. Some have children who would starve if they weren't willing to put their children before their needs. All have made a choice that is best for them along with their families. Everything here is clean. The men are not drunkards. My employees are enthusiastic to perform for me instead of the brothels by the docks. I pay better. There is less chance of the pox. Eager even to have another woman stroke them, kiss them for the money. Money can make choices vanish. Men are not as finicky. Now let's give you another choice. Which would you prefer? For Jake to have sex with Lainie or with you."

Oh God. Oh God. There was no choice. The shudder ripping through her tore at her heart. He would never accept neither as her answer. She could never give Lainie to the man. Could never give herself to Jake. She'd seen him with three different women. He wasn't cruel. Nonetheless, the women wanted him. She didn't.

"Make your decision." His tone was one of a man who won exactly what he wanted. The grin on his face was too smug.

"Me..." The single word whispered through her teeth. She wasn't even positive she spoke...if he heard.

"What did you say?"

Harris knew he heard her. Chandler was taking pleasure in taunting her. "M...me..."

"Louder."

She gulped in a breath of oxygen. Fought to say what he wished to hear. "Me..."

That had to be loud enough for him. She wanted to die on the spot. Jake walked toward her then stopped. He smiled.

"I want the people in the back of the room to hear. Much, much louder." He caressed the back of her neck. Motioned for Jake to take his place. The man's hands settled on her shoulders, slid down her arms.

"Me!" Harris shouted. A titter went up around the room.

"That's my girl." Chandler nodded to Jake who touched her neck with his mouth. Laved then nipped. After that Harris felt him stand.

Chandler stood in front of her. His hands settled on his lean hips. "Ah, so you are agreeing to give your lovely body to Jake? Maybe later. We'll wait to see what your husband does. How much longer do you think it will be before he arrives?" He looked to the door as if to see Ashton slamming through it.

The sigh she let loose was premature. Chandler didn't mean to give her a reprieve. He set his hand under her arms. Brought her to her feet. She thought her knees might give way. With the back of his hand, he caressed her cheek, slid his knuckles down her neck. She shuddered. Her stomach churned. She felt certain she might lose her dinner.

"Place your hand on my arm as if I'm escorting you to the opera. A small bit of playacting is always appreciated. If you do intend to keep Jake for yourself, you must look as if this decision is yours...nay must appear enthusiastic...even zealous. Otherwise Lainie will be chosen. Here, your demeanor is important."

Shuddering, she did as Chandler instructed. To keep Lainie from becoming the victim here, she would do anything he asked. As they moved around the room, Harris felt the fabric of her gown rub against her nipples.

At the contact, they tightened. The room was cold. Everyone in the room stared at her, at Lainie too. When Jake is done with you, you may pick out anyone in the audience to give yourself to."

"No."

"Ah, Harris, it is the way we do things here. You cannot refuse once you've accepted Jake into your body. If not, there is Lainie. The choices are numerous. You are already coming over to my way of thinking. Willingness has so many different sides to it. Don't you think?" Their trip around the room ended. Chandler stopped in the middle of the stage. "Harris has agreed upon Jake for her lover. She wants him to have her anyway he would like. She has told me she is accepting him into her sizzling rainy passage. No, she wants you all to know she is excited to be with him. What do you all think? Do you wish to see the two of them play together? Perhaps when Jake is finished, I'll have Harris pick out a member of the audience she would like to have sex with." He patted her hand.

A wild cheer echoed around the room.

"First, as always, we must have a quick portrait of our newest prize." He pulled the ties to the gown. The diaphanous material slid to the floor. She gasped bending to retrieve the gown. "No. Now that you've agreed, you will play by my rules. You will remain without clothing the rest of the evening."

Chandler held her tight, led her to a chair where he arranged her into a position of his liking. The artist sketched. Jake stood behind her, his hands on her shoulders, caressing. Touching her. All she felt was revulsion. Waiting. She shivered. Goosebumps slid down her arms. Her nipples hardened more. The room was cold. She was chilled to the bone. Since she sat down the room cooled more. She was freezing. Shivering. The door leading onto the stage was open. The cold night air charged inside.

"Open your eyes or it happens now." Chandler's voice was fierce. "I shouldn't need to remind you that you agreed. If you don't act compliant, impatient, there is always Lainie," he taunted her again.

Chandler would never stop. With no choices left to her, she did as he ordered. Tried to reach out to Ashton. Needed his support. The strength she would receive from hearing his voice. So terrified of Chandler and what he planned, she'd forgotten to do so before. She needed to tell him where she was. Roc would come with him. She along with Lainie would be safe.

I'm afraid. Chandler has us. I had to tell him I was willing to let another man have me to save Lainie. Had to make a choice. He wouldn't allow anything else. Where are you? Come for us. Please...

Coming for you. Stall him...

~ *~

When Harris and Lainie didn't return, Ash along with her brother raced to the powder room. He'd told Hawk to stay with Maisie. Hawk wasn't to allow Maisie out of his sight. After a quick knock they burst inside to shrieks from the women. There were two ladies in the powder room. Not the ones they wished to see. He should never have left her alone. Should have shadowed his wife. Stood guard at the door. Followed her inside if need be. He chastised himself knowing full well that his brother abducted them. How the devil did he learn where she was? He must have received word the moment they arrived in the restaurant.

Spies of course. Friends who enjoyed Chandler's new enterprise. They might even get some reward for informing his brother they were in attendance. This was a favorite restaurant for the family. Damn! He was a fool...an idiot. Roc set his hand on his back. "You know where they are? Don't you?"

"Yes, I know who whisked them away right under our noses. What I don't have is an address. Shouldn't be too difficult to procure the exact locations of Chandler Enterprises. We just have to ask the right person."

"I will ask the owner. Wait at our table. I'll be back as soon as I know where to find them." Roc disappeared out the door.

He brought in a huge lungful of air, his nerves stretched tight. A few quick looks around told him only the three of them were in the room. A few questions might garner useful information. He wouldn't hold his breath in hope.

Now, Ash was left with the humiliation of barging into the lady's room. Before speaking, he cleared his throat judging the two women weren't that displeased. "Sorry...my apologies," He rubbed his hand behind his neck then pressed the palms of his hands to his temples. He needed to think hard. This was far too important to mess up. "Have any of you seen? Two ladies." With his hands Ashton tried to describe his wife and Lainie. By the look on the two women's faces who stood in front him, he understood they knew nothing. He was beside himself with fear. They were just here.

"One of the ladies spoke, "There was no one in the room when I came in a few minutes ago. Didn't see anyone leave."

"The women would not have been alone. There would have been at least one man with them. More than likely two." Ash knew this might not prove useful. What he needed was the address. These women would never be able to give that to him.

"I saw two men walking quickly down the hall. They were each carrying a woman. They seemed in a rush. Headed for the back of the restaurant," the second lady said. "I didn't like the way it looked. What was I to do about it? The tallest man, the one who looked a bit like you, said their wives had too much to drink." She lifted her shoulders. "Seemed plausible under the circumstances. Anyway, couldn't argue."

"Do you know who the men were?" Ash found himself pacing, walking off the nervous energy swamping him. "That's important. If you can give me a name, I'll have a better chance of finding the women. By the way, that woman was not his wife. She is mine."

"Oh, let me see. As I said he looked something like you. His face has been featured in the paper." The woman tapped a long slender finger to her chin. "Believe one of the men must have been the Earl of Greenwood. Yes...Chandler Wolcott, the Earl of Greenwood. Do I have it right?"

Ash needed to bellow his anger. He found he was beside himself with frustration. He cleared his throat attempting not to be rude. "The deposed Earl of Greenwood," Ash corrected. "He is doing other things now. I'm the earl. A lady would not wish to know what those activities are. Did you recognize the second man?"

"No, but he was very large, handsome. His fingers were long, bronzed. Just as yours are. He carried the second lady. They were both in a rush. For a moment, I thought they would start running. The earl...no Chandler, slowed his steps. I recall he said, rushing would cause people to notice them."

"Under the circumstances, they would not wish to be noticed. A kidnapping would...well he would deny that. Chandler would say they came of their own accord."

Getting any more information from these women would be impossible. They told him what they knew. There was nothing more. "Thank you."

"Did we help?" The first lady who saw nothing at all fluttered her dark lashes at him, smiling as if he would stop what he was about and pay her more attention.

"Yes."

Behind him, there was a startled gasp as a woman walked into the room. He bowed.

"You should probably go," The second lady laughed as she recognized the delicate situation he placed himself in. She looked him over with a pleasant smile. "You do realize you don't belong here."

"You're right, of course." Ashton continued to back from the room. Once outside he turned to make his way to their table. His family didn't need another scandal behind its name. James would chastise him if he discovered what his second son was doing. No, when he heard the reason, his father would applaud his efforts. Ash understood, Chandler would find a way to turn this into his favor. In order to get the ladies free from his brother, he would be humiliated first. His brother would take great delight in doing so. If it saved Harris, he would do whatever was necessary.

He needed to speak with Hawk. Tell him to take Maisie home then guard her well. While he didn't think Chandler would pursue Hawk's wife, he couldn't be certain. He should take no chances. Long, fast strides took him back to the table. Hawk had taken care of the bill then summoned their cloaks.

"I take it you didn't find the women," Hawk said as he pulled Maisie close. Ever watchful he fastened the cape. "Do I need to worry? I will do whatever you suggest. You do know your brother. It is you he is after. Am I right?"

"Yes and yes," Ashton told him, still sifting through all the pertinent facts. He needed to take great care. "Though I doubt my brother will come for Maise, he would have taken her if she'd been with Harris. Just as he grabbed Lainie. He couldn't afford to have one of the women run back to tell me. Chandler is not stupid. He knows I will come for my wife. Also understands I would do anything, compromise myself to see to her safety. The leverage is his to play with. He will do as he pleases."

"I can take Maisie home then come help," Hawk told him. "I don't wish for anything to happen to my little sister or Roc's wife. Wouldn't three of us be better than just the two of you? Though, sometimes there is greater risk in numbers."

"No. Yes...as soon as we get the address, I will hand it over to you. If any of the Stewarts or the McKennas want to follow along, bring them." He paused for a moment deliberating on this new scenario. "On second thought, my brother only wants to bring me to my knees. Humiliate me along with the title he lost. That has been his primary focus our entire lives. Don't bring help. I will take care of this. Roc will retrieve his wife."

Watching Hawk lead Maisie from the restaurant, he felt a moment of hesitation. His decision had to stand. More witnesses to whatever Chandler planned were not wanted. Not even family. If his brother did wish to bring about the mortification of his woman, he would present her naked to the people who paid so highly to receive this type of gratification. While he understood her family members would turn their heads, he still didn't wish for them to be present. If they saw her in such a state, the fact would also be Harris' humiliation.

He still waited for Roc. The address must not be so easy to procure. Perhaps one needed to know the right people. Chandler wished to make as much money as possible. He would never keep the exact place of his residence unknown. Ash had been told the man advertised. People knew his whereabouts.

Sitting down, he tried to enter into Harris' mind. While she didn't seem to be actively blocking him, her mind was in turmoil as were her emotions. Rather than talking to her, he sensed her emotions building to a tearing point. She'd been ripped out of her comfort zone. He felt her walking around. She stood on a stage very close to being naked, wearing only a sheer gown. His heart went out to her. Tried to tell her to stay strong. He was coming for her. Nothing that happened to her on that stage with his brother would ever change how he felt about her.

Her fear was tangible. As if he was inside her, Ash felt the shaking of her body. The trembling. When he closed his eyes, he watched her looking at herself. Saw what little she wore. Chandler's hands were on her, touching her. He was playing with her, toying with the ties holding her gown in place. He threatened her. Touched a nerve, more than one.

A naked man approached her. Chandler gave her a choice. She refused to answer. Then he heard the words, the threat that would sentence her to the machinations of his brother.

He told Harris to open her eyes or he would untie the bows to her gown. She refused. He jested with one tie, reminding her that she had a choice. What was she willing for him to do? Was keeping her eyes closed to the performers in front of her worth being naked before all of those in the room. The spectators wished to see her. That was why they paid money to watch his chosen couples having sex.

Ash's fist clenched tight. Anger spiraled. He hit his fist into the palm of his hands. His brother rendered him helpless. He was winning. The arguments of their youth meant nothing now. Until he could get to this establishment, he was helpless as was his wife. He watched his brother parade her around the room, showing her off, turning her so the audience could see every part of her through the thin fabric.

Now they stood in the middle of the stage. She looked at Lainie. He gave her another choice. Harris was to choose to have sex with Jake or Lainie would be the chosen one. He saw her shaking her head, tears running down her cheeks. She swayed. He held her up, his hands below her breasts, feeling them. Overcome by what she had to do, she finally spoke. Harris told Chandler she would be the one. She would do what was necessary.

Bloody everlasting hell!

His brother rendered her submission with finesse. Harris agreed to the proposition in front of fifty sniveling low life's. No one could proclaim she wasn't agreeable. In Front of her, fifty people witnessed her submission, the words that would condemn her to whatever Chandler wished. She said she would choose to have Jake take her, have sex with her in any way he wished. It was then he got into her head and could speak to her.

I'm afraid. Chandler has us. I had to tell him I was willing to let another man have me to save Lainie. Had to make a choice. He wouldn't allow anything else. Where are you? Come for us. Please...

Coming for you. Stall him...

How? He sets all the rules. Doubt if you can do anything to stop this from happening. You need to hurry. Please. I think though, from what I've watched, Chandler enjoys prolonging the moment. I heard him tell Autumn Bounty that he wanted the audience to be titillated to a bursting point before the sex occurred. That way the spectators will pay more to see her the next time.

You're right. He leaves nothing to chance. Even has Winter naked in the back of the room watching. She isn't participating, at least not yet. Who knows what he will do? Though I've learned he keeps Winter for himself.

He lost her again. Felt the shudder rip through her. Felt Chandler's hands on her. Where the hell was Roc? They needed to leave here. She didn't have much time left to her.

Jake is watching me, studying me. He is wearing nothing. I see all of him. When I close my eyes, Chandler is beside me yelling at me to open them. I can't refuse. If I don't keep watching, he will declare it is my time, mine and Jake's. He could change his mind because I know he wants it to be him inside me. Don't know how to stall for time. If I run, this will all happen so much faster. Your brother told me to behave. If I didn't, he would have me in front of you. If not that, he would see that three men would take me as close to the same time as physically possible. This way, with me going along with him, it will only be Jake. I don't want to be forced. Just because I said the words, I'm not agreeing to do anything like that. He wants me to be eager. Instead, I'm sick. Could vomit on him if he touches me.

Hold on. I'm going to find out where you are. Hold on...do whatever Jake wants. Play. Flirt. You can do that. Hold him off for as long as possible. I don't want anything to happen to you. What I can tell you is that no matter what happens, nothing will change between us.

Oh, God.

The scene vanished. His heart stopped beating as he searched for her. Ash understood this was the beginning of her seduction. The game would begin soon. He had to get there now. Roc was here, striding toward him.

"Get your coat. Your brother's house is down the street a block. That's why he found us here in the middle of his show. This presentation with your wife is overshadowing the initiation of Autumn Bounty into his repertoire of his select women. Heard he stopped the show just to get the girls. Heard from someone we were here. Thought it was too good to be true. Our wives are going to be the entertainment before the main event."

Ash's hands were shaking. His heart pounded to a death knell. Blood rushed. Energy soared. "You've heard from Lainie?"

He prayed Chandler wasn't going to renege on his words to Harris. There was no promise that Lainie wouldn't find herself subjected to the same choices as Harris. It would be just like his brother to do something so dishonest. If he separated the women, neither would understand if the other was safe. They were both of the kind who would give of themselves to save the other. He tried to reach out. Knew Harris would make the choice to believe his brother. There was no other course for her even though Ash understood both ladies would be told the same. Choose sex with one of the men present or the other one would have to participate.

Shouting orders to the coachman to follow, Ashton and Roc raced down the street. Pushed the men guarding the front door aside. Hit those who tried to keep him from the theater. "Where are they? Chandler, where is he?" A man at a desk in the front pointed to a large wooden door. With a rage he'd never felt before, Ashton thundered to the doors. Threw open the closed door leading into the theater. The large wooden door slammed against the wall, with such a thunder the spectators all turned to stare. Men raced to his side. Grabbed his arms. With ease, he shook them off, throwing them to the floor. The audience's chatter came to a stop. Collectively, it seemed all held their breath. Ash stood in the aisle.

"Chandler!" Ash roared as he strode toward his brother.

His fists tight, he steadied his gaze on Harris. Her smile was weak. Good God, he could see all of her. Just as he'd seen when he was inside her mind. The flimsy material did nothing to hide her magnificent body. The same was true of Lainie. They were both pale, shaking. The women must be terrified of what his brother had in store waiting for them.

"Ashton, my dear brother, whatever took you so long. I thought you would never arrive. It was getting harder by the minute to put off the entertainment. The fans, you know, must have their fun. Now that you are here, I won't have any need for the ladies. Though..." Chandler paused, looking from him to Harris. "It might be a delight to my crowd to watch husband and wife have sex for everyone to appreciate. I'm certain that would be something never seen before in this sphere. I've not scripted such an event."

"I will bury you, big brother," Ash said through his gritted teeth. "I will bury you!" Ashton repeated, so furious with Chandler. "If anything happens to my wife or Lainie, you will end up in Newgate. I promise you that."

His brother's fingers formed a steeple beneath his chin. He appeared unconcerned. "You have a choice, too, little brother. You can have sex with Stella here, who I know you are familiar with, or your wife. Want you to be acceptable to my plans as well as enthusiastic this evening." Chandler turned to his audience motioned with his hands. "What would you enjoy seeing the most? My brother and his wife or my brother and Stella?"

The chant went up. Wife...wife...wife...

It seemed Stella wasn't appreciative of the audience. "Oooo...no...me first. Me before the wife." Naked, Stella flew at him. She wrapped her arms then her legs around him bringing his mouth to hers. She kissed him. Tried to force his lips apart. He pushed her away. She stumbled then stood in front of him posturing. Thrusting out her voluptuous breasts. "Didn't know you would come back tonight. Even though your wife is here now. She's such a little bit of a woman. No curves. Not like mine," She moved so her breasts swayed. "We just...well...two nights ago you were in my bed. We could do it together again. Like that time, I could take you upstairs to my room." She ran her hands down his chest. Turned to the spectators. "Would you like that, a threesome...me and his wife...having sex with this big virile man?"

"Both!" they shouted."

"Wait!" Celine stood in front of the couple. "Don't leave me out. Move aside. He had me last night upstairs. Paid me handsomely, he did. He's so big." Celine stared at his crotch. "He fills me up."

Stella had moved behind him. Celine held his arms. In seconds Stella had his pants unfastened. He wrestled himself from Celine then tore

Stella's hands from his body. Fought the two women's raging hands to fasten his pants again. Good God, what was going on here? He'd never visited this place. He felt heartsick when he saw the glazing over of his wife's eyes. Moisture filled them. Bloody hell, she couldn't believe these women. This had to be something else Chandler engineered to humiliate him. He stiffened, knowing he could endure anything for his wife.

The trust between them that had been so fragile wilted in this evening's events. Two women claimed he'd been with them. When? Dear God, she had to believe in him. Trust was so important. He'd been with her. Always her. No one else. He'd conquer that mistrust. Show her he would never cheat. She was his mate.

I understand this looks bad. I've not been here before. Never betrayed your trust. Would never. We weren't even in London two nights ago or last night. You've got to think about the facts. These women are lying.

I believe you. It hurts to see those women mauling you. Don't do anything stupid. Your brother...

Her ensuing smile brought air to his lungs. His heart stilled then began to beat anew. She believed him.

We are leaving here. Give me a few more minutes. If I have to negotiate, I will. Though...I believe the damage Chandler sought has been done. When I walk out of here with you, he will let me go. Chandler won't wish to see to the end of his profitable enterprise. If he makes either of us do anything we don't wish to, I will see him in prison. Threats to you do not make you willing.

Fine. Don't do anything to your brother you will regret. We will all get over this horrible evening. Life will go on for all of us. I do understand the anger. Can feel the fury simmering, see it in the fire of your eyes.

There will be reports in the morning paper. Are you ready for your portrait to be smeared across the front page? Chandler won't go easy on either of us. His hatred runs deep. The fact that you were naked, posing, will be subtle, meant to prove you were agreeable to this type of entertainment.

Have to be ready for anything. I'm a highlander as well as a shifter. Used to unexpected events. We are strong. Stronger than our enemies. Now get me away from this man and his roving hands. Take me away so together we can heal.

Ash wasn't having any more of this. He needed to be alone with his wife. Roc would also need time with Lainie. The damage done mentally was unknown. There might be grave repercussions. He hoped not.

He strode to the stage. Jake's hands were on his wife's arms, holding her in place. He noticed the artist at the side of the room. Stalked to him. Grabbed the pencil along with the paper from his hands. Ripped and ripped until the sketches lay torn into tiny shreds on the floor. Ash understood the man would be able to recreate his work. Despite his actions, the scene would be in tomorrow's London Times. Chandler calculated this wisely. Planned this to the minutest detail. He would weather the storm created here. He and Harris would meet the consequences of the evening together. His father would understand everything he did as well as why. He'd had no viable choices. No one here had been willing.

"We are leaving. Don't attempt to stop me!" Ashton cried out. Roc was on the stage wrapping Lainie in his coat. He followed suit then swept Harris into his arms, starting for the door, impatient to be gone. Stella stood by, a smug expression on her face. Ash imagined the woman was also looking for retaliation. It was obvious she played an important part in this scene staged by his brother. He rejected her. Stella found her niche here with Chandler. Men, men everywhere to ease all her needs.

"Not so fast," Chandler said, stepping toward them. "Now that you are here you should stay and watch Autumn Bounty. Her beautiful assets are much like Lainie's." Chandler was staring at Roc. "You might enjoy the production. Lainie could take her place. Jake is Autumn's man. He understands how to please women."

"Never!"

Ash's fury began to simmer. "We're leaving. You can't hold us here."

Roc started down the floor. Stopped when Autumn caught his attention. Turned to address Chandler. "This woman is nothing like my wife. Lainie is also beautiful on the inside."

As if on cue the audience rose to stop them. They wanted the two couples to remain in the room. Wanted to see them make love to their wives. Men moved to block the door. Furious, Ash swirled. His voice rang out clear for all to hear. "You wish to bring the law down on your head, Chandler? Keeping us here is against our will. The act would be kidnapping. You, brother, comprehend I've the power to ruin you. Still might. You offend me. If pressed, I will find the means to have this place shut down."

His threat was better than anything his brother could create. The spectators fell away from the door sensing Ashton's victory. No one wished for their sexual games to end.

"Ah, well..." Chandler said with a deep shrug. "I am disappointed in your reception. Thought you would be friendlier. It's quite titillating to have sex in front of an audience. If you tried, you might find the sex act incredible the same as I do. Believe though, I've accomplished what I intended tonight. Your abject mortification. Say good evening or good morning to our father when you see him. If he's no longer up when you arrive home, speak the words in the morning. I do think you'll enjoy the morning news. Might be as gratifying as good sex in front of fifty spectators." He shrugged. "It might not."

Seething, Ash strode from the theater. Roc followed behind him. By the time he reached the bottom of the steps to the brothel, his breathing was under control. He needed to be there for Harris. Couldn't allow his anger to get in the way of her needs. Had to remain focused on her. The trauma tonight was more than she should have had to experience. Tomorrow's papers would have pictures of all of them.

In the carriage, he cradled a shaking Harris in his arms. Kissed the top of her head. Tried to soothe her the best he could. Spoke quietly to her. Ran his hand along her back. She nestled against his chest. Her breathing seemed to ease the longer she was with him.

"Truly, I'm fine." She brought in a long deep breath of air. "I will be. Just hold me."

"Hush, you don't have to speak."

No, have to talk. Your brother is loathsome. Before I arrived, he'd been playing with Winter. In case you didn't notice, she was sitting in the back of the room naked. He left her that way all the time he was gone. All the time we were being tormented. He doesn't care about anyone except himself. She loves him. He only thinks of himself.

I didn't see her. Are you telling me she might have needed rescuing too?

No, Winter wants to be right where she is. She told me so. Knew I was concerned about her. Winter told me she's pregnant with Chandler's baby. Doesn't wish to leave now or in the future. Told me her future is with him. There is nowhere for her to live except with Chandler.

Ash's hands wound into her hair, eased. Stroked. Tension collided with common sense. He could not wrest Winter from his brother's hands. Could not coerce her to leave him. She told him Chandler was her mate.

His fists tightened as his heart lodged in his throat.

~ * ~

Upstairs in his suite of rooms, Winter was still naked sitting before the fire. Bertram sat on a couch watching the woman. Chandler spilled brandy into two crystal glasses. As he strode to Bertram, he handed his man the drink. After that he sat beside Winter. Set his hand upon her leg. Ran a finger along her inside thigh. He looked at her, smiling. Her eyes shimmered, threatening tears. She was everything he wished for in a partner. He imagined he felt a bit like his brother when he thought about Winter. Chandler wouldn't allow another man to enter into her dark warmth. She was his. At this moment, she didn't want him close. He felt her animosity soul deep even when she smiled at him. She didn't like the fact he brought her to the theater this evening. He would make certain his four favorites understood they might be called upon to entertain on more nights than just the one per month. His plans were changing, developing with each new show. It would be up to him. Surprise would be good for business.

"What do you think about tonight?" Chandler addressed his question to Bertram. What he wanted to know was Winter's take on the events. He would wait. She would lie. "For myself, I was pleased. My brother's face... He was spitting mad. Never seen him so furious. The earl could prove to be troublesome. His portrait at our little whorehouse will be plastered on all the papers."

Bertram leaned back in the chair, "You couldn't have planned the events any better. Your brother, true to form, acted the raging beast. His fury was pleasant to see. You had his wife believing she would be violated.

The scene was enjoyable. Played out just right. Get tired of the highhandedness of certain individuals thinking they are better than the rest of us. Knowing they can be brought down a peg or two is justice."

"Would you like a drink?" His attention was now turned to Winter. Her eyes flashed at him. "No? Yes? Do you wish for me to guess?"

"Wine would be nice," she offered with a shrug, her abundant jewels moving. At every turn she provoked him. Understood how to bring him to attention. She was temptation in one small package.

Chandler understood she did that to entice. Not tonight. "Perhaps you might be in need of something stronger. I'll get you a brandy."

He rose, striding toward the decanter, feeling the heat of her gaze on his back. She wouldn't say anything more. He was pleased that his point was made. He would be the one to decide everything. Even as to what she would drink. "What did you think of my brother?"

"As you said, he was furious. He loves his wife," Winter spoke while she looked down, hiding the volatility of her eyes.

He tapped the glass of brandy. Yes, the man does love her. Too bad she doesn't trust him. "What about you? Do you love me?" The question was pointed, directed at his woman. He was quite certain she would sidestep the query.

Lifting her chin, she blinked once. "Clothing would be even better than brandy," she told him, her voice soft.

When he frowned at her, she flinched. As he got to know her, her feelings were becoming more visible. He would not tolerate her responses if they became evident to others. If so, a lesson would be taught.

"Ah...clothing. I do appreciate you the way you are. Naked. Much more enjoyable to this man's eyes. Hope it's warm enough for you." His gaze lingered on the tight hard buds at the tips of her breasts.

Chandler grinned while she swallowed her true feelings. He was certain her objection was to Bertram. In the shows they put on, Winter had no trouble with others watching her. There were no difficulties with Jimmy along with Johnny touching her. Now, in the privacy of his suite of rooms, she protested, albeit silently.

"Yes, I would ask permission to dress. We do have company."

That was a bold statement. One he didn't expect. Sometimes Winter surprised him. For some reason, she didn't appreciate all of Bertram's assets. When he handed the drink to her, he was reliving the night. Having started with Winter naked in the back of the room, he'd been pleased when word came to him Ash along with his wife were at the restaurant, he left hoping to retrieve her. His brother's wife was a beauty. Lainie even more endowed than Harris or Winter. He thought he might enjoy having Autumn the next time it was her turn to be on stage. He would think of the possibilities. Decided he would enjoy having each lady at least once. Perhaps he should take turns with his special ladies. The audience would appreciate the suspense.

"Next week it will be your turn on stage. What would you like? Another threesome with Jimmy and Johnny? Maybe we could add Bertram for a fourth partner."

Chandler walked to her. Set his hand on her shoulder, testing the quality of her skin. "Going to start the bidding higher. Maybe at three thousand pounds. I know the price will go higher. Don't want to be too greedy. Though if people are willing to pay, I would capitalize. What do you think?" This time he was asking Bertram.

His friend nodded. His grin leering at Winter. "Three thousand sounds good to me. Will you allow anyone else to take her? Winter? I would never reject an offer. I would love to experience all her charms. Love to feel the fire inside her."

Pleased with Winter's reaction to Bertram's suggestion. He would consider others to act with him, not to take her. Focused entirely on her, he replied. "I will consider that scenario. A woman should be used to multiple men...women who work for me." He turned to Winter. "You would like others to have you?"

Her stiff back was a different reaction. She tilted her chin to show her defiance while she said the words he would like to hear. "Whatever you wish. I'm your pawn. At your whim." Winter downed her brandy. Chandler understood she wished for more. Thought if she was a bit tipsy, she might not hold herself so aloof.

"You are correct. This is about whatever I would like. Now," he turned his attention back to Bertram, "as to the morning paper...wish I could see the look on the old man's face when he sees the front page. He might have another stroke. We would be well rid of the man who sired me then left me to fend for myself without a second thought."

"What a shame," Bertram agreed while he sipped his drink and studied Winter. "If you choose, I would play a part next week. She is quite a fetching piece. You do know that. What could I do? Arouse her as the woman did that first time. I would enjoy that part of her. Love to taste the secrets between her legs."

Chandler watched her shiver under Bertram's perusal, digesting the words. He should allow Bertram to fondle her. Get her ready for his entrance. Maybe he should watch Winter sip on his friend's sex. He shuddered at the thought of his body responding to the image. To be able to read her with such ease pleased him to know the end. Still...there was something that kept him from saying yes to Bertram's inquiry. Something he didn't understand about himself.

His position with Winter would need to be different. Entertaining in some new way. For the next time, he planned on taking on the role of a sultan. He might inspect her body on the auction block. Once he purchased her, she would come to him on her knees, showing her submission. Ah, but sultans did not share their women. They were possessive of their harem. He could make changes in the script. Perhaps not. The absolute possessiveness he felt for her grew with each mating of their bodies.

He gave her more brandy. Watched her as she looked at him, her eyes imploring. Winter wasn't much of a drinker. She always held back. "Drink all of it." He waited until the full glass was gone. "Would you like to ease my friend before he goes upstairs to be with Sasha? Believe he was never satisfied this evening. He played no role. You could take him into your mouth. Caress with your tongue. Suck a bit. The hot draw of your mouth on his sex would give him his climax. I'm certain Bertram would appreciate the attention to his manly parts. What do you think?"

The slight stiffening of her shoulders told him all he needed to know. She nodded her acquiesces. Winter would never reply to this question. She despised Bertram. Though she would do his bidding. Sometimes he hoped she would get over her revulsion to his friend. A threesome with Bertram would prove enjoyable. Until Winter, they always shared. This little act of no consequence would be one step closer to his wishes. He could insist. He would wait to do so.

"I'd enjoy that. You are agreeable?" Bertram asked, surprised Chandler offered. "I've always admired you, Winter."

Everyone had been well aware of his possessive nature where Winter was concerned. Chandler didn't mind displaying her. Didn't care if others played with her large breasts or tasted her dark secrets. Anything else... He meant to challenge her tonight. Wanted to note the extent of her revulsion.

"Come here, my love." He beckoned to her, holding out his hand. "This will be fun for all three of us. I will enjoy watching. Gazing on others is always stimulating foreplay. When you finish with Bertram, you can come to me." He paused again thinking about all Winter's dislikes. "We could invite Sasha to join us. I'm certain the lady would be pleased."

Understanding there was no choice for her if she wished to stay with him, she rose. Walked to stand in front of Bertram. With quiet dignity, Chandler was coming to admire. She waited for his command. He nodded. Pleased with her easy compliance. She did sign an agreement that she was acceptable to do anything.

"You know what to do." He nodded. His body responded. He wanted her for himself. Sharing was impossible.

When she unfastened Bertram's pants and he leapt free of the confines, Chandler's sex grew, hardened. He was hard pressed to stifle the groan, keeping the sound behind his teeth while he watched. Chandler nodded again. She would begin now. As she moved closer to Bertram's sex. Chandler couldn't keep the word behind his teeth. "Stop!"

Winter glanced up, confusion in her widening eyes.

"Wendall!" Chandler bellowed. "Get Sasha. Now! Come here, Winter. I find I'm not in the sharing mood tonight."

With grace, she rose then walked to him. Chandler was transfixed on her body, of the gentle bounce of her breasts, the curve of her hips, the soft triangle at the apex of her thighs. He sat down then gestured for her to kneel.

"Here she is," Wendall said while he led Sasha into the suite. "What would you have me do?"

"Take your robe off, Sasha. Tend to Bertram's needs. Wendall, you can caress Sasha anyway you like."

Sasha knelt before Bertram then took him into her mouth.

"Put your hands on her head. Keep her there. You wouldn't want to be disappointed if she left you too soon." Chandler understood from his first encounter with his little whore, Winter didn't like to take his seed into her mouth. Celine was different. He wasn't so positive about Sasha.

Tonight, he wanted to see her eyes along with the expression on her face when she did. He spread his legs so she could come between them. Reached over to lift her chin just a bit so he could watch. "Wait. See what they are doing."

Bertram groaned. Wendall fondled Sasha's breast. Tugged on her nipples. She whimpered. Betram thrust his hips forward so she accepted even more of him into her mouth. He moved again then again. The mating was fast. Bertram's teeth were pulled back as he reached for his release. Wendall tipped her over then entered her. She cried out. Surprised. Pleased. He reached his peak.

"That's right."

He smiled. Witnessed Sasha licking her lips. He didn't think Bertram understood how much she loved this. He knew. Bertram's seed erupted into her. Watched as Bertram kept her mouth on his sex until she swallowed.

Winter accepted him into her mouth. He felt her teeth rake the length of him. Her tongue whirled around the tip. She pulled on him, laved him until he cried out. Flashes of pain then ecstasy swept through him. He spilled his seed into her mouth. To his surprise there was no subtle flinch of her muscles. He brought her to stand. Taking her hand in his, he led the way.

Chandler moved back to the large chair she'd been sitting on earlier. "Come to me," he told her. "Sit on me."

She nodded, her eyes flashing as if what he asked was too soon. "I'd like..."

He understood she wished for more brandy. Something to take away the unwanted taste. Was he wrong? "What you'd like is not important at the moment. What I want is you. You see." He paused, watching her stand in front of him. "You aroused me. We will make love then Bertram can go to Sasha. Celine too if she likes. What do you say?"

"Fine..." her voice was soft. Chandler understood she wanted him. This woman was an enigma to him. Every day he learned something else about her. Tonight, he would begin to let her know just how much. He didn't mean to ever let her out of his life. What he knew, the threat of exposure would keep her with him forever.

Just as she waited in front of Bertram for his directive, she waited for him to speak his wants. He didn't care what Bertram could see. He found he wanted to be alone with her. There were stories for him to tell. Her stories.

"Bertram, you may go. Enjoy your night. Sasha won't be pleased with no payment. Make certain she as well as Celine are pleasured. Tell her I will give her to someone else tomorrow that will make up for the loss of income this evening. Soothe her. The lady has a young son who needs to be fed. Some of the money she earns here goes to the nanny who keeps the boy out of this house."

His friend downed the rest of his brandy then left the room. After the door closed, Chandler looked to Winter who tilted her head, confused. She would have thought to be entertainment for both men. Only his mind changed to something more intimate. He'd had his fun with her and Bertram. He'd had enough conflict the last few hours. Needed to be alone with his woman he'd known for almost a month.

"Lay down." She looked to the other room where the bed was then questioned him. Chandler shook his head. "The fur by the fireplace."

"Is that what you want? It's not your usual preference. Why did you send for Sasha?" she questioned.

She seemed to realize her mistake then without saying anything else or waiting for a reply she stretched out on the fur rug. Ran her hand along the rug, letting the fur wind between her fingers. The tip of one breast vanished in the fur. Firelight danced on the exposed silken flesh. The sensual pull of the scene startled him. She moved provocatively, enticing him. This was what he needed this evening. Perhaps he'd wait to recount some of her stories about her past. With every day he learned more about this woman who intrigued him. If she objected to something, he had poignant facts to threaten her with.

"Seems I didn't want any man enjoying your mouth on his sex. Not even my friend," Chandler told her.

"I don't mind taking your seed into my mouth."

"Why did you flinch that first time?" He rid himself of his clothing.

She shrugged. "I was surprised. If you recall, I'd never done anything of that sort."

"On your back. I want your knees up. Spread wide. Need to look at you."

She obeyed as she always would. He came down between her legs.

Chapter Eleven

With very few words said during the carriage ride, Ash dropped Lainie and Roc off at their rented building. During the short trip home, Harris molded her small body against his. Her hand was set on his chest, her face against the hollow of his shoulder. Tears slid down her cheeks wetting his shirt. Soft sobs echoed in the stuffy confines of the carriage.

Ashton didn't like the silence. She would do better if she would speak. Tell him what as well as how she felt. What was on her mind? He needed to hear her thoughts without vaulting into her head unwelcome. Doing so might be the only way he would understand how much she'd been hurt as well as terrified. If he wished, he could keep her from knowing he was listening to her thoughts.

When they stopped in front of the townhouse, he carried her. Strode the steps to his home with Harris in his arms. Smith-Jones greeted him at the door. As if the butler understood what happened, he brought brandy to his bedchamber. Ordered a steaming bath along with food for Harris who was still clad in the diaphanous gown. They had not taken the time to gather her clothing. Someone there might put the gown to use. At the thought, his laugh was harsh. The people there didn't appreciate clothing.

His butler didn't ask any questions. Made his way with quiet footsteps. After his wife slept, he would inform Smith-Jones of some of the events so he would be prepared in the morning to deal with the fallout from tonight. The paper would be destroyed before either his father or Harris could see the drawing he felt certain would be on the front page. He would also speak to his father. Gossip had a way of spreading. James would have to understand so he wouldn't be blindsided.

By the afternoon there would be a myriad of different people at their home wanting admittance, from reporters to politicians then other members of the *ton*, some friends, some foes. Asking for his side of the story, for explanations. Unless Harris was in a better frame of mind, he wouldn't be speaking with anyone. They would have to wait for a comment from him. For all he cared, they could wait forever.

Tomorrow, Smith-Jones would need to be his spokesperson. He would tell the man what he expected. Ash understood his man would never let him down. He needed to trust.

Ash held his breath until the bath steamed in front of them. He undid the ties that Chandler tormented her with. The gown slid to the floor. He hung onto her as she stood. Steadied her when he thought she might falter. She'd been through so much. His heart cried out for her. This was his fault. He let down his guard. Thought they were safe in the restaurant.

"The bath will help ease some of the tension I feel radiating through your back. Would you like me to wash you?" Ash held his breath until she answered him with a nod to her head. Massaging her shoulders, he spoke to her in a soft voice. Kneaded tight muscles. Ran scented soap along her back. "After this a real massage would be in order. Would you like that? I've perfumed oils that might be to your liking."

She'd gone through so much in a few short hours. Chandler should be hung by his thumbs. Stretched out on the medieval rack. His brother had no right. What he did in that whorehouse with willing women made no difference to him. People would seek their pleasures any way they could find them. He held no grudge with that. Women needed to survive. Chandler had no right to involve his wife along with her brother's wife. Now, because of the trauma, he didn't wish to do anything she wasn't certain of.

"You don't have to treat me as if I'm fragile," she said, looking up at him with a shimmer in her eyes. "I won't break if you say something wrong...or right. I can manage the bath on my own though the massage sounds wonderful." She placed her hand on his. "Would you throw that gown into the fire?" She nodded to the one on the floor. Her voice shuddered. "In the fire," she repeated. "I don't ever wish to see it again. Nor do I wish to remember the night. Don't wish to ever speak of those times again."

"Would you like me to retrieve the clothes you were wearing when Chandler took you? I could go tomorrow."

"No."

I dinna want to ever go to that place again or think about what I saw there. If you returned for something as inconsequential as my clothing, I would worry about you. I've more gowns than I need. Assume you have enough money to buy me another dress along with the necessary undergarments even if I've no need of anything.

I'm pleased. If I never see my...Chandler again, that will be fine by me. In my mind, he's no longer my brother. Just a man that I thought I once knew and loved. One I now loathe. He achieved his ultimate goal or so he thinks. I don't feel humiliated. Those who know me will understand my position. We will be honest when questioned. There is nothing else to do.

Neither am I humiliated or mortified. While I didn't enjoy what transpired, all I feel is pity for those who seem to enjoy what he sells. Those who participate. I pray all the women are indeed agreeable. I do understand that many times women are put in a position to sell their bodies in order to survive. Stella didn't need to do so. She made her decision. Once the woman held a good job here, In this very house. Now... Harris turned away unable to say more. She closed her eyes.

Would you rather toss the gown into the fire? Would that make you feel better perhaps. A means to put an end to the transgressions against you. I would do whatever you say, love.

No, don't wish to touch that horrible thing again. From this vantage point, I'll watch the flames rise. Watch the fabric smolder, curl against the heat then burn.

With the gown in hand, Ash strode to the fire. When the fabric touched the flames then ignited, he stood back so Harris could watch the material coupled with the memories disappear. He hoped there would be no more thoughts that would remain. His arms crossed on his chest. Feet braced apart, his anger at his brother simmered.

This recovery was a fragile thing for Harris. He questioned. Made guesses as to the best way to handle the conversations he would have with her. He hoped tonight she would find a healing sleep. Her condition was difficult to read. Ash wished he knew her well enough to embark on the best restorative route. He would understand all her needs. Though he could tell by the expression on her face, her recovery might not take long. She'd not been touched too deeply by the event.

She was strong.

Shifter strong.

He hoped Lainie would mend with as much ease as it seemed Harris was. Looking at her now, he was not as frightened for their future as he had been when he carried her into the townhouse. Lainie was not a shifter. She would need to rely on her husband. Roc would see to the recovery. The pair had been through much over the last year. He fought for her to remain in this time. If not for banning together, Lainie might have been swept back to the future. A future Lainie didn't wish to return to or belong.

"Here."

Ash handed her the towel Smith-Jones set by the fire to warm. He watched her rise from the tub. Reached for the cloth. She was so beautifully formed. He cleared his throat, thinking of all he might have lost. It was all he could do to speak. "Dry off then I'll give you that massage."

"A massage?" she questioned a tentative smile on her face. She wrapped the cloth around her then lifted her arms to undo the pins holding her hair on top of her head. The towel fell to the floor. The long strands tumbled over her shoulders, curling around her breasts.

He wanted to feel the silken glide of her hair between his fingers. "Yes. Seems I would like to touch you, caress you. If you don't want that..."

He waited for her to deny him. A denial wouldn't surprise. She didn't say anything more. Though she nodded to him as if she agreed.

From within a cabinet, he found the scented oil he wanted. After he opened the stopper, the essence of lavender floated into the air. Permeated his senses. He purchased the scent when he returned to London last year. He found the perfumed oil in a store near the townhouse. Bought it to remind him of Harris as well as all she meant to him. Whenever he felt lonely, he would open the bottle. Inhale the essence of her, longing for her. There wasn't a moment he was away from the highlands that he didn't want to ride as fast as he could to her. Hold her in his arms. Kiss her again.

When he looked up, Harris stood in front of him. She was still naked. Had not wrapped the towel around her while she waited. He was surprised by her daring. Her eyes were wide pools, silver-blue, liquid with emotional fire. That response surprised. The breasts he adored were tipped now with hard tight buds. Her lips were pursed as if she was thinking. Her hips curved and were shaped beautifully. The dark triangle at the apex of her thighs beckoned to him. It seemed she was presenting herself to him as a gift. Ash thought she'd never looked more beautiful than she did now. After all she endured tonight, she was giving herself to him. Putting him before her needs. Perhaps not. It might well be possible she needed this to heal. A loving hand. A man who believed in her. Someone she believed in. After this evening, Ash felt certain she trusted him.

Soon they would make love. Put the night behind them. Disregard. "Do you hope to forget what happened in my brother's domain? I'm not certain you are ready to make love. If you are not, I'll truly understand."

Now he had second along with third thoughts about the massage which would lead to lovemaking. He would never be able to caress all her soft evocative parts without thinking of the culmination.

"More than anything I need you to hold me, Ash. Doing so would serve to cleanse my spirit. Wish to become one with you. The healing will begin with your loving hands. I have no doubts about that. Don't tell me no. I am ready."

He reached for her hand. Wrapped his around her fingers. Held the palm to his lips for a short kiss. Brought her down upon the rug in front of the fire. "If that's the way you see it. Know that I'll do anything you wish. If you need me to hold you, I will. If you ask for me to stop, I will. This is for you." Ash held her hand in his, rubbing his thumb gently on her wrist. He tugged. It was a small motion. "Lay down. Are you ready? Now? Do you wish to lie naked for me? Vulnerable? Open?"

From the first second he saw Harris, he knew he loved her. Understood she was his mate. He should tell her. He'd not told her he loved her. Thought it was a given that two people who would live on in future generations would love each other. Ash brought in a big breath of air, letting the oxygen simmer in his lungs.

"Now," she told him before stretching out on the thick fur beside the dancing flames of the fireplace. She rested her face on her hands. He saw her eyes drift closed. Despite her seeming ease, he witnessed the tensing of her back muscles. Saw how very tight she held herself. Without understanding what she was doing, she protected herself.

"I won't hurt you. You don't need to shield yourself from me," he whispered while he brushed her long hair to the side. Touched his lips upon her neck. "I won't do anything you don't want. If you say, no, I will stop." He straddled her, his legs on either side of her hips. Her buttocks were firm, rounded. He kissed the twin sides.

Taken by the beauty of her, his breath caught. His gaze roamed the length of her. She was perfection. If he wasn't kneeling, he thought the sight would have sent him to his knees. It wasn't as if he'd never seen Harris this way. Stretched out. Naked. Tonight, there was something different about her. The strength of her cat shone in her. The light of her eyes was powerful. The way she moved across the floor to lie down beside him was provocative with magic. She fascinated him. Touched him with hunger even while he admired her. Ash didn't believe she was aware of the innate strength she possessed.

This was something all shifters had in common. They were strong. Their inner strength was beautiful as well as undeniable. They would endure despite any hardships. Their relationship would live on forever. Ashton thought of the infant in her womb just beginning to grow. She nurtured him with her body along with the power of her mind. This was the beginning of a new dynasty. His heir would be born in July or August. He would be able to watch her body change as the baby grew. Would feel him kick. Would know the babe's thoughts.

Watching the liquid stream from the bottle, he poured oil into the palm of his hand. Rubbed the insides of his palms together to warm the lubricant. He studied her back, deciding all of her needed to be addressed with loving care.

She rose. Turned to look over her shoulder. A question in her eyes. Her smile was vibrant as well as alive. "Lavender?" she questioned. "You have lavender scented oil? Why?"

He saw the slight smile once more crease her lips. He wished to kiss that beautiful mouth of hers. Kissing would need to wait until he finished here. Distracting him would be too easy. "I would think you would like something a bit more manly."

"Do you like the scent?" His grin was wicked. "Flowers go well on me. Better on you. I would cover your body with the warm perfume. Ease you until your limbs resemble wet noodles. What do you think? Should we both carry the aroma of a flower garden?"

"You know I love the scent of lavender," she laughed. "It is possible when you finish easing me, I can do the same for you."

Her laughter was wonderful to hear. "Bought the scent that year we were apart. Wanted to be reminded of you. Though I didn't need the reminder to think of you night and day. I missed you. I'm eternally grateful we are married."

Ash began to work on her shoulders, massaged. Felt the quivering of her tense muscles. The knots that he needed to reduce. He wanted to do whatever he could to comfort her. She could have nightmares tonight. If she did, he would be next to her. Would take her into his arms. Hold her until all bad memories were vanquished. He prayed she would never think of Chandler again.

With slow strokes, his hands swept down her back. Touched upon each vertebra along her spine. Gave careful attention to the twin dimples above her buttocks. He poured more oil into his palms. Swept across the delicate curve of her hips. Moved lower. Touched upon her inner thigh. Found the sensitive spot behind her knees. Caressed the muscles of her thighs before dipping lower to massage the calf muscles. He took one foot at a time into his hands, rubbing his thumb along the arch. Straddled her to kneed her shoulders again. His sex pulsed against her buttocks. He could pull her up, press into her from behind. Last night she'd been curious about different ways to make love. At the prospect of teaching her, his body hummed with excitement.

More perfumed scent found its way into his hands. Decided he would begin once more at her neck. Massaging. Kneading. Tantalized nerve endings. Across her shoulders, he kissed her. Heard the tiny sound of pleasure ripple into the air. Nipped the back of her neck. Allowed his hands to discover the ladder of her ribs. Touched upon the sides of her breasts. Maneuvered across her waist. Her back arched more at each caress. More sounds whispered from her lips. Each breath she inhaled was witnessed by him. Her lashes fluttered against her cheeks.

"Don't fall asleep on me," he told her laughing as he bent to touch the lobe of her ear. If she did fall asleep, Ash prayed the slumber would be a healing sleep. He should not wake her. Didn't wish for her to sleep until she climaxed. Nevertheless, her body would tell him what she needed most.

"I won't. Not until you make love to me. Must feel you inside me before I drift off," Harris murmured. "Your warm fingers are pleasant. The aroma of the perfume languid. Are you going to allow me to do the same to you?"

"In time." He paused in thought. "Ah, my love, believe your front deserves as much attention as your back. I wouldn't wish to miss a single place," he murmured, his voice growing husky with the building desire rampaging within. "Will you turn over for me? Show me your beautiful breasts. Open your mouth for me to kiss deeply. If you're willing to do the same with your legs, I would see as well as taste all of you tonight."

She did. He was pleased with the tight hard buds of her nipples. The soft pink color that nearly matched her lips. With the child, all this would change. She would grow rounder, more sensitive to his touch. He bent over, desiring more from her. His hands on either side of her head, Ash kissed her. Framed her mouth with his. Touched his tongue against hers. Rubbed. Tasted. He poured more scented oil into his hands. Smoothed the perfume over her breasts, across the crests beckoning him to taste, down her torso. Enjoyed her belly knowing soon the softness there would soon be swelled with his child.

As he did with her back, he moved lower. Fondled her between her legs. Touched silken flesh. Teased. Taunted. She moaned. Arched her back off the floor, seeking more from him. The noise, a soft sound rippling from the back of her throat. His kisses fell upon her breasts. After that her navel. Caressed her thighs then moved back to her lips. He touched upon them. Swept his tongue across her swollen mouth. Dark pink now from the pressure of his lips upon hers. Pushed inside to the welcoming shadowy warmth he so loved. She tasted of sweet wine. Her lavender scent was evocative. Enchanting. Mercurial. Kissed her long, deep penetrating kisses. He could never kiss her enough. She was magic to him.

His hand pressed against her belly. He felt his child beneath his fingers. No bigger than a minute now. He would feel the lad's growth every time he caressed Harris here. It would not be long until he could understand the boys' thoughts. His tongue swirled around her navel. He moved lower, spreading the sweet oil, kissing her. His fingers delved between her legs.

Her heat overflowed his hands. She was ready for him. Damp with her pleasure. Writhing more with each caress.

Spreading her legs farther, he kissed her intimately. Found the small nub of her pleasure. Licked. filled her core with his tongue. He loved the taste of her. Burying his face between her legs was one of his greatest pleasures.

He had not kissed her enough, though her supple body arched for more. Capturing her mouth with his, he fired the flames along with tempest reeling in his body higher then higher still. Her fingers wound into his hair. Nails scraped his neck. Whimpers cascaded from her lips. He ached with the need to fill her.

"Please...don't want to wait...longer." The words were barely a breath echoing from Harris' mouth. He wanted to capture the words within his. Molded his lips across hers.

She was not ready. Not as prepared as he wished her to be. He needed her writhing beneath him. Wished to feel her magic soar when he entered her. She ran her nails along his chest. Touched upon his nipples. Moved lower to hold onto his pulsing sex. Stroked.

"Do you want me inside your hot little body?" he asked as he nipped her chin then across her lips teasing her. Bit each tight bud. Swirled his tongue around them. Sucked upon them until they were both elongated, so very large. He enjoyed how his mouth could change her body.

"Yes... Come inside me. Fill me with your sex. I would like that." The words were followed with another whispered moan. "I need you to fill me, Ash. Thrust inside me until my world shatters into pulsing fragments."

"If you insist," he laughed, watching her body respond so perfectly to him. Thrilled with the easy seduction.

"I do. I do insist."

Her eyes were wide open. There was no lazy drifting of her lashes to hide her emotions from him. The silver-blue crystals simmered with the blessed heat of her desire. She was hungry for him. Her passion rocketed.

Ash sent two fingers inside her. Felt the pulsing of her core pound against him. The wet rain of her honey that would ease his way. She would find her pleasure soon. He wanted that then one more time with her. She would be left, sated with her pleasure to eventually find her way to a peaceful slumber. They would have wine then he would leave her to sleep. He would have to speak with Smith-Jones. Needed to tell the man everything that happened at the brothel. Smith-Jones would be the primary spokesperson for the family. Though he would give one interview to the man of his choosing.

His sex lay across her thigh. She did want him. Having told him so, he would oblige all her wishes and dreams. With slow precision, Ash entered into her. Filled her. Her tight sheath kissed his length. Pulsed against him. Throbbed. Touched upon him as no other woman had before. There was magic tonight. Enchantment in the way she clung to him, in the way she gave him her all. Harris would forget all but this. All except these exquisite memories. She would not remember Chandler's venom.

His thrusts were slow. Measured to create the most pleasure possible. Meant to heat. Destined to evoke as much ecstasy as imaginable. He meant to prolong this until he brought her to a frenzy of need. Beneath him her small body vibrated with the growing tension. Intended to chase away any demons that might still linger in her mind. Her climax would be upon her soon. He thrust harder then deeper and faster until she yelled out. He roared then emptied himself into her sultry heat. He lay still unable to catch his breath. Heard the cadence of each breath. Felt the rise and fall of her chest.

His weight encased her. He tried to hold himself away. Her arms closed around him, pulling herself against him. Dragging him closer. Using his forearms, he pushed up and away from her, relieving her of some of his weight. He didn't wish to crush her. Pushing damp strands of hair from her face, Ash reveled at her resiliency. She fought against an imposing opponent. She won. Tonight, she'd been through more than any one should need to go through. Had seen things meant only for those willing to participate in debauchery.

She was strong. Wasn't fragile. She told him so. He would need to believe her words.

He kissed her lips, a slight brush nothing more. Rolling with her, he cradled her in his arms until her body seemed to relax into his. Her head rested on his chest. His arm lay around her. Ash set himself away from her. Strode to the tray holding the wine then brought it to the floor where they made love.

"Wine? Would you like some? We've more than enough for the evening," he asked but he didn't wait for a reply. "Food? You need to eat. Feed our child as well as yourself. You do have to eat more than before."

Harris would drink. She would sleep. "I'd like some of both. What time is it? I feel as if the night is turning to dawn and I'm still awake? Before...before I would never have been able to sleep. Now... You've cleansed me of the horror though not all the memories. I feel sorry for Winter. She doesn't deserve Chandler's treatment of her. Why does she stay?"

Ash didn't know how to answer the questions. Mates stayed together. That was the fact that kept Winter doing Chandler's bidding. He filled her glass to the brim before handing it to her. She tipped it back, drinking long and deep. He loved the sight of her. Naked. At ease in front of him. When she moved, her body danced in tune with a rhythm she seemed to set. There was a time he wondered if these moments would come about. When she set the glass down, her eyes sparkled.

She was his. He was hers. No matter what he tried, his brother would never tear them apart. Leaning against a chair, Ash pulled her into his arms. They both drank. He filled her glass again, hoping this would be enough to allow her to sleep without bad dreams. She ate cheese. Some meat followed. He doubted if she would eat much more. This would suffice until breakfast. Until tomorrow crashed down around them.

It would. He along with Smith-Jones would shelter her from the worst gossip. The vilest rumors. The sketch would do nothing to ease the script Chandler created around them. Together they would weather the storm. Hold their heads high.

The fire in front of them frolicked, fed by the heat of the night, crackled. Spit embers. Rising, he set another log on the fire. Flames, gold, red as well as blue shot into the air. When he turned back to look at Harris, her lashes drooped across her eyes. The empty glass tumbled from slack fingers to roll on the fur rug.

Satisfied, she would sleep until he returned from the early interviews. Sleep longer into the morning. He would keep her close. Ash scooped her into his arms then strode to the bed. The covers were pulled back. He set her on the mattress. Brought the sheets and blankets up to cover her. He bent to kiss her forehead. Touched with a light stroke across the feathering of her eyebrows. Recalled the sweet caresses of her body when she made love to him.

"Sleep. I'll be back. Dream only of us together."

Quickly, Ash dressed in his buckskins and white shirt. He pulled on knee high moccasins. Searching out Smith-Jones, he walked to his father's office. Now his. Between them there was much to say.

Smith-Jones sat in a high-backed chair, sipping brandy. His eyes now peering at him over the crystal rim. "Been waiting for you. Understand you wished to see to her needs first. Thought you might be down later. She fall asleep?"

Ash grunted before pouring a glass of brandy for himself. He sat next to his friend, his forearms on his knees, he stared into the amber liquid. "There is much to explain. The Times will have pictures of my wife on the front page. She is naked. None of what happened is her fault. My brother... He kidnapped her from the restaurant. Someone told him we were there. Unfortunately for Lainie, she was caught up in my brother's anger. She suffered too."

"We've all heard about the brothel he keeps. Did he mean to have Harris participate? Chandler, for the last three weeks has prided himself with the fact all the women along with the men who participate are agreeable to the scripts he writes. Harris would not have fit that scenario. I imagine her presence was meant to taunt you."

"She was not willing. As I said, Lainie was with her. Though Lainie was allowed to remain clothed. If the diaphanous gown she'd been forced to wear could be considered clothed." Ash tossed back the liquid fire then filled his glass again. More spirits would douse the inner turmoil plaguing him.

"There were reporters?" Smith-Jones asked. "An artist I assume to capture the likeness of your wife? As well as you."

"Both." Thinking about the earlier events caused his blood to boil. He was furious. This should have never happened. Chandler should have never been able to find Harris alone and unprotected. Ashton went on to tell him everything he saw. He didn't know all that Harris went through.

"Chandler gave her choices to make her appear as if she was eager to perform. Choices that were no choice at all."

"He planned the event quite well. Do you suppose he always has an artist at his disposal for his productions, as he calls them? Having one might be useful for blackmail purposes," Smith-Jones mused then looked at him. "Did Chandler threaten you?"

"No. Chandler understands I would never give in to his intimidations or possible blackmail. I'm not afraid of him. Found life needed to be lived with truth. Damn the consequences. I've never been placed in such a precarious position. It's not me I'm worried about..."

"It's Harris." Smith-Jones finished for him.

"Harris, yes, I'm worried about her. Though this evening she proved her metal both as Chandler's entertainment as well as with me when I was terrified for her." She was strong...shifter strong as she told him. "I believe she will survive this with few or no repercussions."

"The newspaper will be destroyed in the morning before your father or Harris rises. I will defer the curious until you are prepared to make a statement. Is there anything else?"

"I would learn when my father rises. He should hear from me what transpired. I'm going to explain everything. If he encounters any inquisitive friends or enemies, he must be able to reply without hesitation. Answer the inquiries with confidence." Ash prayed no one would reach his father with questions before he could relate the facts. He understood except to bolt all the doors, someone would question them.

"Very well. I would guess you wish to spend the remainder of the evening with your wife. She will need you if she wakes?"

"For now. I hope she doesn't awaken to any nasty dreams. If she does, I'll be there for her." He paused then thinking about all that happened. "I want you to save the paper for me. Harris needs to learn about the article as well as see the picture. In the future she might be blindsided by some unfeeling person. Just as father needs to learn the truth of all that transpired, so does Harris. A united front is what we will present."

~ * ~

Harris woke up when Ash climbed into bed with her. She sighed with a soft sound reverberating from her throat. The length of his naked body against hers, felt right. He tugged her close, his arm across her. With one hand he cradled her breast. Touched lovingly. Another sigh filtered from deep in her lungs.

"Did you accomplish what you set out to do? I would know what to expect in the morning," Harris asked, understanding he would need to speak with Smith-Jones.

His man would comprise him of all that happened. Turning in his arms, she ran her hand along his chest, spreading her fingers to touch as much as possible. She moved lower discovering the flat of his belly. Her fingers coiled around his sex, hardening him just as she wished. His hand clamped over hers.

"Little vixen. Do you want me to make love to you again? Whatever you want is yours." He smoothed his finger down the length of her nose. Turned his hand over to caress her cheek before a light touch brought his fingers along the column of her throat. "I would if that is what you'd like."

"No, I suppose not. It's almost dawn. You must need your sleep. a few hours will need to suffice. I would not take that away from you. I understand there will be visits today from people we *dinna* wish to see. Your father, what is he going to think? He can't be hurt. His son, his oldest, is a horrible person."

Ash caught her roaming hand, settled his on top. "I will talk to him first thing in the morning. You are right. I do need sleep even if it's only a few hours." He closed his eyes. "He will understand the monster his son has become. Do believe, though, father understood when he stripped him of the title. If he didn't recognize the extent of Chandler's depravity, he would not have done so."

"I'm eager to get on with our lives. We've spent so much time seeing to the needs of others. I would see this all settled before the *bairn* is born." Harris brought his hand to her belly. "It might be too soon to know. I think I'm pregnant. Can you feel him? You told me you would know when I conceived."

"It's not too soon for us to *ken* the conception of our child. I feel him too, beneath my hand as we speak. Another little shifter for us to coddle."

323

Ash laughed at the look of chagrin on her beautiful face. "You are not pleased that I know?"

"You knew!" She punched his chest. "I thought I would be the first. Believed I would get to tell you." Harris pressed her hand against his. She loved the warmth of his hands, the callouses. His fingers were long, bronzed. They stood out against the white of her flesh.

"Yes, I knew. Felt him inside you this morning after we made love. Thank you for telling me. Now, we've a few hours left to sleep. I wish for my wife to be up and about, showing the world nothing will cause her to falter. You will demonstrate to all of England you are strong. Indomitable. We will stand together."

"Should we do something besides sit in the house waiting for the world to fall apart? Maybe go somewhere with our heads held high?"

Harris didn't understand why she spoke those words. He wouldn't feel that way. Ash was strong. Cat strong. Shifter strong. Just as her brothers would do in a similar situation, he would take charge. "I would let the public see us together. Know that what happened would never drive us apart. Where should we go?"

"We could go shopping for a new gown. You did lose one. Perhaps stop somewhere for a pastry. I do love anything sweet. Like you." Ash cuddled her close. "Did you have any bad dreams while I was gone? I would vanquish them."

"No, not one nightmare. I slept as well as I could without you next to me. I missed you. Was a *wee* bit cold." She ran her feet along his legs. "No place to warm them." Laughed inside when he shuddered.

"You do have the coldest feet," he murmured. "Though the heat of other wonderful parts of you makes up for your frigid toes."

Harris understood Ash needed to sleep. She closed her eyes, thinking forward instead of behind, refusing to live in the past or dwell on anything unpleasant. He'd been talking to Smith-Jones while she'd been asleep.

She was restless, tired of waiting. Energy to get on with the day burned inside. She wasn't about to run from last night. Needed to see the front page of the London Times before Smith-Jones destroyed the paper. She'd seen the artist sketching. Harris understood he would have been ordered to do so. When Ash dozed, Harris knew this might be her only chance. The slow cadence of each breath told her he was sleeping.

When she looked out the window, light was beginning to shine inside casting a warm glow of light upon the earth. While he thought to protect her, she wished she could do the same for him. In this town no one knew her. Ash had an important role to play. He was an earl. He was a member of parliament. People looked up to him. He didn't deserve his brother's wrath. Harris knew her husband never sought out the title or the wealth that went along with the position. Now that he would be the earl, he had more responsibilities. Before, he could come and go whenever it pleased him.

Harris was determined to meet his accusers head on. Those who sought to defile his good name because of his brother. She was certain there would be a drawing of her in the paper today. Chandler had her naked for that very purpose. Ash tore up the sketch. His actions would make no difference. She would know the worst. Didn't want or wish for safeguarding. She was his wife. His countess. She would stand by him with her back straight along with her head held high.

Another hour passed by before she slipped her legs over the edge of the bed. A bath would be nice but she could ask for one later. She didn't wish to wake Ash. Didn't want him to know her purpose. With haste, she dressed. Slipped from the room without making noise. The door closed behind her with a soft sound. For several seconds she waited, her back against the door, listening, attempting to hold her breath.

With silent feet she made her way to the front doorstep. Smith-Jones was behind her. She screeched when he tried to step in front of her. "No." Agile as she was, she ducked beneath his arm. Reached for the paper. He stepped back, his hands on his hips. She clutched the London Times to her chest. Breathing heavy, she stared at him. "You're not going to keep me from seeing this. Don't you dare try to take the paper from me. I won't let you." Harris didn't know what she'd do if he forced the issue. She couldn't fight him.

"You're not supposed to be here," he accused, his voice strained. "I've my orders. Doubt if your husband thought you would be up this early after the ordeal you experienced. No, I'm not going to take it from you.

Though the earl would expect me to do just that. I would like you to hand the paper over to me."

"All you said is true. I'm determined to understand what has been said. Not about to settle for a second-hand rendition. One that would sketch the truth to the way Ash wants me to see it. You cannot keep me from seeing along with reading the damage to my husband Chandler created with his actions. I won't have it. I'm made of sterner stuff. You *ken* I am." Harris swept past Smith-Jones, forcing him to take a step back. She marched into the kitchen, the paper still clutched to her breasts. "No, you don't. You're not going to stop me. I won't hand it over to you."

"Milady, please. I promised the earl neither you nor James would see this before he could speak with you. I've never broken a promise."

She swallowed hard. Stiffened her spine, needing the courage. Didn't like the fact she put this sweet man in a position where he would need to explain himself to her husband. She began slow, her words precise. "I promised myself I wouldn't run from whatever lies are written here. Do you wish for me to break a vow to myself?"

Harris almost laughed at the look sweeping Smith-Jones' features. He was too confused for words.

"You put me between a rock and a hard place, Countess. I've..." He reached out to grab it from her.

She whirled, dancing away from him. "We will peruse this news together. What do you think? Should we enjoy a cup of hot coffee while we do so?"

Harris marched into the kitchen. Found the coffee warm on the stove. She bargained with the fact Smith-Jones would not hurt her. He could do only so much.

"You do know the earl prefers tea," he told her as he poured himself tea, added a dollop of milk then sugar.

"He is learning to drink coffee. That's why the cook has been instructed to keep it warm for us. I must have coffee in the mornings. Tea will never do. When I'm tired, I need the little jolt the coffee gives me."

Behind her the man grumbled. Keeping the newspaper beneath her arm, Harris dished up a plate for herself. In the breakfast nook she sat down with her coffee, food along with the London Times. Anxiety raced through her. She was afraid to look. Terrified of what she might see or read.

Sipping the hot coffee, Harris stared at the paper then Smith-Jones. He was frowning at her. It was clear he didn't appreciate her efforts that went against his boss' direct order. Now, he waited for her to look at the damning article. She knew what was on the paper would be horrible. A deep breath of air for courage, her fingers moved on the newspaper.

"All right then, should we see what the paper has in store for us here at the Wolcott residence? What do you think?" Harris didn't care what he thought. She cared about her husband. Prayed he would not be affected by the written word.

"Yes," Smith-Jones nodded. "We should inspect this. Knowing the truth is often better than going in with a blind eye. Imagine since you are part of what happened, you should also discover the complete truth. Though I don't blame Ash for protecting you. I would do the same."

With no hesitation now that she found her bravery, she spread the paper in front of them. True to what she believed she would see, the immodest sketch of her was boldly depicted on the front page. The headlines were clear.

COUNTESS CAUGHT NAKED IN A COMPROMISING SITUATION.

Harris snorted with disgust. Tapped her nails on the coffee cup. "Well...I imagine I was caught in a compromising situation. Not one of my doing. Nor did I wish to be sketched nude in front of that leering audience." Harris read a few lines of the article then looked at Smith-Jones. "Doubt if my husband would wish to have you staring at this depiction of me. Though..." she hesitated looking from the naked depiction of her to Smith Jones. "The sketch doesn't show that much of me. Suggests...makes certain all staring at the sketch know I'm wearing nothing. Still, the drawing could be harsher. More brazen. I should write a note to Chandler thanking him for protecting my modesty. What do you think? Should I thank his brother?"

Harris found she enjoyed his discomfort. The man was mumbling nonsense. It was clear he was trying to figure out what to say to Ash.

"It needs to be destroyed before James gets up. Though, I understand Ashton will wish to see this as well as read the article."

She handed the paper to him. "You're right about that. Burn the damn thing before Ash sees it. The drawing will make him angry. He might do something foolish. He needs to preserve his position among the ton."

For herself she didn't care what people said about her. They would not spend much time in London.

"Harris!"

Her name boomed from the door told her the newspaper would not burn before Ashton saw the damning contents. She cringed, turning toward the door where her husband stood with his feet braced apart and his arms crossed in front of him. The scowl on his face told her he was not appreciative as to what she was about. Upon awakening he must have raced here. His dressing gown was all he wore. She stared at his bare toes then to his face.

"Yes?" she said, her voice soft, contrite. Sweet. Could even be described as syrupy.

The arctic frost of his eyes terrified her. Despite her bold behavior, she shivered, quivered as he sent the ice of his wrath her way. He was angry. Almost as angry as he was last night at the theatre or whorehouse. The evening before he'd not been furious with her. She stood to meet him, to explain her opinion. He wasn't going to appreciate or listen to her position.

He strode into the room then on into the kitchen. Ash returned with a cup of coffee along with a plate of food. He sat down, sipping, staring at her. His eyes burned with a fever she wasn't certain how to interpret.

After a bite of food then a slow drink of his coffee, he spoke, his voice husky so calm as if he held back emotions. "You were not supposed to see this. I gave Smith-Jones the directive to get rid of it before anyone was up." He looked to his friend as if the man could give him an explanation.

The smile she was trying to hide erupted. She lifted her shoulders in a gesture she hoped would placate her husband. "I was up before him. He told me what you ordered. I ignored that command. Wished to see what the rest of London would wake up to see. Since it is me in that sketch, I've every right."

"True."

Harris found herself shocked he would agree with her. "True? Then why did you come howling into the room as if you were a raging tiger."

"Are," he corrected, his voice suddenly calm. He smiled at her as he began to speak. "I am a raging tiger. Not at you, my love. Never at you. However, I'd like to twist Chandler's neck until he—"

"You cannot do that," Harris interrupted, setting her hand on his. All the panic she felt earlier, rising. "I'm healing. There will be no nightmares. The humiliation was left in his little theater. Would wish for you to do the same. You will make a statement this afternoon. After that we won't mention this incident again. We can carry our heads high. Done nothing wrong." Harris sighed, wishing she could erase the frown lines on Ash's forehead. "This morning while I watched you sleep, I did a great deal of soul searching. Am I embarrassed when I think about all those people looking at me? Wanting to see me in an intimate position with another man? Yes. Will I ever see the lot of them again? Maybe. I hope not. I'm not that person who doesn't have someone who is mine through eternity. They are the people who should be ashamed, embarrassed, humiliated. Not me. They seek sex wherever they can find it having no one to love. I don't wish to ever talk about this again."

Smith-Jones looked away with a smile on his face. Ash picked up her hands, kissed the backs. "Everything you said is right. We need to proceed into the future." Ash turned to his friend. "Told you she is strong. Cat strong."

"What will you tell your father?" Smith-Jones asked while he looked at the door. James would be joining them soon. "James is also a shifter. He should see as well as read the London Times. Come to his own conclusions. What happened should be prefaced but show it all to him. Let him decide."

"His heart?" Harris asked, concerned. that she might have started something that would result in something tragic.

"We will preface the viewing of the paper with a short explanation of what occurred. He will not be so shocked it will harm him in any way. He will be prepared for the worst. Truth is the right way to proceed."

"Of course, truth is the right way to go around here. Tell me what happened. By the way you three are huddled together, something tragic has gone on. Smith-Jones bring some tea and a plate of food. You know what I like. I'm not going to have a heart attack. The three most important people in my life are all sitting in front of me safe. That's all that matters to me."

"Yes, sir..." Smith-Jones said before fleeing the room. He seemed pleased James asked him for help.

Ash explained with brief words what occurred last night at Chandler's establishment. James snorted, sipped the tea his butler brought him. Her heart in her throat, Harris waited for the words.

Clearing his throat, James began, "I should have disowned the boy years ago. Thought he would mature. Grow out of his growing pains. Come to believe in himself. He did not. Now he runs a business which caters to the surliest individuals in our society. I don't know what I did wrong with the lad."

"He's no longer a lad, father. Chandler is a grown man. He makes his own decisions," Ash pointed out as he watched Harris. "You did nothing wrong."

Harris sent an unladylike snort into the conversation. "He's grown up. You can't change the man. He set his course a long time ago. The only person who might succeed in doing so is..."

Perhaps that was too much to tell. She should let Ash decide what his father should know.

"Winter," Ash cut in, waving his hand. "The woman told me she loves him. Winter will either be able to make him a better person or he will drag her down with him. They would have to wed to move on to another life. He can't claim her. "As far as we know for certain, he is not a shifter."

"Part shifter," James corrected with a long-drawn-out sigh. "He is part. That fact, in part, is what has made him so surely over the years. Chandler has hovered between two worlds. He was never able to shift completely. Most of the time he was able to change his upper body to a tiger. Later he grew impatient with himself. Quit trying. I always told him to have patience. In time if he gave himself a chance, he would be able to shift. He did not. You say Winter is in love with him? That love could help him become a better man."

"Winter Snow is also a shifter. Winter is allowing Chandler to abuse her because he is her mate. Believe she doesn't know what else she can do," Ash said, as he looked around the room then focused on her.

Harris was shaking her head at the three men who seemed to be thinking she could do something about Winter. She could not. No one would allow her to enter the building. Ash would never allow her to go there. Chandler would never allow Winter to leave even to visit with her. It was a stalemate no one could solve.

Holding up her hands she spoke. Her words trembled when she began. "Those two will have to figure this out on their own. I won't interfere. If Winter loves the man, she will find a way to wed or for him to claim her. She must understand what is at stake. We cannot interfere. I refuse to interfere."

"She is right," Ash conceded. "We cannot step into the middle of this situation. Chandler despises shifters. We would not wish for him to feel that way about Winter. If he knew, I cringe to think what he might force on her."

The knocking at the door told them visitors were beginning to arrive. They would need to stay strong. Smith-Jones stood. "I will weed out the guests. The few you would be acceptable to speak with will be sent to the drawing room. The others will be directed home."

They were left with a strained silence. Harris decided to ignore the churning of her stomach. Selected a croissant to nibble on. It was too early for her to feel morning sickness. The nausea she felt must be because of the anticipation of the next few hours. She would weather the brewing storm.

"I would like you to stay in our rooms," Ash began while he held her hands in his. "Comprehend you would protest the confinement. Don't know what you could do here. You shouldn't be exposed to more verbal abuse. I'm sure even among the chosen there will be at least one man who will set the blame on your shoulders."

"If I remained here, I would not be pacing, worrying about the reception you are receiving. If you would give me a choice, I would like to stand by your side, my chin held high. Proud of you. I'm not ashamed because none of what occurred was of my choosing. I was a victim. Wasn't that what we spoke of last night?"

Epilogue

A little over a year later.

The bridal suite in the McKenna Keep was filled with food and wine. Heather brought her to the room with the other wives just as tradition called for. They bathed her in lavender scented water. Dressed her in a sheer gown of dark purple. This wasn't the first time since the women made certain after the first bridal feast Clan Chaton tradition was carried forth.

Just as the first time, Ash spent time with the men downstairs while he paced the room and drank more ale than necessary. He told her he was just as eager to join his bride this time as he was the first. Since the birth of their first child, they had very little time together. This would be their first night they could spend in each other's arms, where they wouldn't need to tend to the young shifter. Harris' mother and father were pleased to watch the barin while they had a second wedding night.

There had been no advice given other than to take care. A second child so soon after the first would be difficult. Though not one of the women could say they heeded that advice. Not even Maisie, Hawk's wife. Their second child came only a year after the birth of their first. Harris had to laugh. Despite Hawk's urgings, none of the men enjoyed the necessary precautions needed, even Hawk.

Harris stood now at the back of the room waiting for her husband to be delivered to her. The door was flung open. Ash was carried in by the men before he was set upon his feet. His lazy grin went straight to her heart. She was certain she understood the thoughts racing through his head.

He'd been allowed to wear a kilt, the dress tartan of the Frasier clan. The men rid him of his shirt, as well as the knee-high socks and shoes. Except for the two of them, everyone fled the room.

"*Je t'adore* my love?" Ash stepped forward, his hand outstretched to her. He pulled her into his arms. Framed her mouth with his. She parted her lips for him. The kiss was long as well as sweet. She needed him as much as she needed to draw breath. After his lips left hers, he stared down at her. Pushed hair away from her face. "Was the second wedding as nice as the first?" His question touched her heart. "I'm blessed to enjoy two weddings."

"They were both just as nice. Different because this ceremony was here at the McKenna Keep. I always dreamed of Father Damian performing the service. The claiming ceremony was unique too. I'm happy my family could watch. I did see you again. Watched as we roamed the countryside in our cats."

"I take it we were not in danger." He told her, releasing her to pour them both a glass of wine. Sitting on a chair, Ash pulled her onto his lap. "Drink up. We've no little one to see to tonight. Heather will take good care of the little shifter. Spoil the lad."

She wrapped her hands around his neck, hanging on to the chalice of wine as she did so. "Still bothers me not to have him by our bed. What if he wakes up frightened? Screaming. We both know he has solid lungs to voice his dislikes when he has a mind to do so. He might keep mother and father awake all night."

"Your mother will know what to do. Remember she had two boys as well as a stubborn girl. Besides, our little man took to both your parents. They've spent hours playing with him. They all adore each other."

"Who is calling who stubborn? I believe you've got me beat on that score." Harris grunted her dislike of the name he gave her."

"We should make love. I need to feel all of you. Against me. Beneath me. Above me. In front of me. Your breasts are fuller since you gave birth. I want to savor all of you." Ash was sliding the straps of her gown down her arms, unveiling her breasts. The nipples were hard. Begged for attention as he dipped his head to do just as he told her he wished to do.

Her head fell back giving him better access. She set her chalice on the nearby table. "Make love to me."

After, they lay sated on the big bed. He ran his hand across her belly. "Do you suppose we've another babe on the way?"

"I'm certain we will know soon enough. You did not tease me at the table as you said you would."

Ash stiffened at her comment. "Couldn't bring myself to do so...after what occurred a little over a year ago..."

To reassure him, she set her hand to his chest. "I understand. When you are the one arousing me, I like it. We both understand no one would have seen." She wondered what he would say next. "I could have dropped my fork again."

"They would have known what we did. As it is, they are curious. Your eyes didn't glaze over with your release. We entertained them at our first wedding. Didn't intend to do so tonight. While I didn't wish to wait for the women to attend to you. I did."

She lowered her lashes pleased with his consideration. "Thank you. Since it would have been you touching me, I would not have minded. As it is, I'm glad we did not. I would be alone with you in the privacy of our chamber."

"So, I made the correct choice?" He laughed, running his finger with a gentle stroke along her eyebrows."

"Yes, I love you Ash. Would say the words now even though they should have been said ages ago. You said nothing to me."

"Ah, my love, I've thought to say them too. I love you along with your reckless heart. Harris' reckless heart holds mine in the palm of her hands. I do love you."

"As I do love you."

Coming Soon

Rafe's Every Wish Fulfilled
Sweet McKenna Book Ten

Chapter One

Present
Glasgow, Scotland

Rafe sat in a chair provided for visitors, his fingers drumming on the cold wood of the armrest. The clock struck the hour of one. He'd been waiting three hours for an audience with the head of the magazine where Dallas was supposed to work. All he knew was that she'd been sent on an assignment somewhere north of here. He had to find out where.

His patience neared the snapping point. Restless, he wasn't used to waiting for important information. Dallas went missing from his life over a week ago. This was worse. Before that, he'd not seen her for months. On assignment, she told him he needed to remind himself. This wasn't like the first time she went missing. How the hell did he know that? Gut instinct. In the present, he sensed her before she was gone. Vanished without a trace.

Those two words, "on assignment," didn't tell him anything he could sink his teeth into. To get this far into the building, Rafe had to lie. Told the secretary in the front of the building Dallas was his wife.

Not much of a lie.

Dallas would be his wife as soon as he could get her to a minister, say the necessary words then put a ring on her finger. She would need to agree. After the way she'd been acting, he was worried she would balk at the suggestion of marriage. Now, he didn't have any thoughts about what ran through her head. Before, he could always read her mind. Her eyes coupled with her facial expressions were an open book. He had to see her before he could read that book.

When she disappeared a few months ago, he thought he would never see her again. At the falls he found her car. The trunk held her tripod along with her computer. Nothing else. Not her camera or the big bag where she kept all her necessities. Fool that he was, instead of leaving the car in the parking lot where she could get to it, he drove the car back to her house. She told him she had to hitchhike into Edinburgh for her interview. *Hitchhike! Good God, he put her life in danger.*

"Mr. Frasier…" He jerked to attention. Nerves snapped.

He looked up to see the secretary standing in the doorway leading to the boss' office. "Yes. That's me." She knew it was him. His heart turned over. He was about to get a few answers. He stood. The chair he'd been sitting in screeched against the floor.

"Mr. Johnson will see you now. He doesn't have much time. You need to make this quick."

Just as the McKenna suggested, Rafe had driven to Edinburgh, to the office of the magazine Dallas mentioned she worked for. Cole McKenna, head of the clan, suggested he do whatever was necessary to discover Dallas' destination. That's why he lied. Her boss would never give out information as to her whereabouts to just anyone. He needed to be someone. Someone who would be important to Dallas. A person who could be trusted with private information. The lie was a necessity.

Blazes, he needed to see her. Hold her. Test their relationship. The spark they felt when he kissed her last time he saw her lit his insides on fire. His body roared to life. Before that time there had never been anything substantial between them except an honest friendship. Yes, he loved her. Loved Dallas as a brother loved a sister. Now…now the feelings he harbored for her were far different. There was nothing platonic in the way he felt when he looked at her or thought about her.

After she told him she lived with the man who drove her to Edinburgh before her job interview, he went crazy. Was the name Scratch or Gordon? He couldn't recall. At the time he thought he should shake a bit of sense into her. She wasn't acting with logic.

She couldn't give up on them. Not now when there was something tangible between them. He didn't intend to allow her to dismiss him from her life. Not after the kiss they shared. Not after realizing after all these years Dallas was his mate. In a hazy outline, Rafe began to understand what occurred. The universe was in the process of righting itself. He needed to hear more details from Dallas. If she could explain those months she was away, incognito, he would feel much better. As Cole, the head of the clan Chaton, told him, he needed to tell Dallas everything about him. She needed to understand shifters mated for life. He couldn't leave out one detail. Before they could move on, he would need to show her his cat.

"Have a seat." The man he came to talk to motioned to a chair.

Dear Lord, he'd been so caught up in thought he didn't listen. He needed to pay attention. This was far too important for him to mess up. If this man didn't give him Dallas' location, he didn't have anywhere else to turn. There were no clues as to her whereabouts. Nothing in her small apartment that would give anything away.

Rafe pulled up a chair then sat down in front of the big cherry wood desk that seemed to fill an entire wall. Windows behind the desk caught and held the light. The day was a fine one. Sunlight danced in the room.

"What can I do for you?" he asked as he appeared to be studying him. "Don't want any shenanigans. The last man who came in here tried to bribe me. Be apprised, I don't take bribes from young men. Dallas' whereabouts is privileged information."

Rafe's hands were sweating. "I need," he swallowed hard, a vague attempt to mask his discomfort. "Find my wife. No bribes. Just need to know where she is. Said she was going to call me when she reached her destination. That was how many days?" He looked out the window trying to figure out the day she left. "I've lost track." Wouldn't do to put his foot in his mouth over the day she left. "If she doesn't have cell service, she can't call."

"Strange," the man tapped his pen on the desk. "You've misplaced your wife? How does a man misplace the woman he is supposed to love? Where have you been?"

A half-smile formed on his lips. That was a lame thing to say. "My texts…they don't go through. No cell towers. You see." Rafe held out his hands, palms pointing to the ceiling. "She told me she'd let me know when she arrived at the destination. Last night I gave up expecting a call. At least I'm assuming…" he lifted his shoulders in what he hoped would appear to be a nonchalant gesture. Wasn't certain as to how much acting he needed to do. "Assuming she got where she was supposed to go. I'm worried."

"Dallas…you are looking for Dallas Shaw."

"Frasier, Dallas Frasier now."

"Frasier," he corrected himself looking skeptical. "Frasier, you say. That is what my secretary said. She is your wife. Why should I believe you? There were two other men in here looking for her. One of the men told me Dallas was his wife." His snow-white brows furrowed together while he appeared to study him.

Damn, he never thought of that scenario. Never believed for a moment those two bozos would be looking for her. Would come here. Why not? She did tell me she agreed to wed one of them. Was it Gordon or Scratch? Yes, believe she said Mathew Gordon. Must have known the mistake for what it was.

"They are lying. Both of them. I have proof of my claim as I'm certain they did not." Rafe pulled out a forged marriage certificate that Cole insisted he take with him. He was glad he listened to the McKenna. He thought the certificate would provide the proof he needed in order to gain the information. He handed the paper across the desk to Mr. Johnston's outstretched fingers. "This should provide the verification you are looking for."

Rafe sweated while Mr. Johnston looked over the certificate appearing to read every word. After what seemed an eternity, he gave him the paper. The man nodded.

"You should pay more attention to your wife. Those men who visited before you were…" he paused as if he didn't have the words. He went on, "So, the two of you are married. Miss Shaw marked single on her application. Why would she do that?" The frown lines on his forehead became deeper grooves as he looked for a plausible response. One he could believe. While the man waited for Rafe's answer, he sat back in his chair, his hands folded across his belly. "What do have to say to that?"

The question was not as difficult as it might seem even though her application gave her correct marital status. Cole gave him the needed idea for the reply. He would have never thought of something so simple.

Rafe cleared his throat. Pointed to the marriage certificate. "What is the date on her application? That should tell the true story."

"Dallas applied in February."

"If you look at the marriage certificate, it's dated March ninth. Simple… When my wife applied for the job, we weren't wed. Now we are. I do need to locate her. Don't like her out of my sight. We've plans to go through the photos she's taken. I've been worried crazy since she left. Sick to my stomach. Half out of my head. Haven't eaten. Don't know if she reached that part of the highlands or if she's in need of assistance. Her car isn't always reliable. It's broken down before. Plan on using the money she makes on this shoot for a downpayment on a new car for her."

Mr. Johnston cleared his throat, tapped his pen on the top of the desk. "Your wife was sent to the Isle of Skye. I'm sure you are familiar with that area. Very touristy. Very photographic. I'm certain the photos will do the magazine proud. She is taking pictures of the Fairy Pools along with other highland scenery. The closest village is Carbost. That's where her base camp is located." He picked up a piece of paper then began writing. "Can't imagine why she doesn't have cell service," he muttered seeming distracted.

Rafe hoped he was giving him the address of her hotel or place of residence. Dallas would pick a rental rather than a hotel to stay in for the duration. He needed to be with her. Must convince her they were meant to be together. His heart quickened when her boss handed him the directions. The breath he'd been holding while the man wrote left the back of his throat in slow motion. Relief plummeted through him.

Taking a moment to read the information, he looked up. Smiled. "Thank you. Thank you, sir. I'm certain Dallas will appreciate this. We work well together. Always have. I did make arrangements to join her. She's expecting me. Dallas would be disappointed if I failed to turn up. She would wonder why." He folded the paper before stuffing it into the pocket of his jeans having the feeling he'd said too much.

"Is that all?"

"Yes." He rose to leave making plans now to get to Dallas in the next day if possible, reached over the table to shake her boss' hand. Tomorrow evening he hoped to see her. Hold her in his arms. "Thank you again." Pleased with his accomplishment, he felt like whistling.

Rafe walked past the secretary, tipped his head in acknowledgement then out into the lobby. Outside the air was warm. The day was brilliant with sunshine. A gentle breeze ruffled his hair sending an errant lock into his eyes. The delight he felt was tangible. He felt certain the trip would be speedy.

He reached his home in Carnoch in record time berating himself for not packing his things before heading into the city. If he'd had the foresight to do so, he'd be well into the trip instead of working to get started. Two-stepping the stairs to his bedroom, once there he pulled out a travel bag then tossed clothing into it; underwear, socks a couple of changes of both jeans along with shirts. Figured if he forgot anything he could buy anything he needed in the village where she stayed. Grabbing his tooth brush and shaving paraphernalia, he raced down the steps, tossed his bag into the car.

He was headed north.

Behind the wheel, he tugged in a breath of air, gripped the steering wheel. Focused on the road. So much depended on this trip. He couldn't mess it up. After he explained his position, he would show her his cat. Tell her about shifters. With exact words clarify his theory about why she was sent back to another century. Wondered if she believed in the old folklore. While he knew her better than anyone of her acquaintances, he wasn't certain if she was superstitious. In the present, even north in the more secluded places of the highlands, shifters were rumors. Stories told in the night around campfires.

Where superstition was concerned, there were varying degrees. One could walk to the other side of the road to avoid a black cat…or not. If not, a person would test their luck. Take fate into their hands. He grinned. She always avoided walking beneath a ladder. For him, he didn't pay much attention to minor things. One made their luck. Established their fate. That all worked out well unless the universe stepped in to rearrange an accident.

On his way to the Isle of Sky, he mulled the thought over for a few seconds. While he'd never visited there before, he heard the rugged terrain was beautiful. The Fairy Pools spectacular. She would take gorgeous pictures…absolutely amazing photos. Ones she could frame then sell. He brought his computer to help her go through the photographs. Her next show would be in June. He tapped his fingers on the steering wheel. The exhibit would take place in Edinburgh. He never got a chance to see the pictures she took at the falls. Would be interesting if they shed any light on what happened to her. How was he going to get her to speak of that time? Maybe she would want to tell him all that happened. It might be that she wouldn't remember. That was a very real possibility.

The place where she disappeared from his life. Cole told him he believed she traveled backwards in time. The picture of a woman named Lainie with Cameron Roc Frasier in the McKenna keep haunted him. The woman sitting next to Roc looked enough like his Dallas to be her sister or a twin they were so close in appearance.

One day he brought a portrait he'd painted of Dallas to the keep. When he held it up to the one of Lainie for comparison…there were subtle differences. Lainie's hair was redder than Dallas'. Her eyes were a deeper blue. Lainie's breasts were larger. Her hips wider. Cheeks a *wee* bit plumper. He supposed Dallas kept her body's natural tendencies to become lush curves by exercise. If he had his way, she would stop torturing her body to be a shape it should never be. He loved all her lavish curves. When they made love, he wouldn't have to stumble around in the dark to find her feminine parts.

When they made love…

That event was still in the future.

After the clock on his dash told him he should be in bed, he pulled over. Stopped at what appeared to be a café that might be open all night. Once outside in the crisp spring air he stretched. Brought several stimulating breaths of oxygen into his lungs. A few minutes later after using the facilities then buying a large cup of coffee along with a sandwich, he was behind the wheel again.

The next afternoon, he stopped in front of the rustic log cabin Dallas had supposedly rented. His heart skipped a beat, then another. He wiped his sweating hands on his jeans. Pulled at the t-shirt that stuck to his damp chest. Nerves seemed to splinter while he tried to breathe deep. Never in his life had he been this damn nervous. His steps toward the door faltered, certain his knees would give out before he could knock. With his hand in front of the wood he held back.

Courage. I need courage to face her.

At the front door, he struck with the palm of his hand. Knocked again when there was no answer. Walked around the cabin so he could look in the windows. Pressed his nose against the pain of glass. As far as he could tell, Dallas wasn't there. He thumped his forehead with the heel of his hand. She would be working. He checked the front door. It wasn't locked. Rafe let himself inside swearing at her stupidity. Dallas never remembered to lock doors. Either that or she didn't think securing the door was necessary.

He checked his watch. She would quit only after the sun disappeared for the night. He had two options. One was to cook dinner. He could have everything ready when she arrived home. At the last stop he bought a couple of bottles of wine, chicken he could broil along with a bag of salad. The second option was to take the trail to the Fairy Pools. Meet her. Help her with her gear. They could walk back after sunset. He opted for the first choice thinking he needed to prolong the meeting he wasn't certain about. Had no idea how she would receive him. Would lecture him about the lie he told her boss. He needed to be upfront with her.

A romantic dinner.

They would talk all night if necessary. Convincing her not to run from him again would come before speaking of marriage or showing her his cat. She might need to learn how to trust him again. Rafe never believed between them trust would be an issue. As he proceeded now, he wasn't certain. He had a tendency to get things out of order. Knew there was always a proper order to everything. He just had to discover what that sequence was. He was by nature, far too impatient.

No mistakes tonight.

Whistling, he set about the preparations for the romantic dinner, positive this was the right choice for them. On the small table that sat in the corner of the kitchen next to a window, he spread a white tablecloth. Rafe didn't know why he brought adornment. Now he knew. Even when he tossed clothing into his bag, he thought of romance. Stepping outside he picked a handful of wildflowers. With water and a vase, he now set the fragrant decoration on the table. Setting the mood was always important.

Dinner was ready. The candles were lit. Wine was poured. He paced outside to see the dying brilliance of the setting sun. He was impatient to see Dallas. His body hummed in anticipation. If he closed his eyes, he envisioned her marching down the trail while she struggled with all the equipment. She would be home soon. The tourist information he read said the roundtrip would take about an hour.

He saw her emerge from around a bend. Thought he should step lively so he could help her with the equipment. For the first time since he arrived some of his nerves vanished. This was his Dallas. He knew her better than anyone. Took her to the doctor when she had no one to help her. Understood her like no other just as she understood him. The two of them were meant to be together.

He knew when she saw him. Was overjoyed by the initial reaction. The smile on her face told him a wealth of information. The most important that for at least one beat of her heart she was pleased to see him. Seconds later there was no frown. She stopped walking. Stood still for the longest time while she stared at him. After what seemed to be a thorough perusal, she started to walk.

Rafe couldn't wait to reach her. To pull her into his arms then kiss her would be a dream fulfilled. His long strides ate up the distance between them. He was at her side, taking her camera equipment from her. The tripod he collected under his arm. Her large bag which held the cameras along with the lenses, he slung over his shoulder. She didn't need his help. Even so, she looked as if she wouldn't refuse.

He grinned at her. Touched a wayward lock of hair that had come undone from her pony tail. Pushed the cool silken strand behind her ear. "Hello."

Again, the urge to tug her into his arms for the kiss he'd been waiting for, for what seemed to be his entire life rifled through him. Wished he dared sweep her off her feet so he could carry her to the bedroom. Making love to her had been on his mind for the entire drive. In absolute truth, it had been on his mind when he kissed her that long ago day and discovered the inferno she lit within him. He had to be patient as well as realistic. She might not be ready to take that necessary step. Damn, but they had so much to talk about. There were months missing from their lives. If his guesses held merit, she'd been in a different century. She'd been righting something that went amiss hundreds of years ago.

Tilting her head a bit to the side, she spoke. Her voice soft, "I never expected to see you here, Rafe. Why did you come all this way?" She ran her tongue across her lips as if she too wished for that kiss he'd been thinking about. The erotic gesture left a trail of moisture behind. He needed to taste. Savor. *Damn.*

How could he tell her in a brief sentence? The whys of his

appearance were long as well as varied. The reasons all involved her, coupled with what they meant to each other. The need to see her before she could make a mistake with Mathew Gordon part of those reasons.

"I'm glad to see you too." He ventured with the sarcastic comment instead of the explanation she wanted. She would bristle then retaliate. His Dallas wasn't a girl who would let anyone take advantage of her emotions.

Dallas brushed strands of hair from her face as she resecured her ponytail. Her brows were drawn together, sunset colored brows he wished to trace with the tip of his finger. Her lips thinned as she fought to concentrate. "You know what I mean. Don't get flippant."

He'd started walking again, unwilling to give himself away. She caught his arm to stop his retreat. He turned to listen, hoping she would say something that would please him. With Dallas one never knew how she would respond.

"I'm happy to see you too." With a small giggle. "Needed someone to carry my equipment. Might as well be you." Dallas was skipping to keep up with his longer strides. "You don't have to walk so fast. Nothing is going away."

This wasn't what he would have liked to hear from her sweet kissable lips. Though he did appreciate the small giggle. Before when they did things together, she laughed all the time. Their relationship was carefree, never serious.

Her cheeks were pink, a slight sunburn marring her tender skin. He wished she would tell him how happy she was he came to help her work. "You forgot your sunscreen again." Someone needed to take care of her. He meant to apply for that job. "Your cheeks are burned."

When she replied she sounded in a huff. Dallas never liked it when he took it on himself to lecture her. She was always forgetting necessities as she was too caught up in her photography. "No, didn't forget anything. I applied it this morning. Been out all day. The stuff wears off. Got enough to carry without adding sunscreen to the mix." Her back straight she walked ahead of him.

He loved to watch her hips sway. She was dressed in walking shorts not her usual short, shorts that showed off her long legs to perfection. If she wore the smaller variety, he'd find himself treated to a glimpse of her fanny. Before she picked up her pace to walk in front of him, he was able to revel in the thrust of her breasts. They were large. Would fill his hands if he ever got another chance to hold them, test their weight. He shuddered recalling the last time he touched one breast. The lightning that leapt between them. His memory had him hard beneath his jeans, throbbing with need for this delightful woman who was his mate.

This meeting wasn't getting off to a great start. Not the one he imagined as well as hoped for. Backpedaling would be a good idea. He put his foot in his mouth twice now. Doing so a third time was unacceptable to the path he embarked upon. He caught up to her. They walked side by side for a few seconds. He debated how to begin the next exchange without damning himself to her scorn. "I came because I was worried about you. That's one reason why I followed you here. Your friends Gordon and Scratch were asking about you at the magazine. Wanted to know where you were. Would you have cared if they turned up here to disrupt your assignment?"

"So, you thought you would lead them to me? Those two are the last two men I want to see. They make me shudder. There is something evil about those two. Can't quite put my finger on why they give me those feelings. Though they are real."

They reached her door. He opened it for her waiting for her to pass through. Catching the scent of lilies in the air as she entered, he was reminded of other times. As long as they were getting off on the wrong feet, he might as well add another damper to the evening. Dallas might not be too pleased at the romantic setting. She gasped when she saw the table.

The wine.

Candles.

The flowers.

Smelled the roast chicken.

"You cooked?" She reached up to brush a tender kiss across his lips. "Thank you, and you brought wine." Dallas walked to the table, her hands beneath her chin. After she looked at him, "The flowers are a nice touch too. Romantic. Didn't know you could be amorous."

Decided not to mention the unlocked door. That would have been the third *faux pas* of the day. Too many times to count, they argued about securing her apartment. She grabbed her equipment from him. Stowed the things away.

"I like to cook. You know that. Are you hungry? Not as creative as you." After splashing some into a glass he pulled from the cupboard, he handed her a glass of wine. Stepping back to observe, he waited.

"Hmm… didn't expect to be treated as if I'm royalty tonight. Was going to have a peanut butter sandwich and a cup of tea. Look at my photos then go to bed. Thank you. To answer your question, I'd like to take a shower first. Feel dusty as well as sweaty. I am hungry. Forgot to bring something with me for lunch. Do you mind waiting until I get a hot water treatment?"

"Take your time. Brought my computer. Do you care if I take a look at some of your pictures? We can start going through them tonight for your exhibition." Rafe found he was eager to see what she captured on film. Was eager to sit close to her while they combed through the pictures, debated which ones to use.

"You'd do that?" Her eyes brightened. Her hands were behind her back, unfastening her bra. From prior experience he understood she'd be eager to shed the garment. Didn't appreciate the underwire digging into her skin or the confinement. "Yes, please… Seems as if it has been so long since…" Dallas turned away as if she hid from him. Her shirt along with her bra slid from her. He saw the length of her back. Imagined the rest of her naked. Around him, she was always at ease with her nudity. They were like brother and sister. No longer. Soon they would be lovers then husband and wife.

He huffed in a breath of air, stalling himself from action. The long line of her back beckoned to him. Damn, but he wanted to touch, follow the line of her spine with his lips. "What's wrong?" He knew there had to be some reason for her to run off without an explanation. This was the second time he felt her abandonment, soul deep, unexpected. Now that he understood her position in his life, fleeing him was worse. "You are…different. Tell me what happened those last months. Maybe I can help."

She turned. For several beats of his heart, he saw her breasts, the beautiful pink tips. He sipped air.

"Rafe…please…not now." Her t-shirt held against her chest, she backed away from him. After she grabbed her glass from the table then drank, she fled to the bathroom. Left him staring at the empty space she'd occupied but a second before.

"Not now…" Rafe murmured, sifting air through his teeth. What did he do wrong this time? "Now, now!" His fist tightened. He needed patience. Told himself that time and again. It was just so bloody hard to watch her struggle with her emotions. To understand part of the conflict along with the turmoil she fought. In the past, Dallas would have confided in him.

When? When will she talk?

Over the last few months, they'd both been through more than any couple should be put through. Now she didn't want to tell him anything. Wouldn't speak of the months they'd been separated. He needed to understand what happened to her. Where she disappeared. Felt as if he stumbled around in a fog.

Fuck…he found her car at the waterfall. He didn't see her again for over a month. After he saw her on the street, she vanished again.

Unexpected, she showed up at his door one night. When he kissed her that evening, held her in his arms, he felt the spark he'd been looking for all the years he'd known her. While she was gone from his life, she changed. Dallas told him she felt the same electricity between them. The leap of energy. Not more than a few minutes later, she told him she was living with some man. All she was doing in Carnoch was picking up her car. She fled as if she was afraid of him. How the bloody hell could this woman be afraid of him? He'd taken her to the doctor when she couldn't ask anyone else. Held her hand when she was in pain. She meant the world to him.

Patience.

More tolerance than should ever be necessary is what is needed now. If I want her, I must give her time to adjust to this new revelation. Give her time to come to me the way I want. The two of us have always been friends…never lovers. Now I want something different from her. She might be afraid. Dallas is my mate. Soon my wife. My life.

You can't expect anything from her on the spur of the moment. With no warning, you showed up at her front door. Surprised her. Cooked her dinner. Had romance in mind. She needs time to process this unexpected visit. You aren't her boyfriend. Never have been. What do you expect?

He sat down with his glass of wine. Nursed the drink. After his emotions slowed to small vibrations, he pulled out her camera then took out the card. Put the card into his computer to download the first images.

The tourist guide was right. This was a beautiful spot, magical. Her images captivated. Held him enthralled. He pulled a few aside for Dallas to look at after dinner. She had enough for the magazine article as well as her exhibit. He would help her choose those to frame.

She was out of the shower. He heard her soft singing. She always sang in the shower when she was at his home. For a lifetime then beyond, he could listen to her voice. Dallas walked from the bathroom in shorts, very short shorts, and a t-shirt. The kind he liked to see her wear. Hell, he painted her while she wore nothing. Now, she didn't wear a bra. Beneath the pink cotton T, he saw the outline of her breasts, the rose-colored nipples pressed against the fabric. Watched them sway as she walked. Around him, she still seemed comfortable with her almost nudity. Well, he wasn't as comfortable as he used to be. His penis jumped against his jeans. Being around her was taking on a new angle, a hard edge he had to find a way to hide.

That was the nice thing about their relationship. They were at ease with each other in every way. Dallas posed in the buff for him. He did have a buyer for the last painting. The profit would have paid his mortgage for five years. He didn't sell. Couldn't part with the oil. The offer came to him while she was gone from his life. While he didn't know where she was, he couldn't bear to have the painting out of his hands. He hung it in the attic where she posed, where he painted. At night he would walk the steps to the room. Gaze at Dallas. Wish.

After she posed for him then dressed, she never wore panties. She would always stuff them in the big bag she carried with her. He wondered now if she wore anything beneath the shorts. If he guessed, he would guess she wore nothing. The image sent more lightning ripping straight to his groin. He found he was damn uncomfortable. Needed an adjustment to his pants. Nice that she was at ease. The night was going to be a long one. What he hoped for on the long drive, wasn't going to unfold. There would be no lovemaking tonight.

Clearing his throat, he stood, "Ready to eat? I'll dish up. Give you a bit of everything." Rafe pulled out a seat for her then topped off her wine. "You've amazing pictures in the first batch. How many are you obligated to give the magazine? Do you have a choice?"

"Fifty. They have first pick of the photos. I've got so many it won't be hard to find ten or so for the gallery. More to wrap in plastic and mount on cardboard for possible sales. The wine is good."

They ate in silence. Rafe didn't know how to talk about the past months. How to broach the subject that seemed to send her off in a rush in the opposite direction from him. He supposed she needed to feel relaxed in his company again. As it appeared now, she was stiff, restrained.

She pushed the remnants of her food around on her plate. He gave her more than she would eat. Tried to convince her he loved all her curves. Wouldn't mind if there were more. Dallas was always careful about how much as well as what she ate. Made certain to exercise. Complained about the cellulite on her legs. When he got the chance, he would taste each tiny dimple.

With a long-drawn-out breath of air, she set down her fork then picked up the wine glass. "Look, I understand we've talk that needs talking about. I ghosted you. You should hate me. Want you to understand the ghosting wasn't intentional. I had no say whatsoever in what happened to me. Never meant to leave without telling you wear it was I was going. In a blink, I was in another world sitting on my butt looking at a man I'd never met before."

That was a start. Maybe she needed to tell him where she was as much as he needed to learn the truth. "Where did you go?" His curiosity spun out of control. So far, she told him nothing about those months when he couldn't find her. This was the first hint of communication. "You could have picked up your cell. Called." He braced himself with his forearms on the table. "I was worried. Terrified something horrible happened to you. Helpless. A man doesn't much appreciate that vulnerable feeling."

She lifted her shoulders in a tiny shrug as if there was nothing she could do. The movement sent other parts of her in a visual dance treating his eyes along with his senses to a titillating display of female curves. "No cell tower where I was. Nothing. No electricity. Nothing. No cars. Only horses." Dallas shuddered. "I dislike riding horses. Found myself perched on one…a horse. The ground flew by. I held tight."

"That's all possible. Were you on some kind of assignment you never mentioned to me. I know there is no service here which is why I couldn't call you. Why I didn't give you a heads-up that I would arrive this afternoon. Didn't mean to catch you unaware. You expected to be alone. I intruded. Do you want me to leave?"

She set the glass on the table a strange look in her eyes. "How did you find me?" She topped off her wine. "Need something more to bolster me up. Somehow, I understand what you're going to tell me, I won't like. So, let's get this over with."

"Lied to your boss." He didn't intend to make any apologies. Would do it again in a heartbeat. "Told the man you are my wife."

She hissed air in through her teeth. "He believed you?"

~ * ~

The bastard! At least her boss didn't believe Mathew. Even so, she was surprised to discover her boss told Rafe her exact location. Mathew was a sneak. Oily. Hateful. Not very much time passed before she understood her mistake with the man. On first meeting him, she trusted him to do what he said, helped her out of a tough situation. While he was a cad taking advantage of her weakness. He tried to coerce her into his bed. Only one kiss convinced her his bed was the last place she wished to be. The kiss disgusted. Left her to shudder with displeasure.

When he found her hitchhiking, she was so disoriented she didn't know if she was coming or going. She was confused. The world seemed to spin in too many different directions. After she hopped into his car, Tinley moved to the back seat. During the ride into the city, she had this uncanny notion she knew these two. The men were less than stellar. It was here, at the Fairy Pools, that she realized where she first saw the men.

At first, she was so muddled in her mind that Mathew was able to sweettalk her into staying with him at his apartment. Within a span of a day and a half, she moved out. She could do so only because her boss at the magazine gave her an advance to meet her needs until she left for the photo shoot.

For days after she settled into the cabin, all she could do was walk the trail to the pools. She would sit for hours staring at the rippling, sun dappled water as the cold liquid spilled over the rocks. Tried to remember all that happened to her. Felt the breeze blowing off the craigs change as if something supernatural touched her. The sunlight dimmed. All around her the scene seemed surreal. Little things came to mind. A touch. A caress. The man who set her upon his horse was real, flesh and blood man. The first few days she believed this was the remnants of a dream. The dream wasn't a dream at all. What she experienced was real. When she closed her eyes, even when she didn't, she saw his features.

The man in the mist rainbow behind the falls…his face was still etched into her memory. Why not? He could be a brother to Rafe. Tall handsome as sin, the man captured her attention the moment she saw him, feet braced apart. His hands placed square on his hips. He came to rescue her from Scratch and Gordy. Gave commands. Laughed when she acted as if she wouldn't obey. Asked her if she would rather be with the two men. Until she started to retain her memory, she never made the connection between the two who accosted her in the glen and the two who picked her up on the side of the road. A cloud covered the sun. Shadows deepened. Tourists came and went. Laughed. Chatted. Spoke of the beauty. The enchantment of this mystical setting helped her remember some of her past. There were moments when she felt certain fairies fluttered around the pools. They would slip their toes in the water. Splashed each other. When she tested the water, it was like ice to her fingers. Still, a few of the tourists braved the icy cold to swim.

Scratch and Gordy.

Tinley Scratch and Mathew Gordan.

Good God, she peppered sprayed one of them. Couldn't remember which man was the recipient.

Sunshine broke from the clouds. Chased away the shadows. Even so, given the eerie feelings surrounding her, she could not rid herself of the darkness in her heart that seemed to also possess her soul. The man who rescued her from those two, tossed her on top of his horse as if she weighed nothing. Nothing! A woman of her size? The ride through the forest trails terrified her. As she clung to his massive forearms, he whispered to her that he would keep her safe. Told her to relax when doing so was impossible. She recalled the cave where he took her. Where they spent the night and one or two after that. The exact time was hazy in her mind. Parts of those months she remembered. Some parts she did not.

She sat on a nettle. The man, Roc was his name, Roc Frasier. He rubbed cortisone cream on her butt. He touched her in ways no man ever touched her before. Mentally as well as physically, she felt the spark she and Rafe lacked. Reveled in feelings that were new to her. Found if he wished or asked, she would have let him take her virginity. In her large bag she had all she needed to protect herself from disease as well as pregnancy.

While she showed as well as explained these things to Roc, she had the sudden feeling he was angry. Why would he be furious with a woman who wished to protect herself? That was something she didn't understand. He didn't like the birth control pills or the condoms. He was familiar with condoms.

Never would understand his position on the birth control. Rafe wasn't like that. Understood the necessity for both.

It rained the next day forcing them to remain in the cave. While she wanted him to take her to Inverness, Roc refused. Told her in time he would take her to the city. She didn't remember how many days it rained. How many days they stayed in the cave and talked. When the weather cleared, she sat in front of him on his huge horse. They traveled to Carnoch. Discovered he lived in the same home as Rafe. By that time, it became apparent to her that Roc and Rafe were in some way related.

The Fairy Pool was silent. There were no tourists for the moment. The day was passing. The sky would grow dark soon. She needed to return to her cabin. With her bare foot, she kicked the water sending sprays of glistening drops into the surrounding air. Watched as the tiny droplets fell back to the pond sending ripples across the surface.

It was in those first few days she began to forget things she should know. There would be lapses in her memory. She would begin to say something then stop, forgetting what she meant to say. It was during those first days that Roc swept her off her feet, literally as well as figuratively.

All these remembrances were things she should tell Rafe. He should understand why she never contacted him. She didn't know if he would believe her when she told him she traveled back in time to the year seventeen-fifty-six. There were days that she didn't believe the reality herself. Now, everything blurred together, the past along with the present. She felt as if she was evolving into a different person. The time in the past century transformed her personality.

He was right when he told her she changed. How could a person travel through time without becoming someone else? Sometimes she pinched herself in order to be positive she wasn't dreaming. Rafe couldn't understand. If she told him what happened to her, he would believe she was daft. She wasn't. What she went through wasn't a bad dream she would wake up from.

Rafe was here…in Carbost. He came to talk about their different relationship now that she returned from her adventure. Her adventure…one she fell into. Slid down a hill to land at the feet of a handsome Scotsman…a Frasier. She wasn't ready to talk. Didn't know if she ever would be prepared to spill her story. Didn't know if anything she told him would be true. All she seemed to have at her disposal were guesses. Her mind tripped from one image to another one.

After her shower when she waltzed into the living room as if everything was the same as it used to be, she realized her mistake. Rafe's eyes seemed to glaze over while he stared at the outline of her breasts. He never before looked at her as if he wanted to devour her. She was reminded of the jump of adrenalin between them when they touched. The electricity that skidded from their fingertips. She even felt that spark when he touched her to take her camera equipment.

In their life before, he never paid much attention to her body parts. Never stared at her breasts. When she dressed this way in front of Rafe, she didn't think. All she wished for after a long day of walking and shooting pictures was to relax, to be comfortable. With bra along with panties beneath her clothing she would be anything but at ease. She opted for comfort. He was still staring. His gaze traveled along the length of her. Good God, before she went to take her shower, she stripped off her bra along with her t-shirt right in front of him. Her breath caught at the realization she all but invited him to touch.

Now, with Rafe, this was all new to her. Never before had he been interested in her as a girlfriend, as a lover. Rafe never consumed her with his eyes. He was eating her up. Now his eyes kept focusing on her breasts. Her nipples hardened beneath his passionate examination. Through the thin fabric of her t-shirt he would see her response. She felt as if she should cover herself. Instead, she tilted her chin up and decided that she would ignore the potent stare that flashed her way. Dallas intended to brazen this out. She understood what he wanted. She wanted the same. Terrified didn't do justice to what she felt having never been with a man in that way.

Earlier today when she saw him striding toward her, she felt as if a gigantic weight had been lifted from her shoulders. Pleased to see him didn't do justice to how she felt. She understood Rafe would listen to her. Listen to whatever she could tell him. Would never judge even though he might be a bit skeptical of what she was going to recount.

After she saw the candles, the wine, the vase of flowers... The romantic setting he created for their pleasure. Her heart filled with love. She understood they had some things to consider...to hash over before they could become lovers. Comprehended he would not believe she traveled through time... Assumed he would not believe Gordan and Scratch... He would imagine they meant her harm. That much they would be able to come to terms with. They would agree. Gordan along with Scratch were trouble for her. What Rafe wouldn't understand was why.

Her short time in the shower allowed her to regain a dash of composure. Hot water soothed her knotted nerves along with muscles that had been tense for months. She kept telling herself he would never commit her to some asylum for the insane after she apprised him of some mind jarring revelations. After all, he lived in the highlands his entire life. He would just have to understand her truths. Something unexplainable happened to her. She survived. Scotsmen were a superstitious lot. Maybe that rumor was just that gossip. Rafe wasn't superstitious. So much for that thought.

"You've not said anything in the last twenty minutes." His voice came from out of nowhere, a soft melodic purr. "Where have you been? Your eyes have this glazed over look. You've been deep in your head. Can I help?"

Startled by his sudden intrusion to her musings, she jumped. "Oh! Oh, my...suppose I was caught up in my thoughts." They were looking through her photos. "I...my mind was on something else." She smiled at him hoping to ease the moment into something more doable.

Rafe sat back, his hands behind his head, a half-smile quirking his lips. Lips she now thought about kissing as well as how they'd taste. "Care to share? Were you thinking about me...us?"

He was giving her the opportunity she needed to divulge her thoughts, memories, the time that changed her. She looked down, hiding her eyes from him. "No...don't wish to tell you what's in my head right now. I..." She ran her tongue across dry lips. Drank long and deep of her glass of wine hoping the liquid would ease her parched throat. Nothing seemed to help.

Dallas wasn't surprised to hear him curse beneath his breath. He sat up straight. She'd heard all his words before.

"If you don't want to talk maybe you can explain these…" Rafe pulled up a page of photos. Pictures of Roc. "Who is this man to you?" his tone harsh, his words filled with anger. "Who the hell is he?" For some reason his anger didn't reach soul deep. She was glad of that.

My savior.

Unable to stop herself, she groaned. In the cave she shot photo after photo of Roc. She wanted to have pictures to remember him by. Thought that with the exception of Rafe, he was the most handsome man she'd ever seen.

"That's not fair of you. I… It's not right that you question me about this man. He has nothing to do with me." Dallas couldn't tell him she fell in love with Roc Frasier. Now, she didn't recall enough about him to understand how that happened. If her feelings weren't deceiving her again, she was in love with Rafe Frasier. They looked so much alike. Acted very different. They were both demanding. There were more similarities.

"Not fair!" he shouted before quieting his voice. "Not fair… You take over one hundred photos of this man. Who is he!" Rafe moved away from the computer screen so she could see better. Pointed. "Who is this man? I deserve an answer."

"Someone…someone I met." She drank more wine. Let the liquid slide down her throat. Wished the alcohol would soothe her nerves. "A man who is dear to me. A man who is in my past. I will never see him again except through these pictures. You've no business going through those photos. No business questioning me." She felt a sudden rise of moisture to her eyes. Pushed the sensation away.

Rafe placed her hands in his, his eyes focused on hers. His lips were pressed into a grim line. "Do you not recall giving me permission to take a look at the pictures on this card?" He set his finger on the card. "Rest assured, I would never go into your photo pool without authorization." He rubbed the backs of her hands with his thumb.

She felt the shimmer of heat glide across her skin. Knew the sensation as something new between the two of them. Lightning jumped across their fingers. Dallas tugged. Needed distance to think. For a few more beats of her slamming heart, he held her hands. With another curse, he let her go.

"Who is he? I would have you tell me," he demanded again. This time his words held no venom. He sounded resigned to the fact she took so many photographs because she needed to remember. "He looks a lot like me."

She doused her lungs with oxygen. Held the air inside until her lungs burned. Thought she couldn't hold it any longer. This…she supposed…was the time to begin the tale of her journey. "You will think I'm crazy. Everyone will believe I've lost my sanity. Suppose as my best friend you deserve to learn about it first. I'm not certain I believe all that I'm going to say to you."

"Who is this man who is plastered on this camera card? This man who you seem to be thinking about while we are working?" he asked again. Appeared he didn't intend to give up on that single question.

"His name is…was…" That was a great start. You could have said is… He was staring at her as if he was still furious about the photos.

"Is or was?" Rafe picked up on her misstatement which wasn't a misstatement at all. "Is he living?"

"Was. His name was Cameron Petroc Frasier. I called him Roc. He called me Lainie. The man rescued me from Gordy and Scratch at the falls when I was lost. Had nowhere to go." The walls in the cabin spun. Darkness closed in on her. She closed her eyes for seconds inhaling deep breaths of air while she counted.

"Did you sleep with him?" his question sounded possessive of her, condemning.

A slap in the face could never have been so hurtful. Yet… did she sleep with him? She'd wanted to be in his arms, in his bed. There were several times he held her through the night because she was terrified as well as lonely. Understood she wasn't in her century. Didn't believe she would ever be able to return to a century she understood.

"How dare you?" She found a serenity in her answer she didn't expect. "What I did with Roc…"

Rafe held up his hands as if he knew he transgressed. Shook his head as if to give emphasis to his mistake. "Is none of my business. I understand.

We've always been straightforward with each other. Imagine I trespassed into territory where I don't belong." He wrapped his fingers around the stem of his glass. "I'm sorry…" He drank.

The look in his eyes told her he didn't mean his words. The man wanted to know if she was intimate with the man. Not that she could remember. The long sigh she let out reflected her distress. She would tell him what she could. "Yes, I slept with Roc but not how you're thinking. At least I don't recall intimacy. I was terrified when I realized I'd… Never mind. Let's just say we never had sex that I can recall. That was the gist of your question. My mind was fuzzy after the first few days in Carnoch."

Dallas might have laughed at the look on his face if she wasn't so distressed from the question. If Roc had agreed, she would have gladly given him her innocence. She wanted him from the first sight of him. *Coup de foudre*…love at first sight. He reminded her so much of Rafe. Rafe who could never love her. Even though there was no spark, she would have given Rafe whatever he asked for.

When she caught sight of Rafe this afternoon, she felt that same sudden onslaught of lust. The feeling wasn't love. She already loved Rafe. Couldn't feel more for him than she already did. What she wished for was so much more. Love coupled with lust.

Lust.

Raw hunger for this man she'd known for most of her life was a new feeling. Desire. The need to be seduced by him. A real kiss from Rafe would never be refused.

"That you can recall?" The pause between sentences was significant. "I suppose that will have to do for now. I'm going to find a way to understand what is happening. It would help if you would speak to me."

He would know the truth if or when they had sex. It could be tonight. There was only one bed in the cabin. The couch would never be comfortable for either, less for Rafe since he was taller. Dallas wasn't at all positive she wanted to share a bed with him. Her newfound feelings for him were just that…too new.

With a thready breath of air puffing from her, she felt resigned. "You've got the gist of it. Why don't you tell me what you've been doing all this time?" She was prepared to be out of the line of fire for a few minutes. This interrogation wasn't to her liking since everything she recalled or didn't was a muddled mess.

His broad shoulders lifted upward. "The same as always. My life didn't change when you left except that I didn't have my friend to talk to. You are listed as a missing person. Suppose we should tell the authorities you've been found."

"That's been done. After I moved into my apartment, an officer came to interview me. Couldn't tell him much. I was here then I wasn't. Somehow, I returned but couldn't recall how." She found her hands were shaking. She didn't understand the emotions eating her up. "He...the officer blamed me for deceiving the good people of Scotland. He was going to charge me with..." She waved her hands in the air. "With lying. Deceiving the public. Using officers for my gain when someone else might have needed one."

"That day you disappeared, I expected a phone call from you when you reached Inverness. It never came."

"No cell towers..." she reminded him.

"You were going to have dinner at that restaurant you liked..." He stood. Began to pace the room. Rafe reminded her of a cat on the prowl.

"I slid down the hill behind the waterfall," Dallas blurted out wishing she dared tell him more of her memories. "I didn't deceive anyone. Didn't hurt anyone or lie... Never lied to you. When all this happened, we were like brother and sister. Nothing more. Nothing less." Moisture threatened to fall for a second time. Her throat felt clogged. She headed for the door. Escape seemed preferable to answering questions. Distance from this was something she needed. She raced from the room tears spilling from her eyes. Behind her she heard Rafe's muffled curse.

Outside she didn't know where she was going. She headed down the trail before deciding that wasn't a good idea. She didn't want to encounter people. Had to get away. Needed distance to think. He confused her. One moment she thought she understood what was happening. The next she didn't know.

The night sky was darker than she expected. Stars twinkled high in sky, shining, brilliant. A planet sat on the horizon. The moon gave meager light to the path. Oh, dear, she wasn't dressed to be running around where people could see her. She didn't care. She did though. Escape was what she needed. The night was too dark to see much of anything. She stumbled.

Caught herself. Wiped moisture from her face.

Dallas heard his steps behind her. She stopped knowing she would never outrun him. He would follow. Understood he was there to protect her from herself as well as the Gordy and Scratches of this world. Why didn't she have the courage to tell him all he wanted to learn. Rafe wouldn't care if what she told him was crazy. He was a patient man. He loved her as a brother loves a sister. While he might think she was a *wee* bit touched in the head, he would humor her.

After she stopped, he rested his hand on her shoulder. Squeezed as if to reassure. The touch was gentle. He stood behind her. She felt the warmth from him. Felt secure, safe. She recalled feeling much the same way with Roc. The two men, of two different centuries, were so similar. "Come, Dallas, we should get back to the cabin. The breeze is cool. You don't want to take a chill." He nodded up the trail. Two men were walking toward them talking seeming oblivious to them. "Don't think you would like just anyone to see you wearing these clothes."

She sniffed. Brushed more tears off her cheeks with the backs of her hands. He was right about that little bit of reality. He turned her. His finger beneath her chin, lifted. Brushed a gentle kiss across her lips. She warmed. Heated. Desire for this man she'd known most of her life flared. Was disappointed when he drew back. She wanted more of a kiss. To her a million lifetimes passed by them. Now her life pivoted back to normal.

"I want you. Don't ever doubt that, Dallas. Not tonight, not until we understand what happened to you. Since your disappearance, things have changed between the two of us. You asked what I did while you were away. I'll tell you. We'll have more wine. Some of the desert I brought. Instead of questions to you, I'll field questions from you. Would you like that? I will answer all the questions you put in front of me."

He turned her so her breasts pushed against his chest. His hands circled her butt. The men walked by. Nodded. Said good evening with smiles on their lips. The two gentlemen were gone. They were alone. His arm around her, Rafe walked her back to the cabin.

Once inside the warm interior, Rafe sat down with her. Needing his heat along with the comfort he offered, she snuggled into him, her head on his chest. Took consolation from the steady beat of his heart. The pulses of their hearts seemed to blend together. Almost as if they beat as one. She set her hand on his chest. He covered her fingers with his. With him she felt complete. Damn the questions. She didn't want to think.

"I hoped you would tell me more of your life over the last few months. Can tell now that you're too distraught to talk first. I've the distinct feeling you no longer trust me with your secrets. That hurts. I will begin by telling you all of what I know. Some of what I guess. With Cole McKenna's help, we pieced together what we believe happened to you. A hypothesis of sorts. I needed a few answers."

"You did? You went to Cole? I do trust you. It's just that I'm afraid. As you said things have changed. Afraid of what we might feel for each other. Uncertain too." She pushed away from him, looking into the silver blue of his eyes. "What…what happened to me? I remember some of that time. Understand a few facts that I wish I didn't." She almost sputtered that she traveled back to another century. Almost told him she fell in love with another man. If she said those words that would hurt him too. Prudence helped her hold her tongue. The last thing she wanted in the world was to upset this man who'd given her so much.

"This could be a very long story. You understand until you returned there were no sparks between us. We both felt as if there should be. To both our dismay, there wasn't anything. We loved each other. Even though you were willing to gamble on a marriage, I wasn't. For us, I understood, there was too much at stake. Things have changed. Those sparks I searched for are between us now. Not just sparks but flames, an inferno."

"Yes. Now I feel warmed through to the marrow of my bones when you hold me. Heat flares. That small kiss ignited every part of me. I don't fathom the changes. None of this makes sense. If you can help me figure this all out, I would be grateful."

"Me too. I'll try to put some of this into its proper place. At the keep, there are portraits of all the McKennas, the Stewarts as well as the Frasiers. They line the stairway. The couples…let's just say there are some resemblances throughout the centuries."

"I've never been there. Is there some significance…in the portraits." She tilted her head while thinking. "Was I there? It seems that I…no…" If she heard the wobble in her voice, it was certain that Rafe did too. "I just don't remember details. I see flashes of things then what I thought I saw or felt is gone. I don't believe I'm supposed to recall anything. There is something strange, eerie. Maybe supernatural at work. It's almost as if I was turning into a different person." Just like that. She snapped her fingers. "I'm me! I want to stay me…" she murmured.

Smiling down at her, he shook his head. "Nothing of what I intend to tell you will make a difference to us now. What I'm going to say to you is that your picture wasn't on the stairway when I visited the keep. I know for a fact that in this lifetime, you have not been to the McKenna keep. Believe you were there…"

"I…this lifetime…?" Perhaps Rafe understood more than she gave him credit for understanding. "Did he guess she traveled through time…twice?"

"Yes, when I was looking for you, I visited Cole. He showed me a portrait of Cameron 'Roc' Frasier painted with his wife Lainie. Elaine is your middle name. Is it not? Did you tell me he called you Lainie?"

"Yes, yes, he did. When I told him my name, he picked up on my middle name. Said that was what he intended to call me. Told me I didn't look like a Dallas. Whatever that is supposed to mean. So…?" With a start Dallas realized she was eager for Rafe to talk to her. The pressure to let out all her emotions vanished.

"Lainie resembled you so much so you could have been sisters or pass for twins. Roc looked a lot like me. What do you think? Do I look like that man on your camera card?" he persisted in this. Maybe he knew more than he let on. "I should not have grown so angry. Suppose I was jealous."

"What I remember of those days it's true. The two of you are much the same. What does that have anything to do with except coincidence?" She remembered a story Roc told her when she mentioned she would return to this time. "Roc told me…he said…no… it's too unbelievable. I didn't agree with what he said. I was determined that he take me back to the glen where he first found me. I needed to find a way home. He didn't want that. Didn't wish for me to go home. Even then he spoke of marriage." She gasped realizing what she told him. Rafe had this way of drawing her out.

With his fingers supporting her chin, he lifted. Smiled with his eyes. "What don't you believe?" His eyes focused on hers. He appeared so sincere. "You wished to find a way to get home? Roc was against doing so? Because he loved you. Sensed something else."

"You won't think I've gone insane?" This tale was so preposterous.

Roc showed her his cat. Did he? Was that a dream? He prowled around the bedroom just as Rafe prowled in his human form around this room a few minutes ago. In his cat form, Roc teased her. Could Rafe change into a cat? Could anyone change shape? Was this all a product of her vivid imagination?

"I saw him naked." She thought her eyes would cross with the blurted revelation. She'd never seen Rafe naked. Never slept in a bed with him even just to be held. Until these last few minutes, never wanted to see him wearing nothing. Now she imagined how he would appear in the buff.

"Some of your memory returns?" Rafe chuckled as he bent to kiss her again. The brush of their mouths was soft, sweet. "I believe I'm still jealous. Jealous of a dead man. That seems at odds with logic."

"How do you know that he's passed?" More questions. Her breaths turned ragged. The walls once again began to spin.

"I'm going to start with the beginning of this story. You've heard of the Clan Chaton?" he stroked her back. Touched one vertebra at a time as his finger traveled up then down the length of her spine.

Dallas began to melt at his touch. Was this how a man seduced? "Gossip…tales told to frighten children. Yes, I've heard of the clan of the cats. What does that have to do with anything? Superstition is all it is. Rumors passed down over generations." Dallas wished he'd get to the point. Bits and pieces of thoughts flashed through her head. Nothing she saw in her mind made sense.

"They, shifters, mate for life then into eternity. It's always that way. If something happens, future generations will not know their mates. Will never connect or feel the…spark," his voice was so serious. He held her hands, rubbed the back of her wrists as if to soothe.

Curiosity soared through her. *Never feel the spark?* "Shifters don't exist," she insisted. "How can a person change from a human into a sleek black panther?" She felt as if grasping at straws would be easier. A niggling thought in the back of her mind began to take root. Again, flashes of remembrances warred with the present. Fought reality or dreams, she couldn't be certain.

"Or a tiger? There are other cats that change from human then back." His voice continued in a modulated rhythm. Continued to sooth, reassured even while she questioned. She closed her eyes for a few seconds more than a blink.

"I'm listening. It's obvious by the look on your face you're serious. Go on." If Rafe believed, she would have to find some way to also give credit to his facts.

Rafe ran his hand along the back of his neck. Heaved in a large breath of air. For the first time since she saw him again, he seemed nervous. She sat next to him. He no longer held her. The crease of his brows told her he was worried. His lips pulled into a thin line told her the same.

"We think…Cole and I believe that something happened to Lainie Shaw back in the seventeen hundreds. She was Cameron's mate." Rafe cleared his throat before continuing the story. "Shifters mate for life then on into eternity. Believe I just said that. If something happens and the male doesn't claim the female in his lifetime, they will no longer…"

"No longer what?" She thought he might be teasing her. "Rafe, no longer what!" She cried out again as he seemed to be hesitating. This was something she needed to know.

"The shifter will no longer be able to claim the female. They will continue living during other times, but they will never mate. They will continue to search for the one woman who is supposed to be theirs, never finding her. Maybe as in our case, finding but not realizing the truth."

She waved her hand in the air. Stared at him for a few seconds her insides fluttering. "That's utter nonsense." Again, that feeling of his truth assailed her. She'd heard those same words somewhere before.

Imagination or reality?

"You fell through that time portal for a reason. Slid down the hill to land at Roc Frasier's feet. You had to bring Lainie Shaw home to Roc Frasier. Otherwise, Roc would never find his mate nor would all the next generations. I'm part of that generation as are you."

"No…"

"You are my mate."

~ * ~

On the stairway of the McKenna keep, Cole McKenna stood in front of the portrait of Lainie and Roc Frasier. Together, they seemed to smile down upon him. The two found happiness because fate stepped into their lives. Their story had been told through the generations of the clan. The tale was one of loss then discovery. Bitter despair then happiness. Roc worried over ever finding his soul mate just as Rafe did now. Dallas Elaine Shaw stumbled from another time to help bring Lainie and Roc together. The how didn't matter. The why was obvious.

Cole marveled at how fate stepped in to help the struggling couples. By now, Rafe would be learning about Dallas' adventure. Cole wondered what part of it she could recall. Bits and pieces…bits and pieces that would forever leave Dallas wondering about the past. He hoped the couple would find happiness. Now that Roc and Lainie came together, there was little doubt in his mind that in time, Rafe would marry Dallas, claim her so future generations would also find happiness.

A wedding soon in the keep would be wonderful. It had been a few years since a celebration such as this one had taken place. His sister had been the last recipient of a clan marriage celebration. While his mother berated him to look harder for his mate, he waited with patience. Cole knew she would come to him in time. Indeed, he knew who she was. Too young at the moment for him to marry or claim as his in the way of the clan. He needed to remain patient while he waited for her to grow up. In the past he would not have needed to wait.

Striding down the stairs, he decided to take a look at the woman who would one day say vows with him. Who he would claim in the master chamber of his tower room. In the present, she was a little hellion turned seventeen almost a year ago. At eighteen, he could claim her as if…he would try to wait at least another year. Patience was never his strong suit.

As if she owned the place, she ran wild through the keep. Acted with a free spirit. On more than one occasion she'd been called a hellion. He did enjoy watching her. When she was younger, she would stick her tongue out at him when he reprimanded her for her unruly behavior before dancing away. Once when she managed to upset a cart of apples and the owner slid on them, he threatened to take her over his knee to give her a child's punishment for her reckless gallop through the village. She laughed at his threat then dashed off in another direction. He could have caught her. Chose to watch her escape. Didn't wish to give her the wrong impression. Despite his threat he could never lay a hand on her.

The girl was a flirt. Understood her female power over the males of her age. Knew how to lower her lashes as well as toss her hair over her shoulder. Coiled the young lads with care as well as wanton abandon around her little finger. Phoebe knew she was beautiful. She was used to getting her way in all she did. He needed to guard her well. When they wed, he needed to know that he was the only man who tasted those sweet charms she flaunted. Her father was careless with her. Seemed he didn't know how to handle the wild child that she was. With a delicate touch, is what he had in mind. If she continued to test her wiles on all the young men of the village, he would need to revise his commitment to wait for her to mature. If she did show signs of maturity within the year, he would begin a tender seduction. Hell, he didn't know if he could wait another year. Eighteen was old enough.

Her golden hair she tied into a ponytail that hung down to the middle of her back. When the strands were not tied back, the silken waves tumbled around her shoulders all the way to her delectable, curvaceous rear. She wore shorts that showed off her sassy butt. Showed too much of her was his opinion. He held no sway over how she chose to cover her body. Even though he wished she would wear more, he would never dictate.

Her breasts were small beneath the tight-fitting top she donned this morning. Today, she went braless. The tight buds pushing on the fabric seemed to beg for attention. Her legs long and well-shaped appeared to go on forever. He needed to talk to her father about moving her into the keep. Into the castle would be better. There were unused rooms in the north tower. The two could live there in comfort. Would live beneath his observations. He would have a bit more control over her activities. If he mentioned the connection to his mother, she would take Phoebe under her wing. Guide her. Teach her what her father could not.

As to date, she'd not directed any of her burgeoning charms his way. Had not flirted with him as she did the young lads. She would think of him as an old man. He was ages away from being considered decrepit. The thought gave him cause to smile. He meant to teach Phoebe that he was hers. From time to time, he would remind her he was the head of the clan McKenna. He wasn't certain what she knew about the Clan Chaton. Rumors still abounded. Most of the time, the clan hushed those rumors. Phoebe, he knew, was no shifter.

Phoebe's back was to him. Animated, she spoke to the school

teacher's son. He was a nice lad. Calm. Mature for his lack of age. Would never do for this woman who lived life with energy that would bedevil a lesser man. Her vitality overflowed her small form. Cole wasn't worried about the boy. What he lost sleep over was the blacksmith's son, Rex. Rex turned twenty-one a few weeks ago. Had his eye on Phoebe. He was a young man filled with his self-worth. He watched her with lust-filled eyes. If the young man seduced, the innocent that Phoebe was would lose her virginity to Rex. He couldn't allow that to happen. Cole wasn't at all certain how to go about keeping Rex away from his mate. Given some thought, he would come up with some diversion.

Bloody eyes, why did Phoebe have to be so young. So, beguiling as well as beautiful. He was twenty-six. Not that old but almost ten years her senior. By this time next year, he would be ready to settle down with this young woman. Doubted if she would be prepared for marriage. Seduce her. Take her off guard with his many charms. Make her want what he alone could give her. Perhaps he would begin the day after her high school graduation. He could take her swimming to the loch near the village. Perhaps show her how a man kissed a woman. Give her a small taste of something she might not wish to live without.

"Phoebe?" Cole approached her with a smile. "You're looking very pretty today. Any new conquests?" He looked to the school teacher's son then back to her. The boy blushed a deep shade of red.

"Cole! What a pleasant surprise?" Her tone held a wealth of sarcasm. He supposed he deserved the mockery. In the past he'd spoken few words to her. Had attempted to ignore her along with her outthrust tongue. Though, it had been a few years since she resorted to that means to show him her dislike. This year, he saw major changes in her body as she turned from girl to woman. He did appreciate all her new curves, the shape of her hips, the bounty of her breasts. She should wear a bra.

"Not so much. You are always in this part of the keep after school. You are in your junior year?" He tried to put her age with the grade. He knew full well what grade she was in at school. Had been watching her for the last three years. Wished to see how she would respond to him.

"Senior year," she told him while she tossed her hair then smiled. The smile was one of a siren. "You forget I'm almost eighteen. Will be so before graduation." She lowered her lashes at him. Turned her shoulder a bit giving him a full view of her shapely yet unconstrained breasts. When she opened her lashes again her aquamarine eyes sparkled with mischief. Bloody eyes, the girl-woman could seduce a saint.

What was she planning now? He knew there was some type of plot hatching in her head. "I…" she moistened her lips. Let her tongue slow-glide across the pink lips he'd like to savor. Smoothed the fabric of her tight-fitting top until it was stretched taut across her ample breasts. His body reacted. Her nipples accentuated by the calculated gesture.

Much to his dismay, he wasn't immune to her flirtations. His body began to tighten while he imagined tasting what she offered. "Want to go for a walk?" Cole held out his hand needing to feel the warmth there.

A walk with her might be a huge mistake. He wasn't ready to show his intentions. Before he could do so, she needed to graduate from high school. He needed to get to know her better. The time was coming when he would begin his quest for her hand with serious determination.

"Why, that would be nice. Would rather go for a ride…in your car," she amended with a flourish of her arms. "That convertible is…" She winked at him. "You know what I mean. Awesome."

The groan rumbling up through his chest had to be tamped down. He hoped he didn't know what she meant by the inuendo that she covered up with a quick addition to her statement. If she did understand, it might be too late. Maybe he didn't have time to wait until she graduated. Shaking his head, he caught her elbow. Began to walk.

"You should not be making such scandalous inferences. Do you know what you're talking about?" he berated her. Of course, she knew. Most young women understood the act of mating better than they should. He would like to be the man to teach her. Didn't want her to rely on social media for her information. "Come now, a good walk through the rose garden will do us both good. I've need of some exercise. Saturday we can go into the hills. Maybe to the lock to swim." He needed to turn on his McKenna charm. Whether she was ready to wed or not, he must bind her to him.

"Why are you being so nice to me? You've never been pleasant before. Never asked me to go anywhere with you." She skipped along beside him, deciding not to take his hand. "You've always berated me for my behavior. Why the change?"

Before this she was a little girl. "Why shouldn't I be nice?" he questioned, rumbling different thoughts through his head for a decent answer. "You're a sweet girl."

She stopped, staring at him as if he'd gone daft. Her hands on her hips, those perfect little breasts thrust forward, moving with each breath of indignant air she inhaled. Enticing. Her brows drawn together, leaving scowl lines marring her perfect forehead. To trace that soft line would be nice. "Liar, we both know I'm not a sweet girl. So, I repeat, why are you being nice to me?"

"Just wished to talk." Guess he was not showing his charming side. Berating her did nothing to give him an advantage. She called out his lie.

"Talk about what? I'm telling you..." She was shaking one long delicate finger at him. "Even though you are head of the clan, I don't give away my favors to anyone. Not even you. Want the man I marry to be the only man to know me. Even if I say a few outrageous things, the words mean nothing. You hear me? Nothing!"

Cole couldn't stop the huge grin from framing his mouth. He would forever be pleased with her answer. "Don't wish to take anything from you that you don't wish to give. Indeed, that was one of the topics I wished to speak with you about...the way you flaunt yourself to the village lads." Well, he put his foot in his mouth again. Needed this beguiling child-woman to graduate soon. Oh, but she would give her favors to him. That moment was only a blink away. He could wait now that he understood her conscious.

Also by the Author
at
Rogue Phoenix Press

Connal's Eternal Love
Sweet McKenna Book One

A few days shy of All Hallows' Eve Connal McKenna, Laird of Clan Chaton stands on the parapets of his castle. Bonfires line the hillsides while his clan prepares for the upcoming festivities. Drawn by the whispering of the wind, Connal McKenna feels a strange restlessness in his soul. Setting out to discover the wickedness that is calling to him, he discovers his mate. With gentle words and sensuous kisses, the auburn-eyed highlander conquers his mate, the beautiful, defiant Wynnie Adair who he comes upon during an evening ride. She must ultimately put her trust in the only man who can save her from the ruthless plans of her father and succumb to his gentle coaxing.

In Brady's Arms
Sweet McKenna Book Two

Forced to run from the only home she knows, beautiful, headstrong Lillian Townsends seeks shelter in the wild highlands where the McKenna clan live. Trying to avoid a betrothal contract signed by her stepfather to an aging lord, she is desperate to find a means to sidestep the inevitable, including a marriage to the oldest son of the laird. Lilly is enamored of the young lord who pursues her with unrelenting determination flashing his devilishly handsome charms. She is hard pressed to resist.

Besotted from the first moment Brady McKenna sees Lilly, he is determined to find a means to coax her into his arms and bed. With only the promise of carnal pleasure as his mistress, Brady relentlessly pursues the woman who has unwittingly forged a place in his heart. She is like no other woman, proud, defiant and enchanting. Despite his father's advice to stay away from her, he cannot. He boldly seeks her out and makes her his own.

Nobody but Walker
Sweet McKenna Book Three

The Highland Lass...

She was brought up, adored and loved by a doting mother and father ardently protected by her brothers. She was everything sweet and innocent until she was faced with betrayal and an unexpected and out of wedlock pregnancy. When she gave her love to a man who couldn't return her passion and commitment, she was left devastated and furious. Faced with the loss of her child if she didn't comply to his demands, Crissie McKenna followed him to Belfast then on to his country home to discover he was already married.

...The Irishman

Stunned to find out his one and only encounter with the woman he wanted to love forever created a child, Walker Endicott, Earl of Briarwood, claimed his child as his only heir. Walker threatened all her previously held values even while he thrilled her senses. From the moment he first saw her to the second she ran after him begging him to make love to her, his captivating masculinity held her fascinated. In his arms she would know tempestuous passion, bitter despair, and a soaring joy that would humble them both before the power of love.

Roby's Moonlit Night
Sweet McKenna Book Four

Once she'd been a pampered child with high expectations for her future blessed with love. Then she became an innocent pawn in a terrible game of greed and power. Now, with a noose around her neck, Pippa was to hang before she had the chance to unveil the men who drove her from her home, before she had the chance to live.

Roby McKenna was a man blessed with endless charm and wit. While he searched for his eternal love across the Atlantic in a new land, he would have to come home to find her. His silver blue eyes could sparkle with amusement or harden to steel gray with displeasure. He had all the women a man could want or need. As he grew older, mistresses were not enough. A quirk of fate brought him to the gallows, a spark of destiny made him claim the condemned Pippa as his bride.

Made for Houston
Sweet McKenna Book Five

Leah Kennedy is as wary of people as she is strikingly beautiful. However, the shocking death of her father that forever changed her girlhood has left her terrified of the very love she desperately longs for. Only in the untamed splendor of the Scottish crags does she feel safe from the feelings she stirs in men and the cruel mockery of Selkirk's villagers.

Debonair, well-educated doctor Houston Stuart has turned his back on social privilege along with professional honors to set up a medical practice in the lowlands of Scotland. There, serving those who need him the most, he hopes to forget the bitter memories and disillusionment that disturb his days.

Coincidence brings the cultured doctor and this fey mountain girl together. Something as bizarre as destiny disrupts the obstacle of birth and breeding, stubborn pride and fear which has kept them apart...as each seeks to heal the other's wounds with a raw passion neither can deny and all the odds against them cannot defeat.

Say You Love Kit
Sweet McKenna Book Six

Fascinated...

When the woman stepped through the door of the pub, the sun

setting her fiery red hair glowing around her delicate features, Kit Stuart finds himself captivated by the sight. The moment he sees her he knows she will be his. Convincing the fire-haired lady of that fact isn't easy. After she calls out another man's name when he kisses her that night, he is instantly enraged as well as jealous. The road they travel is fraught with secrets that neither can tell. Trust is an elusive quality that neither can give.

Intrigued...

Forced to run for her life, desperate and afraid, Aila MacDuff willingly enters into the Kinnel Stones, a mysterious place where people disappear then appear magically in different times. At the first sight of Kit, she finds herself inexplicably drawn to him. She's been told to search for her mate and that she will know when she finds him. Aila doesn't know what this man's name is or what he looks like. Nonetheless, she is certain he will be similar to her mate from one hundred years earlier. Despite the fact she is falling in love with Kit, he can't be her mate. Her mate is a shifter. Kit is not.

It Had to be Riley
Sweet McKenna Book Seven

Her anger assured retaliation...

Shawna's only concern with the contemptable scoundrel she had been forced to wed was the return of her dowry. She had not seen her husband in three years, and now Riley Stuart furiously repudiated there had ever been a marriage. He even went as far as to tell his family he'd never seen her before this day.

... Her passion promised love

In the heather clad hills of the beautiful Scottish crags surrounding the small village so near to the Mckenna keep, the ferocity of her loathing yields to the intense hunger of unquenched longing. In the powerful arms of the dark and handsome husband she thought she reviled, Shawna shivers with the honeyed torment of awakened desire and powerlessly submits to the wild, enchanting ecstasy of burning passion. Together they abandon themselves to the exquisite pleasure of the love their hearts cannot escape.

The Magic of Hawk
Sweet McKenna Book Eight

With her extraordinary silver-mauve eyes, Maisie McRae struggles with the return of her lost love. She finds solace living with her half-sister and existing on dreams. After three long years the man she once dreamt of marrying asks her to make the same foolish mistake again. Holding herself aloof from the arrogant man, Maisie refuses to let his sweettalking words seduce her into his arms.

Smitten from the first instant Hawk Frasier sees Maisie, he is determined to find a means to entice her into becoming part of his life. A missing letter keeps the unlucky couple from realizing their dreams. Defeated by her rejection, Hawk searches for a way to ignore the woman. Unable to forget the way she feels in his arms, Hawk returns from the colonies, ready to try again. Despite the chance of a second rejection, he forges ahead. Boldly, he seeks her out and makes her his own.

Roc's Steadfast Heart
Sweet McKenna Book Nine

Dallas Elaine Shaw, on a photo shoot for the magazine she works for, tumbles down an incline to find herself catapulted into the eighteenth century. Facing three men, one of those men, the one with laughing silver blue eyes commands her attention. The other two stare at her with leering, malicious intent. She finds herself rescued by the man with the intense eyes. Terrified of horses, she discovers herself riding in front of the arrogant man who saved her. In a few short minutes, he sends a multitude of sparks simmering within her.

When Roc Frasier sees the woman sprawled on the ground, he thinks he's gone to heaven. This is the woman all his dreams are made from. Her body holds the enticement of lush bountiful breasts, curved hips he could hold onto. She is his dream come true. What he doesn't understand is this woman has traveled through time. She comes to him to complete the interrupted circle of life. This woman is his soulmate. His life's blood. She wants nothing more than to leave him, to return to her time. She can't. They are each other's destiny.

www.ingramcontent.com/pod-product-compliance
Lightning Source LLC
Chambersburg PA
CBHW060348260626
47160CB00006B/2243